RED
RENEGADE

Also by Freddie P. Peters:

In the HENRY CROWNE PAYING THE PRICE series
INSURGENT
COLLAP$E
BRE∕KING PO!NT
NO TURNING B∕CK
SPY SH∕DOⱲS
IMP∅STOR IN CHIEF
HENRY CROⱲNE P∕YING THE PRICE BOOKS 1-3

In the NANCY WU CRIME THRILLER series
BLOOD DR∕GON

Dear Reader,

I'm thrilled you've chosen RED RENEGADE, Book 6 in the HENRY CROWNE PAYING THE PRICE series.

Think about getting access for FREE to the exclusive Prequel to the HENRY CROWNE PAYING THE PRICE series: INSURGENT.

Go to freddieppeters.com

RED
RENEGADE

FREDDIE P. PETERS

HENRY CROWNE PAYING THE PRICE BOOK 6

CHAPTER ONE

"Twenty minutes out. I repeat, twenty minutes to drop point." The captain's voice drew the men's attention. Henry opened his eyes and checked one final time the equipment was in place.

He finished zipping up the grey synthetic thermal suit over his white and grey splodged PCU, used as extra protection by the ALPHA team for their High Altitude High Opening jump. Fergus, his buddy in the team, gave Henry one thumb up. Henry nodded back, giving him the O sign. When the time came, Fergus would be checking the level of Henry's oxygen tank, and he would do the same for him.

The temperature in the aircraft cabin had been dropped substantially to accommodate the men's heavier protective combat uniforms, necessary to counter the frigid temperature they would encounter during their HAHO. The training for a HAHO insertion into China's part of the Gobi Desert had been gruelling, pushing Henry to the limits. But the SEAL team had been more patient than he had expected, making sure he'd reached the high standard such a jump required.

"You're a determined bastard, H. There's no doubt about it," a grinning Master Chief Rodriguez had admitted to Henry a couple of nights ago, when OPERATION TECH LEOPARD had been given the green light.

Henry had smiled back and tapped his beer bottle against Rodriguez's. "Yup. Although I may not feel so smart when my feet are dangling at 30,000 feet over the Gobi, or we are about to hit the sands of one of the most hostile deserts in the world."

"Forget about the desert, it's the Chinese patrols along the border with Mongolia that you need to worry about. If we hit one of these, getting sand in our boots will be the least of our worries."

Someone tapping on Henry's shoulder made the memory vanish. The medic on board the flight was doing the rounds, checking the vitals of each man on the team. All six of them had been on a hundred per cent oxygen inhalation regime for forty-five minutes. Starting the jump at such high altitude would mean being oxygen deprived for a period of time. Each jumper would be fitted with an oxygen bottle, but the risk of nitrogen getting into the blood remained, increasing the chance of decompression sickness. This would mean losing consciousness during the jump and likely certain death.

The medic flashed a small light into Henry's eyes. She nodded and moved on to Fergus who grunted, but let her do her thing.

"Ten minutes to the jump, people... Ten minutes." The captain's voice came over the intercom.

Fergus stood up, still connected to the pure oxygen main tank. Henry followed suit and they checked each other's individual tanks.

"Remember," Fergus said into his oxygen mask, "you must fit your tank's mask to your face as quickly as you can to avoid any nitro seeping in."

"Sure." Henry could have reminded Fergus that he'd gotten the message loud and clear during his training but Ferg was a good guy who just wanted Henry to be safe.

Henry fitted his helmet and checked one more time that his weapon was taped down firmly to avoid any part detaching during the jump. He pulled on the harness of his chute and switched on his Tactical Assault Kit, an Android app that would help him with geospatial location, comms and navigation.

Master Chief Rodriguez disappeared into the bowl of what should have been a commercial airliner. He emerged a few moments later and gave the men a thumbs up.

Henry took a deeper breath and clenched his fist a few times.

"We are going dark," the captain announced.

The cabin lights went out. Henry adjusted his night vision goggles and the cabin became a greyish surround. Henry could make out a form at the back of the plane. One of the tactical support staff was clad in thick gear and had also donned a small breathing apparatus. He got himself ready to open the hatch on the aft side of the aircraft. They were almost there.

"Two minutes to jump, ALPHA team... Good luck."

Henry swiftly disconnected from the main O2 tank. He put his oxygen tank mask on. Fergus slapped him on the shoulder... time to go.

The plane's speed slowed and the man standing at the back of the plane opened the cabin door. The roar of the engines' noise coupled with the smack and intensity of the cold air rushing through the cabin caused Henry to stagger back. He straightened up just before Fergus turned to check on him.

Master Chief Rodriguez walked to the edge of the black hole to the outside and without looking back, gave the ALPHA team a sign: his hand up, fingers outstretched... five seconds. The men stacked up in a line. Without hesitation, Rodriguez jumped into the darkness that surrounded the plane.

Henry activated the infrared beacon atop his helmet as he jumped into the frigid winds and the deafening noise of the jet engines. He found a stable body position and started looking around. Below him, he could see one other beacon flashing. They had staggered the jumps to avoid triggering the Chinese radar signal cover detection and the only way to find his way to the target location, apart from his navigation instruments, was to follow Fergus's light.

Henry pulled on the opening toggle; the chute deployment jerked him in his freefall. The sound of the aircraft above had completely disappeared, replaced by the intense sound of the gale swirling around him. The wind was giving Henry and the men of ALPHA team a much-needed push to reach their target landing.

Their plane had followed the usual commercial route from Seoul in South Korea to Dalanzadgad in Mongolia. That was the best way to fly over China without arousing suspicion. Still, the team needed a drift of fifty miles, pushing the limits of how far a HAHO could take them.

The needle of the altimeter strapped to Henry's wrist was moving down gradually, indicating his descent. His glide path was steady, and he just needed a few adjustments from his chute's toggles to follow Fergus's beacon.

He had another fifteen minutes in the air before touchdown in the hills of the Ganqi Maodu province, thirty miles from the Zhaga detention camp. Henry checked his Tactical Assault Kit for confirmation of his whereabouts. He located Fergus's beacon one more time, switched off his own and pulled on the toggle hard to the right, changing his steady drift to a sharp, 90-degree turn – his final course.

* * *

"They've just left the aircraft," Lieutenant Pike of the US military confirmed. Putting down her headset, she moved closer to the map of China and the surrounding countries that had been pulled up on screen at the beginning of OPERATION TECH LEOPARD. She turned to Steve. "Your man is on his way to China, Agent Harris."

"And so is your team." Harris didn't like her insinuation, but he had to admit that to the US military, Henry might not have looked like the most obvious choice for such a high-grade mission. "He's survived Islamic State in Rakkah and Putin in Moscow. I'm sure he'll be fine."

"Except that the place he's headed to would give a hardened Apache warrior pause," Pike replied smugly.

Ignoring her taunt, Harris walked to the map spread out on the large screen at the far end of the op room and followed the flight path of the aircraft once more.

"The aircraft left Seoul at 11pm as expected. The flight plan was lodged as a charter flight to Dalanzadgad airport, carrying a team of fossilists on an expedition to unearth yet another large dinosaur skeleton." Harris followed the progress of the aircraft that showed as a small moving arrow on the map.

Pike grinned. "Just as well the Gobi Desert is such a hotbed for extinct dinos."

Harris looked at his watch and made a quick mental calculation. Henry had been gliding with the ALPHA team over China for more than five minutes. He was unquestionably one of MI6's best assets but his insertion into a country that was starting to flex its military muscles against the West would yet again push Henry hard.

Pike nodded. "They now have twenty-four hours to retrieve the package and return to the extraction point inside Mongolia."

"I'd rather refer to it as retrieving the stolen tech intelligence and its creator. After all, it's supposed to be the most advanced piece of military hardware in the world and the man, one of the most innovative scientists." Harris checked his watch again.

"And I'd rather keep referring to it as the package. The less we say about him the better," Pike replied tersely.

"You might be right, but you and your superiors assured me that these premises were completely watertight and that nothing could penetrate the security measures put in place." Harris's tone did not quite carry the sarcasm he wanted to convey.

Pike shrugged. "Better safe than sorry..."

Harris said nothing more, satisfied with his reply. The part of OPERATION TECH LEOPARD the US military hadn't been told about, involved Rob Walker's kidnapping. The man, whose work it was to create advances in semi-conductors used in high grade military weapons, had disappeared almost a year ago. He had been traced to Zhaga prison camp where his tech knowledge would be siphoned out of him, slowly yet surely. Rescuing Walker would take time and a different tactic than a quick extraction.

Harris pushed Pike a little bit more. "My CIA contact is also telling me that this hardware intel breach would compromise the tech strategy that Taiwan and the US are pursuing together to stave off Chinese aggression."

"I guess that's why we are in Taiwan and not Gham," was all Pike added.

Harris nodded. The US military was still interpreting the operation as an intelligence extraction. That was fine by Harris.

His CIA contact Jack Shield had briefed him about Rob Walker's kidnapping shortly after he and Harris had completed a Russian joint MI6/CIA mission. The two agencies didn't always like working together but Steve and Jack had had a track record of getting results where no-one else could.

Jack had joked over dinner one night, "May we be successful for a bit longer otherwise Hunter III will have my head on a plate."

"That's a bit dramatic, even for Hunter. He'll just send you to the lower-level, third floor basement and you'll be filing documents for the rest of your meagre career."

"You're probably right," Jack replied, finishing his fish and chips at the same pub they always met at in London's East End. "I think I'd rather he had my head on a damn plate than be sent to the third floor basement at Langley."

Back at Vauxhall Cross, MI6 headquarters, Steve and Jack had taken the lift down to basement level three, not to visit the archives but to enter the most secure part of the building, and had a private conversation about their next operation.

Jack walked over to a small table and helped himself to coffee. He sat at the main table. "Rob Walker is the mastermind behind a cooperation programme between the US and Taiwan in the production of semi-conductors. He is a prolific tech scientist. He and his team have designed a new super-fast chip that makes a huge difference in the way information is transmitted to other devices that use the chip."

"I presume you're referring to the types of chips used in high-grade military wear, such as drones and combat aircraft." Steve got coffee too and sat next to his friend. "It's a bit ballsy to kidnap someone like that."

"You bet. And underneath the nose of the CIA as well. We feel very sour about that."

"How did you manage to locate him?" Steve took a sip of his coffee. "You have an asset high up in the Chinese government?"

Jack grinned. "This is what I like about you, Steve. Not afraid to ask a question, even if I can't answer it. And I know you'll make something of it, whatever I say."

Steve looked ahead, savouring his win. He pushed Jack a little more. "So, the CIA has someone informing them, someone high up in the army and the Chinese Communist Party, in fact so high up that you can't say – code name?"

"Seriously, Steve!"

He shrugged. "Well, was worth a try."

The satellite phone ringing brought Steve Harris back to the present and the op room. The call made Lieutenant Pike frown. The agreed contact time was supposed to be in a couple of hours when the ALPHA team had established an observation position close to Zhaga camp.

Pike picked up. Her face turned pale as she listened to the message being relayed to her.

"You have a window of two hours," she simply said before hanging up.

"Problem?" Harris asked.

"Your guy has gone missing."

* * *

The ALPHA team would not notice Henry wasn't following them until they touched ground. And even then, they would assume he had drifted outside the landing zone. He was not a SEAL, after all.

He checked his altimeter once more; he had a little more than ten minutes of drift left. The Tactical Assault Kit strapped to his chest was helping him with navigation; a clear sky and high moon made the approaching ground visible. The switch of direction was taking him straight into the cliffs, rather than the softer terrain on which he was supposed to land.

He pulled on the left toggle, trying to adjust his drift to match the new coordinates and landing zone. The wind had changed direction and the elevated terrain, the cliffs and gorges made the air flow unsteady. There was a reason why the ALPHA team had stayed clear of this location to land.

A gust of wind caught him. "Shit..."

Henry tried to manoeuvre the chute away from the ridge, but the wind made it almost impossible to steer. His ground speed was still too high for him to release the chute and drop – something he had learned to do but had been advised to resort to only in extremis.

The chute canopy overhead was fluttering, the rock face almost upon him. Henry pulled as hard as he could, to the right this time. The chute grated the rock, sending bits of stone flying into his face. Henry's descent slowed with a shudder, compromising his control of the canopy. He yanked the release strap and tumbled down amongst the gravel and sand. His body somersaulted in the air, amid a cloud of dust. Yet his feet found some purchase on solid ground and Henry stopped his abrupt fall.

As the wind settled around him, the sudden calm startled Henry. He didn't dare move, fearing it would reveal a catastrophic injury. The flutter of the chute caught in the boulders above him forced him to sit up and pay attention. He moved his shoulders and neck, then gingerly his legs, and collapsed back on the ground laughing.

He'd made it in one piece, unhurt – rookie's luck.

Henry stood up and consulted his Tactical Assault Kit once more. Rodriguez's voice came through delivering a short roll call that would soon be missing one. Henry took a breath and switched off the comms before his name could be called. There was no time for hesitation. His teammates were twenty miles away. He was alone.

Climbing up the hill, he grabbed the limp canopy and started rolling it up on the ground. He didn't want the piece of material to catch in the wind and start dragging him with it.

Henry unstrapped his rucksack, took a shovel out and dug a quick hole into which he pushed the chute, the assault kit, night goggles and rifle. He emptied the contents of the rucksack, retrieved a new set of clothes, jeans, T-shirt, and light windproof jacket, walking shoes and another rucksack that did not spell military but a well-travelled explorer.

He checked his new legend passport one more time, in the name of Henry Newborn. The stamp showing he had entered Mongolia a fortnight ago was on the back page, a habit of the Mongolian passport control according to MI6's fake passport team.

Henry stuffed the mobile Steve, his MI6 handler, had given him before he left Taiwan for South Korea in his new rucksack. The phone was encrypted, and he would use it for a short conversation with Steve once he was on his way to meet the smuggler he was meant to rendezvous with in a couple of hours' time. After that, the phone would be cleaned by the Comms team in Vauxhall Cross and it would become useless.

Henry's mission to salvage the stolen intelligence also entailed rescuing Rob Walker, the man who knew more about military tech advances than any other scientist. And the first step was for Henry to get captured by the Chinese and sent to Zhaga.

He slid the Glock 19 into the waistband of his jeans at the back. Not exactly what an amateur fossilist would have with him but it would do until he met with the smuggler who was to guide him to the Zhaga prison camp and organise his capture. Henry tossed his military uniform and pack into the hole and quickly covered it up.

It was now 2am. The sun was due to rise at 6am. Henry had just enough time to find the meeting point where the smuggler going by the name of Zu would be waiting for him.

He started walking in the dark hoping the famous Gobi pit viper wouldn't show on his journey.

The crushing sound of his walking boots echoed around him. Henry stopped after fifteen minutes. The GPS he was using on his phone was the same used by the Tactical Assault Kit he'd buried in the sands after landing. He had tested it extensively during his MI6 training, but in this harshest of places, Henry's confidence in the agency's technology felt overoptimistic. A small deviation would send him miles away from his meeting point and there would be no ALPHA team to rescue him – he had just compromised the mission. There would be only one response from control and command in Taiwan: immediate extraction and no prospect of returning back to China.

* * *

Henry stopped on the ridge of yet another rocky hill and got his bearings. He'd been walking for almost an hour but the meeting point was supposed to be less than a quarter of a mile away.

He belly-crawled to the top, and prone on his elbows, brought the binoculars to his eyes and scanned the horizon. There was nothing there, no movement, no life, just an impressive vastness of dunes encircled to the north by the rocky cliffs he'd been following since he'd landed.

Henry adjusted the field of vision to get a closer look at something that seemed out of place. A piece of heavy sand-coloured tarp flapping in the wind, strapped around a bulky shape.

"What..." Henry pulled the binoculars from his eyes in a swift move of disbelief. "... the fuck?"

He replaced the glasses and tweaked the field knob. There was no one waiting for him at the rendezvous point but a car, an SUV that looked dusty and well used from what he could see.

He waited ten more minutes, scanning the horizon again for danger. Nothing. Henry got up slowly and made his way to the car that had been left for what he presumed was his attention. Rodriguez had kept telling him that all plans go to shit as soon as a team hits enemy territory, but

Henry hoped the plan he and MI6 had put together would hold for a little longer than two hours.

Henry stopped a few times, checking for human presence and booby traps, before finally reaching the vehicle. To his relief, the desert was dark and still eerily calm.

He pulled the cover off the SUV. It wasn't dusty as he had thought. The tarp must have been thrown over the vehicle less than twenty-four hours ago. The vehicle itself was another story, old and covered in muck. It had seen better days. Henry walked around the car, checking again for signs of trip wires, but it was clean.

He circled the vehicle once more, feeling something wasn't quite right. He paused and moved to the front.

The number plates didn't look Chinese.

He bent down to take a closer look and noticed a small flag on the right-hand side of the plate. The Mongolian flag. He smiled and straightened up. It was clever to provide him with a vehicle that would give more weight to his cover story.

Henry opened the door of the car and inspected the interior. The keys were on the dashboard. There was a map of the region on the driver's seat with a new set of coordinates.

He ran his hand underneath the dashboard. The SUV wasn't wired. He sat in the driver's seat and turned the ignition on. The engine responded without hesitation. Unlike the exterior that made the vehicle look as though it was ready for the dump, someone had fired up what went under the bonnet.

He released the handbrake and depressed the clutch slowly. The SUV started to roll down the slope, bumping on the rocks that formed part of the terrain.

He looked at his watch. Another three hours before daybreak.

CHAPTER TWO

"Viper One-Six, this is Viper One-Zero, over." Master Chief Rodriguez pressed the talk button through the thermal suit he still wore. He adjusted the boom mic of his headset and repeated the call.

Still nothing.

His four men were standing around him, all accounted for except one. They had rolled the canopy of their parachute in a tight bunch and should have been digging to bury any evidence of their illegal entry. But the news that one of their team was missing had stopped them in their tracks.

Fergus was the first to break the silence. "Fuck... this can't be happening. I checked his equipment just before the jump. It was all fine."

"I know, Ferg, the doc gave him the all-clear too. The switch from the O2 tank to the portable tank took a few seconds." Rodriguez unzipped his thermal suit with an angry hand. "Even if he's unconscious somewhere I should still be able to geo-localise him."

Fergus unclipped the Tactical Assault Kit from his chest and tried to get a read on Henry's position too. There was no signal.

"Keep trying," Rodriguez said. He turned to the rest of his team. "You know what you need to do, so do it."

Two of them started digging the hole in which they would bury any equipment they couldn't carry. The last of Rodriguez's men was assembling the portable radio Rodriguez would use to communicate with command and control in Taichung.

Both Rodriguez and Fergus moved to a more elevated section of the flat sands they had landed on. Their kit did not detect any infrared signature. There was no one around.

Fergus took out a set of binoculars and scanned the horizon.

"This doesn't feel right," he said to Rodriguez, who was still searching the land around them.

"I know... Henry's no SEAL but there was no reason he should screw up his jump."

"Suggestions, Rod?"

"A number... none of them I'm happy to discuss just yet."

Fergus slowed his methodical sweeping motion and returned to the point he had just gone over. "Fuck." He dropped to the ground, out of sight, and Rodriguez followed immediately. "We've got company."

Rodriguez rolled to his side whilst Fergus raised his body a fraction, focusing his binoculars on the vehicles approaching. Rodriguez brought his Tactical Assault Kit to his face. There was still no heat signature. The hostiles were far enough away for now not to notice the ALPHA team.

"What are the chances of meeting border patrol in one of the most deserted parts of Inner Mongolia at 2am?" Fergus mumbled, adjusting the field of vision of his glasses.

"None." Rodriguez looked back at his team. They too had dropped to the ground, awaiting instructions. "Two cars, almost certainly border patrol, speeding towards the hills," Rodriguez said in a low voice that carried just enough for his team to hear. "Finish the digging, bury our stuff. We need to be ready to move."

"They're not looking for us." Fergus was leaning on his right arm, following the movement of the two large trucks and the trail of dust they were kicking up behind them. "And they're going pretty fast."

"Patrol cars gunning towards a godforsaken place in the desert, looking for smugglers they couldn't care less about?" Rodriguez had taken his own binoculars out of his rucksack and was following the convoy also.

"Slim chance..." Fergus slid back a little to gain a better viewing position.

"Keep tracking these fuckers. I need to make a call to base." Rodriguez retreated to where his men had almost finished covering their tracks. He crouched next to the portable radio that his comms specialist had just activated. It was ready for encrypted transmission.

"ALPHA team to base, do you copy, over?"

There was only silence. Rodriguez repeated his message.

A reply came. "Base to ALPHA team, we read you clear, over."

12

Rodriguez covered the receiver with his hand. "One man is MIA. I repeat, one man MIA."

There was a short pause. Lieutenant Pike confirmed the message. "One man missing in action. Acknowledge ID, over?"

"Viper One-Six. I repeat, Viper One-Six, over."

"Chance of tracking Viper One-Six?"

"Two hostile vehicles are moving to a clear target and we assume it is Viper One-Six."

"Can you extract?" Pike asked.

"Hold." Rodriguez muted the call. "Ferg, where are they?"

"Still speeding in a straight line. I'm about to lose them."

"Base, give us two hours before we abort."

"ALPHA team, you know the rules. I need to escalate –"

"Two hours... Comm's breaking up..."

"Two hours, confirm ALPHA team," Pike said.

But the line went dead before Rodriguez could reply.

* * *

Henry could not quite figure out why the SUV had been left for him or why Zu had changed the meeting plan. Zu would need a car to drive to this remote part of the desert. Perhaps providing him immediately with a car registered in Mongolia would add to the credibility of his story when he encountered border patrol.

He was visiting the sites of a dinosaur dig in the Mongolian part of the Gobi. He had sponsored the expedition and wanted to see the results for himself... and then he got lost. It wasn't a bad cover story and it would serve its purpose.

Henry checked the GPS on his phone. He was almost at his destination. He slowed the car to an almost stop and scanned the horizon. The landscape had not changed to desert and dunes yet. Unlike the desert of Iraq and Syria that kept throwing rolling hills, gravels and rocks in your way, the texture of the land in the Gobi was sandier and harsher.

The rock cliffs and gorges stood to his right, the flat land to his left, with dunes of sand in the far distance. There was little room to hide a vehicle unless he used the low recess of one of the hills.

Henry slowed to a stop, spotting the roof of a truck in the distance. He thought about finishing the distance on foot to make a silent approach, but it was too late to have second thoughts about trusting Zu. Henry accelerated gently, moving the SUV closer to the new rendezvous point.

The truck looked in as bad a condition as the SUV Henry was driving. The colour must have been red at some point; the patched wings and mismatched doors had been picked for practicality rather than aesthetics. The driver's window was rolled down and a silhouette was sitting upright in the seat, head tilted slightly back.

The hairs on the back of Henry's neck bristled. There was something odd about the angle of Zu's face. Either he was asleep or...

Henry stopped the SUV and took a moment to survey the truck's surroundings. There was no movement and it would be hard to hide in such a bare and unforgiving landscape.

He took his Glock out, opened the door of his vehicle and stepped onto the ground. He rolled down the window of his car and pointed his gun in the truck's direction, using the door as a shield.

"*Ni hao...* Hello." Henry's voice sounded too loud in the silence of the desert. He waited for a moment. "Xiansheng Zu..."

The man didn't move.

Henry tightened his grip on his weapon, unwilling yet to consider what seemed to be the obvious explanation for Zu's silence.

Henry moved towards the truck, gun at the ready. Before reaching it he slowly crouched to the ground, one eye still on the other vehicle and its driver. There were two sets of tracks and only one that had departed from the area.

When he reached the truck Henry wasn't surprised by what he found. Zu's head was hanging to the right; a bullet through the temple had done the trick. Henry bit his lip and stood back a little, then circled the vehicle to check for any clue to help him understand what had happened.

He opened the passenger door of the truck. The blood-splattered seat was empty and so was the glove compartment. Henry felt underneath the seat, finding nothing. He returned to the driver's side.

As he opened Zu's door the man's body slid a little, and Henry thought he heard a sound. He put his fingers on Zu's neck but found no pulse. Zu was dead. A further check on the rest of the car confirmed it was empty.

Henry closed Zu's door and slumped against it. His mind raced with possibilities. He stood up slowly forcing himself to focus. He had a car, a mobile with a line to Harris and a GPS. He could still make the ALPHA team exfil window in Mongolia – just.

The wind had started to rise, carrying sounds coming from the east. The strange noise that Henry had heard while checking on Zu came again, this time more distinct.

He ran to the SUV and pulled binoculars out of his rucksack. He stood on the front guard of the car and skimmed the horizon with them. He couldn't spot anything at first, but the darkness of night was receding and as his eyes became accustomed to the change in luminosity, he spotted a trail of dust in the distance.

Whoever they were they were heading in his direction, and he doubted it was to retrieve Zu's body. He needed to leave now. He carried a Glock and Zu had just been gunned down. It would be easy for the authorities to draw the wrong conclusion, even more so if he was to flee towards the border.

Henry cleaned his Glock with his shirt and left it in Zu's car. He ran back to the place where he had spotted the tracks of the second vehicle. They were heading east.

He returned to the SUV and started the engine, then turned the car away from the border between China and Mongolia, towards the trail of dust he had spotted headed east.

He still had a chance to salvage the mission.

* * *

Rodriguez re-joined his team. "We've got two hours. Let's think about what we've got."

Fergus nodded. "Another four hours of darkness, so good cover 'til then."

"If we abort, we need to allow for an hour and a half to reach the border with Mongolia," one of the team said.

"So, two hours sounds reasonable?" Rodriguez repeated.

The men grunted an OK.

"We are on foot, and they have a car. We can't catch up," Ray said.

"That's not the idea. But they're likely to come back the same way they came. We can intercept them on the way back." Rodriguez half turned to reply.

"And we definitely have time to walk there. It's less than a couple of miles south," Hulk added.

Fergus laid his tactical kit on the floor. "We have the advantage of surprise..."

"You can say that again, Ferg. The last thing these suckers are going to expect is us jumping from under their feet as we are lying in wait for them in the desert sands." Everyone chuckled and Rodriguez took heart that they might just pull it off. "OK... what does the terrain look like?" he asked.

"Very flat desert sand, now that we're moving south," Fergus replied. "We find the tracks left by the two vehicles and we bury ourselves nearby. We'll hear them coming. It's an easy enough intercept."

"That sounds solid." Rodriguez pursed his lips. "Any objections?"

Everyone nodded. "Ferg, map the course and send it to our kit," Rodriguez said, standing up. "How much ammo have we got?"

"More than enough, Rod. We're not supposed to fire anything, remember?"

"Let's bury some of it. I'll leave my spare Glock in there as well, in case H makes to the rendezvous point."

"Is that a good idea?"

"Nope, but I sure would want my team mates to leave a little help behind if I was stuck behind enemy lines," Rodriguez shot back.

"What if the Chinese find that stuff?"

"Then they find the chutes as well and they won't be able to trace anything back to us, as you know."

"Chutes yes... guns and ammo, that's another issue," Fergus added.

"That's my decision to make." Rodriguez turned away from the team to where they had buried the parachutes. He dug a deep-enough hole, wrapped the gun and munitions in the chute's material and covered it again.

16

When he returned the ALPHA team was ready.

"Let's sync our watches again. We have less than two hours to find Henry."

Rodriguez signalled his team to stop. He pointed to his eyes, then to Fergus. Fergus nodded and moved in the direction of the tracks they were looking for. The rest of the team crouched, waiting for him to come back from his recce. There was nowhere for them to hide on this flat land. They would see any hostiles coming for sure, but they in turn would be spotted too.

At least it was still dark, and the ALPHA team had the advantage of the hunter tracking their prey.

"We're almost there. I've picked up the tracks on the infrared binoculars... I'd say one klick away," Fergus said.

Rodriguez drew a few lines in the sand. "We approach in two groups... Ferg and Hulk you go first, position two hundred metres due south of our target; you bury and wait. Go for the tyres as soon as you hear my group engaging the enemy."

Both men nodded. "Chief."

"The rest, you're with me. Don, I want you to stay back from where we'll be buried by five metres. You keep an eye on any additional company this godforsaken place may throw at us."

"Roger that." The last two men in his team waited a couple of minutes and they started walking again towards their objective.

Rodriguez found the tracks of the two vehicles Fergus had spotted. He crouched to look at the imprint of the tyres in the sand.

"The tyres are worn... vehicles rather heavy, though." Rodriguez ran his gloved hand through his hair. The trucks were likely border patrol, although he still couldn't exclude it being a smuggling gang using the rather porous line between Mongolia and China.

The mission had a zero-casualty, low-engagement protocol – the reason why the ALPHA team had been involved in the first place. He hesitated for a short moment before walking to the place where his other team members had dug in.

Rodriguez flattened to the ground; lying on his belly he dug himself a little farther into the sand, enough to be able to position his rifle and shoot. He checked that his scope was clear. He moved to the right where he anticipated the vehicles would come from and checked his watch.

They had forty minutes to make the extraction, after which Henry was on his own. And if so, it would be the first time the ALPHA team had left a man behind.

* * *

Henry turned on the low beam lights to follow the tracks of the second truck. Any other vehicles would now spot him within minutes. He clenched the wheel a little tighter. It was a big gamble to think the mission was still on track following Zu's death. He slowed down a fraction, fighting the desire to turn back and head towards the Mongolian border.

He kept one hand on the steering wheel and fished his rucksack out from the passenger seat, to retrieve his mobile. He pushed the device into the cradle fitted to the dashboard and pressed the call button of the last number he'd called a few days ago.

"Where are you?" was the first thing Harris said when he answered the call.

"Gobi Desert, Chinese part... aboard a crappy-looking SUV."

"On your own?"

"Unfortunately, Zu won't be much help, I'm afraid."

Henry heard Harris pull in a breath. "You mean he's dead?"

"Bullet through the head is usually bad for one's health," Henry shot back.

"You didn't tell me which direction you're heading in, though."

"I was coming to that... I'm driving east. There are a couple of cars headed my way and I'd be surprised if they're not coming to collect their prize."

"You mean they're coming for you?"

"That's the only explanation I can think of. The border with Mongolia is renowned to be worse than a sieve for traffickers, with routes through the mountains and desert but not in this area, so they can't be looking for illegal crossings. The terrain is steep and the gorges narrow. We discussed that. If I were a smuggler, I'd choose an easier route."

Harris was thinking. "OK. I buy that. But Zu's death is a blow. What makes you so sure these guys don't mean to do the same to you?"

18

"So far Dragon has given the CIA some very accurate information. I'm taking the risk that Dragon might have been outed and that he's spilled his guts to the Chinese authority. If that was the case though, there was no reason to do away with Zu. Chinese intelligence would have wanted to interrogate both Zu and me."

"But if you're wrong, it's going to hurt." Henry heard Harris light a cigarette.

Henry smiled. "Are you supposed to be smoking in whatever office you're calling me from?"

"Minor detail. I was not talking about MI6 and the CIA's reputation by the way... I was talking about the way Chinese intelligence extract information. They're not so worried about human rights there."

"Don't get me wrong, I'm not looking to add this experience to my CV. But if the Chinese are already after me, the border between Mongolia and China is not going to stop them. Even if I make it to the exfil site, they'll be following close and then I'll blow the exfil of ALPHA team."

"We can warn them," Harris said.

"And we'll end up having a shooting match, killing Chinese border patrol or intelligence guys on Mongolian soil."

"The Chinese shouldn't have followed you..."

"And we shouldn't be in China in the first place."

"Point taken."

"It also assumes that they won't catch me before I get to the border. They know the terrain and I don't." Henry mechanically looked into his rear-view mirror. "This was always a one-way ticket."

"You know that's not quite true. I've got enough time to instruct control and command to tell the ALPHA team you're rendezvousing with them."

"Then we all pile into the SUV and exfil to Mongolia?"

"They're about to do that anyway on foot so a lift would be welcome." Harris sounded unusually willing to accommodate.

Henry slowed down the vehicle. "Should you not be convincing me I can do this?" He had less than fifteen minutes to change his mind.

"I've trained you and I know you, H. If anyone can pull this off, you can. I have no worries about this. But you're on the terrain, not me. You can read the situation better. If you commit now, you've got to do this based on what your current position is, not because I tell you I can extract you."

Henry stopped the SUV. He had been gripping the steering wheel so tightly his knuckles had turned white.

Harris was patiently waiting on the line for his reply.

"I still think this is the right call," Henry said slowly. He nodded as though Harris could see him. "My legend is credible. We need to get the package out of China. I can do this."

"OK. Let's stick to what we've agreed. You're going dark until you find a way to communicate that doesn't compromise your situation."

"And I'm hanging up now. The welcoming party will be with me in less than five minutes." Henry didn't wait for Harris's reply. He cut the call and moved the SUV forward at a slow pace.

The two trucks that were speeding towards him had switched on their lights. They would have known that whoever was in the car had no chance of escape.

Henry stopped the car again and decided to wait. The two trucks arrived at speed and for a moment he thought they weren't going to stop and might ram his vehicle. But the drivers braked hard, sending dust and grit flying.

For a couple of minutes no one moved.

Henry took a breath, almost regretting having left his Glock in Zu's car. He opened the SUV door slowly and put a foot on the ground. Every move he made was measured and deliberate. He put his hands up to show he wasn't armed and walked away from the car.

"*Wo milu le...*" Henry said in a hesitant voice that he was lost.

There was no response.

"*Wo milu le –*" He had no time to finish his sentence. The doors of both trucks opened to the noise of guns being racked and boots hitting the ground. Six men encircled Henry in seconds. One of them walked straight up to him, a rifle pointed at his chest.

Henry had no time to repeat what he had said. The butt of the man's rifle hit his stomach with force, winding him. He hardly saw the second punch coming that threw him against the bonnet of his SUV.

The other men soon joined in, pummelling him with their own blows.

CHAPTER THREE

The distant sound of voices slipped into his mind. Pain jolted through his body as he tried to move. Someone grabbed his hair and started shouting in his face. The rank smell of stale breath and cigarette almost made him heave.

"You American... lost?"

Henry made an effort to open both eyes but his left one remained shut. Before he could protect himself the blows to his head had landed just above his left cheek, and his eye had started to swell.

"No... British. I look for fossils... dinosaur," he mumbled, his head held back against the front guard of the SUV. He'd dropped to the ground during the attack, to avoid blows to any vital organs, as he'd been shown in training.

The man holding his hair banged Henry's head against the metal bumper and stepped back.

He spoke to the other men in Mongolian. There was no reason for these people to use Mandarin, even though the Chinese government was now insisting Mandarin was the official language of Inner Mongolia, a part of China. Henry strained to understand but his knowledge of the language was basic.

He kept his head down, observing the small group, now that they had established he was no threat to them. The low headlights of his car were still on, making it easier to see the details of the men's uniforms. They looked old and tatty, not what one would expect from a well-run unit. Nor did they look like the photos Henry had seen of the border guards that the Chinese newspapers were bandying around.

Their Type 95 automatic rifles, a variation of the infamous AK47, were slung negligently over their shoulders. Two of the men were instructed to inspect the SUV. They found Henry's rucksack and brought it to the man Henry understood to be the leader. He emptied the contents on the ground, and went through them with the tip of his boot.

He clicked his fingers and one of the guards picked up what he was most interested in: Henry's passport. The leader looked at the front page and moved to the back page where the Mongolian entry stamp had been affixed. Henry almost smiled. MI6 had yet again done a good job at producing a state-of-the-art fake document.

"...'enry Neuborn..." The leader articulated slowly.

Henry nodded.

"...fin-an-sheal con-sal-tan..."

"Yes... but I'm here to look for fossils –"

One guard slammed the butt of his rifle into Henry's arm. He winced. He was not meant to speak unless spoken to.

The leader repeated "fin-an-sheal con-sal-tan" and a sudden realisation brightened up his features. He moved closer to Henry and rubbed his thumb against his first two fingers. An international sign that didn't need translation: money.

Henry hesitated. This was not the response he had anticipated. Kidnapping for ransom might be less common in China than it was in Iraq but there was always a first time.

"No money with me," he replied in Mandarin, patting his pockets.

The leader understood straight away, not surprised by Henry's command of Chinese. All he was interested in was getting cash out of him. The man rummaged through what he had dropped on the ground and found Henry's wallet. He took out the single credit card that was there.

In a sudden move he bent down to Henry and the same reeking smell as before hit Henry's nostrils. "You get money for me." The leader's expression had turned from aggressive to eager.

"For all of you?" Henry asked, looking around at the other five men.

This was the right question to ask. The idea of keeping all the money Henry could get his hands on made the leader stand up.

He turned towards the group of men and started delivering some fast instructions in Mongolian. A couple of them didn't appear to like it. The tone changed and it sounded more conspiratorial than before. Henry didn't need much knowledge of Mongolian to understand the gist of what the man was saying. He was taking Henry to get some money... perhaps to a place where Henry could withdraw cash. The others were not invited on this trip.

There was more arguing but the man finally got agreement and turned to Henry. "You come with me."

"Can I pick up my stuff?" Henry mimicked picking up the items on the ground.

The man picked up the rucksack and threw it at him; Henry rapidly gathered the items together, grabbing a few handfuls of sand in the process.

After he stood up, one of the guards threw him against the bonnet and tied his hands together. He shoved him in the SUV along with his backpack. It appeared that the leader was also taking Henry's SUV.

The other trucks disappeared the way they came, and Henry was left waiting in the SUV whilst the leader watched his men go. He jumped into the vehicle after a couple of minutes and started the engine.

"Where are we going?" Henry pulled on the makeshift handcuffs.

"No talking."

This was fine by Henry. No matter where they went a single man would be easier to overcome than six. He just had to bide his time.

* * *

Rodriguez moved to the left and signalled Don. Don shook his head. There was still nothing coming. Rodriguez checked his watch again. twenty minutes had passed.

The faint rumble of vehicles driving towards them focused Rodriguez, Don and Ray. Fergus and Hulk from their position would have heard as well. Rodriguez stuck his eye to the scope of his M16A2 rifle. He moved a little to the right and the left but saw no sign of the vehicles coming their way.

Rodriguez turned to Don who signalled he was to look due east.

Don signalled three with extended fingers and a hand sign to watch for army trucks.

"What the fuck... another convoy?" Rodriguez mumbled. "This is the fucking desert, not some LA motorway." He slid down towards Don who had crawled up to speak to him. "How far is this new lot?"

"Two klicks, maybe more," Don replied. "The wind is carrying the sound of their engine."

"And since they are arriving in the opposite direction to the one we are expecting the trucks carrying Henry, we won't hear the trucks coming."

"Correct."

"No need to track the group we're waiting to hear," Ray said, his eye still to his scope. "They're on the approach."

"We let the two convoys converge and observe," Rodriguez whispered and climbed back up to his position.

The convoy of three trucks arriving from the east accelerated. Rodriguez changed the angle of his rifle's scope to survey their progress. They were moving fast and he could see the quality of their vehicle was better than the first lot of trucks they'd encountered.

The two trucks coming from the west slowed down, but after a moment of hesitation something made them accelerate. Rodriguez guessed that they had been contacted by the eastern convoy and had been asked to meet.

Two hundred metres from the ALPHA team position, both convoy of trucks stopped abruptly, East facing West. One of the trucks advanced only a few metres farther. Men stepped out and took position on the ground.

"Shit... they're ambushing their own people," Rodriguez whispered.

"What if Henry is in one of the two trucks?" Ray asked, surveying the scene through his scope.

"We don't know that yet."

"But that's why we're here, right?"

"We are going to extract him, not get involved in some turf war," Rodriguez hissed.

"So, what do we do? Give up on him?"

"I didn't say that... but at the moment we've got five trucks of either border patrol or military and everyone is well equipped. We wait."

Ray mumbled something. Rodriguez returned to his observation of the three-truck convoy and the other two approaching vehicles.

A small man stepped out of the truck that had moved ahead. He walked a few steps to the side of the vehicle. Rodriguez could see him clearly through his scope. He could also distinguish his own men Fergus and Hulk, buried deep in the sand, uncomfortably close to the hostiles' position.

The two trucks from the west slowed to a crawl and when one of the east trucks flashed its lights a few times, the trucks stopped.

"No one's getting out," Ray murmured.

"No matter what they do they don't stand a chance," Rodriguez replied in a low voice.

The small man standing by the side of the first convoy truck lifted a hand. He was speaking into a radio. There was impatience in the way he stood next to his truck, and he must have conveyed that in his conversation.

Five men stepped out almost at once but stuck close to the vehicle. The headlights from the three-truck convoy came on in one strong beam. The five men recoiled, sheltering their eyes with their arms.

The shooting started and the bodies of the men twisted from the impact of the bullets. The sound of the guns echoed like thunder across the bare landscape.

Rodriguez sensed his two men freeze. None of them were sure whether Henry was one of the dead. The small man stepped towards the carnage. He was calling again on his radio.

Among the slain bodies one man stood up, wavering. The truck's lights had been switched off and the injured man stumbled forward in the dark. The small man took a gun out of its holder. The injured man was begging and the interrogation started. It didn't last very long.

The battered man was dragged into one of the army trucks while the small man returned to his vehicle. The convoy started its engines, about to resume its journey towards the west.

Ray moved his rifle a fraction. "Rod, this is now or never."

"Neither party has Henry."

"How do you know?"

"Because that's where the three-truck convoy is going... The men are looking for him. We could try to follow them."

Rodriguez gritted his teeth. "We're out of time."

"But we –"

"I *said* we're out of time." Rodriguez followed the trucks for a moment using his scope. There was a no-casualty-low-engagement protocol on the operation, and he cursed that decision.

* * *

Henry shifted in his seat a little to discreetly check the time on the dashboard clock. It was past 4am and the sky had already started to take on a lighter colour, announcing daybreak. His abductor had not bothered to tie him to his seat, perhaps knowing that no one would survive in the desert unless that person had been born there.

The man had taken a route that headed towards the southeast. From his research, Henry recalled that there was a good motorway past the Zhaga camp that linked the main city to the border, some 200 km away. If they reached the motorway around daybreak at 6am they could be in Bayannur before lunchtime.

Henry moved a little restlessly and the driver gave him a nasty look.

"Water," Henry asked in Mandarin.

"Later."

The man returned to his driving. There was no track to follow and the SUV was bouncing heavily on the gravelled ground, although the terrain had started to feel smoother. They were getting close to the sandy part of the desert where a heavy vehicle getting stuck was a strong possibility.

"No... I need water now." The leader had to keep him alive at least until he'd found a way to get money from him.

"Later."

Henry slumped back into his seat. He would give his captor a little more time to relax and get fooled into thinking he wouldn't try to escape.

They had been on the road for thirty minutes now. The driver's attention was locked on the terrain they were crossing, and Henry continued with the small loosening motion he'd started on his restraints as soon as they'd driven off. The ties around his wrists had enough slack that he could use them as a weapon.

The leader hesitated before slowing down. He changed course closer to the south. Henry felt the man had made a rash decision. He would be driving through the dunes, to reach the motorway more quickly, and this would be risky.

"I need water." Henry's voice was a mix of pleading and annoyance.

His captor didn't respond.

Henry slammed both bound hands on the dashboard. "I want water... now!"

26

The man hit the brakes hard and started shouting in Mongolian. He pulled his gun out but not fast enough. Henry slammed into him, his body squeezing the man against the car door. The gun flew across the dashboard, dropping into Henry's footwell. Henry managed to push the man against the steering wheel. In a quick move Henry slung his bound hand around the man's throat, pushing his knee into his back. The man tried to hit Henry a few times but in the cramped space his blows didn't have the room needed to inflict damage.

Gasping for air, the man flung the door open and collapsed outside the vehicle. Henry let go of him before he did and slid into the driver's seat. Not bothering to shut the door, he reversed at speed and turned back towards the place they'd come from.

With his hands tied, Henry just managed to reach the gear box and drive. He would get rid of the makeshift cuffs when he'd put enough distance between the vehicle and the leader who was now running after the car in a hopeless attempt to catch up.

With the car lowlights on, Henry was certain he'd correctly followed the SUV's tracks in the opposite direction for the last twenty minutes. He stopped the car, bent down to reach his rucksack in the footwell. He retrieved the Swiss army knife he'd managed to salvage earlier and started cutting through the wire that had been used to tie him up. He pulled hard one last time and the left wrist cuff snapped. He would take care of the other cuff later. He had another ten minutes or so to drive before he reached the place where he'd been ambushed. Henry placed the knife back into his rucksack and slung it into the footwell of the passenger seat.

He was about to drive off when he spotted a convoy of three trucks in the distance that had stopped. He bent again into the footwell, to retrieve the gun that had fallen into it. He checked the chamber: eight rounds. Nowhere near enough to stand even a remote chance...

Henry breathed deeply, hesitated.

It was the second time in a couple of hours he was disposing of a gun. He opened the window and slung the gun out. 'Don't carry a weapon if you're not going to use it' had been Harris's advice when he was training him. Henry was about to test whether the advice had been wise.

He drove towards the incoming trucks for a few minutes and then stopped. The convoy was on the move and Henry estimated they would reach him in less than ten minutes. The drivers took their time, confident it seemed that whoever was driving the SUV wouldn't escape.

Henry sat back and waited for their arrival.

The first truck stopped 100 yards away from the SUV and for a short moment nobody moved. Then someone jumped from the back of the truck and staggered along the side of the vehicle, moving slowly into the lowlights of Henry's car.

He immediately recognised one of the men who had assaulted him a few hours ago. This time he was the one who looked battered and bloodied. The man stopped and turned back, as though waiting for more instructions. He need not have bothered. The sound of three gunshots was the answer to his question.

Henry gulped some air and cursed Harris.

What had he been thinking? At least he might have stood a chance with eight bullets than none.

"Come out of the car... hands on your head." The English was flawless, perhaps with a slight accent that Henry thought sounded more public school than Chinese.

He opened the door of the SUV slowly and slid out even slower, putting his hands on his head as he did. He didn't want some trigger-happy guard to put an end to his mission.

"Move to the front of the car..."

Reluctantly, he left the protection of the car door. Someone switched the headlights to full beam, blinding him. He recoiled but forced himself to keep his hands where they were.

Men jumped out of the trucks, encircling him fast. Another guard opened the SUV door, rummaging through Henry's vehicle.

"My passport is in the rucksack..." Henry tried to sound calm, but even an innocent man would be worried about what he was witnessing.

Still blinded by the truck's lights, Henry didn't move.

"Are you Henry Newborn?"

He assumed his rucksack had been handed over to whoever was talking to him.

"Yes... I'm British and I'm looking for fossils in the Gobi. Dinosaurs... *Kǒnglóng.*"

There was some sniggering amongst the men who had their rifles pointed at his chest.

"No," the voice said. "You're a spy."

* * *

Harris had just returned to the Taichung Control and Command room after having taken a couple of calls from MI6's HQ in London. His local team had confirmed that Henry's mobile phone had been cleaned of all systems that may be traced back to Vauxhall Cross.

"Any news?" he asked Lieutenant Pike.

"ALPHA team should have crossed the Mongolian border ten minutes ago. I'm hoping to receive a transmission shortly after 6am," she said, checking the digital clock on her screen.

Harris checked his watch. Less than five minutes to go. He took his cigarette packet out, disappointed to find there was only one left in the pack.

Pike glanced at Harris sideways. "Nasty habit."

Harris was about to tell Pike to mind her bloody business but thought better of it.

"Been trying to stop for years... People like you who don't smoke don't understand."

"Who said I didn't smoke?"

Harris's eyebrows arched. "How did you manage? Lots of ..." Harris had opted for strong will rather than sweeties.

"When you join a SEAL team, that's the first thing you do – stop smoking. The smell on your breath and clothes can give you up. I cleaned up then."

"You've been on SEAL ops?" Harris couldn't disguise his surprise. Pike looked like a nice girl, a bit uptight, maybe, but he attributed that to her operating in a high-octane environment dominated by men.

"Yes, sir."

Harris gave her a nod of admiration. Hardly any woman made the grade to become a SEAL operative... A story for another time over a beer, perhaps.

29

Pike checked the clock again as a few people moved back into the room. Her boss and the head of the US unit that had been dispatched to Taiwan were talking in a low voice. The pair stopped as soon as they reached Harris and Pike.

The clock passed the 6am mark and the phone remained silent.

Harris took the last cigarette out of its pack and was fingering it nervously. He knew what the score should be. They had lost Henry and couldn't, or rather shouldn't have found him. But Harris was stuck in Taiwan and the ALPHA team was on the ground. So much could happen that he could do nothing about.

The other two US military in the room were chatting among themselves, ignoring Harris.

Shit, it's my guy's neck on the line.

He wondered how much of that had been Hunter III's work. The head of Special Ops had not appreciated Henry taking liberties with the understanding between MI6 and the CIA. There was to be no recruitment of American nationals on US soil. This hadn't stopped Henry getting Nick Fox, a young genius hacker, to join his team. Oops on that one.

Harris smiled at the memory.

The time moved past 6.10am and Pike's commander moved closer to Pike, armed crossed over his chest.

"What's the window for extraction?"

They all knew the window was tight, but it was a way to confirm the ALPHA team was late on their comms rendezvous.

"Two hours, sir. The chopper is on the ground, hundred klicks from Gashuun-Sukhait border crossing."

"And then?"

"Straight to Ulaanbaatar for a direct flight to South Korea."

Everyone nodded. The plan had been discussed many times. The chopper was not a military one but it was good enough to carry the men, and there was no other way to extract the team than to choose a commercial flight that would fly over China. This time a standard flight would do.

Another number flipped over on the screen. 6.13am.

Harris rubbed the back of his neck.

The shrill sound of a phone made Pike smile. She picked up. "Good to hear your voice, ALPHA team."

She handed the handset to Commander Richards. "I hear you, Lima Charlie ALPHA team."

Commander Richards listened intently. His jaw clenched a few times and he glanced at Harris. "Master Chief Rodriguez, prolonging your presence on Mongolian soil is not an option."

Harris was not hooked into the conversation, but Rodriguez seemed to have a different view.

"Negative, Master Chief. ALPHA team is to make its way back. I'm expecting a full debrief after you reach South Korea."

Commander Richards hung up and turned to Harris. "Your man is still missing." Richards sounded genuinely sorry. "The ALPHA team tried a rescue, but they couldn't find him in time."

Harris nodded, looking suitably shocked. "Anything else you can tell me?" he asked Richards.

"We'll have to wait for the debrief in South Korea."

"I presume CIA Chief of Ops Hunter III will be patched in?"

Commander Richards frowned, as if to hint what a silly question. TECH LEOPARD was a CIA-MI6 op.

Harris brandished his last cigarette. "I need a fag." He walked out of the building to a place he had spotted that was perfect to make calls without risk of eavesdropping.

The number he called rang for a while. "Yup..." Nick Fox eventually answered.

"Where were you?" Harris shot to Nick.

"S-sorry..." Nick stammered. "Working on an assignment from your team, sir."

The image of the young man, collapsed on the ground after his release from Russia, flashed in front of Harris's eyes. Nick still needed to get over the ordeal of abduction.

"Pack your bag. I need you in Taiwan."

"Today?"

"No, yesterday." Harris softened his voice. "There is a late-night flight. I'll call the team in DC. They'll get you on and meet you at the airport with your ticket."

"OK... I'll get ready."

"And bring some good hacking equipment."

"My best stuff is here at home. I've got all you need –"

"No doubt, but I need you here."

"How much hacking are we talking about, anyway?" Nick's interest in his next big challenge was palpable.

"Nothing you can't handle." Harris smiled. "Just the CIA's Chief of Ops mail account."

CHAPTER FOUR

The vast complex was ringed with 25-feet-tall bare concrete walls, watchtowers and humming electricity wires. The main entrance was equipped with face-scanning turnstiles and rifle-bearing guards in military camouflage.

A large gate had opened to let the truck in; after, Henry had been shoved out. The men who'd looked after him during the journey didn't need to handcuff him. Henry knew by the way they moved that they were trained to kill in more ways than one.

Henry had expected to be interrogated on the spot in the desert. Instead, he'd been handled roughly by a couple of guards and bundled into the back of one of the trucks. The journey had taken less time than he'd expected. He'd avoided looking at his watch, knowing it would give an excuse for the guards to rob him and rough-handle him a little more.

No doubt there was going to be plenty of that wherever he was going. Why not give the body a rest in preparation for the upcoming onslaught?

A small man jumped from one of the other trucks. The guards straightened up and moved back a little. The atmosphere changed from rough but confident to harsh and focused.

The man walked up to Henry, taking him in, assessing. He looked much older than his voice had sounded in the desert. There was no readable expression on his face.

"You are a financial consultant?" he said. Again, the fluent English, the manners, so out of place in this prison camp in the middle of the desert, made Henry nervous.

"I am... But I'm here to –"

A sudden smack with the butt of a gun reminded him that he was to answer the question and nothing else. Henry yelped in pain.

"What do you advise in?" the man asked.

"Large financial deals and equity market investments."

The warden had stopped a few paces from Henry. Henry could now see his features clearly in the light of daybreak. Despite the mask of impenetrability, Henry saw resentment and anger. This camp was not a promotion for him no matter how high-profile it might be. It was a punishment.

"I don't believe you..." He turned his back to Henry and started walking to the main building. "Take him to the basement," he added, this time in Mandarin.

"This is a mistake. I want to speak to the British Embassy," Henry yelled, as the guards pulled him towards a smaller building to the left-hand side of what looked like the main prison complex.

The guards laughed – a cranky, nasty laugh people make when they know what awaits you. Henry knew as well. He had spent months training for it but whether he was truly ready he was about to find out.

Two guards were waiting by the door. Henry noticed that their uniforms looked older. It reminded him of the men who had first attacked him. Perhaps there was a pecking order amongst the guards of the camp.

One of them unlocked a heavy door and pushed it open. The smell of detergent was almost overpowering. One of the guards who had accompanied Henry shoved him in but didn't enter himself.

Henry looked around the room and saw a desk and a man sitting at it.

The man, lean and much older than the guards he had seen so far, stood up. He squinted at Henry, then turned towards another room, the door of which was open, and shouted what sounded like orders.

Someone else arrived with a large bucket. He moved to Henry and gestured to him that he had to undress. When Henry hesitated, the older guard shouted an order, swiping up a baton from behind the desk.

"OK... fine." He held his hand up in a sign of agreement.

He took his time to undo his shirt, shoes, trousers. The older guard moved closer and tapped his hand on his wrist. Henry unclipped the expensive watch he was wearing. He placed it in the bucket and stood stock still in his underwear.

The older guard started shouting again. Henry tried to play dumb. He knew where this was headed but he had hoped it might happen in his cell rather than in the hallway of the prison building.

The discharge of electricity from the older guard's baton hit his abdomen and knocked him to the ground. Henry rolled to his side, surprised, and bunched up in a ball. He had not suspected it would be electrified.

The older guard stopped his attack eventually and kicked the bucket with his foot. The metal object thudded against Henry's back. Henry staggered to his feet, removed his underwear and placed it in the bucket.

The older guard took his time to consider his handiwork, then jerked his head towards a flight of stairs leading down. He waved his hand again and Henry started moving in that direction. He was certain this set was not leading to Heaven.

* * *

The steps felt slimy and cold against Henry's bare feet, and the metal creaked under his weight. Through the metal grid, he could see that two guards were waiting for him at the bottom of the stairwell.

He wondered how many naked westerners had walked these corridors. Not that many, he suspected, but there was one he knew must have: Rob Walker. The man must have been terrified. It was un-comfortable enough for Henry who had been trained to expect the worse. Walker must have been given the full intimidation treatment too.

The guards' gaze focused on Henry's genitals, an intimidation tactic that inevitably worked. Henry fought the desire to protect himself, running the risk of inviting reprisals. When he reached the bottom of the staircase he stood still.

The guards recoiled a little under his calm. He was neither scared nor aggressive, showing a passivity that didn't trigger any reaction. One of the guards shook his surprise off and smacked Henry across the back with his baton, shouting more instructions. Henry didn't need a translation to know what they meant.

The guards walked him along a brightly lit corridor with cells on each side. The sound of low voices from some reached him. Then a shriek burst out, bouncing off the walls of the dungeon. Henry clenched his fists and slowed his walk. The guard shoved his baton into his back and Henry started moving again.

The two guards and Henry reached the end of the corridor and a door. One of the guards moved past Henry, reaching for a set of keys that was hanging from his belt. He unlocked the door and opened it wide.

Henry looked inside, expecting a cell, but instead another corridor appeared. It looked as though this area was part of the foundation of the building. The lights were dimmer and the stench unmistakable. Henry doubted many people came out of the place alive.

The guard who had opened the door recoiled; even he didn't look happy to enter the place. The second guard took over whilst the first waited outside.

Another shove of a baton encouraged Henry to walk down the small passage. The second guard opened another door that had simply been bolted shut. He pushed Henry into the cell and slammed the door behind him.

There was nothing in the cell – no bed, no mattress, not even a chamber pot. He shivered. This deep underground, the temperature had dropped noticeably. He might have been fine with clothes on, but the coolness of the place would soon chill his naked body.

He took stock of what he could in the room. It was larger than he'd anticipated. Carrying out a slow walk along the walls, he checked for graffiti or carvings. There were none. The occupants of the place mustn't have had enough time or the ability to leave marks.

He crouched and ran his fingers over noticeable grooves in the floor of the cell. These had been caused by something large and heavy being dragged across the concrete slabs. Henry took a quick intake of breath. Some machine had been moved around in here and he doubted it was meant to improve the prisoner's comfort.

He stood up, took a final walk around the cell, placed one ear to the metal door. There was no sound at all.

Henry returned to a place he thought he might sit in comfortably. He lowered himself to the floor, leaned against the cold wall and brought his knees to his chin, arms around his legs. It was the best position to preserve strength and energy, both of which he would need if he was to survive the next twenty-four hours.

Only a few minutes had elapsed before a door opened somewhere in the corridor. Henry heard voices; someone was angry, and he thought he recognised the warden's voice.

The door of his cell slammed open and two men in white forensic suits came in. One of them was carrying a set of heavy chains and the others were bringing in two chairs and a trolley upon which a couple of boxes sat.

The chain was flung up at the ceiling, catching on a hook Henry hadn't noticed.

The men moved around the room with precision, placing the chairs and the trolley at angles that seemed to have been decided for maximum efficacy.

Like being a patient and witnessing the preparation of the operating theatre before a major op, Henry observed everything without moving.

The men in white suits lined up against the wall as soon as they had finished. There was a pause, as though everyone was making sure the room had been organised exactly as instructed. The warden entered.

He took one step into the cell, stopped, took time to consider the way the room had been laid out, spat out some instructions to the line of men. They disappeared into the corridor without closing the door.

"Who are you, Mr Newborn?" The warden turned to him, the same cold expression on his face as before.

"Perhaps a set of clothes before we speak? It would feel more civilised." Henry stood up slowly.

A shadow moved across the warden's eyes. "As you'll come to know, Mr Newborn, I don't do civilised."

* * *

"You have reached the office of Mr Henry Newborn. Our office is closed at the moment. Our opening hours are 8am to 7pm Monday to Friday. This answer phone is checked regularly so please leave a message after the tone and one of our team will call you back as soon as we can." A long tone followed and the recording kicked in.

Warden Tang put the phone down without hurry. He'd already visited the website registered under Henry's consultancy name. The site looked sober yet polished, just enough to elicit interest but not enough to truly reveal the extent of Mr Newborn's reach in the world of finance.

Warden Tang pursed his lips. So far Mr Newborn had regurgitated the same story. He was a successful financial consultant who had developed an interest in fossils, hence the financial support for the excavation of a new dinosaur skeleton in the Mongolian part of the Gobi Desert.

It was a credible story and yet Warden Tang wondered why he had received a tip that a foreigner had crossed the border. Why the idiot Zu had tried to capitalise on that information on his own, organising a second-rate team of second-rate guards to collect the wealthy individual he had gotten wind about. Zu should have known better – nothing that happened in Zhaga or in the desert within a 500-mile radius escaped Tang's surveillance drones.

He returned to the website and clicked on the page called Our Team. It was a predictable display of professional yet approachable faces. Each team member had a small bio attached to their name and a phone number.

Tang hesitated. His phone records were regularly checked, and his mobile was being monitored, he was sure of it. Visiting the website and making one call to the Brit's offices may be acceptable but making a call to a number of other phones might be pushing his interest too far.

Tang took a burner phone out of his uniform and proceeded to call the mobile phone of a man called Nick Fox, Newborn's senior consultant, or so the website said. A voice with a distinct American accent had recorded a message that sounded very similar to his boss's and Tang hung up.

He continued down the list, calling each of the people mentioned on the website. They were all incredibly busy or they simply didn't exist.

Tang checked his watch. He smiled briefly at the thought of soon relieving Henry of the expensive Rolex he had spotted on Henry's wrist when he'd first met him. It was 7.30am in Zhaga. He calculated it was 7.30pm in Washington DC where Newborn's office was meant to be. As far as the London office was concerned, it was 12.30am and Newborn's staff would be sound asleep.

Tang stood up. Perhaps he needed to check whether the latest round of waterboarding had yielded any different answers. He thought about one of his favourite books and remembered a passage from it.

Sun Tsu said:

Miliary might concerns the state,
For it will dictate who lives and who dies,

The Tao of existence and destruction,
One must study it.
The text spoke of a link between knowledge and victory.

Warden Tang sat down again and dialled Nick Fox's number, leaving a very short message to be called back. He needed to know more.

Tang left his office and returned to the lower part of building he had left only half an hour ago. His people were experienced and his instructions were clear. Whatever they did, the Westerner had to be kept alive and his intellectual faculties intact. He was no use to Tang brain-dead.

The sun had risen over the horizon an hour and a half ago and the temperature was rising too. September was a good month to visit the Gobi – if there was any good time at all. Tang took his Ray-Ban sunglasses out of his uniform top pocket and adjusted them over his eyes. He crossed the yard. One of the guards opened the door for him as soon as he reached the building. He walked in, climbed down the stairs and arrived at the door of the interrogation room.

The westerner was still naked and drenched in water. His face had slumped to the side and he was mumbling something Tang couldn't understand. As soon as Tang entered, the men in white protection suits moved away.

Tang grabbed a chair that was stored in the corner of the room far from the water that was now draining through a hole in the ground. He dragged it next to Henry with a screech and sat down heavily.

"Who are you, Mr Newborn?"

Henry's face rolled painfully to the side. "Financial... consultant." The words were almost inaudible.

"And you got lost in the Gobi looking for dinos... *Kǒnglóng.*"

The Chinese word for dinosaur made the other men snigger. Warden Tang turned back and shut them up with only one look. He snapped his fingers and they disappeared.

Henry nodded in a slow move.

"I so want to believe you, but I found the explanation..." Tang leaned forward. "How do you say, I forgot the expression... far fetch."

"Call the..." Henry swallowed with difficulty. "...office... anyone, please."

"And what will it prove?"

39

Henry's eyes opened a little more. There was desperation and fear in them. "Ask for... references... clients..."

Tang sat back.

Why not? He could play along. Pretend he was a Hong Kong Chinese man wanting to do business with Newborn Consulting and who knows, maybe he would actually do business with them?

Tang left the room without a word to Henry.

He said to the men waiting outside, "Clean him up, find him some clothes and move him to Section One. Something happens to him you know what'll happen to you."

Everyone nodded in unison. They didn't want to end up in the room they'd just left, for they knew they wouldn't come out alive.

* * *

Harris made his way to the British Rep Office in Taipei. There was no point in staying behind in Taichung. As far as he could tell he knew more than control and command knew about the true purpose of the op and that Hunter III had not revealed anything to his army colleagues. It would stay that way for a while, Harris suspected.

The Rep Office had provided him with accommodation, and he liked the idea of not having to worry about being spied on. It could happen there too but was less likely than in a hotel. Harris had wondered whether the office would be less well equipped than a proper Embassy. Taiwan was still being contested by China and its independence status was not yet recognised by international law. But Harris needn't have worried. All he required had been made available to him.

He yawned. A few hours' sleep would be welcome now. Nick Fox would be arriving in sixteen hours. Harris had time to plan his next move.

His mobile buzzed and he took it out of his crumpled jacket, irritated.

"If it's Pike calling me back –"

But it wasn't Lieutenant Pike. It was MI6 surveillance centre.

Harris made an effort to focus on the call. "What is it?"

"Good morning, Steve. We've received a warning on our systems. Someone called Henry's office. Didn't leave a message, then called every cell phone listed on the website. Didn't leave a message first time around, but must have changed their mind and called Nick Fox's cell." The news from his MI6 surveillance colleague changed Harris's mood.

"Sorry, Deborah, it's been a long night."

"No worries... I have the recording for you. I've sent it to your encrypted account."

"Could you play it for me, please?"

"Sure." The line went dead for a few seconds and then the recording started.

"Mr Fox, I have read with interest the list of services you offer. I would be interested in discussing in depth. Please call my number." The man gave a string of digits and hung up.

"Have you traced the call?" Steve asked.

"Of course. It's a burner phone, geolocalised in China, Ganqi Maodu."

"You're a star, Deb, and now I've got to make an urgent call."

Harris didn't wait for her to reply. He killed the call and dialled Nick's MI6 phone. The phone rang a few times. Harris tapped on the glass of the windowpane nervously. "Come on, Nicky, pick up the bloody phone."

Voicemail kicked in and Harris swore loudly. He didn't care if he could be heard.

He tried the number again. Perhaps Nick was still in the airport lounge looking at one of his gadgets and he wasn't paying attention to his mobile. The phone kept ringing. With his own device stuck between his ear and his shoulder, Harris opened his email on his laptop and found the message confirming Nick's travel arrangements.

The plane to Taiwan was boarding and take-off was in thirty minutes.

"Shit... He needs to reply to this guy."

Nick's phone went to voicemail. Harris left an urgent message. He dialled another number.

"Jack, I need you."

"In trouble already? You know that Hunter is running OPER-ATION TECH LEOPARD himself, right?"

Harris grunted. "I do. I'm at the receiving end of it, remember?"

"So, who's in trouble, Nick or Henry?"

"Henry... and I need to speak to Nick who is on his way to Taiwan. The plane is about to depart and he needs to return a call."

"It's life or death, I presume?"

"Literally..."

"OK... I'm on it. I'll call you as soon as I have news." Jack hung up. Surely the CIA could get a word to Nick on time?

Harris brought up on screen the list of flights departing from Dulles International Airport in Washington DC. He found the Cathay Pacific flight Nick was due to be on. Boarding had ended and departure was imminent.

Harris ran his hand through his hair. Nick was embarking on a 16-hour journey and calling him would be almost impossible.

CHAPTER FIVE

The hot water coursed down Henry's back and despite the other water treatment he'd just endured, it felt good to be allowed a shower.

After his interrogation, the warden's men had thrown a grey jumpsuit at him and as soon as he was dressed, they had dragged him out of the godforsaken building in which he had spent two terrifying hours. He'd been prepared for what to expect but he hadn't known until he'd gone through it that he would survive the ordeal.

One of the guards who had been assigned to him shouted something. Henry nodded, turned off the shower and wrapped a large towel around his body. He moved out of the communal cubicle to the place where he had dumped the grey jumpsuit.

A fresh outfit comprising of a pair of faded-blue trousers and an even more discoloured T-shirt was in place of the jumpsuit. His expensive hiking boots had vanished, replaced with a pair of trainers that had also seen better days, but at least they didn't reek as he had feared they might.

Henry took his time to dress, fighting off the memories of a time during which he thought he would never escape prison. HSU Belmarsh in East London was a prison within a prison and although it couldn't be compared to the Zhaga Camp, the prospect of spending 30 years behind bars there had pushed Henry to the limit.

The police officers that are guarding Henry on his way to the UK Counterterrorist HQ look at him and decide he won't be trouble, stuck in the back of the van that is taking him to Paddington for interrogation. The cuffs are pretty tight around his wrists – such a very small but effective restraining tool. The van seems to be stuck at a set of lights or are they stuck in a traffic jam?

Henry shuffles on his seat. He is impatient to get on with this ultimate test...

It all happens in one instant, a surge of energy never experienced before. An uncontrollable force throws Henry against the walls, the floor, the ceiling of the van; his ears are incapable of taking in the deafening noise. Space is torn open and his consciousness ripped from him the instant the bomb goes off.

Henry closed his eyes and breathed in a slow and controlled breath. Now was not the time or place to lose it. The past would not make him vulnerable.

Henry gave the guards a sideways glance. Their focus was elsewhere, more interested in sharing images or whatever else was on one guard's mobile.

He looked around. If he was quick, he could use the small stool on which his fresh clothes lay as a weapon and he could dispatch these two idiots. A small bubble of anger rose in his chest at the idea. He let it pop without responding to it.

Instead, he sat on the stool and fixed his shoes. He slung the wet towel over his shoulder. He doubted it would be changed for a while.

The guards, noticing he was waiting for them, started shouting again. Perhaps it was a way of reassuring themselves that any delay in delivering the new inmate to his cell was due to the inmate's tardiness rather than their idleness.

Henry stood up and made his way towards the corridor. One of the guards shoved his baton into his ribs. Henry turned in a sharp, sudden move that startled the guards. Everyone froze and the man who'd used his baton reached for his gun.

Henry relaxed, subservient again. The guards stood down. He was just at the beginning of his mission. Patience. The time would come to settle scores. He resumed his slow walk along the corridor. After a short moment one of the guards called Henry's name and he stopped.

The door of a cell was open. Henry took a sharp turn into it, expecting it to be empty, but the warden was there sitting at a small table, waiting.

His body was set at an angle to the table, legs crossed, interlaced fingers resting on his lap. A long stick was finely balanced on his legs. He could have been waiting for service at the terrace of a café or having a drink with a friend. A mobile phone was on the table, screen facing down.

"I have made a call to your office and decided to leave a message for your senior consultant." There was a hint of sarcasm in the warden's tone. He moved one hand in a proprietary way to rest on the phone.

Henry hadn't been given his watch back, but he estimated the time to be around 8am. His mental calculation was quick: 8pm in DC. "It's late. I'm sure he has gone home by now."

"You will address me as Warden Tang or sir." Tang's eyes drilled into Henry's.

"Yes, sir." The words stuck in Henry's throat, but he managed a passable show of humility.

Tang seemed satisfied though and he carried on. "8pm is not that late in your line of business, or so I was led to believe."

"It depends. A lot of the work can be done from home." Henry was stalling for time. Harris and his team had been prepped to expect verification of identity and a challenge from the Chinese authorities. Where were they?

Tang pouted. His thin face might have been more attractive were it not for the harshness of his stare. "I am not a patient man."

Henry tried to guess where the warden's accent came from, higher education no doubt. He sounded so British and yet there was a slight inflection that didn't quite add up.

"Let me call Nick... He'll call back if I tell him this is urgent."

"No doubt, but no. I want to see how... commercial your senior consultant is."

There was no doubt Tang was toying with Henry. Perhaps he had already decided what he was going to do or perhaps he genuinely wanted to know more, but Henry was certain that the purpose of the current conversation was to play with hope and fear.

"But I am willing to try one more time." Tang picked up the phone from the table, scrolled down a list of numbers and pressed the recall button. He switched on the loudspeaker.

Henry's throat went dry. He knew Nick's voicemail message by heart. They had agreed on its content together. It was suitably corporate and suitably bland – nothing that would reveal Nick's true position as prime hacker and genius tech geek. But he didn't see how a second call would convince Warden Tang if the first hadn't.

The phone rang a few times and the voicemail kicked in.

"You have reached Nick Fox's voicemail. I am currently on a flight and unable to take your call. Please leave a message after the tone and I will reach out as soon as I can."

Tang frowned and killed the call. This was not the message he'd heard earlier.

Henry made a mental note to thank Harris for his quick response, or perhaps Nick was learning to think more like a spook. "It will be difficult –" Henry started.

Tang cut him off angrily. "I haven't asked for your opinion yet."

Henry nodded and lowered his eyes.

Tang hesitated then returned his attention to the phone. "Where is your man going?"

"Very probably London. He goes regularly."

Tang stood up. He brushed past Henry with a physical assurance that Henry had seldom witnessed in such small men. Henry was a good head taller than Tang and yet there was no fear in showing Henry he had the ability to hurt him.

The door closed behind Tang, leaving Henry to wonder what the warden had decided.

"Wait...!" Henry slammed the flat of his hand against the metal door, barely making a sound.

Memories of HSU Belmarsh flooded his mind: the bells that rang for lockdown, the shuffling of feet on their way to the canteen, the constant sense that something bad could happen to you even though it rarely did. Although when it did, it never finished well.

Henry closed his eyes tight. This was the same and yet different. He would escape Zhaga just the way he had escaped Belmarsh, but this time he wouldn't be the only one escaping.

* * *

Harris was dozing on his bed. He hadn't bothered to undress which meant that his suit would look a mess tomorrow – never mind. The buzz of his mobile made him sit up in one snappy move. The number of the caller was held back.

"Yes..." Harris managed in his most grumpy tone.

"It's Nick." He sounded uncertain, and Harris had to rein his desire to tell Nick he needed to be reachable at all times even when he was on a goddamn plane. But Nick was a newbie who had had his fair share of being thrown in the deep end.

"Are you calling from the plane?"

"Yes." Nick's voice was muffled and low.

"Cathay has got phones in business class so you can make in flight calls, so don't look uneasy. Just make it sound as though it is a call with a client."

There was a short silence. "This is the way I would speak to a client."

Harris smiled. "I suppose that's how you would be speaking to a client about a possible hack."

"I would prefer not to speak about it at all. It's all done through –"

Harris interrupted. "You gonna have to make an exception then because you need to call a prospective client in China."

"The guy who left an odd message on my phone?"

"Who told you?"

"I went to the toilet and checked."

Harris revised his advice and asked Nick to speak in a whisper. Lord knew what the passenger next to him thought of the conversation.

"Yes, that guy and you know who he might be." The aircraft phone wasn't secure, so Harris kept it cryptic.

"Henry briefed me."

"OK, then... make the call."

"Steve..." Nick Fox's voice was so low Harris strained to hear him. "I don't want to screw up like last time."

"You didn't screw up last time. You held your own like a pro. You just needed a bit more training. H would never rely on you in this new op if he didn't think you can do it, and neither would I."

"OK, OK. I'll make the call."

"You don't need to say much. Just take some notes and ask for a second call."

"I'll ask him for a proper client onboarding call and can tell him I'd like to get Henry's opinion."

"And if he asks why, seeing as you are a senior consultant?"

"I'll give him the list of SEC rules that require multiple engagements to open a business account."

"Sounds a very good plan... I'm sure you can make up something."

"Why would I do that? There are enough of them. I can select –"

Harris interrupted. "You mean you know all of them by heart."

It was not a question but more a reminder of what type of brain Nick had: read something once, remember it forever.

"That's an excellent idea," Harris said. "You don't want this guy to think you don't know your stuff and I doubt he's going to become a client. He just wants to check Henry's business is legit."

"It is legit..." Nick replied.

Harris smiled. That was the spirit. Harris only wished he was in the same room as Nick when he made the call.

* * *

The cell was plain but clean. The main building at Zhaga camp was not like the one Henry had just left. It had been constructed recently with a view on efficiency. He was the sole occupier even though there was another bed in the room.

Henry had stretched out on the bed after Tang had left the room. They would come back for him later and he needed to try to relax after the heavy ordeal of the waterboarding. He'd learned that skill during his first operation in Syria, to ease the tension as soon as he was not in imminent danger.

The bed had a wafer-thin mattress and was barely long enough to accommodate his tall body, but it would do. At least he had some clothes on and the beatings had stopped.

Henry looked around. The table at which Tang had sat was still there dwarfing the space. It would no doubt be taken away later. The cell window was high up with a thick glass pane, through which Henry could see a set of tight bars. The metal door looked impressively solid. A toilet had been squeezed in one corner.

He turned to the left, facing the wall and this time saw a few inscriptions had been scratched on it. Chinese characters that Henry would decipher later, others he didn't know but wondered whether they were Mongolian. He almost skimmed over a mark that was very faint. He frowned, moved closer to the wall and ran his fingers over it. There was no doubt; two letters had been scratched into the paint: RW. Henry breathed in and out. What were the odds he would be thrown into a cell that Rob Walker had himself been in? Low. Warden Tang liked to play with his prisoner's mind.

Henry thought about the plan he and Harris had etched, with the input of Dragon, the CIA's most valuable asset in the Chinese Communist Party. Henry was not quite clear why Zu had been killed and the first lot of border guards dispatched only to die, but he suspected that good old-fashioned greed and double-crossing had something to do with it.

Still, Warden Tang almost calling Henry's bluff by calling him a spy from the outset had been an unexpected twist. Why would a foreigner like him lose his way in the desert? The question had to be asked and Tang was proving to be an unexpectedly clued-in adversary. Dragon had mentioned that Zhaga was about to be sent a new warden and that was the reason why the extraction of Rob Walker had become urgent.

Henry would have liked to know more about the new incumbent, but the information had been difficult to get, and Dragon had been less able to communicate with his CIA handler. Henry doubted the previous warden had such impeccable English. It was British English with the precise, yet affected pronunciation only a public school could deliver.

The sound of footsteps stopped Henry's train of thought. He sat up and grabbed the edge of the bed. The key turned in the lock and two guards entered. They were the same people who had accompanied Tang earlier.

One of them jerked his head, indicating that Henry should stand up.

The other guard grabbed Henry's shoulder, turned him around and handcuffed him. He prodded him with his baton and they left the cell.

There was only one floor in the main building, and they walked the length of the corridor, accessed a door that led to a covered bridge and kept moving. They were now in the open but there was barbed wire along the sides of the bridge. It would be impossible to jump to the ground below.

The building they were walking towards had a tower-like quality. It was narrower, octagonal in shape, and taller too. The guard in front of Henry used his badge and another door opened. The new space was austere and the wall only had one portrait hanging from it: Xi Jinping, President of the People's Republic of China and leader of the CCP.

The walk to a set of rooms was short. The guard knocked and waited for a command to open the door. He opened as soon as Tang inside gave the order and the two guards and Henry moved a few steps in but no farther.

The guard bowed low and waited for more orders. Tang was sitting at his desk in front of a PC that looked new and expensive. The warden was finishing something; Henry guessed what it might be. He was reading a document on his computer screen.

The sudden slam of the guard's baton into Henry's back told him that he too was meant to bow. Henry imitated the guard, bent at the waist, now unable to see what Tang was doing at his desk.

The warden stood up. Gave a short set of instructions in Mongolian.

One of the guards left Henry's side and grabbed a chair from the corner of the warden's office. He plonked it in the middle of the room and returned to his place, bowing again.

"Sit," was all Tang said.

Henry straightened up slowly and moved to the chair. He must have been too slow because one of the guards grabbed his shoulder and slammed him into the seat.

Tang dismissed the guards with a wave of his hand. He leaned back in his oversized armchair and stared at Henry for a couple of minutes.

Henry waited. Tang tapped his fingers on the table. He might have liked Henry to ask a question, giving him the opportunity to impose punishment, but Henry kept his cool. The pain of this morning's treatment was still coursing through his body. Avoiding another beating was a good idea.

"Your Senior Consultant has disappointed me," Tang said.

Henry arched his eyebrows in surprise and his stomach tightened. Had Nick not returned Tang's call, or worse, had he been too transparent?

"I'm surprised."

"He was not selling your company very well at all."

"In what way?" At least Nick had returned the call.

"He was too keen to speak to you."

"I find that hard to believe."

"Are you saying I'm lying?" Tang straightened up.

"Of course not, and I apologise if Nick has not been up to your high standards. It might be that what you are asking for is too –" Henry hesitated, wanting to find the right word, "– adventurous."

Tang's impassive face wasn't giving much for Henry to read. But his tight posture spoke volumes. The man was on high alert. He wanted to hear more.

"Perhaps Nick wanted to speak to me about what it would take to do business in the Far East with a high-profile customer."

"Are you saying I want to do business with a western imperialist like you who is intent on destroying China's future?" The harsh language was there but the tone wasn't.

"But you need to know whether I'm lying and whether my story stacks up. What better way to do that than to check that I can deliver what I promise on my website?"

Tang glanced at his computer screen. "What does complex corporate structure mean?"

Henry shuffled on his seat to disguise the rush he felt. Tang, like many men of power, could not resist the thought of making the sort of money that would make them even more powerful. Greed was good!

Lunch was almost over by the time the guards led Henry to the canteen. Men were dressed in the same standard uniform of grey cotton shirt and trousers. The only difference was the colour of a large elastic band that each wore on their right arm. The yellow-coloured armband wearers looked as though they had finished their meal and were queuing to dump their trays on a large conveyer belt. The green band wearers were still eating but only a couple of inmates were at the food counter helping themselves.

Henry joined the small queue. The prisoners tried hard not to look at him. Like in any prison, being invisible and making no contact with someone who could be a threat was key to survival.

The menu was predictably poor: rice, some form of meat in a stew with a few veggies. Just enough to keep the prisoners from starving, not enough to give them the energy to do more than the job they were assigned to – whatever it might be.

Henry took his tray and sat alone at a table at the back of the long room. He could see that some of the people who were dumping their trays on the conveyer belt looked different to the ones who were finishing their food. The yellow and green band wearers seem to belong to different ethnic groups.

As far as the Chinese authorities were concerned there was nothing in Zhaga but sand and the occasional poisonous snake. The camp did not exist, no satellite images, no record anywhere... until Dragon had started leaking information to the West.

A large community of Uyghurs had been sent there on terror charges. It was impossible to know whether these charges were well-founded or not, but the people deemed most rebellious were usually sent to Zhaga.

Then there were the Hong Kong rebels, those pro-democracy and free speech dissidents who had not yielded to the pressure the Chinese state had put on them. Worse was to come for Hong Kong, no doubt. Foreign agents caught spying or foreigners believed to have been caught spying also formed part of the contingent.

Henry thought he recognised the typical Uyghurs' features in the people wearing the yellow armband. He couldn't make out who the green armband people were, but he thought he'd caught a few Cantonese words when he'd walked past a table. Perhaps the Hong Kong lot.

Henry ate quickly. At least his conversation with Warden Tang had earned him a meal and the chance to see a bit more of the huge prison complex. He also hoped that what he'd told Tang about equity markets and how to hide money through shadow companies would lead him to the man he was here to rescue.

Rob Walker.

CHAPTER SIX

One of the guards that had accompanied Henry to the warden's office flung a black band across the table at him. He took the piece of elastic and rolled it up his arm.

The guard shouted something whilst jerking his head. Henry was to follow the man. Some of the inmates had started sweeping the floor and the tables. Henry noticed that they wore an orange band.

He followed the guard out of the canteen and into the main yard. It was midday and the sun was now beating hard on the gravelly earth. Henry squinted. He had walked into the canteen from one side of the yard after seeing a glimpse of what he'd guessed were the inmates' dorms – rows of them. But now the size of the camp became clearer. The large buildings that stood on the opposite side of the canteen made the camp look vast.

The guards eyed him a few times, and Henry wondered whether they were concerned or simply waiting for him to make a mistake so that they could inflict more pain. But nothing happened and as soon as he reached one of the buildings someone else took over.

The officer in charge of work assignment took one look at Henry and shouted to the guards. They came back grudgingly and showed him out of the first building. Whatever the officer saw was either not to his liking or perhaps he felt Henry was better suited to another task. Henry knew what to expect: a good deal of forced labour and hours that resembled those of a London banker, minus the money and the perks. Henry almost smiled.

The noise that was coming from the building they approached told Henry all he needed to know. It was the sound of heavy machinery, of construction work one would expect from an assembly line.

The two guards slowed down and pushed Henry ahead with their batons. Through the wide-open gates, he saw men working in rows, helping to cast large pieces of metal.

Armed guards stood inside, doing the rounds. They were wearing ear protection muffs and sunglasses. One of them used his radio to call someone else. A couple of minutes later, another officer arrived on the scene from inside the factory. His demeanour was confident in a way that differed from the guards. Henry wondered whether this was the construction yard master.

"You speak Mandarin?" the man asked in a heavy accent.

Henry nodded. "A little."

The man took another look at Henry and turned away. "Follow me."

Whatever was being built here was large – very large. The factory looked like a mix between assembly line and shipyard. A piece of metal that probably weighed over a tonne was hanging from a crane. The part must have just been completed. A few inmates were guiding it along the chain tracks; no one wore protection of any kind. Henry wondered how many men died regularly here to help construct whatever it was they were building.

The Yard Master kept walking until he'd reached another part of the factory. The noise was less intense and papers were strewn over a long table. Men were poring over what looked like engineer's sketches. Computers had been placed at several intervals on the long table. As Henry glanced at the sketches, he recognised the technical specifications for a large structure. One of the men who'd been sitting at the table stood up and had a quick conversation with the Yard Master. He nodded a few times and moved towards Henry.

"You are good with numbers?" he asked in Mandarin.

Henry shrugged. "It depends what numbers."

The engineer pointed to the screen.

Henry moved forward, seeing typical drawings used for building work. He nodded. "I think I can make sense of them."

"You can replace one of the prisoners we lost," the engineer simply said. "Come."

There was no point in asking what had happened to the prisoner. Henry wouldn't get an answer and if he did, he probably wouldn't like it.

One of the seats was empty at the table and Henry sat in it. The other men had briefly lifted their heads when he'd walked in but had returned to their work. Henry noticed that their armbands were predominately green.

"This piece needs to be scaled up for construction," the engineer said. "The ratio is one to 12. Translate the numbers and write them on the drawing in red."

The calculator that the previous inmate had used had been left in the middle of the drawing. Henry sat down, spread the papers a little wider and started the calculations. He could have done them in his head. He'd done much more complex operations mentally when he'd worked on the trading floor but showing off his skills wouldn't gain him any points here.

The man seated to his left gave Henry a couple of side looks but didn't acknowledge him otherwise. He worked solidly for an hour without looking around. The shape he was helping to scale up didn't look like anything he'd seen before. It wasn't a building; Henry couldn't quite figure out what it was – yet.

Henry sat up straight and rolled his neck around a few times, to relieve tension and to get a better look. He scanned the large hangar, catching sight of the narrow mezzanine that stood several feet above the working space. Armed guards were walking the gangway, machine guns at the ready.

The prisoner to his right stood up and went to a small water dispenser. The man to his left who had glanced at him a few times scribbled something on a scrap of paper. He laid his hand over the words and briefly removed it for a few seconds.

The name Bo Chan was written in English. The man took a rubber and erased the words, with barely a movement of the hand. Bo had just shown Henry how to communicate without being noticed.

The man on Henry's right returned. Henry would have to wait to respond. Or perhaps assess whether he should. The other thing he'd learned at HMP Belmarsh was that no one could ever be completely trusted.

Someone else from the same table Henry was sitting at raised a hand. The engineer who had spoken to Henry waved him forward. He took a wad of sheets and approached the engineer's desk. The engineer took a quick look at what had been produced and seemed satisfied. He folded the papers, put them in a basket that was almost overflowing with documents, turned to a filing cabinet and extracted more drawings from it. He gave the new wad to the man and sent him back to the long table.

Bo cleared his throat softly – a subtle sign that Henry should stop snooping and start working again.

Henry gave a small nod. As far as he could tell, he was the only one wearing a black band. So much for trying to remain inconspicuous.

After another hour of work, Henry finished the calculations he had been given to do. He stood up, gathered his papers, and waited. The engineer had disappeared. Henry turned around to check where he was. He was about to move to the engineer's desk and drop his work on it when a baton slammed into his back, catching him by surprise.

"Sit," was all the guard said.

Henry drove an angry hand to the site of his injury and sat down. For a few seconds he assessed the situation. Could he take the guard on? The men around the table must have sensed the change in mood because everyone had stopped what they were doing.

The guard stepped back, perhaps surprised by Henry's anger and undecided as to whether he should use his baton again or call reinforcement.

The engineer returned to the table without anyone noticing and started shouting orders. The workers returned to their numbers. Henry snapped out of it and gathered his papers. The guard was the last one to draw back, still in two minds about his next move. The engineer ordered him away and he withdrew, unhappy.

"You work fast," the engineer said when Henry handed him his work. "But even if your work is accurate, I won't save you a second time."

Henry gave a small bow in response. He had been stupid to rise to anger. There would be plenty of similar treatment, probably every day, and he had to remain calm. He returned to the table with a second wad of papers to complete and worked at it solidly until a bell rang.

He waited to see how the other inmates responded to the bell. Everybody finished their last calculation, wrote it on the drawing they were working on and stood up in a clockwise motion, starting at the top of the long table. They then formed a row and waited to hand over their wads of paper to the engineer.

Other men came out from what Henry assumed were other working stations. He couldn't see Rob Walker among them. Yet if Tang wanted a man who could do numbers, surely Walker would be an ideal choice.

Now that everyone was waiting for a signal to move, Henry had time to assess what the hangar was all about. At the centre of it, men were casting large pieces of metal. The heat was intense as liquid steel was poured into huge casts and then allowed to set. Inmates worked without tops, and they were drenched with sweat.

Prisoners like Henry were housed to the side of the hangar, away from the main casting pit. He scanned the length of the building, realising that he couldn't see the far end from where he stood. The other interesting feature was the rolling cranes that transferred the finished pieces to another part of the building, probably the part of the site where the pieces would be assembled.

Despite his effort, Henry couldn't spot Walker anywhere. The shrill of a whistle focused everyone. Guards moved alongside the prisoners, and everyone started walking together. Henry counted twenty men in his row. Another row of men emerged from the other side of the building. The men working on the engineering drawings must have been split in such a way that no one saw the entirety of what was being constructed.

A few minutes later Henry's row reached the outside. The sky had started to darken a little and he estimated it to be around 7pm. Despite the advanced hour the inmates in the pit looked as though they weren't finished yet. Even here, the white-collar prisoners were having it a bit easier.

A second whistle brought everyone to a stop. Another group of men, this time coming from the left, lined up next to Henry's row. At the sound of the third hiss, they walked towards the canteen and entered the building. Still no sign of the westerner.

His own group started moving and Henry followed.

The smell of food made his stomach rumble. It wasn't an appetising smell but the portion he'd received at lunchtime was not enough to keep him going 'til the evening. Looking at the thin men around him, Henry knew he too would shed a few pounds if he stayed at Zhaga for any length of time. But that was not his plan.

Everyone lined up and started helping themselves to what was on offer. Henry gave a quick glance over his shoulder as he bent to grab a tray for his food. Bo Chan was waiting behind him to do the same. A brief smile crossed the man's lips, but his face returned to a neutral expression before Henry turned back around.

Henry chose the same table he had chosen at lunchtime. It was away from the centre of the canteen but close enough to where other inmates had congregated. Henry knew the drill. A newcomer needed to get the other prisoners to trust him before he sat at their table, and he'd sussed that his black armband didn't mean anything good.

More people were arriving, and the tables around him filled in, apart from his own. That was fine by him. He didn't want to reveal how much Mandarin he could speak, and his grasp of Mongolian was rudimentary. The only man making the occasional eye contact was Bo and Henry responded with a nod. Whether Bo was an inmate working for the warden to extract information or a genuinely open-minded man, Henry would engage and see what he could get out of him.

The canteen hummed with the sound of people eating. There was no conversation and Henry took his time to eat his food, not knowing what would happen after that. He was not sure how to return to the cell he'd been put in after his interrogation.

The men who had arrived first started to drift off. Another group was arriving, and this time Henry guessed it was the men who'd been working in the pit. Henry felt the heavy weight of someone's eyes on him. He turned and saw Bo was looking at him. The man jerked his head in a quick move. Time to leave.

Henry gave him a confused look. He didn't know which way to go. The room was emptying faster now, and soon he was one of the few men left from the first shift. The sudden move of so many inmates coinciding with the arrival of the second shift sent a warning. Henry forked down the last of his dinner and was about to get up. Four men walked to his table and sat around him. Their band was a fluorescent orange and the tattoos on their arms didn't bode well.

"You... spy?" said the lead man sitting in front of Henry. He was pointing at Henry's armband.

He wondered how much damage this muscled guy could inflict with a couple of chopsticks. Perhaps a lot.

* * *

58

The alarm on Harris's phone had been chiming for a couple of minutes. He rolled on his side and started searching for his phone with an unsteady hand. He tapped the screen a few times, eyes still closed. He managed to find the right spot and the sound stopped. Harris grunted, rolled onto his back, clutching his mobile to his chest.

He was about to drift off again but managed to open one eye and check the time.

"Shit..."

He had only given himself a four-hour rest time but it was far from enough. His mouth felt dry, and the taste of tobacco lingered. Harris looked for his cigarette packet and recalled he hadn't had time to buy a new pack – just one cigarette left. The policy at the British Office in Taipei was strict: no smoking in any of the bedrooms, but Harris didn't care.

He swung his legs over the side of the bed and moved to the chest of drawers where he had emptied the contents of his pockets that morning before going to bed. He reached for the fresh packet he had bought at a dispenser in the foyer of his building and picked out a cigarette. He struck the wheel of his old Zippo lighter a few times, hesitated, took a long drag to light the cigarette and inhaled deeply. The nicotine kicked in and his body relaxed a fraction.

It was 2.30pm in Taiwan and Nick's plane wouldn't be landing until the following day, mid-morning. Harris needed to gather more information from the Op control and command room. The ALPHA team debrief was planned for 3.30pm, assuming the team had managed to cross the border between China and Mongolia and reach the US Embassy in Ulaanbaatar, the capital of Mongolia.

Harris sat on the bed and wondered whether someone would have called him, had there been any issues. Hunter III was far from done with getting even, and he remained unhappy with the idea of running another joint operation with MI6.

He shrugged. It wasn't his fault that Rob Walker was a British tech scientist working for the most prominent tech lab in Taiwan and that Harris handled one of MI6's most successful assets, Henry Crowne. Harris then smiled. He had taken a risk in recruiting Henry, the former investment banker who'd been charged with money laundering for the

IRA. Harris had stuck to his instincts about Henry, and it had paid off. There was no mission risky or complex enough that Henry wouldn't tackle. Islamic State at its centre of power in Raqqa, Syria, or Putin and his henchmen in Moscow. Redemption came at a price and Henry was willing to pay whatever price was demanded of him.

Harris pulled one last time on his cigarette, realised he'd let the ash drop on the carpet and swore. He put his hand underneath to catch the rest that was about to crumble and ran to the toilet, dropping the cigarette butt into it. He did a passable job at cleaning up and flushed the lot down the loo.

He took a quick shower but didn't bother to shave. More important was getting something to eat before he headed to TECH LEOPARD's command and control at Taichung airbase.

Harris slid his laptop into the secure vault of his bedroom. The British Rep Office was not as grand as an Embassy, but it nevertheless had all the kit he needed. He left his bedroom and moved through a security station, presenting a badge he'd been given by the British representative who was running the British Office in Taipei.

In the lobby he nodded quickly to the two women who looked after reception. A few people had started to queue outside for visas and other documents. The two security guards at the door were drip-feeding visitors inside according to a set timetable; very few people were allowed in at any one time.

Harris gave another nod to the guards and a good afternoon. One of the guards opened the door and Harris found himself on the top floor of the building that housed both the British and Australian Rep Offices. The view from the 30th floor was impressive, but Harris didn't have time to linger. He called the lift, stepped in as soon as it arrived and pressed the ground floor button.

He left the building, crossed the street to a little food stall he had spotted the night before and bought himself a large portion of braised pork rice. Harris loved the small eats culture of Taiwan; everywhere you could find street food, and the choice was endless. He crossed Song Gao Road again and walked over to the taxi rank just outside the Embassy. Harris had enough time to eat on the way to the Taichung airbase and check his messages.

60

He picked the first cab in the rank, gave the address and proceeded to have his lunch. His cover story was that of a businessman selling tech systems and the small industrial estate that was a 10-minute walk from the airport was a perfect cover. Harris started scrolling through his emails on his encrypted mobile phone with one hand, the other busy wielding a set of chopsticks. There was nothing of interest either from his team back in London or from the TECH LEOPARD control room.

He sat back, set the phone on the seat next to him and thought about where the operation was headed. No news from London had somehow been expected. Nick had spoken to the mysterious Chinese man who'd rung his mobile. Nick had been made clear that onboarding a new client required Henry's approval. It hadn't gone down well, and Nick had almost been spooked but not quite. Holding back had been the right thing to do. Harris had assured Nick that whoever the Chinese man was, he was doing a classic background check.

What Harris found puzzling was the quality of the man's English. Dragon had not mentioned that the Zhaga camp's warden was a man who'd been educated either in Hong Kong or England. It was a point that the CIA needed to clarify. Or perhaps this warden was new.

Harris finished his food, wiped his mouth clean and glanced at his watch. ALPHA team should be making contact with Op Command and Control in twenty minutes. Harris would be there five minutes before the call was due.

The taxi dropped Harris at the indicated address. He walked through the small industrial estate, along the perimeter road of Taichung airbase and presented himself to the sentry guard at checkpoint. The sentry swiped his pass. Harris's photo came up on the man's iPad. He took his time to make sure Harris was the man on the screen. But something was slowing the process.

The guard read something on the screen of his tablet and returned to the sentry box to inspect Harris's pass. The man placed a call and Harris knew there was trouble.

He looked around. There was no other way to access the site and even if there was, he couldn't get in without the say-so of Commander Richards.

"Please wait here, sir, someone is on their way." The sentry's words had the requisite tone, respectful yet unequivocal. Harris wouldn't be allowed in without an escort.

Harris bit his tongue. He needed to keep his fire power for whoever was about to turn up. He hoped it would be Pike. Despite the constant bickering, there was something straight about her that Harris felt he could trust.

Harris spotted the heavy frame of Commander Richards making his way towards the entrance point.

"Fuck... they're sending the heavies," Harris muttered.

Richards nodded to the guard and the man disappeared into his box.

"I'm sorry to have kept you waiting," Richards said mechanically. He moved aside, gesturing with his hand that Harris should follow.

"Not a problem." Harris tried his best to stay polite. Richards didn't give a damn about keeping Harris waiting. "As long as I can hear what your guys in Ulaanbaatar have got to say."

Commander Richards's back stiffened a little. "Well, this is the issue. ALPHA team has encountered a setback and we are assessing the situation."

The situation, Harris guessed, was that after the ALPHA team had not been able to find Henry their mission had been aborted. This was fine by Harris and part of the grand plan. ALPHA team was to be used only for Crowne's infiltration. They weren't going anywhere else, and the CIA had reluctantly agreed to keep the SEAL team and the military in the dark about phase two of OPERATION TECH LEOPARD. Henry would be captured and end up in the same camp as Rob Walker.

It was a big risk but Dragon, the CIA informant, had been very clear. They had to minimise the risk of any leak. The Zhaga camp was a very special place, the knowledge of which had been unknown until Dragon had disclosed it.

"Does that involve my man?" Harris asked.

"We're not sure yet."

"I know ALPHA team lost him on landing."

"You mean he didn't manage to land in the target zone." Richards was looking straight ahead. Harris noticed they were not taking the usual route to the control room.

"This was always a possibility and ALPHA team had rehearsed for that event," Harris said.

The time for recrimination and fault allocation would be coming soon and Commander Richards had started the process of covering his back.

They moved past the building Harris had spent the best part of two days in since the beginning of the operation. He stopped and waited for Richards to notice.

"Have you moved the control room?"

"No..." Richards said as he turned around.

"Do I have to call Hunter to be let in?"

"This is at the request of the CIA's Head of Special Operations." Commander Richards chose Hunter's full title. It was all becoming too formal and unfriendly.

Harris's nostrils flared. "Are you telling me my operative is lost in the middle of China's Inner Mongolia and I can't be part of the debrief with ALPHA team?" He wasn't giving up so easily. He still wanted to know what the ALPHA team saw and did before they'd decided to abort the mission, whether Hunter liked it or not.

But Commander Richards wasn't budging.

Harris glanced at his watch. They had less than ten minutes before the planned call with ALPHA team. Or perhaps they'd already had the call and not told Harris.

He ran a hand over his tired face and laughed. He should never have gone back to the British Office for a kip. Whatever Richards or Hunter were prepared to disclose from the debrief with the ALPHA team, Harris would only be given the bare minimum.

Hunter was having his revenge and relishing it.

CHAPTER SEVEN

Henry shrugged. "I'm not what Warden Tang thinks I am."

His fluent Mandarin slowed down the muscled guy sitting before Henry. He was not going to be defeated by a few words in his own mother tongue, though.

"Why... black band," he said, poking at Henry's arm with the chopsticks he'd picked out of Henry's bowl.

"It's a mistake. I'm just looking for dinosaurs," Henry carried on, in English.

The word dinosaurs made the man frown and Henry translated. "Kǒnglóng."

The man slapped his hand on the table hard and started laughing. It was the cue the others had been waiting for. They started shoving Henry around, almost unseating him. It took all of Henry's will power not to react but instead looked scared. These bad boys would know how to fight but the element of surprise and Henry's training might just give him the edge.

The leader stopped laughing suddenly. He grabbed Henry by the shirt and pulled him closer across the table. "You lying."

His dark eyes bored into Henry's, showing the sort of violence Henry hadn't seen since his Middle East mission into the heart of Islamic State territory. If Henry had learned anything in Raqqa, Syria, it was that there was a time to stay quiet and a time to fight back.

The slam of a guard's baton on the table interrupted Henry's plan to drive the man's head against the table, guaranteeing a split nose.

Everyone froze. The men who had surrounded Henry vanished. The man who had grabbed Henry looked up puzzled for an instant, but he withdrew as well. It seemed that his instructions to ruffle the newcomer up had just been superseded by more important matters.

Another guard materialised next to Henry, and he poked him with his own baton to make him move. Henry and the two guards exited the canteen. He found himself back in the yard and heading towards the squat buildings he'd seen earlier.

The constructions were arranged in two rows and the stones looked grey beneath the giant projector lights that were sweeping the camp at regular intervals. Guards with dogs, and rifles slung over their shoulders, were now walking the perimeter.

Henry slowed down a little but a fresh poke to his back sped him up faster than he would have liked. Climbing the 25-foot wall wasn't an option and the wires that were entwined on top of it made it a definite no-go escape route.

The guards walked Henry along the row of the first building and turned left at the corner. They moved alongside what looked like the exercise yard. It looked empty but Henry couldn't be sure. A few minutes later he was brought to the front of another construction with a heavy iron door. From the outside there was nothing to differentiate it from the other buildings.

One of the guards radioed in and someone opened the iron door.

Two other guards were waiting inside. They barely looked at the newcomer and spoke only a few words to the men who were bringing Henry in. From where they sat, they had an overview of the rows of cells that lined the long corridors and steel stairwells. Henry hadn't realised but part of the building was sunk into the ground. The bottom cell likely didn't have any windows.

TV screens were also arranged along the far wall and the guards made no attempt to hide the extent of their surveillance.

One of the guards opened the first door and the clunk of keys from his large keyring sent a chill down Henry's spine. Memories of Belmarsh made him hesitate but the now familiar prod in the back pushed him forward.

True, the security protocol at Belmarsh had him crossing over seven doors, each with their own checks to move in and out of the High Security Unit where Henry did time, but at least he'd been in London. Why was it he was so certain he could escape this godforsaken place and take Walker with him?

Henry found himself in front of another steel door that wasn't locked. The guard who seemed to be in charge opened it wide and shoved Henry into the cell. The door closed behind him with an ominous clunk.

Henry clenched his fists. It was tougher than he'd expected to be behind bars again.

He sat for a moment on the bed, unclenching his fists slowly. The cell was like the one he had been moved to after his interrogation, with a slim bed that barely accommodated his tall body, walls that looked as though they had just been bleached, a small window fitted with a thick pane of glass and bars, and the requisite toilet squeezed into one corner.

The neon light above Henry's head flickered a few times. He stood up, keen to inspect the cell further. Soon the light would be switched off and the cell would turn pitch black.

The walls between the cells were thick, as was the steel door. There would almost certainly be no communication between prisoners once they were in their respective holds. Henry had expected to be sharing but this was not the way this building worked. Isolation was a tool of control.

He ran his fingers over the stony walls and noticed dust on his fingertips. He rubbed his thumb over them, surprised. Henry inspected the wall close up. Someone had used some heavy machinery to sand down the stones. The memories and messages of the man who had occupied the cell before him had been thoroughly erased, as though he'd never existed.

Henry followed the walls of the room, looking for a weakness to exploit. There was none he could see, until he arrived at the toilet corner. The pipes that brought in water and were used to flush the content looked a little loose. Henry crouched and gave them a gentle push.

There was a little give. He tapped on the pipe and felt a small vibration under his fingers. Now he needed to establish whether the sound travelled to the cell next door or perhaps below.

He was about to tap a series of knocks when the lights went out without warning. Standing up slowly, his hands felt the wall. He found the door and stuck his ear to the hatch the guards used to peek into the cell. Everything was quiet.

Henry waited a moment for his eyes to become accustomed to the darkness. The light that surrounded the hatch gave him a focal point to get his bearings. Henry was about to move away from the door when he heard a faint noise, one that grew stronger quickly.

He recognised the heavy clunk of the steel doors being opened. A couple of loud voices followed and Henry strained to understand what was being said. The guards were dragging something or someone along the corridor. They walked past his cell and stopped. Opening the door of the cell next to his, the guards slammed it with a noisy bang within seconds, and disappeared.

Everything fell quiet again and Henry wondered whether he had just found out where Rob Walker was being held.

* * *

The shrill sound of a bell woke Henry up. He had finally drifted to sleep in what he guessed was the early hours of the morning. Images of Belmarsh kept resurfacing and the fear of spending the rest of his life behind bars had woken him during the night. He doubted he would serve a lengthy sentence in the Zhaga camp, though. If the work didn't kill him, someone would.

The setup of the prison camp reminded him more of the organisation of the harshest prisons in the US where gang protection was the only way to survive. Henry stood up just as the door to his cell was being unlocked. The guard opened the hatch to make sure Henry wasn't too close to the door, then pushed it open so that it crashed against the wall.

The man who was shouting at him was new, but he looked as vicious as any of his colleagues. Henry took one step outside his cell. The inmates were waiting outside their respective doors while the guards were opening them one after the other.

It was strange that Warden Tang assumed the guard numbers wouldn't be overwhelmed by the inmates. The locks at Belmarsh were usually activated centrally through the guards' main control room, but of course the door could also be opened with a key if needs be.

Henry cast an eye to his left towards the prisoner who had been brought in late last night. His face was bruised, and he wasn't holding himself straight. Blood had dried up on the sleeves of his shirt and he looked as though he hadn't had a shower for a while.

The man must have felt he was being observed. He shifted on the spot but didn't look at Henry. Henry stopped his investigation and waited for what came next. There hadn't been any prisoner instructions given and there wouldn't be. Observe and adapt, or else, was clearly the motto at Zhaga.

One of the guards gave a loud whistle and everyone started to shuffle towards the main exit in an almost perfect row. The prisoners seemed careful not to walk too close to one another and Henry adjusted his pace to match. The man who had been beaten up was walking behind Henry and he could hear him drag one of his legs.

This must have been a serious beating, or perhaps an interrogation.

The line in which Henry was in poured outside, but instead of walking towards the canteen, the inmates walked into what Henry had suspected last night to be the exercise yard. They moved into the pen in exactly the same order. The first man stopped, turned towards the buildings in a military half-turn and everyone copied.

A second row of men was now entering the pen. All in all, Henry estimated there were 50 men lined up, awaiting orders. He sensed an odd mix of military discipline and utter fear among them. He noticed that every man was wearing a black armband.

The loud speakers posted at each corner of the pen started to shriek and the voice of Warden Tang bounced around the yard.

"You are here because you broke the law of the People's Republic of China. The shame you brought to your family and country is unforgivable. But you can repair the damage you've caused through hard work and by learning the true values of the People's Republic of China…"

The speech delivered in Mandarin went on for a few minutes. No one moved or dared show they were bored. Henry imagined that the same brainwashing and attempt to justify the rehabilitation of these fallen men was a daily occurrence and that everyone listened.

The smack of a baton on Henry's head caught him by surprise. The two men on either side of him froze. The shouting from the guard who had delivered the blow didn't give Henry any indication as to why he'd been hit. But the man on his right bowed his head lower and Henry followed suit. It was not enough to listen to the garbage Warden Tang delivered. The prisoners needed to look contrite too.

Henry kept his head bowed until the sermon was finished. When everyone moved their heads up, Henry gave a furtive nod to the man who had saved him from more beating. The man with the bruised face didn't acknowledge Henry, but Henry recognised the distorted features of the man he'd been looking for. Rob Walker had been subjected to yet another of Tang's interrogations.

Henry wondered how many more beatings Rob Walker could sustain before he talked, or perhaps he had already spoken about his latest tech research and Warden Tang was extracting the very last details from Rob.

One way or another, Henry needed to get him out of Zhaga as soon as he could.

Henry's attention refocused when music started. One of the prisoners had stepped to the front and was making slow moves which Henry recognised as Tai Chi. Everyone copied as best they could.

The choice of exercise intrigued Henry. After all, Tai Chi was the precursor to the performance of martial arts and he assumed that the last thing Warden Tang wanted was an army of prisoners proficient in kung fu. On the other hand, it was probably a good idea to keep the inmates exercised and in reasonable health so that they could perform whatever task they were assigned.

Some guards started to snigger when some of the prisoners couldn't quite follow. Henry cast a look to his right. Rob was doing better than he'd expected for a man who had just had a severe thrashing.

All the guards were now enjoying themselves... laughing and jeering. Whatever Warden Tang gave with one hand he took back with the other – allow exercise but be humiliated if you don't perform well.

The performance lasted fifteen minutes and by the time they had finished, most men had lost track of what they were exactly doing, to the delight of the guards. Rob had kept up well and Henry was impressed. The man might be a tech wizard but he was fit also.

As soon as the exercise stopped, the inmates walked out of the pen, in the direction of the canteen. Another lot of prisoners had moved into the other pens. Henry noticed that their armbands were green.

Henry's row of inmates started to queue for food. Most people with black armbands looked Asian. Rob and Henry were the only westerners in the lot. Another uncomfortable position for someone who was intent on making himself invisible.

Rob reached the stack of trays before Henry. He took one and slid it along the food counter. Henry did the same and waited for a sign that Rob wanted to talk. But the other man simply went about his business, presenting his plate to be doled up with two scoops of rice and one scoop of something that looked like meat floating in a thin brown sauce. Rob moved on, grabbed a tin mug, poured tea into it and left the queue to find a seat at a free table.

Other men moved in small clusters, but the black armband lot didn't seem to chat or trust each other. Perhaps it came with the territory. By now, Henry had sussed that the black-armband-designated inmates had been caught for spying, or at least were accused of it.

Henry chose a table that was away from Rob, sitting at an angle so he could observe him without being too obvious. Henry hadn't anticipated it would be easy to approach Rob, but he hadn't expected the man would be so abrupt in wanting nothing to do with him.

As Henry knew from his time as a high-flying investment banker and then an inmate at Belmarsh prison, building trust took time, time he suspected neither he nor Rob had.

* * *

Mattie Colmore pressed the send button and collapsed back onto her bed. She'd been working all night to refine the article *The Times of London*, her employer, was about to publish. The exclusive interview she'd managed to secure with a North Korean defector had cost her months of hard work.

The man she had managed to track and gain the trust of was the only high-ranking military personnel to successfully defect to South Korea and live to tell the tale.

Mattie admired the courage and determination of the man. Now that he had given Mattie the right to tell his story, she wondered whether she was once more pushing the boundaries too far. But the truth had to be told and the unspoken support China was handing over to North Korea had to be exposed.

Mattie stood up slowly and walked to the window of her hotel bedroom. Metro Hotel, Myeongdong, overlooked Jung-gu in the centre of Seoul, the perfect location for a comfortable enough hotel that was not flashy and from where she could access the entire city. Mattie leaned against the window to watch the traffic move past her hotel.

She turned her wrist to check her watch. At 7am the streets of Seoul were buzzing with activity. She had just enough time to shower and jump on the subway to meet an old friend of hers at a little café near Seongdong-gu. She had spoken to him about another project she had in mind and this one would involve China directly.

Mattie moved to the bathroom, removed her T-shirt and pants in a couple of quick moves. She stepped into the shower without bothering to turn the hot tap first. She'd had plenty of cold showers in the various parts of the world she'd visited, places where hot water was always a luxury – when there was water.

Being a war correspondent for *The Times* had put her in some very tight spots, spots she had sworn to her boss she would avoid... until the next time – and she felt that that next time was just around the corner.

Mattie slid on a pair of jeans, a blue T-shirt and light jacket. She pushed her laptop into her rucksack and made her way to the closest tube station, Euljiro 1-ga. She had one train change and would arrive at the university quarter in about twenty minutes.

Mattie started walking in the opposite direction to where she intended to go. She crossed abruptly and retraced her steps on the other side of the street. She hurried towards the underground station entrance and was lucky enough to catch a train that was about to depart. Anybody following her would have found it hard to board the same train.

She didn't want to be followed to her meeting with her reliable source. Some extra precautions were warranted. Who said that only spooks could lose a trail? Mattie smiled at the thought.

She arrived in the Seongdong-gu district a little later than antici-pated and made her way to the Mealdo café, taking odd routes and using other decoys. She pushed against the glass door and entered.

Mattie never used the same café twice and she had spotted this new find whilst strolling through the university district of Seoul. She sat herself at the back of the café and checked her watch. Her contact was late, but then again he always was.

A friendly waitress walked over to her with a small iPad strapped to her arm and asked, in fluent English, whether she'd like to place her order. Mattie looked around, glad to discover she was not the only westerner in the place – the advantage in choosing a café in the student quarter.

"I'm waiting for a friend, but I'll have some hot water in the meantime."

Mattie took her laptop out of her rucksack and logged in. She had not yet expected an email from the political editor at *The Times* but there it was in her inbox already. Did the man ever sleep? The piece was good to go and would come out in a couple of days' time.

The waitress arrived with a glass of hot water, careful to deliver the metal handle in such a way that Mattie could grab it easily. Mattie took a sip, oblivious to the scalding temperature of the liquid.

The same feeling of emptiness settled in as she re-read the editor's mail. The work was done. She had no aim, no project to drive forward, and she hated that floating sensation she always experienced at the end of an assignment.

Mattie was about to check her watch again when the slim figure of the man she was waiting for appeared in the shop window. He looked at the menu that was displayed and took the opportunity to scan the place, hesitant. He must have spotted Mattie because he pushed the door more confidently and walked straight to her table.

Mattie smiled. "Hello, Han. How are things?"

"Fine, fine...What are you having?" Han slid his slender body into the chair that was next to Mattie's and close to the wall.

"I've not decided yet. Was waiting for you."

The friendly waitress reappeared and before she could ask the question, Han ordered. "Two yuja teas and some hotteok, please."

Mattie nodded. "Lemon tea and pancakes... sounds good."

"That's right." Han took out his mobile from the flimsy rucksack he was carrying and placed it on the table.

Mattie waited. Since meeting Han, she realised patience was the only way with him. He was taking risks for her, and she appreciated that. Accommodating his quirkiness was the least she could do. "Have you had time for a holiday of late?" Mattie asked.

Han shook his head. He never had time to do anything apart from work. He could have lied about it but somehow Mattie believed him.

The waitress brought the tea and cakes. Mattie and Han started with a quick sip of tea and Han launched in. "I have something new for you... A camp where political prisoners are being held. It's not official. People disappear and are never seen again," Han said in a whisper.

"And where is this camp?"

"Somewhere in Inner Mongolia."

Mattie drank some tea and frowned. "This is a pretty big scoop."

"It is." Han forked a large piece of pancake, shoved it into his mouth and chewed thoroughly.

"I know you wouldn't come to me with something as big as that if you didn't believe there is something in it, but how sure –"

"Very sure," Han interrupted.

"Can you at least give me an idea as to how you found out?"

It was a question she didn't like asking Han. It exposed other people and he had made it clear from the beginning he wouldn't compromise anybody else. But this was explosive news and for Mattie to follow this lead, she would need to enter China.

Han kept forking pieces of pancake into his mouth, chewing fully until he'd finished his first cake. "My company does business in Inner Mongolia, new contract."

Mattie nodded. "A contract that involves this camp?" She didn't expect a reply from Han, although he might have corrected her if she'd got this very wrong. Mattie toyed with her own food, nibbling on a small piece, thinking. "It's not easy for a journalist to get to China. I need to find a way, a project that presents China in a good light and deals with that region."

Han had finished his second pancake. He pointed with his fork to the uneaten cake on Mattie's plate. "Are you eating that?"

Mattie shook her head and pushed her plate towards him.

"Nomads," Han said.

Mattie's eyebrows lifted. "Nomads... you mean Mongols?"

"It's Inner Mongolia." Han shrugged.

Mattie grinned. An article on the descendants of Genghis Khan, those who now live in China – the perfect topic.

CHAPTER EIGHT

A sharp whistle sounded and all the inmates stood as one. Two rows formed within seconds and the small rumble of a few words being exchanged during breakfast disappeared.

The second whistle told the men they needed to start walking towards the factory. The doors of the large hangar were already opened and some of the prisoners were busy at work. The two rows of prisoners wearing black armbands arrived near the entrance and each row moved in a different direction.

Henry selected the correct row by luck, sparing himself another beating.

Rob moved fast as soon as the guard called the prisoners and Henry noticed he too was going towards the same office to the right of the main factory pit.

They were still a few yards away when the heat of melted metal struck Henry. It hadn't felt so intense the day before, or perhaps then they hadn't been casting new pieces. The thunder of heavy equipment moving around, intended to drive the melted steel towards the large cast, cut through the camp's silence.

The line of men to which Henry belonged started entering the factory, most of them veering to the right. A couple of men stayed behind, awaiting orders it seemed. Henry walked past the men headed for the same long room he had worked in the day before, moving alongside the thick glass wall that separated offices and the pit.

Henry slowed down a little, fascinated by the sight of what was happening inside the foundry. The metal pieces that had been cast in the early hours of the morning had cooled down enough for the cast to be removed. A large pool had opened in the ground and the large piece of steel was being pushed towards the liquid. Henry remembered that quenching metals, the act of plunging them into various liquids, was done in stages, with the aim to strengthen and improve the grindability of the steel.

The pool must have been there all along, but Henry hadn't noticed it yesterday. It had probably been closed, covered by the two horizontal sliding doors that were now open.

Two men moved to the side of the pool. They started pulling on the chains that were driving the steel forward. The effort made the men's muscles bulge but the taller of the two seemed to struggle. Another two men joined the first team and the piece started to glide towards their destination.

Henry noticed that a tall and emaciated man was wrestling with the chains. The bones of his spine were sticking out of his skin like a fin and his feet were skidding on the floor. The piece finally reached its landing place over the pool and one of the men slammed his fist on a large button at the side of the pool. The piece started its journey towards the water. The men pulled back to avoid the scalding water that would start spitting as soon as the steel entered it.

One of the men who had been observing the scene moved to where the four men still stood, securing the chains they had used. He walked straight up to the tall man, grabbed him by the legs and threw him into the pool, as though he was a stick of wood. The tall man barely struggled, too stunned by the rapidity of the move.

The other three inmates froze for an instant, hesitating over whether they should save him. But even the shrieks of their mate didn't convince them to act. In seconds the incandescent metal would hit the water, bringing it to boiling point. With their shoulders slumped, they followed the attacking man who'd disposed of their pal, like subservient dogs.

The fizz and sound of spitting water covered the man's yells for help. Henry's stomach churned and he swallowed a few times to control the nausea he felt. Someone pushed him forward. The inmate behind him grumbled a few words he didn't understand, more concerned over not delaying the prisoners moving to their daily jobs than by what was happening in the pit.

Henry nodded and accelerated the pace, still reeling over what he had seen. No one had budged or seemed affected by it. It clearly wasn't the first time they'd witnessed a man dying because he could no longer carry his weight. The image of the gang master throwing the other man into the pit flashed in front of Henry's eyes again. He recognised the thug who had tried to attack him the night before in the canteen. He was wearing an orange armband, and so were all the men in the pit.

Henry took his seat at the same long table as the day before. Bo Chan had arrived already and so had the inmates wearing green armbands. There must be a set sequence of arrival and different task allocations for different groups.

The prisoners wearing an orange band worked primarily in the pit and they worked all hours, perhaps even round the clock. This meant that even at night there would be activity around the camp – not so good for a night-time escape, then.

The prisoners with black armbands like Henry were spared the harsher tasks but were kept away as much as possible from the rougher lot. Perhaps they were more valuable commodities, worth interrogating or even exchanging.

Bo gave Henry a quick side-look. He must have guessed what Henry had witnessed. Henry returned the glance. He had questions but he also needed to be careful. "Trust no one" had been his motto at Belmarsh, and it had served him well.

Henry grabbed the calculator he had been using. Someone had assigned new drawings to the men and they were on the table. Whatever it was they were helping to build was secret enough to warrant extra precautions, even in the middle of one of the most inhospitable deserts, in a camp surrounded by 25-foot walls and round-the-clock surveillance.

Henry didn't try to locate Rob. He wasn't going to speak to him in this place so there was no point in looking for him.

Henry worked for two solid hours. He delivered two sets of drawings to the engineer in charge of the works. After, he took a small break, walking to the water cooler. He stood at the machine for a moment, not bothering to face the room but instead concentrating on the thick piece of glass that was the wall of the office. The glass had been put there no doubt to isolate the workers from the noise of the pit, not out of consideration, but to improve their ability to concentrate on their task.

Henry wondered whether any of the guards or the engineer had noticed that the glass acted as a mirror due to the angle of the overhead neon lights. He didn't need to face the room to see what was happening there. Henry refilled his cup. He gulped it down quickly. Perhaps a second cup would drive one of the guard's batons into his back, but it was worth the risk.

As Henry threw the empty cup into the small bin, he spotted Rob Walker at the end of the same table he was working from. He was only five men away from Henry. So close and yet so far.

The harsh look from the engineer when Henry returned to his seat burst the small bubble of elation he'd just felt. It said "don't do it again". A warning about the second cup of water or the reflecting glass, Henry wasn't sure which.

* * *

Flight CX848 from Dulles International Airport, Washington DC to Taoyuan International Airport, Taipei was on time. Harris read the message on the Taoyuan arrivals board again. The first good news he'd had in the last eighteen hours.

The meeting with Commander Richards had not gone to plan. Harris had been shunted into a small room at the back of the Taichung Air Base and debriefed in the most succinct of ways.

Yes, ALPHA team had made it out of China and to the US Embassy in Ulaanbaatar, Mongolia.

Yes, they had aborted the original mission.

No, they hadn't been able to locate Harris's asset, Henry Crowne, also under his alias of Henry Newborn.

Everything Harris already knew since this was exactly the way OPERATION TECH LEOPARD had been structured by the few who had top-level clearance for the operation: Harris, Crowne, Hunter, CIA Chief of Special Ops, and the Chief at MI6. Even Jack Shield, the man Harris trusted above everyone else at the CIA, had not been invited for the full debrief by his boss, Richard "Dick" Hunter III. Harris had vigorously protested for his inclusion, but Jack was in Hunter's bad books and there was no changing his mind.

That was the official list and the one Hunter relied on, but Henry had had a beer with Nick Fox, the young hacker Henry had recruited under the nose of Hunter in Washington DC, and Harris had had a beer with Jack Shield because Harris didn't give a rat's ass about Hunter's opinion – within reason. Harris suspected neither did Jack, but they hadn't bothered to compare notes on it. There was no time. The unofficial team now included two very able people and Harris was ready to use them to the full to get what he needed: news about Henry.

Harris walked into a small bar that was selling hot beverages and pastries. He ordered a coffee and reluctantly passed on the tempting pastries. Taipei, and Taiwan in general, was an incredible place for small eats but he knew that his waistline and his wife would complain if he kept indulging.

He took a seat at the bar on one of the high stools and waited. His instructions to Nick had been clear: go through customs, go to the taxi rank and wait for him there.

Passengers started to walk through the sliding doors in bursts. The typical airport crowd was waiting outside these doors. Families reunited, as well as lovers or friends. Also emerging were the expected businessmen and women who were looking for their names on the boards held high by chauffeurs waiting for them.

Harris stirred sugar in his coffee and took a sip. He nodded approvingly at the young man who'd served him, who nodded in return.

A young man wheeling a couple of small suitcases passed through the sliding doors for arrivals. He stopped to get his bearings and turned right to follow the sign to the taxi rank. Harris hadn't seen Nick since the fateful day of his exchange with a Russian spy-turned-defector at the border between Russia and Finland.

It had been one of the toughest exchanges Harris had ever done in swapping Nick, a clever yet inexperienced operative, for a young woman who'd paid for her defection with her life, in front of their eyes. Henry had been there too...

Harris forced the memory away. He had no time to reminisce. He finished his coffee in a couple of gulps and made his way to the taxi rank. Nick had taken out his mobile and was busying himself with it. It looked a natural act... a young businessman looking for an address or other information before deciding on which means of transport to take.

Harris came alongside him, taking his own mobile phone out of his inner jacket pocket. Nick kept going with his own business, although Harris knew he had noticed him through a subtle move of the head. Harris smiled to himself. Nick had grown up since Finland, and he had to give Henry credit for that.

The taxi queue became much longer, and Harris started walking in the opposite direction, towards the airport train station. It wasn't his intention to jump in a cab with Nick – far too obvious a move.

Nick waited for a few seconds and made his move, following Harris at a distance.

When they arrived at the overground station, the ticket hall was buzzing with people. Harris slowed down and waited for Nick to catch up. He started queuing and when his turn came he acted slowly so that Nick, who was behind him, could see what he was doing. Harris mumbled to himself the way a man would when concentrating on a difficult task. He repeated the words "express train" and "Taipei Main Station" out loud. After collecting his ticket from the machine, Harris made his way to the platform. A couple of minutes later he boarded. He didn't need to check, Harris knew Nick would be on the same train.

The express train took about 16 minutes to reach Taipei Central Station. Harris disembarked and Nick caught up with him in a smooth, covert way. This time they stood together at the taxi rank and boarded the same yellow cab.

"Zhongzheng District," Harris said.

Nick raised an eyebrow but said nothing.

"Small change of plan," Harris volunteered. He had initially indicated they would stay at the British Rep Office in Central Taipei but now that Hunter had decided to play dirty, Harris was forced to change tactics.

Once the cab had pulled out of the station and they were approaching Zhongzheng, Nick looked amazed, Harris noticed.

Nick bent forward to get a better look out the window. "Wow... they've got everything..."

Zhongzheng, also known as Taipei's tech district, was spread out in front of them, a mix of skyscrapers and more traditional buildings, as well as billboards advertising the latest in technology.

Harris smiled and wondered whether Nick was referring to the architecture or the tech stuff... He got the cab to stop at the intersection of a main road and something that looked like a small alleyway.

Nick took his suitcases out and both men made their way to a terraced house that was wedged between two shops. The bottom part of the house was a small business that dealt with mobile phones.

Entering the shop, Nick couldn't help himself. He stopped and looked around in wonder. Harris had to grumble he was not *a kid in a toy shop* to get him to move.

They walked to the back of the shop where an old woman welcomed them with a set of keys and a smile. Harris thanked her and he led Nick to a small door. They entered a diminutive courtyard. Harris passed through in a few steps and used one key to unlock the door of another slim house.

The old stones gave way to a modern space. The room was already equipped with screens and computer devices. Nick dropped his cases on the floor like a sack and walked over to them immediately. "Lovely..." he said, running his hand over the adaptive keyboard and the computer hardware. Nick turned to Harris with a grin. "This is serious material... I could do a lot of hacking with that."

"Yup," Harris replied, dumping his rucksack in the far corner of the room. "How about hacking the CIA?"

"I thought you were kidding?"

Harris grinned. "Couldn't be more serious."

Nick covered his face with his hands and Harris wondered whether he'd been too direct. Nick was an American citizen after all. Then Nick slid his hands down to uncover the broadest of smiles. His focused thinking face followed. "Right... I'm gonna need a lot more than this stuff. I'll make a list and you tell me how much I can spend."

"How *much* is how much?" Harris said with half-closed eyes.

"Don't know, $10,000... $100,000."

"What – $100,000 for tech stuff?"

"And how much do you think the CIA spends on its *tech stuff* as you say?" Nick sniffed.

Harris rolled his eyes. "I said hack the CIA, not build a competing tech system."

"Well, there is the *hacking* and there is the *after hacking*. I presume the idea is to get away with it so that we can actually use the intel I manage to download. The idea is also for us not to be spotted the moment I break into their system, right?"

"Good point…" Harris pouted. "And that's going to cost 100 grand?"

Nick frowned and then his mind clicked. "Oh, yeah… Grand… yeah $100,000… it might."

Harris ran his fingers through his hair. The Chief at MI6 was not going to be amused with the bill from this op, but then again, if Hunter had played ball…

"OK, done, but you'd better –"

"– get a receipt?" Nick cocked his head.

"Forget it," Harris grumbled.

Henry had trained Nick too well. Nick was becoming the same pain in the arse as Henry could be.

"What's the target of the hack, then?"

Nick was already taking possession of the equipment Harris had assembled. "You've done well on getting some quality kit."

"I asked some MI6 contacts in the decryption team. My contact there is always happy to help. To get back to your question, we're hacking the email account of the head of Special Ops."

"That sounds tricky… I like it." Nick nodded, absorbed now by the task of setting up his various passwords and face recognition access software.

Nick stopped suddenly and turned in his seat to face Harris. "Hang on… you mean Hunter III?"

"The very same." Harris nodded.

"But… we are on the same team."

"You would have thought so. However…" Harris paused, trying to choose his words carefully for once.

"He's still pissed I joined your team rather than the CIA."

"That's an understatement," Harris returned.

Nick shrugged. "Tough. Can't win them all."

Harris couldn't help his smile. Henry had indeed done a splendid job on Nick, a budding pain in the arse perhaps, but a more assured team player too.

Nick was back at his screens. "You haven't told me anything about Henry yet."

"It's because I know as much as you do."

Nick froze for an instant, then carried on setting up his equipment. "You mean after the call with the Chinese guy?" he asked.

"That's right. I would have liked to hear what the ALPHA team had to say for themselves."

"What about the CIA –?" Nick stopped himself from saying more and looked around.

Harris moved next to him. "It's OK. This place is one of MI6's safe houses. It's very secure and I ran a debugging check this morning on my way to the airport." He continued. "You mean Dragon, the CIA informant?"

"Any intel coming from him?"

"That's now my issue. Hunter is blocking me from the intel. Well, he can't completely, but he will decide when and what we hear. I can also guarantee you that it won't be in real time."

Nick turned to Harris and frowned. "How can we help H if he needs us to?"

"Unfortunately, I've come to the conclusion that Hunter will quite happily sacrifice Henry if it means saving the skin of Dragon."

"What does Jack say?"

"He doesn't know yet. At least I haven't told him. But I think Jack will keep tabs on what's happening with TECH LEOPARD as much as he'll be allowed to."

"It still won't be in real time." Nick's fingers flew across the keyboard as he spoke. Harris marvelled at the young man's ability to multitask.

"That's right. We are flying blind on this op now and I'm not having it."

Nick fell silent for a moment and then stood up. "Not for long, though. It'll take me a day or so to get into Hunter's mail."

"You sound very confident."

"Well." Nick shrugged. "It won't be the first time."

Harris narrowed his eyes at him. "That you sound very confident or that you've hacked the CIA?"

"Yeah, got into their systems once but I guess it wasn't worth it as I was doing it as a test run, you know... just to see whether I could."

"And did that involve anybody else in your best bud circle?"

"You mean like The Piper?"

"Just like him. I know this hacker guy was helpful the last time we used him but –"

"Yeah I know, I need to be careful," Nick interrupted, a look of concern on his face.

"Couldn't agree more."

"I still don't know whether The Piper is a guy or a girl... don't want to offend The Piper. That would be –" Nick started.

Harris interrupted Nick with a wave of his hand. Harris didn't care about gender appropriateness although it dwawned on him that perhaps he should. He just didn't want some other whiz hacker to blow his operation.

"Yep, got this. I don't want The Piper to blow us out of the water, all right?"

"He wouldn't," Nick said, looking offended at the suggestion.

Harris bit his tongue. Not the right time to tell Nick about *never trusting anyone*, especially a hacker, and especially a hacker Nick had not even met. That conversation would come a little later.

Harris changed the topic. "We need someone on the ground since Hunter is not forthcoming with intel."

"You mean in China?"

"Exactly so."

Nick scratched his head. "There is a big hacking community in Hong Kong."

"Nope. No more pals of yours. I have someone in mind. Have you heard of someone called Mattie Colmore, war and political correspondent for *The Times* in London?"

CHAPTER NINE

When the bell rang, Henry waited for the other inmates to move. Bo Chan on his left was faffing around with the large piece of paper on which he'd drawn the spec he was scaling up.

The inmate next to Henry had left, eager to join the canteen's queue before anybody else.

"Orange bands?" Henry murmured.

"Drug and gambling gangs," Bo Chan whispered, standing up slowly.

Henry didn't thank him. It wasn't worth the risk getting caught conversing with one's neighbour. Bo Chan left, and Henry waited a little longer to join the flow of inmates. Henry stood up eventually, making his way to the front of the building. Rob hadn't moved yet, still working on the drawing he was also upscaling. Rob wasn't going to make it easy for Henry to approach him.

Henry sped up his pace. There was no reason to linger, even less so when he walked past the pit hosting that morning's summary execution. The piece of metal that had been quenched was no longer in the pool but the dark liquid that had been used to cool the steel down was still there. Henry wondered whether the tall man's body had been removed, and if so, where it would end up.

As he reached the front of the hangar, the heat of the sun made Henry gasp. Once more, the men who went to the canteen first were the prisoners working on the drawings for the engineer. Bo Chan had caught up with the crowd and was lining up with the other inmates. Men started stacking up behind Henry. He resisted the urge to turn back and check whether Rob was with them.

The guards moved them along and the orderly line dissolved as soon as they entered the canteen.

As he was about to take a tray, two guards walked up to Henry and with a jerk of their heads, indicated he had to follow them. Henry looked puzzled. One of the guards slammed his baton into Henry's side, making him leave the tray on the stack and start walking with them. He wondered whether he would have the opportunity to give one of these punks a good thrashing before he left the camp. Probably not but who knew? He might.

Henry did his best to look worried. His last conversation with Warden Tang as well as the sudden upgrade in treatment, from a suspected western spy to an inmate doing the softest of jobs in the camp, had convinced Henry that Tang wanted to spare him, at least until he had established whether Henry could be of any use to him.

The two guards walked past the row of dorms and took a turn towards the interrogation building Henry had been thrown into when he was first brought into the camp. Perhaps Tang still wanted to satisfy himself that Henry was who he pretended to be.

Henry found himself slowing down. The bruises from his last interrogation hadn't started to heal. Another beating would be tough to take, but then again, that was Tang's plan. Find the point where pain didn't kill you but made you talk.

To Henry's relief, though, the guards stopped in front of the entrance that led to the warden's office. Another set of guards took over from there. Henry recognised one of them from the day before. He had spoken a few words of English.

Warden Tang was waiting in his office, ensconced in his oversized chair.

Henry had learned from his mistakes. He bowed as soon as they entered the room, and remained so. He waited to be told to sit again but this time, Tang dismissed the guards before he spoke to Henry.

The sound of a heavy chair being dragged away told Henry Tang had stood up. He was walking around but Henry could only guess at the warden's movements. The door opened behind Henry and the smell of food made his stomach lurch. Someone walked past him towards the far end of the room. The sound of a tray being set down on a surface told him Tang was having his lunch. The person who had walked in walked out without a word.

Henry was still bent over, waiting for orders.

"Explain high-risk high-return investments," Tang said, his mouth full of food.

"Do you have a white board?" Henry asked, still in a prostrate position.

He heard the warden stop slurping what Henry imagined were noodles. "To do what?" Tang asked after a moment.

"To draw you a diagram of what it all means."

Warden Tang was about to be introduced to the dark, yet highly lucrative world of money laundering.

* * *

The small internet café was exactly what she needed. Mattie didn't use her laptop but rather the computer she'd been assigned by the café owner. Her hood was low over her face but in this place where youngsters met and spoke tech and hacks, this was the standard outfit.

Mattie started a systematic Google Map search of Inner Mongolia. It might have taken days, but Han had been forthcoming when it came to what locations to exclude. She now had a vast rather than insanely vast area to survey.

Mattie systematically moved up and down the map using layered mode. It was the only way to see the terrain as it was in real life. Mattie was amazed at how precise Google Maps was but she'd never been sure that the maps were that current until a posting in Afghanistan. The British Army had shown her that this was what the US Army used to carry out drone strikes.

"Why build a tool from scratch when the maps of Google Earth can provide you with exactly what you need, without time delay?" had been the comment from one of the US army officers she'd interviewed.

She moved the mouse around for a couple of hours, only taking a couple of breaks for a cup of tea and a small cake. After having scanned two-thirds of the desert where the camp was supposed to be, she stretched her back out and closed her eyes, to give them a rest. She was missing something.

Han was not the sort to waste her time. Of course, there could always be a first time, but her instinct was telling her he knew the location. Mattie kept her arms lifted over her head in her stretch. She stopped suddenly. Surely, the Chinese authorities must know that a camp as hidden as this one could still be discovered, if only by fluke?

"What if I don't want a place to show on a map?" Mattie muttered to herself, her eyes back on the map of Mongolia.

"You freeze the pane." A young girl was sitting next to Mattie on a similar computer. She couldn't have been more than sixteen from what Mattie gathered, skinny legs hidden beneath multi-coloured leggings, a short purple skirt and pink and purple hoodie, the cap of which was covering only half of her spiky purple hair.

"And how do you spot it?" Mattie asked with little hesitation.

"It's tricky... either you get software that scans the map for you and tells you, or you need to spot a slight inconsistency when you move the mouse over the frozen pane."

Mattie turned to the girl who was speaking to her and yet still looking at her screen. "Where can I buy that software?"

"You can't."

The young girl picked up what looked like a strawberry milkshake and sucked on the straw; by the hollow sound of it she just had finished her drink.

"Let me buy you another one and perhaps you can tell me more about Google Maps. I'm Mattie by the way," she said, extending her hand.

The girl turned to face her. She was heavily made up, emphasising her brown eyes. Her nose and eyebrow piercings looked tasteful as did the small tattoo on her neck.

She didn't shake Mattie's hand but instead gave her a grin. "With an extra ice cream scoop?"

Mattie nodded and smiled. "Sure."

"Cool... I'm Bora."

"That's a nice name." Mattie stood up and walked to the small counter where she ordered a strawberry shake with an extra scoop of ice cream and a yuja lemon tea.

Bora nodded when Mattie returned. "It means purple in Korean."

It was Mattie's turn to grin. "I would never have guessed."

"I know... my parents think it's too much, too."

"I never said it was too much."

"It's OK. I'm not that bothered about what they think, anyway."

"Your English is flawless," Mattie said, approvingly.

"Mum's English, Dad's Korean. It helps."

The drinks arrived and Bora started sucking on her milkshake. She nodded her thanks to the waitress.

"Cho, wat du u du?" Bora asked, her speech blurred by the milkshake she was quickly slurping.

"I'm a journalist."

Bora gave up her straw to speak to Mattie properly. "Cool... Do you find hot stories?"

"Well, I try to find stories that people may want to read." Mattie shrugged, as detached as she could manage.

Bora nodded, straw back in her mouth. "Cho u need a schoop?"

Mattie laughed. "All journalists need a scoop."

Bora finished her drink with the same uncouth sucking noise as before and nodded.

"You need a good hacker." Bora turned back to the computer screen that had become idle. She pushed the keyboard out of the way and dug her laptop out of a rucksack she'd shoved underneath the desk. She logged in a few seconds later and turned towards Mattie.

"What are you looking for?"

Mattie smiled. "An ancient Egyptian city in the Sahara Desert."

"Cool... I'll take a look and let you know when I find it."

Bora moved away from the desk to a part of the café that was much quieter. Mattie sighed. To be young and enthusiastic again. She returned to her screen and started the slow process of scanning a large chunk of the Inner Mongolian Desert in search of a small discrepancy that would identify any frozen panes.

Another hour passed and she hadn't detected anything. Perhaps Mattie could speak to Han again. He may know someone who might help her find this elusive software Bora was talking about. Mattie hardly noticed that Bora had returned and was standing next to her.

Bora was all smiles. She handed over a USB key and slung her rucksack over her shoulder. "Thanks for the milkshake. That was awesome."

"No worries and thanks for this." Mattie waved the USB key at her.

Bora headed for the door, and turned back before opening it. "Don't lose it."

She sprang out onto the street and disappeared into the crowd.

Mattie shook her head with a smile. Lord knows what she would find on the USB: a lost city in the Sahara, perhaps?

She plugged the key into the computer. The usual warning about the origin of the device flashed up on the screen. She hesitated a moment, worried about viruses, but thought that Bora didn't need her help if that had been her intention.

There was a single file with a single name: *a hidden place in the desert.*

Matttie clicked it open and was presented with the coordinates of a location in a desert that Google Maps no longer displayed: 40.8173° N, 111.7652° E, Inner Mongolia – China.

* * *

The white board that Tang had made available to Henry was covered in what had fast become a complex diagram. Henry had explained to Tang the three stages of money laundering and the warden had gulped the information down as though it was fresh air.

Placement injects the money into the legitimate financial system.

Layering conceals the origin of the money through a series of transactions.

Integration: the cleaned-up money is withdrawn from a legitimate account and used for whatever purpose the criminals have.

Tang was full of questions. Good questions:

What jurisdictions were the easiest in which to open a bank account?

How quickly could a shell company structure be put in place?

What types of assets were the best to use to layer the money?

There was now no doubt in Henry's mind that Tang was not only smart, but also a well-educated man. The burning question now was what had the warden done to be sent to this hellhole?

"The best jurisdiction to open an account with minimal documentation used to be Panama, but with the internet it's easier to open an account online and not bother with the travel."

Henry was sitting at the table with Tang. The warden had discarded some of the food that had been brought to him. Yet Henry had not been invited to help himself. He clenched his stomach to prevent it from rumbling. Henry was damned if he was going to beg for food.

"You said it was easy online, but it depends how secure the online services are," Tang said, finishing a small plate of fresh mango.

"If you are referring to whether the internet is policed in such a way that it makes it difficult to open an account, there are ways to get around that as well."

Henry wasn't going to pretend he wasn't aware of China's constant surveillance of the internet and of its citizens. It was what Henry did best: make the unspeakable a matter of open discussion. You want to talk fraud, let's talk fraud.

Tang shifted on his chair a little. He was perhaps not expecting so much straight talking that early.

Tang asked, "And Panama is also good for complex corporate structures that will help with the layering you mentioned?"

"It is but not exclusively. Closer to Asia there is the Philippines and Singapore, if you know what you are doing."

Henry wasn't going to disclose all in one go and Tang must have sensed it.

"How can I be sure you know what you are doing?" Tang asked.

"I help you structure a small transaction and you test the waters."

Tang said nothing, his face as impenetrable as ever.

Henry waited too.

"Gems and gold are good." Tang nodded. It was not a question but rather a statement.

"Of course, easy to move around and sell. Same for large yachts or very expensive cars."

"You would put together a structure? Not in Asia... Panama."

"It's easily done."

"And the cost?" Tang looked off in the distance.

"My company, Newborn Finance, will bear the cost. A gesture of goodwill." Henry felt like adding "or a bribe".

Tang gave Henry a wary look. He tapped his fingers a few times on the table and pushed the dish that he hadn't finished towards Henry without looking in his direction. Tang was thinking.

There was no spoon or chopsticks. Henry would have to use his fingers and try to avoid making a mess, but Tang had made a gesture he couldn't refuse. His stomach told him it was time to put his pride to one side. Henry managed to scoop the noodles and pork that were left into the large bowl without splashing too much sauce on his shirt.

"You start tomorrow. I contact your assistant again," Tang said.

Henry nodded, mouth still full. He hadn't had time to eat much but it was better than nothing.

Warden Tang stood and walked back to his desk. He pressed a button on his phone and gave a quick set of orders in Mongolian.

Henry managed one more mouthful before the guards arrived. He stood up and bowed to the warden. The guards stood on either side of him.

As Henry was about to leave his office, Tang spoke. "I still think you are a spy."

The guards closed the door behind him.

Tang had spoken in English; whether the guards understood it or not they didn't show it.

Fuck.

Henry thought he'd made progress, but he had to reassess. Or perhaps he had underestimated Tang. Tang was greedy without a doubt, but greed was not blinding him. He would keep putting pressure on Henry to get him to where he wanted him without giving away much. A few crumbs, just as he had with his leftovers.

Henry and the guards reached the row of dorms. They passed the buildings and started walking along the edge of the exercise yards. Some orange-band-wearing inmates had been allowed into one of the pens. Some were crouched on the ground, playing dice it appeared. Others were smoking and having a chat.

The thug who had been aggressive towards Henry and dispatched one of the inmates this morning had his back to the wires. Henry and the guards walked past him. He must have heard their steps because he turned around to see who was being brought back from the front yard.

Henry avoided looking in his direction, but he could feel his eyes on him. What Henry had also learned in Belmarsh was the power of fear.

Never provoke but don't show fear if provoked.

He waited until he had arrived at the man's level and turned his head to look at him. They locked eyes long enough for the guard not to see Henry's action. He noticed the tattoo of a tiger on the man's chest and lifted an ironic eye. A flash of anger crossed the thug's face but then he laughed and blew Henry a kiss.

Henry had just made a friend, too good a friend, possibly.

The guards kept walking as though nothing had happened. As they passed the canteen and headed for the hangar, they crossed with four men carrying a piece of tarp heavy with a load. It was only when they came close that Henry spotted two feet sticking out of it.

This morning's dead man was being carried away. Henry slowed down and followed the sad group with his eyes. They walked to the bottom of one of the towers and two guards Henry hadn't noticed opened a door. The men kept going towards a place that was outside the perimeter.

He caught a whiff of rot in the air and Henry knew exactly what would happen to the corpse. It would be thrown into a mass grave and doused with chemicals to deter scavenging animals.

Henry had almost ground to a stop. He realised it and sped up to make up for lost ground. The guards didn't seem to care.

A good lesson for a new inmate to learn.

When they entered the factory, the large doors dividing the pit from the rest of the building were open. Henry had caught a glimpse of what might lie behind when he'd first arrived, but the large piece of steel that was being transported through had obscured his field of vision.

But now the doors were still wide open and the new piece of steel that had been quenched and then lifted from the pool had been moved inside the next hangar. More inmates were busying themselves around the chunk of steel. It looked as though it was being placed in position, ready to be assembled to a larger structure.

Henry slowed down again but this time the poke of a baton into his back told him not to linger. Too late, though. Henry's photographic memory had registered the details of the other hangar and all that he'd seen in it.

The two guards hurried him along by prodding him again. He entered the room he had left before lunch. It was almost an hour after the other inmates had started work again.

The engineer lifted his head when he arrived, taking stock of what must have happened. Henry looked fine, no limping or bruises to the face. The engineer said nothing, but Henry could almost guess his thinking. He had returned from Warden Tang's office unscathed. Why?

A few of the prisoners lifted their heads almost imperceptibly. Rob Walker was one of them. His eyes followed Henry until he sat down, and the look he gave him was not a friendly one.

Even Bo was guarded when Henry took his seat next to him. Warden Tang knew a thing or two about manipulation. Isolate Henry first and then make him dependent on Tang for protection once the other inmates and the gang masters had turned on him.

Henry resumed his work, going through his next assignment, and submitted it to the engineer. He was given another drawing with more calculations to make. Henry returned to his desk and started work again, but more slowly this time.

The speed at which he was working had enabled him to finish more sheets of paper than most in the group. He went through the new drawing thoroughly and brought back to memory what he'd previously worked on. He thought about what he'd seen in the second hangar before the guards had forced him to move, and it all clicked into place. What they were building was big, and it required plenty of space to be assembled. The ship Warden Tang was getting the prisoners to build had more than 20 decks by Henry's reckoning. Henry made a quick extrapolation about how long a ship needed to be to carry so many decks. He estimated 1,000 feet. Henry frowned. That couldn't be right. He did the maths again and came up with the same number.

The ship they were helping to build was 1,000 feet long, over 20 decks high and yet here they were in the middle of the desert. A build like that was ludicrous. The quality of the steel that was cast wasn't good enough to produce a seaworthy vessel – but perhaps seaworthiness was not the point.

Henry returned more fully to the calculations he was meant to make and noticed Bo glancing at him a few times. Henry hesitated. Should he trust Bo with his latest discovery? Only one way to find out. He could also snuff out Tang's attempt at isolating him.

Henry scribbled a couple of ideograms on a scrap of paper.

We are building a ship, they said.

Bo almost smiled. He responded on another scrap.

US aircraft carrier.

CHAPTER TEN

The smell of food wafting on the street made Harris's mouth water. The small street he and Nick had walked along when they'd first arrived in the Zhongzheng tech district had still been asleep, but now at midday, the food stands were in full swing.

Harris had dragged Nick away from the computers he'd been patiently configuring for maximum efficiency. The young man had grumbled that he wasn't hungry, but Harris didn't care. Nick hadn't been to Taipei before and he needed to know about the environment in which he was operating.

"I'm about to let you loose on the streets to search for some extra tech equipment. I want you prepped and ready," Harris said, as he slung his rucksack over his shoulder.

Nick looked miffed. "I've travelled out of the US before, you know."

Harris almost mentioned Russia but that would have been mean and below the belt. "No doubt, but not as a spook."

"No, better, as a hacker."

Harris rolled his eyes. "What? Participated in a hacker's convention, did you?"

"You bet. DEF CON in Vegas."

"Vegas *is* in the US."

"But hackers come from all over the world to win the DEF CON Black Badge."

"What's that, the Olympic gold medal of hacking?"

"Black Badge goes to the winners of some of the most challenging contests, like Capture The Flag." Nick nodded, his eyes lit up with excitement.

"I don't mind sounding ignorant but what is this Capture The Flag stuff, bringing down the US government?"

Nick nodded again. "Teams of hackers compete to attack or defend computers and networks using software and network structures they've designed. Great fun."

"And I presume you've got one," Harris said with a grin.

"No..."

Harris's smile dropped away.

"I've got several." Nick sighed. "But I didn't participate this year."

"Under the principal of *staying under the radar*, as advocated by your boss, Henry Crowne?"

"Yeah." Nick was still moping. "But he says I might be able to compete next year."

The thought put a spring in Nick's step.

"As long as we can get him out of China, that is." Harris was only half joking.

Nick was about to ask a question but Harris interrupted him. "Time to choose some food."

Harris turned into a street and strolled along the stalls that were lined up. He showed Nick the different types of food available, from beef noodle soup to braised pork rice, and from radish pancakes to pineapple cakes. Every little kitchen on wheels looked more appetising than the last and the queues of locals lining up to get served said it all.

They stopped in front of a small stand, the front and side of which was covered with pictures of the finished dish on sale. The Chinese characters that were scribbled all over the ad board no doubt told the crowds how good the food was. But Harris didn't need a translation. Like in many instances he trusted his nose.

Harris turned to Nick suddenly, who had taken an interest in the next-door counter. "Where are we?" Harris pretended to look alarmed.

Nick was about to respond, but then the shock on his own face said it all. Another lesson learned.

Harris nodded. "That's right. Pay attention to your environment even with a trusted person. What happens if we are attacked and I'm gunned down?" There was no reproach in Harris's voice, just calm like his matter-of-fact statement. Nick still had to learn.

Harris approached the stand and ordered his food. Nick chose the dish being sold by a food stand a little farther up and they started their walk back to the safe house.

"I know you think you can't remember but you have an excellent photographic memory," Harris said, taking a bite of his pork bun. "Bring up the images now and find the way home."

Nick closed his eyes for a few seconds. He opened them and looked at Harris, jerking his head at another lane that took them away from the path they'd come from.

Harris frowned. "You sure?"

"Yeah... just remembered, I got a glance at a map of the market when we arrived. This is a short cut."

Harris shook his head and smiled. Crowne would have been proud.

Back at the safe house, Nick ate his food with one eye glued to his laptop screen.

Harris had finished his lunch before they'd arrived back and went to the kitchen to brew a cup of honest English tea. While waiting for the kettle to boil he checked his emails again. A one liner from his contact in Seoul told him matters were progressing but that there might be some delay.

Our friend's trip in the planning, need to confirm ticket.

Perhaps the hacking of Hunter's emails could wait. More urgently, Harris needed a visa to be delivered in the next twenty-four hours.

He plonked a cup of tea in front of Nick. "Do you remember I mentioned a journalist to you this morning?"

"Mattie Colmore, one of the *Times of London* correspondents. You said she might be useful, so I did a bit of digging while I was waiting for the systems to respond during the set-up phase."

Nick was about to launch into the details of what he had discovered when Harris stopped him. "What you won't know – because nobody does, and I hope the hacking community hasn't stuck their nose into it – is that Mattie was rescued as part of an operation Henry was running to infiltrate ISIL in Syria."

Nick took a moment to process the intel Harris had just dumped on him. "I read she'd been kidnapped and was part of a prisoners' exchange."

"Which was not the original plan. In fact, there was no original plan since Henry had gone to Raqqa, the HQ of Islamic State, purely to gather information about their finances."

"So, what happened?"

"He decided to play James Bond and rescue Mattie Colmore."

"And the information?"

"Why do you think I mentioned James Bond? He brought back enough intel to persuade the allied forces to mount a new operation and herald the end of IS."

"Wow..." Nick picked up the mug of tea and took a sip. "Nice cuppa."

Harris couldn't suppress a laugh. "What comes next, you speaking Cockney?"

"Doing *me* best." Nick grinned.

"Anyway," Harris continued, more serious. "The hostage for prisoner exchange was Henry's brainchild and Mattie Colmore knows it."

"She owes him her life?" Nick looked both impressed and a little scared.

"Almost certainly. She at least didn't suffer the way most female hostages had at the hands of IS and Al Baghdadi."

"You said she is in Seoul."

"She is. She's just finished an exclusive interview with a high-ranking officer who's recently escaped North Korea."

Nick nodded approvingly. "She must be a tough nut."

"Yup, she knows how to find the hot places and can't wait to get involved. She covered the Middle East for years, even got embedded with some of the Kurdish Peshmerga female fighters, and now she's paying attention to China and its circle of influence."

"She and Henry must have got on really well."

Harris flashed a wicked smile. "I think they did." The innuendo was lost on Nick. *Just as well.*

"So, what is she going to do?" Nick asked.

"She's already doing it. Well, she doesn't know it yet." Nick raised a surprised eyebrow. "I can't discuss the op with her for obvious reasons, but I can get her to China – and after who knows? Perhaps she'll find out about a mysterious camp in the Inner Mongolian Desert."

"You mean, you're gonna use her to get intel about what's happening there? But that's –"

"Dangerous?" Harris nodded. "Mattie Colmore is a bright woman and a resourceful one. She'll handle it. Besides, it's either that or we sit on our hands and wait 'til Hunter decides to feed us some intel – if he decides to feed us some intel."

"Is that the only way, to use Mattie?"

"I can't even get one of the best satellites we run with the US Army to give me an image of the camp. The pane that would normally contain the location has been frozen and the Chinese have put some of their best hackers on it to keep it that way. So far no one has managed to break through their wall."

"I haven't tried." Nick pouted.

"And you won't. We don't need to attract the Chinese government's attention to the fact that our operatives are interested in the Zhaga camp."

"OK. Is Mattie in China already, then? I thought she was in Seoul."

"She is in Seoul and about to apply for a Chinese visa... A bit of help from us would be very welcome."

"Won't the Chinese authorities realise she's a bit of a controversial figure?"

Harris shook his head. "Not if she travels under another name."

"Travelling under legend takes time to prepare."

"That's where we can help, or rather you can help. She's done this before."

Nick was thinking. "She needs papers and enough details that would satisfy a background check... I've never faked an ID before." A world of possibilities was opening in front of Nick.

"You're a fast learner. You'll be fine." Harris grabbed his rucksack and pulled his own laptop out. "I'll send you the details straight away."

Nick settled in front of his screens. "I guess the CIA can't know."

"That's an understatement. If they find out, they'll close the op and let Henry and Rob fester in China."

"I gathered that. How about the Chief at MI6?"

Harris took a short breath. "Not going to tell him either, otherwise he might ask me to get Hunter in the loop. You know, their special relationship and all that."

"So completely under the radar then?"

"You can call it that."

Nick winked. "Sweet. Just like a good hack then."

Harris's phone rang. He frowned and moved out the room. It was Han calling. "I said to call only in an emergency."

"It *is* an emergency," Han replied.

* * *

The new hotel Mattie had chosen was completely different to the Metropole. This one was less expensive, and it showed. It was clean enough though and Mattie had stayed in much worse places, where the only toilet was a hole in the ground outside.

She threw her rucksack on the bed; it skidded across the nylon bedspread to land on the floor.

"Shit..." She sat heavily in the flimsy armchair and heard it creak under her weight.

Mattie toyed with the idea of calling Han, but she needed to think. Things had been moving surprisingly fast. First Han's lead and then the fortuitous meeting with Bora, which she wasn't fully comfortable with, and now China's announcement that it was declaring a moratorium on western journalists entering the country apart from a select few.

Her chances of being granted a visa were already slim but now they were non-existent.

Mattie unpacked the bare minimum from her small suitcase. Decided on a shower and a change of clothes. She would then take a stroll along the streets of Seoul and see whether she could get inspiration during her walk.

She was just wrapping herself in a bath towel when her phone rang. She didn't recognise the number, but a voicemail had been recorded on her device.

Han sounded even more serious than usual.

"Must meet," is all he said.

She shrugged at the vagueness. Perhaps he too had seen the news and wanted to alert her.

She sent a text back. *As agreed previously, 1hour.*

They never finished a conversation without agreeing where the next meeting point would be. This time it was the Seoul Grand Park and more precisely, its zoo. Mattie would have to cross the river to get to the park, but an hour was ample time from where she was.

She got dressed in her jeans, light sweater and running shoes, stuffed her laptop in her rucksack and made her way to her rendezvous point. She knew she was rushing into this new project too fast, but she always did. At least she was still in Seoul and safe. She'd worry about information falling into her lap, the way it usually did, after she had her visa to China – if she got it, that was.

Han was already waiting for her outside the tigers' enclosure. Mattie slowed down. She was usually the first to arrive at their meeting. If it had happened the other way she couldn't remember. She did a quick mental check and shook her head. No, it had never happened before.

He must have felt her gaze because Han looked in her direction but didn't show any sign that he was waiting for her. He returned to watching the tigers stroll along the sandy earth to the far end of the enclosure and then back.

Mattie reached him with the same detachment he showed and sat next to him. "I know about China closing its border to journalists, bar a few *regime-approved* ones," Mattie said.

"I was worried you might not know." Han picked up his rucksack and took a flask out of it. He took two cups from a small plastic bag and handed one to Mattie. Han poured some yuja tea into both cups.

Mattie nodded her thank you. "I haven't seen the details of the embargo, though," Mattie added whilst sipping her tea.

"It's almost impossible to get in unless you have a project that is authorised by the interior minister. Really, Mattie, with your history and what you're about to publish, you shouldn't go."

Mattie sighed. "You know me, Han. When I get my teeth into something meaty I find it hard to let go."

"And that almost got you killed..."

Mattie dropped her gaze. Images of Raqqa swarming with IS fighters only intent on causing harm, the abducted women she'd had to leave behind and the man who had jeopardised his entire operation to save her flashed in front of her eyes.

"I know." Her throat tightened at the memories. "But the truth has got to come out."

Han topped up their cups. "Maybe."

"Maybe what? The truth has got to come out," Mattie said, more forcefully than she intended.

"I'm simply saying, sometimes it's not possible to do the right thing."

Mattie finished her drink in a couple of large gulps, stood up and walked to the wall of the enclosure. It pained her to see such beautiful and powerful animals cooped up in such a small space. "You should be roaming free in nature," she whispered. She stayed there for a few minutes. The story she had been handed was too big to drop. She returned to the bench and sat down. "What did you say about government-approved projects?"

Han was still sipping his tea. "That's all I know. Journalists may be allowed in on government-approved projects."

"Do you think that a project on the Mongol tribes of Inner Mongolia might work? You mentioned them to me, remember?"

Han shrugged. "Depends on what you're going to say about them."

"If the interviews prove that minorities in China are free and well-treated, perhaps that'll work."

"I don't know, Mattie. I'm still not sure you should go."

"Argh, Han... Then you shouldn't have brought me this piece of intel." Mattie sat back heavily on the bench.

"I wish I hadn't."

"Forget wishing for what can't be undone. Can you find out?"

Han finished his tea and collected Mattie's empty cup. He put them in the plastic bag and returned it to his rucksack.

"Maybe."

Mattie gave him an expectant look that said *come on.*

"I'll try... but no promises."

Mattie smiled. "You're the best."

* * *

Which aircraft carrier were they assembling in Zhaga? Henry recalled a couple of names: the *George H. W. Bush* or the *Ronald Reagan.* Those were part of the Nimitz class of carriers. But that technology was old, dating back to the mid-seventies. The US was developing a new class that would soon overtake Nimitz. The *Gerald R. Ford* new tech was set to be launched in the next few years.

Henry slowed down his work to give more thought to what it all meant. The level of sophistication required to produce one of the most expensive and complex pieces of armament, the US Navy needed to be exceptional. Would Rob Walker know anything about it?

Taiwan was without a doubt the number one producer of highly sophisticated computer chips and no weapon or systems could work without them. Rob and his team had been designing some new high-performing chip...

Henry looked up when Rob went to the water cooler. The man was limping less than yesterday. Just as well; what Henry had in mind when it came to escaping required strength.

Rob didn't face the room like most inmates did when they got water. Henry was convinced that he had also noticed how the large windowpanes reflected back the space.

Rob sipped his water slowly and took his time in returning to his seat. Henry could have sworn Rob had been surveying Henry's position in the room, but that was perhaps wishful thinking on his part.

Henry stood up shortly after Rob. He had just finished the upscaling of yet another drawing and went to the engineer's desk to present his work. The man took it from him and replaced the document with another one. Henry stuck the new roll underneath his arm and moved to the cooler.

This time it was his turn to survey the room. Rob's head was bent over his drawing. The two men on either side of him looked equally absorbed in their work.

Henry returned to his own work without thinking about Rob again. He couldn't afford to make a mistake.

When the bell rang, the inmates finished their work and started to line up, ready to leave. Henry raced to finish the last couple of calculations on his piece. Rob had been amongst the last stragglers at lunchtime and Henry bet that it was his habit.

Only a few men remained when Rob stood up to join the others. Henry finished his work and moved to the engineer's desk to submit it. The engineer took it from him and jerked his head towards the moving line of prisoners.

"Mistakes are harshly punished. Better slow and steady," he said, as he placed Henry's work, now rolled up, in the OUT tray.

Henry nodded and jogged to catch up with the moving line. He was only separated from Rob by one man. The line moved into the hangar. Henry couldn't help casting an eye towards the pit, reminded of what he'd seen that morning. Rob did the same; only a few of the others seemed to remember. It was perhaps a frequent enough event that after a while no one noticed or cared anymore.

When Henry arrived in the canteen all tables were taken and almost full. He took a tray; Henry presented a bowl and one of the cooks slapped some food into it. He looked around for space and spotted Bo surrounded by other men wearing the same green band as him.

Rob had chosen to sit at the end of a table with a mixture of men wearing black and green armbands. He didn't speak to them and they didn't seek to engage either.

Henry slid his tray onto the end of the table where a seat had just freed up. He sat down without a word. The group of men who'd been chatting in a low voice stopped. A few had finished their dinner. They left, headed in the direction of the exercise yards.

Bo sat down and another inmate stayed behind. Henry slid a fraction closer to the men on the bench.

"What does the green armband mean?" he whispered to Bo.

Bo slid a little along the bench, closer to Henry. "Hong Kong dissidents."

"You been here long?"

"Three years."

"Warden Tang?"

The warden's name sent a ripple through the small group who'd stayed behind.

"Very new, only six months."

"Rumours?"

"Facts." Bo's voice had risen a little; he stopped himself before he said more. "From Hong Kong, Tang tried to play on too many fronts and make money from the governments as well as the insurgents."

Henry nodded. He must have made a lot of money out of his shady dealings and most of it he would have lost, but perhaps there was a little left and he needed to extract it from wherever he'd hidden it.

"You?" Bo asked.

"British, Financial adviser. Wrong place, wrong time," Henry said.

"Not a spy?" Bo's voice had increased in volume. No matter what Henry said others wouldn't believe it.

Henry smiled briefly. "Of course not."

Bo nodded. "Of course not." He stood up. "The crazies are about to arrive. We'd better go."

"You mean the guys with the orange armbands?"

Bo needed to give no answer. The canteen doors opened and a group of men burst into the place, the gang master leading them.

Bo and Henry moved as one. The few inmates who'd lingered too long did the same. There was a short queue at the conveyor belt that took the trays away.

More guards arrived in the canteen to control the horde that had just arrived. Some of the prisoners wolf-whistled at the remaining prisoners who were still trying to leave their trays.

The gang master was the loudest. "Hey... spy," he shouted at the top of his voice.

Henry turned back to check that Rob had already gone. Bo pushed Henry towards the door. The guards didn't carry batons Henry noticed, but guns.

"Hey... spy." The gang master moved towards the centre of the room. The wolf whistling from the others rose to a new level.

Henry looked back as he was leaving to see the grin on the gang master's face and the suggestive move of his hips.

"Grinning Man is the craziest of them all," Bo whispered. "He does the warden's dirty work."

"Like getting rid of people who're no longer useful?" Henry whispered back.

Bo gave a quick nod and said nothing more until they'd reached one of the exercise yards.

"Every other day," Bo said, anticipating Henry's question about why they hadn't been allowed into the yard the night before.

Henry briefly closed his eyes in acknowledgement and looked around. Guards had assembled around the perimeter, no doubt observing the crowd and the groups that were forming friendships and chatting.

104

At the far end of the yard was a volleyball pitch. A small group of men had started playing and Rob had joined them. Henry moved to their corner and leaned against the mesh wire of the pen. After a few exchanges the ball rolled out and in his direction. Henry picked it up and sent it back with a decent enough throw.

Rob caught it and gave Henry a thank you nod. Henry kept observing the exchange until the ball came his way again. This time the man responsible for the mistake jerked his head, inviting Henry onto the pitch.

He obliged.

Rob was playing for the other team. Henry slotted in where room had been made for him. Rob was tall and athletic-looking, despite an obvious loss of weight. The teams only had time for a few exchanges before the guard's whistle told them it was over. Everybody shook hands on the pitch. Rob was last.

His handshake was firm and brief, and Rob gave Henry a message. Trust would not come easy.

The inmates formed a line and moved out of the pen slowly. As Henry was about to leave two guards stepped forward and stopped him with their baton.

"Come."

Henry's fists clenched at the disruption but he had little choice. Warden Tang wanted a word and he wanted all to know.

CHAPTER ELEVEN

"Do you think Mattie would ever want to join the service?" Harris asked in earnest. He had moved to another room in the safe house to make his call to his asset in Seoul.

Han laughed. "If she pulls this one off you might want to ask her."

"She volunteered to use her pen name to get her visa?"

"I hardly had to suggest it. I just had to tell her she should think twice about going to China. She immediately told me to use the name under which she publishes other articles."

"That was a bit of a risky strategy."

"On the contrary, you tell Mattie not to do something and you can be sure she'll do the opposite. It's a father thing."

"Ah, yes, I remember the Right Honourable Harold Colmore MP. I can sympathise with her. I met her father once and once was enough."

"And I did my research on him. There is no love lost between them. He's a Conservative MP and Mattie votes Labour. She let the entire world know that as soon as she became a successful journalist."

"Have you approached your contact at the Chinese visa bureau in Seoul?" Harris asked.

"Speeding up the application will come at a price, but that should work."

"I don't want 'should', Han I want a 'will'." Harris squeezed the phone a little harder.

"Everything has a price with officials like the one I've cultivated."

"But won't he be suspicious if we offer too much?"

"Not this one... and I have an ace up my sleeve." Harris could hear the grin in Han's voice. "He's been caught with a couple of male prostitutes in an embarrassing position, if I can say it that way."

"You can say it whatever way you like as long as you get him to do as he's told."

Harris loved working with Han. The man knew what made people tick the moment he saw them.

Han continued. "Mattie has prepared a summary of her fake project. Exactly what the Chinese government is looking for. The story of the Mongol Tribes who live in Inner Mongolia, focusing on their traditions; how free they are to live their nomadic life, blah, blah, blah – enough to show that the Chinese government doesn't discriminate or abuse minorities in China."

"Are there many Mongols in the district she needs to target?"

"That's the beauty of it – not many because it's mainly desert, so it'll be easy for the Chinese government to make sure that whoever goes there is on their best behaviour."

"It sounds almost too neat." Harris took a cigarette out of his packet and lit it with a deep drag.

"Depends how she enters China."

Harris blew out the smoke. "Could she enter from Mongolia?"

"She could..." Han hesitated. "In fact, that's a good idea. Mattie says she's travelled before to meet some of the tribes in Mongolia. The story is that she now would like to speak to the Chinese Mongols."

"Tell her you're working on her visa. I'll do the rest." Harris took another pull and finished the call.

He moved back to the room Nick was working from. Nick had gone out with a tech shopping list that had made Harris's eyes water. He'd come back with some of the hardware, sporting a grin on his face and muttering, "Now we're talking."

"Now that you're happy with all your various toys, let's get to work." Harris dumped his cigarette in a half-drunk cup of tea.

"Swell... what do I break into?" Nick turned away from his screens.

"I want you to gather information about the checkpoints on the border between Mongolia and Inner Mongolia, preferably the one closest to the Zhaga camp."

Nick frowned. "That's easy..."

"I haven't finished. Then I want you to create a record of Mattie Colmore visiting Mongolia on a research trip, to support an article on nomadic life. She has a pen name. We are using that. I've called London to get more details so that we don't cross any wires. The files are on their way to you."

"Great stuff." Nick cracked his fingers and faced his computer. "When do you need this by?"

"Tomorrow lunch."

Nick opened his mouth to protest, but Harris cut him short. "Come on, show me you're as good as Crowne says you are."

* * *

The whiteboard in Tang's office that Henry had used to draw an example of a typical money laundering structure had been moved to one side. A new board was in its place. The steps that Henry had discussed with Tang before were listed on it with comments and questions.

Warden Tang had done his homework and Henry was suitably impressed. Tang could have of course waited 'til the following day, but Henry could see the point of making a show in front of the other inmates of getting him to Tang. Isolating Henry would guarantee greater cooperation. No one survived in prison without a few mates to watch their back. Zhaga camp would be no exception.

Henry was allowed to sit almost immediately after he'd come in. He had followed the correct ritual when addressing Tang in front of the guards, but Tang didn't care about protocol once the guards had disappeared.

"That's a very good list you have here." Henry didn't need to lie.

Tang nodded. He knew it was and whether the compliment was received as such or viewed as grovelling, Henry couldn't tell.

"I'm expecting you to answer most of these questions. For the very few you can't, tell me the points that need clarifying and I'll speak to your assistant, Nick Fox."

Henry turned to the board and went through the list. Tang had written everything in English and Henry wondered whether this was wise. It meant that very few of the guards would understand the content but that wouldn't deter unwarranted interest from them.

"When it comes to choosing who owns the shares in a company set-up or who holds the trust, you can use nominee accounts. The same law firm that incorporates the company or forms the trust can act as nominee." Henry nodded, answering one of Tang's last questions.

"Who are these nominees?"

"The company you want to talk to is a branch of the law firm MosFon. MosFon Nominees (PACIFIC) Ltd has huge experience in doing this."

"Your assistant could contact them."

"It might be better if I did this myself." Henry didn't hesitate in volunteering. Had he been up to his old tricks of setting up another screen company for the dissident IRA, he would have taken care of that business himself.

"Why not Nick Fox?"

"Because I prefer to keep some of my more exclusive contacts there to myself."

The word "exclusive" must have rung a bell. Warden Tang shifted on his seat. "How long before these contacts of yours start asking questions about why you're no longer around?"

"I rarely meet these people. In fact, the less I do the better. They know me or of me. I did the groundwork many years ago to enable that."

That was also true but Tang's question chilled Henry to the bone – a direct way of assessing how long Henry could be useful for.

"We start tomorrow," Tang announced without giving further details.

He used the walkie talkie on his desk to call the guards and Henry found himself on his way back to his cell. The camp had fallen quiet. The crazies had perhaps not been permitted time in the exercise yard. Although Henry doubted it was a good idea to stop the gang men from getting rid of their pent-up energy before locking them up for the night.

The guards took their time in returning Henry to his cell. One of them lit a cigarette on the way. The muffled sound of a scuffle ahead stopped Henry. He was a few paces in front of the guards who either hadn't noticed or didn't care. The two men kept walking slowly, enjoying their smoke.

The noise became more persistent. A few men were out when they shouldn't be. A choked cry made Henry turn back to the guards. One of them told him to keep going with a snappy move of the hand.

When Henry rounded the corner of the warden's office building to reach his own, he came into full view of what was happening. A gagged man was on the ground and two other inmates were kicking him. Henry's sudden presence stopped them. The man got up and made a run for it.

Instead of pursuing him the gang men waited. He had nowhere to escape and for them it was a bit of extra fun. A third man appeared from the shadows and gave a short whistle, which launched the thugs after the running man. They sprang with the agility of hunting dogs and caught their prisoner as he was about to reach the far end of the alleyway that led to the dorms.

They dragged him back by the legs to the place where the gang master stood, and Henry recognised the Grinning Man. The guards had stopped short, preferring not to turn the corner of the building that was sheltering them from the scene. They were not getting involved. Instead, they lit another cigarette and started chatting in a low voice.

Henry froze when the Grinning Man slammed his fist into the man's face. The Grinning Man dropped his knee onto the man's chest and the power of the blow caused the man's skull to crack against the ground.

And then the Grinning Man didn't stop. His fists worked one after the other, ramming into his victim's face with such ferocity that the man stopped crying almost instantly.

It took Henry a minute to decide what to do. The guards were still chatting. The gang men had withdrawn to let their master enjoy the kill. Whatever happened now Henry was a marked man. The gangs would know he'd witnessed the slaughter; so would the guards and the warden.

Henry inhaled deeply and all his training came into focus. He launched at the Grinning Man with a savagery he hadn't summoned for a long time.

* * *

Harris left the safe house. Nick hadn't slept all night and yet this morning he didn't look any worse for it.

Harris turned left, away from the main road and into the smaller streets of the tech district. He'd spent a large part of the night on calls to London. Elaine Wong had spent the day gathering as much intel for

110

Harris as she could. Her assignment to Harris's team from GCHQ might be just what Harris needed to create a path for Mattie Colmore.

"Her pen name will work," Elaine had told him. "She publishes articles on minorities that live in remote areas of the planet. She's freelance on this so *The Times* has no say in how she gets involved."

"That sounds promising," Harris replied. "Just send the data to Nick Fox. He is working on her profile and background story in Mongolia."

Harris heard her tapping on her computer keyboard. "Done."

"Any news in the subterranean world of intelligence about Zhaga or a western spy getting caught?"

"Absolutely zip. I've chased GCHQ and DATA OP here at MI6. There is no news."

"Maybe no news *is* good news. My CIA contact told me there wouldn't be any." Harris sounded more upset than angry.

There was a short silence from Elaine, a hesitation that Harris sensed before she spoke. "If the CIA won't share, perhaps we could try to find out ourselves."

"You mean find out the identity of Dragon?" Harris smiled at the thought of crossing Hunter. "If we blow Dragon's cover you and I will finish our days with a begging bowl outside Waterloo Station."

"Only if we fail," Elaine corrected.

"Let me give Hunter one last chance to be a good citizen and share some intel with us. Otherwise..."

"Otherwise...?" Elaine's eagerness was not what Harris needed. He needed a solid head that would tell him he was already sailing too close to the wind.

"We'll talk about it."

"Great." Elaine sounded cheerful. "That's a yes then. I'll do a bit more digging on what asset MI6 has in Inner Mongolia and come back to you."

Harris had grumbled an *I didn't say that* but too late. Elaine was off the phone.

Harris arrived at the food market. He went through a detection routine that took him in and out of some of the small lanes with food stalls. After 20 minutes he decided he hadn't been followed and sat at a small table at the back of a café he'd spotted the night before.

OP TECH LEOPARD was taking a direction he hadn't foreseen. No operation ever worked as it was supposed to but there was a limit as to how much freewheeling MI6 allowed men like Harris. True, he handled some of MI6's best operatives and that gave him some extra leeway, but Harris was fast approaching the red zone, and after that he would truly be on his own if the operation went sour.

Harris had discussed Hunter's stubbornness with Jack and Jack had summed it up perfectly. Dragon was the most valuable asset the CIA had in China, or perhaps the most valuable asset the western world had in China. No agency would dare blow his cover and MI6 more than any other.

Still, there was no good reason for Hunter not to share.

Harris ordered a coffee and dialled a number from a burner phone he'd been given before leaving Taichung Air Base. There was one ring before Hunter picked up.

"Any news for me... please?" The word please almost stuck in Harris's throat but he managed to be civil.

"None. We have no contact."

"When are you expecting contact, if I may ask? My man has been out there for a couple of days."

"As per our agreement, I'll contact you as soon as I hear anything. I must go now." The line went dead, and Harris cursed. He'd used a burner phone for nothing and would have to get a replacement from Taichung.

"Fuck. This moron is going to get my guy killed." Harris stuffed the phone into his pocket. The waitress brought him a coffee and he paid immediately. Harris took a sip. He thought about the number of moving pieces he was now having to juggle under the radar. Elaine would be solid in London, Han in Seoul and Nick with him in Taipei.

Mattie Colmore was his wild card, but she'd been resilient in Syria and Harris trusted his instinct when it came to people.

Harris sipped more of his coffee. He thought of Henry and what would happen when he discovered Mattie was involved. He would cross that bridge when he came to it.

A young couple that had sat almost at the same time as Harris attracted his attention. They were dressed in jeans and sweaters and had placed their mobiles on the table they occupied. There was nothing remarkable about them. They were chatting amicably, just the way a happy couple would.

The coffee they had ordered arrived and the man paid as soon as they'd been served. The young woman's phone must have rung, because she picked it up for a short conversation and put it down again.

Harris took his time to finish his coffee. The tables around him were almost empty and it was an odd hour to stop for a drink. He caught the eye of the waitress and ordered another drink. When it came, he asked discreetly where the toilets were. Harris dug a bank note discreetly out of his pocket and left it underneath his cup. He stood up abruptly and strode in the direction of the gents. From the corner of his eye, he saw the young man stand up.

Harris moved to the last cubicle. There was a small window above the seat. He bolted the door, yanked the window open and eased himself onto the window ledge. Harris heard the door of the toilets open and someone walk across the room. He climbed out and into the tiny alleyway just as the man was trying to open the cubicle door.

Harris started running and discovered he faced a dead end. He climbed onto a large tin dustbin that almost collapsed under his weight, then onto a sturdy wheelie bin and landed on the other side of the wall.

He hailed a cab and got into the back before anyone could catch up with him.

"What was that about?" Harris turned to check whether anyone had followed him out of the passageway. But the cab joined the flow of traffic and Harris couldn't see the entrance of the place any longer. He leaned heavily against the seat of the cab. He picked up his encrypted MI6 mobile and dialled Nick's number. "Where are you?" he asked him.

Nick yawned. "Still in front of my computer. I've almost –"

Harris interrupted. "Pack up your stuff. We're moving." He killed the call.

The cab stopped him two streets away from the side street for the safe house. Harris entered a small restaurant with a connection to a stingy-sized inner yard. Once more he climbed over the wall, and found himself in the safe house courtyard.

By the time he entered, Nick had already packed up his laptop and some of the new equipment.

Harris shook his head. "Clean that lot... We'll get new equipment. We don't have the time."

"That's going to cost us *time*."

"I'm aware, but we need to leave now. This safe house has been compromised and I don't know by who yet."

"All right."

Nick took a couple of USB keys out of a small leather pouch. He plugged in the devices and uploaded a program on the computers. The screens' well-organised icons twisted in on themselves, and the background image shrank like a wilting flower.

Harris stood at the main door of the house, listening for sounds coming from either the small yard or from the shop that was the front for the safe house. He heard voices coming from the small tech shop. The old lady who ran the shop started to protest.

"Come on." Harris slung the rucksack he hadn't unpacked over his shoulder and opened the door. Nick stuffed the last of his equipment in his.

"Over the wall." Harris kept his voice low.

Nick heaved himself over the wall silently. Harris was about to follow when the door that led to the courtyard from the shop burst open. Harris jumped over the wall just before a pair of hands managed to grab his legs.

There was no need for instructions. Harris took the lead.

He raced into the back of a small restaurant connected to the other yard in which he and Nick had landed and climbed a set of stairs off to one side. Nick was right behind him. Harris could hear his footsteps following.

They climbed two flights of stairs and ran to the end of a corridor. Harris opened a rickety window that gave way after a few pushes. He stood on the window ledge for a few seconds. There was only a small gap between the window and the rail of a small balcony. Still, the drop below was large enough to focus his attention.

He jumped and grabbed the rail, finding space for his foot on the bottom of the balcony. Harris rolled onto it and made space for Nick to jump after him.

Nick balanced on the window ledge.

"The rucksack first," Harris ordered.

Nick threw his rucksack across and Harris caught it. Through the window, he could see a figure running down the corridor. Nick could hear the footfalls, too, because his eyes widened and he launched at the rail. His hand caught it but his foot slid off the bottom part of the balcony.

Harris leaned forward and yanked Nick up and over the railing. The sound of stones hitting the pavement below surprised them both. A sudden jolt announced that the balcony both men had landed on was coming loose; another jolt propelled them across a French window.

An Asian man dressed in a black tracksuit was about to jump but the sight of the dislodged balcony stopped him short. Nick picked up the rucksack and he and Harris ran for another set of doors. They kept going through a maze of corridors, windows and across inside bridges until they finally hit a small street. The place was busy enough that Harris could slow his pace down.

Nick came alongside him, out of breath but the rucksack securely on his back.

"Who are they?"

"No idea, yet." Harris had to confess.

Nick nodded. "Where to now?"

"Safe house number two," Harris grumbled. "I had anticipated we might need to change location mid-way through the operation but not so quickly."

"I take there is no safe house number three, then?"

Harris shot an angry glance at Nick and raised his hand to hail a cab.

There wouldn't be any conversation about OP TECH LEOPARD during their cab ride. Harris needed to think about whether there had been a leak or if he'd been too slack.

CHAPTER TWELVE

Henry's entire body was in turmoil. Slowly, he moved his position on the bed to try to ease the pain. For a moment he couldn't remember where he was.

The weight of his body slamming into the Grinning Man's back sends them both flying. Henry rolls to his side and gets up before his opponent does. Surprise will soon be replaced by anger but for the next few seconds Henry has the advantage.

The back leg kick he delivers into the man's torso, followed by double fist slam to his lower jaw, propels the Grinning Man farther into the yard at the back of the prisoners' dorms. The man knows he must get up. Henry can read it in his struggle to recover.

The guards race to the scene, dropping their cigarettes, but they hesitate to interfere. The man who kills for the warden is fighting the man who's advising him on his latest venture. Better wait and see who comes out on top.

Henry stands up, hands at the ready. The Grinning Man knows how to fight. His training comes from the bare knuckle fights of the gangs of Macau and from martial arts – after all, China is the birthplace of kung fu.

The Grinning Man looks around at the other gang members. He has been challenged. This is his fight alone.

Henry's Krav Maga training that combines defence and attack with maximum physical aggression kicks in. He already knows his opponent has a weak left knee and that his lower spine is stiff. He starts with a crouched sweep that he doesn't complete. The other man throws a reverse leg kick to target Henry's face, but Henry catches his left leg and he brings the man down, slamming his spine on the ground.

The Grinning Man can't help but groan. Henry is already twisting his left leg around the weak knee and uses both feet to create a vice. The sound of bone snapping is sickening. The yell of pain startles everyone. The Grinning Man is rolling on the ground in agony.

The guards finally round on Henry, but the beating they give him is half-hearted. The gang men take their fighter away amid shrieks of pain.

Henry widened his eyes. It surprised him he was back in his cell and not in the interrogation room that had welcomed him three days ago.

The answer might be simple. There may be plenty of men ready and capable to replace the Grinning Man but there was only one Henry Crowne. Newborn as he was known to the warden – financial adviser and money laundering expert. His sudden smile caused Henry more pain and he reprimanded himself for being so cocky.

Or perhaps the warden was reserving a surprise interrogation for him that needed careful preparation. Henry groaned at the thought. He would find out soon.

The light that had started to seep into his cell through the small window told Henry it was time to get up. In a few minutes the bell would ring, the doors would open, and the inmates would make their way to the canteen. Henry doubted he would be part of that crowd.

But he was wrong. No one came for him.

Henry sat for breakfast at the same table he'd occupied the night before. A couple of inmates he didn't know came to sit at the end of it. Bo Chan turned up. He looked pleased with himself and sat down only one seat away from Henry.

"Everyone is talking about you."

"How so?" Henry brought the bowl of food close to his mouth and started slurping pork noodles.

"The Grinning Man isn't grinning anymore."

"News goes around fast. I'm surprised."

"I've just got the right contact at the canteen."

"Hong Kong friend?" Henry kept his attention on his bowl.

"Another lawyer like me."

"What has he done to deserve the canteen and you the drawing room?"

"He wrote better subversive material than me." Bo sighed. "I'm very miffed about it."

Henry finished his food and moved on to his tea. "Can it get any worse than the canteen?"

Bo gulped air and nodded. "The graveyard. For that I'm very grateful my prose was not that good."

More inmates arrived. Rob was amongst them.

Henry looked in Rob's direction. "How come he wasn't with us, the other westerner, when the doors of the cells were released?"

"Shower day... once a week." Bo finished his food and looked around to check who was watching. He jerked his head indicating he had to go, and stood.

Henry stood up as well. "What's his name?"

"Rob Walker... tech engineer."

Henry pouted an OK.

Bo moved faster than him towards the conveyor belt, to leave his tray. Henry didn't hide he was in pain and when Rob walked past him, he gave the engineer a brief nod. Rob looked Henry in the eyes and blinked in acknowledgement.

Small progress, Henry thought.

When Henry entered the foundry, he joined the usual line of inmates that were assigned to the drawing office. A few heads inside the pit turned to look at him. He didn't need to see their faces to know what they were thinking...

Revenge or challenge.

＊ ＊ ＊

Their new safe house was closer to Taipei New City. The feel was very different, more residential, and yet international enough that two foreigners would not look out of place.

The apartment that had been set up for them was part of a series of blocks of flats that were linked by hanging bridges. Nick hadn't said one word during the journey. Instead, he'd opened his computer and carried on working.

Harris went to survey the property first and when he returned, they both moved into their new space, quickly surveying what they'd been able to salvage from their abrupt departure.

118

"My laptop is fine... I've salvaged a few USB keys with content, and I've been sending data to Elaine for confirmation." Nick stretched, then guzzled down a can of Coke he'd bought from the vending machine in the foyer.

Harris eyebrows shot up. "You mean you haven't lost a lot of the work you've done?"

"I have... a few hours' worth of work. Although Mattie's profile is ready to go." Nick appeared to give it more thought. "What's worrying me is the hack you want me to get on with, you know, on Hunter –"

"Hold on..." Harris lifted his hand, keen to backtrack and stop himself from getting too excited. "You built Mattie Colmore's profile and background story in Mongolia last night?"

"Well..." Nick hesitated and Harris's hope sank. "More like this morning." Nick checked his watch. "Got some good HUMIT from Elaine at around 2am and I took it from there. But as I said, the bit that worries me is –"

"– Yep, I get it. The CIA hack." Harris ran a hand through his hair. "But you're telling me we're almost good to go with Colmore's legend?"

Nick looked at Harris, puzzled. "Just one more hour to finesse some of the details but yeah, we're there."

Harris collapsed on the nearest chair and let his head fall on the headrest.

"Shit, this is the best news I've had on this op for at least three days."

Nick didn't seem to share Harris's enthusiasm. He returned to his open laptop. "Who were those guys?"

"As much as I hate admitting it, I don't know."

"Can't be the Chinese, otherwise Dragon would have been caught and Hunter would have tried to pin this on us."

Harris managed a smile. "Couldn't have put it better."

"The Taiwanese have got to be on our side, right?"

"Good point but our side, as you put it, is not playing happy families at the moment."

"OK, so the Taiwanese are on the US side."

"And I would be too if I were them. The Yanks are the only ones who will come to their defence if China invades and make a difference. Even if Japan and South Korea are willing to help, the Taiwanese need the US."

"But why would they or even Hunter want to get us out of the safe house?"

"For the very reason that he doesn't want us to do what we are about to do."

Nick frowned. "That's mean. We're just trying to save Henry and we wouldn't have to get our own intel if he just played ball."

Harris nodded. "Hunter is a mean bastard, but he's not the only one. I just got a lot meaner myself since this morning."

Harris got Nick to draw up a list of the equipment he needed to replace. He would get it himself as soon as he'd called Han to finalise the plan to send Mattie Colmore to China via Mongolia. His timetable was still on track. He hadn't planned to stay in Taiwan more than four days without news of Henry, and with some luck he wouldn't be.

Harris left Nick alone, who was on a call to Elaine. He picked up his encrypted phone and called Han. "We had a little setback, but I'll have the details of Mattie Colmore's journey plus entry point at the end of the day."

"Mattie and I met again," Han said. "She's asked me to confirm with the Chinese Embassy that the project about Mongolian tribes will work. As soon as you give me the go on this, I'll get back to her."

"How about your Chinese contact at the Embassy?"

"He thinks the project is just what the government needs and so are the dollars that will line his pocket."

"Keep him warm. It's only a matter of hours."

Han hesitated and Harris picked up on it. "I know, it's a big risk for Mattie, but if I don't use her, one of our own might not come back."

Han sighed. "I was almost convinced, Steve. You should have added 'and won't bring the intel we need with him'."

"Very cynical of you, Han." Harris pretended to be shocked. It was not Han's business to know what Harris's operative was up to.

Harris returned to the main room where Nick was still working. The young man had opened his second can of Coke and Harris realised they hadn't eaten for quite some time. The safe house would have tins and frozen food that were regularly checked and replenished. He went to the kitchen and found a packet of biscuits. He returned to the main room and plonked the open packet on the table Nick was using as a desk.

Nick helped himself absentmindedly and kept working. He returned to the biscuits several times and Harris left him to it.

Harris turned his attention to his next task: sourcing the tech equipment Nick needed for the hack. Harris also needed to make an appearance at the British Office on Songgao Road. The staff might worry if he didn't return for a second night in a row.

Harris consulted the list Nick had given him. He didn't want to return to the tech district just yet. The men who had almost caught them would have called in reinforcements to check the district thoroughly. They would also be waiting for him at the British Office and Harris would have to find a way to lose them again or not be detected at all.

He needed help from a source he hadn't considered yet.

* * *

Henry resumed his work on the long table that accommodated all the men working on the aircraft carrier project. It was almost pleasant to be working on such a simple task in a place like this. Henry completed it at his usual pace and went to deliver his drawings to the engineer.

The man took the papers from him and did something he hadn't done before. He unfolded the drawings and started checking the calculation.

"No mistake..." The engineer nodded. "And I see you don't double-check your numbers, either."

"I'm good with numbers." Henry didn't want to elaborate further.

"I hear this is more than just being good with numbers." The engineer lifted one brow at him then returned to the calculations.

Henry shrugged. "It's part of my job back home." Was he about to get another client? He almost smiled at the thought. At this rate he might consider opening an office at Zhaga camp.

"So, you are a mathematician?"

"It was a long time ago."

"But you understand mathematics and can read complex drawings?"

"I'm not an engineer, if that's what you're asking."

The engineer rolled his chair back, considering Henry fully. He half closed his eyes, as though he was making up his mind about him. He rolled his chair back farther, picked up another set of papers and handed them to Henry. "You'd better watch your back. The gangs don't like to have their man challenged and defeated. They'll want a return match."

Henry bowed slightly. "Thank you. I'll bear that in mind."

The engineer waved him back to his seat. Henry noticed on his way back that Rob had followed their interaction. He cursed. He didn't want the engineer telling him what he knew and jeopardise the small progress he'd made with Rob Walker.

Henry ran the conversation over in his mind. Was the engineer trying to determine if Henry had found out what it was they were putting together? But did it matter? As far as the engineer was concerned, Henry was there to stay for a very long time.

The shrill ring of a phone surprised Henry. The engineer picked up his mobile and answered immediately. His body tensed at what was being said and his eyes darted around the room, as if to check all was in order. He stood up and walked to the far end of the long space, where the completed rolls were to be taken and stacked, and arranged them in a neater pile with his free hand. His conversation remained low, and he was nodding as though receiving precise instructions.

When the call finished almost everyone had slowed down what they were doing, waiting to hear about the news.

The engineer returned to his desk. He didn't sit down but instead banged his fist on the top of the desk, then waited for everyone to lift their heads. "A very big honour has been bestowed upon us today. We have the visit of General Ling Ma of the People's Liberation Army and high-ranking official in the Chinese Communist Party. General Ma will be coming to inspect the work we are doing here to advance the future of the People's Republic of China."

There was murmuring around the table.

The engineer banged on his desk again. "Silence! Back to work."

The men took a moment before returning to their calculations. The tension escalated in a room that was used to a more sedate mood.

Henry found a small scrap of paper and wrote.

Is this common?

Never, Bo replied.

Henry returned to his work, keeping an eye on the men around him, keen to see who looked concerned.

Rob stood up shortly after the announcement to submit his papers. Henry lifted his head just as Rob was returning to his desk. This time the man didn't avoid Henry's gaze; Henry read fear in Rob's eyes and something else he didn't expect: hope.

They came for them just before lunchtime. Four men were dressed in a very different way to the guards – dark olive suits, red epaulettes and gold stripes on the sleeves and sides of their trousers. The uniforms were pristine, freshly pressed and as crisp as the men inside them. The guards were bullies in camouflage while these young men were trained and precise.

Two of them stood at the back of the main room, rifles to their chests, while the other two walked over to the men they had been instructed to collect. Henry was the closest.

"Henry Newborn?" Henry nodded slowly as the man used his legend's name.

With a sharp movement of the hand, the man indicated that Henry must follow. He then moved over to Rob. He asked Rob's name and gave the same instructions.

Henry turned to see Rob join him and caught the look of sadness in Bo's eyes.

They walked out of the foundry where another large piece of steel was being quenched. This time Henry didn't turn his attention to the pit. His mind was racing through all the permutations possible.

Had Dragon been found out and the plan scuppered? Or had Dragon had a change of mind? After all, a dual nationality tech engineer at the prison, one of the best in the world at designing semiconductors, was a coup, but doubling down with a British agent was a once in a lifetime opportunity.

Then again why wait three days? The delay meaning positive news was of meagre comfort compared to the prospect of being outed as a spy in China.

The small group walked past the canteen, the exercise yard and the row of dorms. They walked past the entrance of the building that housed Warden Tang's office and took a sharp right.

Henry's breath caught in his throat when he realised where they were headed. They were on their way to the dark place: the interrogation rooms.

Rob had been walking next to him, almost in a trance. He stopped suddenly as they turned the corner, forcing the two men behind him to stop abruptly. His body had stiffened up so much that Henry could see the muscles of his arms bulging underneath the sleeves of his shirt.

One of the soldiers was about to use the butt of his carbine on Rob, but before he could, Henry shook Rob out of his panicked state. "They'll start right here if we don't move and it'll be even worse. Come on."

Rob shook with fear and he closed his eyes for a moment. He nodded and they resumed their walk to the building of doom.

Warden Tang was waiting for them. He had swapped his uniform for a more formal one and his face looked as inscrutable as ever – although the glance he gave to Henry seemed to hold a warning.

The men walked down the same stairwell Henry had three days ago. The smell of disinfectant was overwhelming. Warden Tang must have cleaned up the mess of the interrogations he conducted regularly, in preparation for the general's visit. Henry wondered why. After all, the place was meant to do just that: interrogate the political prisoners, dissidents and foreign agents that were transferred to Zhaga.

Their small group walked past the cells lining up the corridor. Henry recognised the vault he had been thrown into. Rob's fists had been clenched since they'd entered the building and Henry felt the tremble of his own body.

Warden Tang turned around and looked at Henry and Rob. His gaze finally fell on Henry and he pointed his finger at him. "You, follow me."

Henry moved forward, sandwiched between the two soldiers who had brought them there.

"General Ma is doing you the great honour of meeting you," Tang said in Mandarin. "You will bow and not look at General Ma unless invited to straighten up. You will only speak if asked a question."

Henry nodded. He was pretty sure there would be plenty of questions and equally sure he would end up on the floor or be strung up to a hook within minutes. At least it was giving Rob a reprieve.

Warden Tang opened the door of the vault and moved to a room different to the one Henry had first been interrogated in.

The lights were bright and the rows of equipment lining the walls were impressive. Henry felt his jaw tighten. This was where his training was going to show. He knew it was only a matter of time before prisoners were cracked open like a nut. He hoped he had enough determination and resilience to last a little longer than them.

Henry was led over to the table in the centre of the room; one soldier stood on either side. There were two chairs, one of which was equipped with the types of restraints Henry had seen too many times in the prisons of IS, in Syria.

Past memories of men, barely alive and hanging from hooks, their feet hardly touching the ground, almost made him retch. Henry swallowed down the bile and pushed the memories away.

Without warning the door opened. A young man entered and assessed the place. He didn't bother to great Tang. Henry caught sight of his uniform insignia. He was a first lieutenant, no doubt assigned to the service of the great General Ma.

Satisfied all was in order, he moved back to the door and held it open, standing to attention.

The person who entered the room was smaller than Henry had expected. At 6ft 2 Henry was taller than many men in the West, and that was equally true in Asia, but he had expected General Ma to be more imposing. Henry remembered to bow his head, and then waited.

General Ma stopped at the entrance of the room and after a few seconds, moved a couple of steps in.

"You are Henry Newborn?" The pronunciation had hardly any accentuation but what surprised Henry more was the tone of the voice.

He heard someone moving towards him. Then General Ma was across the table from him, repeating the question.

"Are you Henry Newborn?"

Henry couldn't resist raising his head to make sure he was right. "I am."

The hit to the face he received for his insult made him stagger back. General Ma might be a woman, but she had the strength of a man.

CHAPTER THIRTEEN

The Sanchong Fruit and Vegetable Market was buzzing. Harris had found a seat at a small coffee stall just near the main entrance. He was waiting for his guest, who he was certain would turn up. The question for Harris was whether Master Chief Rodriguez would come alone or be accompanied by some of his CIA colleagues.

It hadn't been too difficult to locate Rodriguez at the accommodation he and his team occupied. Harris had guessed correctly that the ALPHA team had not been sent back to the US but remained on standby for a possible future extraction. Harris didn't want a face to face with Rodriguez but just needed a way to test the waters. Would he find an ally in Rodriguez?

Harris stirred sugar into the coffee he had just purchased, and recalled the steps that had led him to here.

He had bought a pack of envelopes and a few stamps from a convenience store. Then he had found a postcard of Taipei skyline from another shop. After, he'd jumped into a cab heading in the direction of Taichung Air Base. The ride took him little more than an hour, but Harris needed to deliver his note in person. He'd simply hoped he wouldn't be too late for the midday mail run.

The building the US army rented was guarded and secure. Gaining access was possible but Harris would have to disclose his identity, and his visit would be reported to Commander Richards, and inevitably Hunter.

Not an option.

Harris placed the postcard on his knees and scribbled the number of his new burner phone as well as two more words.

Please call – Harris.

He'd placed the card in the envelope, wrote the name and address of Master Chief Rodriguez's home at his US base in Colorado, then affixed a stamp. Harris took a thick, ballpoint pen out and drew an image on his thumb that looked like the official mark mail received once it had gone through a sorting office. Harris then pressed the image on the envelope and studied his handiwork.

Not bad for a quick fake.

He'd let the ink dry and put the envelope back in his pocket, checking his watch. Han would be waiting for his call, probably busy getting Mattie Colmore's fake passport produced in anticipation of it. Harris had smiled at the thought of Han's confidence.

Harris then shook his head... Sending someone who wasn't a trained operative was indeed a big risk, but he'd had made up his mind. He was putting all his money on Mattie and Henry. Rodriguez was also part of that plan – as long as he turned up, that was.

Harris thought more about the timing of his arrival at the US Army building. He had been in luck.

The cab had dropped him a few streets away from the US Army complex. Harris lit a cigarette and started to walk. He recalled that there was delivery of mail to the army personnel twice a day. Henry had mentioned it when he was training with them. Harris couldn't remember why he'd mentioned it, but the intel was now proving useful.

Harris looked at his watch. He had five minutes or so until the van turned up. He crossed the street and walked to the opposite building. He'd kept going until he judged he was far enough, and then turned back. Harris sat on a low wall that encircled another residential property and took his mobile out of his pocket. He then placed it to his ear and started a one-sided conversation.

The van he had been expecting was late. Or perhaps it had been early, and he'd missed it.

Harris ran his hand through his hair. There was no plan B. He stood up, irritated, and started walking back towards the US building. He was about to cross the road once more when the van turned the corner.

Harris watched it stop at a set of traffic lights and gear up again towards its destination. Harris started to jog slowly, mobile against his ear. He crossed the street just as the van was parking, came round the back in a swift move and crashed into the army person delivering the mail just as she was shutting her door. Her bag of post flew out, the contents spreading on the pavement. Harris apologised profusely and tried to help, but she'd pushed him away in anger.

"Can't you watch where you're going?"

"So very sorry, my wife is expecting and I was on a call to her sister." Harris donned a look of emotional mess and seriousness.

The woman was still suspicious, but her attitude softened a little. "Don't touch the mail. I'll deal with it."

"Again... apologies. Can't I help?" Harris had looked away from the scene, as though anxious to reach his wife, yet concerned for the trouble he'd caused.

"No, that's fine, I'll sort it. Just go." She shooed him off.

Harris thanked her again and resumed a hasty walk that turned into a run. He couldn't have escaped fast enough after he'd dropped his letter into the post strewn on the pavement.

It had only taken fifteen minutes for Harris's burner phone to ring.

"Where are you?" was all Master Chief Rodriguez said.

"Taipei. Not that everybody is pleased about it."

"Is he alive?"

"Not sure, but to find out I need your help." Harris wasn't going to pretend.

"Why haven't I seen you in Taichung?"

"Long story but short answer. CIA's not happy with me or H. If you want the longer version we need to meet."

"Where?"

"Before I tell you I must warn –"

"– that this needs to stay under the radar?"

"That would be preferable but not necessarily ideal for you."

"Where?"

Harris hesitated and then shrugged. He could always pretend he was desperate for intel about his operative. "Sanchong fruit and veg market... near the entrance."

Harris thought he heard Rodriguez swear in Spanish. "Are you serious?"

"It's a very nice neighbourhood in New Taipei. No one will notice us as long as you dress in civvies."

"What do you take me for? I know infiltration, Harris." He groaned. "I'll be with you in one hour."

Harris looked at his watch. The hour was up. In the distance, he spotted the bulky frame of Master Chief Rodriguez walking through the crowd.

On the way to Harris, Rodriguez stopped at a few stalls to get his bearings, doing what Harris suspected was an assessment of his surroundings. He didn't make his interest obvious enough that a stall keeper might ask him what he needed, but kept it focused enough so he looked as though he was genuinely browsing.

Rodriguez noticed Harris and moved a little faster towards him. He nodded a greeting and sat down at the small table just inside the open-air café.

"Thanks for coming," Harris said with honesty. "And alone."

When Rodriguez didn't answer, Harris worried he'd gone too far by inviting him here. But then Rodriguez lifted a hand and ordered a coffee. They sat in an uncomfortable silence until Rodriguez was served his drink.

"If you want my help, I want to know the whole story," Rodriguez said. "I know, although I've not been told as such, that this op went down because it was supposed to."

Harris raised a surprised eyebrow.

Rodriguez continued. "I've been in this business for far too long. I know when an op has been well put together and I know that the minute we hit the ground things start diverging from the plan – but not the way it has with TECH LEOPARD."

"I'll put my cards on the table but there is one piece of this puzzle I can't disclose." Harris toyed with the spoon for his coffee.

Rodriguez's dark eyes flashed in anger.

Harris nodded. "I know. I ask you to come to me and then I tell you that you've not been told the truth, but that I can't tell you the whole story, either. But please hear me out and then you can decide."

Rodriguez shrugged. "This coffee is surprisingly good so I might as well finish my cup."

Harris took a small intake of breath. "The op is not only for the recovery of an ultra-sensitive piece of intel but also to rescue a tech engineer held in captivity."

"You mean, the tech guy created what we are trying to retrieve?"

"That's right. He went to a conference in Singapore and then just disappeared."

"Who is the CIA protecting?" Rodriguez asked as he brought his cup to his lips.

"That's where my own intel stops, I'm afraid." Harris almost dropped his spoon, but then placed it gently on the table.

Both men stayed silent for a moment.

Master Chief Rodriguez drained his cup and set it back in its saucer as slowly as he'd picked it up. "What do you need from us?"

Harris could have punched the air, but he remained calm. "I had to leave my safe house in the tech district a bit faster than I would have liked. I couldn't bring all the equipment I had gathered there with me."

"Your safe house was busted, in short." Rodriguez extended his muscular legs out. "You know who these guys were?"

"No idea yet... could be closer to home than I'd like to admit."

Rodriguez cracked a smile. "So, you've got beef with the CIA?"

"A whole herd of them to be honest."

Rodriguez's smile broadened. "Wow... Here I am in the middle of Taipei talking to a Brit about going against my own government."

"I know, I'm sorry. It's not ideal."

Rodriguez grew serious again. "But we don't leave one of our own behind. H is a part of ALPHA team."

"You know what that means if it all goes tits up?"

"No pension, no honourable discharge, with a bit of time spent in the hold..." Rodriguez pursed his lips. "We need a plan to get your tech stuff back."

* * *

The pain had subsided a little. Henry's body hadn't been brought to such limits before. Electricity was a blessing for civilisation and a greater one for torture.

General Ma had ordered Henry to be strapped to a chair. She'd made it clear she would be respected just as much as a man would.

She had then dismissed the soldiers that had accompanied her, as well as her aide, and called a much older man into the room. He looked like a benevolent grandfather, Henry thought. That was until he'd placed electrodes on his body and electricity started coursing through them.

Henry had gritted his teeth at the start, but now there was no point in holding back. He wasn't supposed to be trained and telling the truth was supposed to come quick.

"I am a financial adviser..." Henry's words had been slow and laboured and his head had dropped to his chest. "Check with my assistant."

"I still don't believe you."

Ma was sitting a short distance away from him at the table. She had hardly moved during the time the old man had been working on Henry. She had lit cigarette after cigarette, waiting for Henry to admit that which could not be admitted.

It was an effort for Henry to shake his head. "I made a mistake... driving."

Ma laughed. "You westerners, you think you can deceive us with your stupid plans, but the People's Republic of China can't be fooled so easily."

Henry then braced himself for yet another round of electrical shocks. The old man hadn't bothered to strip Henry. He had poured water over Henry's clothes, and it had proven more effective than Henry could have imagined.

The two large pegs that looked like jump leads had been moved to Henry's crotch for the last round of questions; when his body arched under the pain, he hadn't been able to suppress a scream.

His mind was fuzzy and yet the truth remained buried deep. There had been no thinking, no anticipating, just a split-second processing of the pain he endured.

Ma finally stood up and came next to Henry. "What happens if I bring your friend into this room and start torturing him, too?" she whispered close to his ear.

"I don't know him."

"Think about it – you're the second westerner to end up in Zhaga. Why?"

A shudder gushed through Henry's body. General Ma was getting uncomfortably close to the truth, or perhaps she already knew the truth and Dragon had been outed.

Henry's resolve softened for a moment, but he knew better than to give in. General Ma was an experienced interrogator. She was fishing and prodding to see what would come out from the doubt she'd seeded in Henry's mind.

Henry managed to shrug. "I don't know him."

"We shall see."

Ma left the room and the old man followed. Henry lifted his head to check what was happening but when the aide returned he dropped it back to his chest. The man took the seat his boss had just vacated.

"Are you thirsty?" the aide asked.

Henry moaned, "Yes," and the young man disappeared.

Good cop – bad cop?

The sound of water being poured into a glass made Henry realise how thirsty he was. His arms were still tied and he couldn't reach the glass that the aide placed before him. Henry's burning throat screamed for some of that water.

"General Ma will make you talk. No matter how well trained you are," the aide said.

Henry lifted his head and mumbled the same phrase he had repeated for what felt like an eternity. "I am a financial adviser..."

In a sense that was true and helped him keep up the pretence of his legend. Henry had been the best at his job in investment banking, working for a big international institution.

The young man rose to his feet and leaned against the table opposite Henry. After a short moment he took the glass and held it to Henry's lips. Henry gulped down as much as he could. Ma's aide poured a second glass. This time Henry slowed down as he drank.

"Thank you."

"I can't do very much for you unless you give me something."

Henry dropped his head again. "What do you want? I know nothing that could interest you." He'd thought hard about what the offer truly was.

The young man returned to his seat and sat down heavily. "There must be something you know that could help you."

Ma's aide was no longer asking about Henry or even Rob. The conversation had moved on and that move was indeed helpful. Henry wondered whether he'd just met Dragon. But he shrugged the idea off. That was far-fetched and dangerous.

Henry thought about Tang. He could reveal Tang's interest in money laundering.

"Anything?" the aide pressed.

"I've just arrived..."

Ma's aide seemed to be thinking about what this could entail. "But you'd like to help?"

Henry gave a feeble nod.

"I need to hear it."

Henry forced his croaky voice up a notch. "I'd like to help."

"Perhaps this is a proposition that General Ma will consider."

The young man stood up and Henry heard him move to the exit. He opened the door and Henry thought he'd heard the cries of another man. Whether that man was Rob Walker, Henry didn't know. What he did know was that Rob wouldn't hold out for long, whatever it was that China wanted with him.

The silence around Henry felt ominous. He started moving the muscles of his back and shoulders slowly, certain that a second round of interrogation was inevitable. But nothing happened and no one came for him. Henry kept stretching the muscles of his legs, trying to loosen up their rigidity.

This was another form of torture. He could be left here for hours; his bladder was starting to feel uncomfortable, and the two large glasses Henry had just drunk wouldn't help.

Henry braced himself for another more subtle but no less effective game of will breaking. He looked up slowly at the ceiling. There was nothing obvious on first inspection.

He repeated the exercise, like a man in pain seeking relief by finding a better position. On the fourth attempt he saw what he was looking for: a small groove in the brick work that would almost certainly house a camera.

After what Henry estimated to be an hour, he started to shout and moved around on the chair. No one came but he kept the act going for a little longer, which would make him look more and more desperate to the observer.

"I want to talk," Henry eventually shouted. This would get Ma's attention or at least her aide's. But when nobody came, it looked as though Henry would be ignored. *Fuck. How many times do I have to beg before you answer?* He inhaled deep and kept going with his desperate man pretence.

The door opened but instead of General Ma, Warden Tang appeared. He looked less self-assured than he'd been the night before.

"Are you ready to admit you're a spy?"

Henry shook his head. "No... I'm not a spy."

Henry lifted his head and met Tang's gaze with a coolness that surprised the warden.

"I won't say anything about our little financial lessons and in return you make sure Ma and her aide leave me alone."

Tang bridged the gap between him in a couple of steps. He slapped Henry's face hard, drawing blood.

Henry spat blood at Tang's feet, undeterred by this show of power. "There is a camera filming us as we speak. You kill me now and Ma will know there was a reason, and that reason has nothing to do with me being a spy or not."

Tang pulled back a little. Concern flashed in his eyes, but was quickly replaced by the same inscrutability as before.

Henry murmured, "I'll help you get the financial structure off the ground and transfer the money you have to a place no one, not even the Chinese government, can find. Or, my assistant will contact the authorities and Ma will find out."

A thin smile spread over Tang's face. Henry couldn't tell whether he thought the threat was ridiculous, or was smiling at the prospect of disappearing with a large sum of money and leaving the shackles of the regime behind.

Before Tang could answer, General Ma entered followed by her aide.

"I hear you have something to say."

Tang's face didn't lose its composure but the side glance he gave Henry told Henry what he needed to know.

Henry said, "I can help you track the billionaires in China who launder their money outside your country."

Tang didn't expect this, and neither did Ma's aide. General Ma, however, appeared much more clued in than the two men around her gave her credit for.

"This has value to us how?"

CHAPTER FOURTEEN

The flight from Seoul to Ulaanbaatar had been uneventful. Mattie had declared on the immigration form she would be staying for less than thirty days and walked through immigration at Chinggis Khaan International Airport without any issue. When the woman at border control asked her what the purpose of her visit was Mattie had said tourism. She'd booked a bedroom for two nights at the Holiday Inn in Ulaanbaatar and this seemed good enough for the official.

No one at customs asked her for anything either. This was welcomed. Mattie had concealed rather effectively the second passport Han had produced for her. But Lord knew what a nosy custom officer might have made of the secret compartment in her rucksack and the passport and burner phone in it.

Mattie walked out of the airport and checked her watch. It was 11pm and she needed to find a cab. Chinggis Khaan Airport was literally in the middle of nowhere and almost thirty miles from Ulaanbaatar's centre where her hotel was. There were a couple of hotels nearby, but Mattie felt a European holidaymaker wouldn't choose a one-star hotel and certainly not a yurt camp.

The heat had slipped from the day and Mattie zipped up her aviator jacket. She joined a queue of people who were waiting for cabs, again deciding against catching the bus into town. A cab ride wouldn't be expensive to a foreign traveller, and she didn't want to attract undue attention on public transport.

It wasn't her first time in Mongolia, but she still spent time marvelling at how arid yet majestic the landscape was. The airport had been built at the foot of a steep mountain that, even under the softness of moonlight, looked as though it had been carved with a hatchet. Ulaanbaatar was on the other side, protected on all sides by the difficult terrain.

When her turn came, a young man with a broad smile and broken English took her only bag. She noticed he was in a T-shirt and didn't seem to feel the dropping temperature. It was barely above freezing and too cold for what he wore. From the back seat, Mattie chatted with her driver during the journey, picking up on what was happening in the country and what it was like to live so close to a mighty neighbour like China.

"So far good... but China, strong, more strong," the driver said, turning around to give credence to his words.

"It's the problem with many other countries that are smaller than China. China exercises influence there no matter what." Mattie leaned in between the two front seats. She'd rather have her driver concentrate on the road that wound around the side of the mountain than look at her.

The chat carried on until they'd reach town. Mattie took his card in case she needed a driver. He gave her the same broad smile as when she was getting into his vehicle.

The room at the Holiday Inn was like any other in the hotel chain in any part of the world. Mattie gave herself permission to visit the mini bar. She passed on some strange white wine that was produced in China. Instead, she chose a Jack Daniels, poured the content of the mini bottle into a glass, and took a large sip.

Mattie took the burner phone out of her rucksack and dialled the number Han had given her.

The phone rang twice, and a distracted voice answered. "Yeah... Who's that?"

The person with a New York accent sounded young, too young. She hesitated, wondering if she'd made a mistake, but what was the likelihood of her dialling a number in Mongolia and getting an American?

She took the risk. "I'm a friend of Han."

The focus of the person on the phone switched immediately. "So, you made it?"

"Why shouldn't I have?"

"Sorry..." There was a muffled laugh. "I didn't mean it that way. I thought Han was kinda having me on."

"Well, he ain't." Mattie thought she'd imitated the New York accent rather well.

"OK... Do you want to meet now?"

"At almost 1am?"

"It's Ulaanbaatar – the middle of the desert rocks at 1am."

"Name the place, then."

"I'll come and pick you up."

"I'd still like to know where it is we are going."

"Sure. It's called Dund Gol on Baga Toiruu, just across the river from you."

"And what does it do, this Dund Gol?"

"It's a cool bar that also stocks Soviet and post-communist old vinyl, some Polish psychedelic rock... Although I'm not so sure about –"

"Fine," Mattie interrupted. "Give me a call and I'll meet you outside the Holiday Inn."

"Won't be long."

Mattie fell onto the bed. She wasn't particularly tired, but she was worried. Han's contact sounded a tad too young to be credible. Or was she simply being an old fart? The thought made her smile.

"You gonna turn out to be just as bad as your dad, if you're not careful," Mattie castigated herself gently.

The last time she had spoken for any length of time to the Right Honourable Harold Colmore MP had been on her return from Syria. It had been a heated conversation about her taking risks which put him in a difficult position. Her return from Syria after being taken hostage in Raqqa had been all over the press.

"I didn't ask you to rescue me," Mattie shouts at her father.

"I say, this is rich of you. You are very glad to be back among us though, I surmise." Her father's small, grey eyes flash in anger.

"The fact that I am back has zero to do with you... and you know that."

"You're just an ungrateful little cow!"

"No Dad... I'm a realistic little cow! The man who saved my skin wasn't there on your say-so. In fact, I rather think your intervention with the US almost destroyed his operation."

"Well, then, next time I'll know better."

"No, you won't. You'll do again exactly what you did a few weeks ago. You'll measure the political impact of my capture and if it's bad for your bloody career as an MP, you'll send a rescue party."

"Get out of my office!" Harold Colmore MP smacks a wad of papers off his desk as Mattie slams the door behind her.

Mattie breathed in deep. It had been one of the most chilling experiences in her life as war reporter. Her mind drifted back to Raqqa, her escape through Syria, and the two men who'd risked their lives for her: Wasim and Henry.

She shook her head to dispel the memory. It wouldn't do her any good to reminisce. She was walking into danger again and she needed to be focused on what came next.

Her mobile rang. Her contact had arrived. Mattie slid her feet into well-travelled boots. She put her aviator jacket on and moved to the hotel foyer.

When she reached the outside, she spotted a man on a bike. There was no one else around. As she approached him, he slid his visor up and extended a hand.

"I'm Genghis. Welcome to Mongolia."

* * *

Rodriguez and the ALPHA team had piled into a couple of cars. Harris was driving the first one. He had hired two large SUVs as soon as he'd left Rodriguez. He and Nick had brought the team to the new safe house and now they all were driving back to Zhongzheng, Taipei's tech district.

"You sure they haven't moved the tech stuff?" Rodriguez asked again.

"Positive," Nick said. "I always put a tracker on my equipment."

"And they won't have cracked the passwords on these techy bits?" Fergus moved forward, his face popping between the front seats.

"It takes time to crack the passwords I create," Nick replied.

Fergus shook his head. "I still can't understand why they haven't moved the stuff out?"

"Because whoever they are, are operating below the radar – just like us." Harris had thought it through ever since Nick had confirmed the equipment was still there. The old woman who'd been renting the place to the Brits would know what to do. Call the police, make a complaint she'd had people try to rob her but say nothing about her Brit guests.

The safe house had become a hot spot for a short while only. It was a matter of time before the assailant returned though.

"Let's go through the plan again," Harris said, as the SUV crossed the river and got closer to the safe house.

Rodriguez started. "Fergus goes to the small tech shop that's fronting the old safe house. He'll keep us in the loop of any potential intrusion and can stop, or at least slow down, any attempts to enter the place from that side."

Harris looked into his rear-view mirror to check the second SUV was following and nodded.

Rodriguez continued. "Nick stays behind in this SUV1 and Don in SUV2, ready to drive off." Nick gave him one thumb up. "Hulk, Ray and I follow you through the route you took to get out. Ray will do a perimeter check, as I'm sure the hostiles have posted surveillance there."

"These guys don't know you, though." Harris slowed the car a fraction to give himself time for this last recap, before they went into action. "The tech district is full of foreigners and the shops are open late. We just need to drip-feed into them and meet on the first floor of the second shop."

Rodriguez nodded. "Yes, I like the idea. But if we can spot the watchers and neutralise them, we'll have more time to get the stuff out, rather than worry they may have spotted us and we didn't notice."

"Sounds good to me." Harris indicated right and turned into the main avenue that led to the safe house. "ETA five minutes. You may want to tell your guys to saddle up."

Rodriguez and his men checked their comms. "This Viper Zero-One. ETA five minutes." He then called the rest of his team in the second SUV.

Everything went quiet in the vehicle and Harris felt the focus of the men around him change. He also gathered himself for what would be coming next.

Harris stopped the car. Rodriguez called his team one last time.

"Let's sync watches. It is 23.07 hours."

Fergus jumped out of the SUV and started moving toward the alleyway next to the safe house.

"I'll circle once around before I park," Harris said.

The two-car convoy drove past the shops they had targeted as entry points. Harris found a spot on the second pass and parked. Ray left for his recce and Don parked SUV2 nearby.

Ray returned ten minutes later. "One car only, two men. They're parked at the top of the side street opposite shop one."

Rodriguez moved in his seat, readying to help his men if need be. "OK. Hulk, Ray, you know what to do."

Ray put a dark hoodie on. He slid a rucksack over his shoulders and took a can out of the bag he'd brought with him.

Hulk had already left SUV2 and was walking slowly in the target's direction. Ray caught up with him and both men walked in sync, yet apart.

Ray was the first to open the door of the surveillance car and throw his can into it. Hulk was only a second behind him and followed suit. Both men turned around but instead of leaving, they leaned against the doors of the car preventing anyone from getting out.

"What is that?" Nick couldn't help asking.

"Special brand of nerve gas. Not lethal, just prevents you from moving for a while. We use that in some hostage situations when we don't want hostages to panic and run and get themselves shot," Rodriguez volunteered.

Ray and Hulk crossed the road after a couple of minutes. Rodriguez left the car first and Harris followed a minute later. Each man drifted into a couple of shops that Harris knew connected to a maze of corridors that eventually led to the safe house courtyard.

Harris left Rodriguez to browse through the latest headsets in the front of the shop. He walked to the back of the shop where a display of the latest iPhone was attracting customers. Even at midnight the shop was busy.

He waited for the assistant to be busy with a customer. Then he slid into the small corridor in the shop's backyard. A few tables had been set up there for people to bring a drink and test their new purchases.

Harris didn't reach the yard but instead took a sharp right and climbed as fast as he could up a narrow set of stairs. Rodriguez followed and within a couple of minutes, Ray and Hulk had joined them.

The team started to move soundlessly, Rodriguez opening the way ahead. He stopped a few times to listen and check. But the maze of corridors didn't hold any surprises. There was an eerie calm that unsettled Harris. True, it was almost midnight, but it felt somehow artificial.

Harris tapped on Rodriguez's shoulder to ask him to wait. "This is too quiet."

"Agreed, but we can't just go back. I think it'll make matters worse."

"Let's get to the roof," Harris suggested.

They had discussed the idea as an option.

Rodriguez nodded. "Let's go."

This time Harris led the way. They climbed another four flights of stairs and found themselves overlooking Tech City from a vantage point that gave them a clear view of how vibrant Taipei was at night.

Harris stopped and Rodriguez took over again, moving alongside a couple of roofs.

"We're two houses away," Harris said as they crouched down.

"Got that." Rodriguez turned to his men. "I'll be surprised if we haven't got company on the roof that leads to the safe house courtyard. Hulk, you're with me."

Rodriguez and Hulk slid below the parapet to find footing on the pipes, air-con units and building architraves that lined below the roofs. They moved slowly, avoiding making a sound. Harris couldn't help being impressed by how these muscled men worked their way through the façade of the buildings, hanging on to almost nothing.

Harris saw Rodriguez slide slowly over the parapet of the house they were targeting, followed by Hulk, then nothing for more than five minutes.

"Shit. This is taking forever."

Ray shook his head. "If they met too much resistance, they would have found a way to let us know."

"I bloody hope you're right." Harris craned his neck to check again.

"I am." Ray jerked his head and Harris turned back.

Rodriguez and Hulk were standing on the next roof.

"What took you so long?" Harris grumbled to Rodriguez.

"I just wanted to make sure the bows we tied on the hostiles looked pretty enough."

They all walked along the roof tops. Harris spotted a couple of men tied up in neat bundles, cloth stuffed in their mouths, which Harris guessed were their socks, going by their bare feet. Their eyes were also covered. They looked uncomfortable, and Harris grinned.

Rodriguez led him and his men down a set of stairs and as they reached the bottom, he turned to Harris.

"The safe house is empty. Let's get the stuff you need and get out of here."

* * *

Rob was already sitting at a table in the deserted canteen when Henry entered. A bowl of rice that had started to go cold was awaiting Henry–likely a request that leftovers be saved for the latecomers.

Henry walked to the counter, took the food and the mug of tea that had been left for him there. His performance must have been convincing enough for Ma to order they had some food. Although Henry couldn't quite make out what part Rob was playing if Ma was now convinced Henry wasn't a spy.

He started eating from the bowl before reaching the table and sat with Rob. The man lifted his head and for the first time Henry saw fear and exhaustion on Rob's face.

"I'm surprised we both can sit down," Henry said, trying to make light of the hours of electrical shocks they had endured.

Rob dropped his bowl on the table and for a moment Henry thought the man might throw up.

"I'm sorry." Henry stopped eating and gave Rob a worried look. "I'm trying to cope in the only way a Brit can."

Rob shook his head. "I lost my sense of humour a few months ago."

Slowly, he resumed his eating, but Henry could see it was difficult for him to swallow.

"How long have you been here?"

"Since June and I think we are in September, so four months."

"We are in September." Henry nodded, unsurprised. Denying inmates a sense of time was an effective way of breaking their link to the outside world and their hope of being rescued.

"What do they want with you?" Rob whispered, as he was finishing his food.

"My expertise in finance seems to be of interest," Henry said between two mouthfuls.

Rob glanced at Henry again but this time with a frown. "I thought you were caught at the border between China and Mongolia?"

"I was..." Henry kept at his food. "And they gave me a good thrashing when I first arrived to force me to say I was a spy."

"Why would a spy enter China through Mongolia? It makes no sense."

"This is what I said to them. What about you, though?" Henry gave a quick glance around the canteen. The guards at the door were having a smoke and no one seemed to care about him and Rob.

"I'm a tech expert." Rob's face dropped a little, but then Henry saw his guard come up again.

"Has it got anything to do with the construction of the US aircraft carrier?" Henry was almost certain it had nothing to do with it, but it allowed Rob to perhaps give a version of events that made him comfortable.

"It might be. I'm not sure."

"Look..." Henry moved his bowl away and picked up his mug. "If you don't want to talk about why you think you're here that's fine by me."

Rob looked taken aback by Henry's lack of interest.

Henry sipped his tea and added, "I can see that trusting people in this environment is tough and dangerous, too."

"The new warden is good at pitching the prisoners against one another."

"I've already got my fair share of that. But the warden is a very greedy man too."

"He needs results."

"You mean in getting the prisoners to talk?"

Rob nodded. "This is what this place is all about: break people, get them to talk about whatever it is the Chinese state wants them to talk about."

"The Hong Kong people are there because of the pro-democracy movement?"

"That's right."

"And the other spies to give intel on their network?"

Rob picked up his own mug and groaned when he attempted to sit up a little straighter. "You've assessed this place pretty fast."

"It's my background – assess risks fast and find a way around them."

"Still, it took me a while to gather all that."

Henry pressed on. "What about the gang lot?"

"They're used as workers on the US carrier project and also to instil fear in everyone. They are merciless bastards, most of them."

"I've noticed that too."

One of the guards cast a look at them and Rob finished his mug of tea quickly.

Rob started to get up. "And what's your way around the risk you've spotted?"

Despite his bruised face Henry managed to crack a smile. "Escape, of course."

CHAPTER FIFTEEN

Harris ran as quietly as he could towards the backroom of the safe house where Nick had left the laptops and computer desktops. The old lady was standing in the small courtyard nodding away, keys in hand. No one else but the tenant she rented the room to would be allowed in there, she'd assured Harris.

She would not have stood a chance had she not called the police, but still Harris had to admire her tough-as-old-boots attitude.

Harris walked around the room and sighed with relief. The four pieces of equipment were all there, intact.

Rodriguez followed Harris into the backroom. "They must have been under strict instructions not to cause too much damage and avoid attracting the attention of the Taiwan Intelligence Services to be deterred that quickly."

Harris nodded. "I also think these men are not as well trained as I had expected them to be." He began stuffing the laptops into a spare rucksack he'd brought with him.

"That is also true." Rodriguez retreated to the door, glancing at Ray and Hulk who were guarding the courtyard. The old lady had disappeared, unfazed by the appearance of these balaclava-clad men. As long as Harris was there, she didn't seem to mind which company he brought.

Harris moved to the desktops. He crouched, opened the hardware, using an old Swiss army knife that had seen better days, and removed the hard drives. He stuffed them in his jacket pockets and stood up abruptly, knocking over a chair in the process. Harris cringed at the noise whilst Rodriguez and his team's attention ratcheted up a notch.

"Have you got everything you need?" Rodriquez asked.

"I'm done." Harris patted his rucksack containing the Radeon cards he'd removed from the computers Nick had prepped before leaving.

"We're going back the way we came. You leave the old lady's shop with Fergus and meet back as agreed."

Harris slung the rucksack onto his shoulders, walked through the courtyard. Before disappearing into the shop he turned back to see Rodriguez and his team enter the small corridors that led to the staircase they'd used to access the safe house backyard.

He hoped the men the ALPHA team had neutralised were still sucking on their socks.

Harris slowly pushed open the door that led into the tech shop. The old lady was sitting at the counter; one of the young men who assisted her was chatting to another young man clad in a white T-shirt, a baseball cap on backwards, and a pair of headphones slung around his neck.

A couple of other customers were browsing the impressive choice of iPhone covers. Fergus was reading the product description of set of ear buds, his body turned towards the door and one eye on the small alleyway outside.

Harris was about to move to Fergus's side when the other man gave him a quick shake of the head. Harris stopped dead and turned towards the old lady. If there was going to be a fight, she needed to get out with her staff and customers.

Harris turned to her and asked, "At what time do you close your shop?"

She slid down from the high stool and moved to the door without hesitation. It was a code they'd agreed on when Harris had rented the place. Using the set of keys that dangled from her neck, she locked the door and flicked a switch that turned on the bright 'closed' sign in the shop window.

The two Asian men who were about to enter slammed their hands against the door in protest. The old lady ignored them. She turned towards the bemused customers in the shop and gave them instructions on how to leave via the back entrance.

Fergus walked past Harris. "Let's go back the way you guys came in."

They returned to the yard. "Rodriguez and the team just left."

"I know, that was the plan." Fergus stopped in the middle of the space.

146

Harris could hear banging on the shop door. "We haven't got much time."

It was only a matter of time before the door caved in, that was unless the police arrived soon. Or perhaps this time it wouldn't matter.

"Viper Two-Zero to Viper One-Zero, do you read, over?" Fergus said, adjusting his comms. He walked over to the staircase his teammates had just climbed up.

"Viper Two-Zero to Viper One-Zero, do you read, over?"

Harris thought about which alternative route they could take if this one was compromised.

Fergus's face lit up – he had a response – and yet his face fell immediately after. "Roger that. Seeking alternative extraction route."

Harris surveyed the façade of the buildings surrounding the courtyard. Fergus followed his gaze, walked over to the external piping to their right, and gave it a hard shove.

"Let's go." He began to climb, placing the toes of his boots on the brackets that held the pipes in place.

"Shit," Harris mumbled. He tightened the straps of his rucksack and followed Fergus up the wall.

Fergus reached the first floor quickly and paused. He tested the next pipe that would allow them to walk across to a small balcony, but a large piece of concrete came off just as he was applying weight to the pipe. Fergus steadied himself and lifted his head. They would have to ascend to the next floor.

The screaming sound of an alarm told the two men that the door of the shop had been forced open. Fergus moved up more quickly, and Harris pushed on behind him. He could feel the lack of grip from his sport shoes on the metal; perspiration was making his hands slippery.

Fergus reached the second floor just as a series of shouting voices rolled across the yard. He didn't have time to test the pipes and took a gamble, simply using the metalwork to aid his jump onto the balcony's parapet. Harris went after him. He launched towards the place where Fergus had found a grip, then heaved his body over the rail.

Harris's rucksack got caught and instead of reaching its target, he was yanked back and his jump fell short. His eyes widened as he began to fall, and he suppressed a cry.

A strong hand caught him. He looked up to see Fergus holding on and bracing himself against the parapet to grab Harris's other arm. Harris's feet found grip against the side of the balcony and Fergus yanked him over the edge just as the light in the courtyard was switched on.

Both men flattened against the wall into the balcony recess. It was only a matter of minutes before the fallen concrete was discovered. Harris slid down slowly to where the door leading to the balcony was locked. He pulled his Swiss knife out and wedged it between the doors.

A few seconds later the doors opened with a sigh and both men stepped into a room that looked like a lounge and kitchen combined. Harris had half expected they might find someone asleep, but no one was around.

They both crossed the room without a sound and reached the main door of the flat. In the distance, Harris could hear voices and the banging of doors. This time the backroom of the safe house wouldn't be spared.

Fergus stepped into the corridor first, followed by Harris. They used a small lift that took them to the first floor. There was no one in the diminutive hallway. Fergus opened the door to the street and left first. Harris followed, both on their way to the SUV that was waiting for them.

* * *

It was not the usual 6am bell that woke Henry up but the noise of his cell door opening abruptly. The two soldiers that he'd seen accompanying General Ma were standing in front of him. One of them grabbed his trousers and shirt with some disgust and threw the items on the bed. Henry couldn't blame him; he'd been wearing the same clothes since his arrival and quite a lot had happened to him since putting them on.

The dorm was still quiet when the guards took him out. They walked past the rows of other dorms, turned the corner of the front yard. Henry feared they would be going back to the interrogation rooms. But the men walking either side of him took a sharp right and he found himself climbing the stairs that led to Warden Tang's office.

General Ma was already there with her aide but there was no sign of Tang. He wasn't invited to this meeting, it seemed.

Henry walked into the room and stopped a distance away from Ma. He remembered to bow and wait to be told he could either straighten up or speak.

"I see you learn fast," Ma said mockingly.

Henry said nothing and this time she laughed. "Go ahead."

"I am a fast learner, ma'am."

The title he used brought a smile to the austere face of General Ma. Her eyes glittered with intelligence. Henry would need more than humour to win her over to his cause.

"I have had my aide do research on your identity and what you offer as an adviser. I also understand that Warden Tang has led his own inquiry."

"Warden Tang wanted to establish whether I had come here to spy on China."

"And have you?"

"No. I lost my way." It was not far from the truth. He had no intention of spying on the Chinese. All he wanted was to get Rob out of the country along with the technology he was developing.

"What an unfortunate... How do you put it –" she searched for the right words "– turn of events."

Henry shrugged. "It's easy to get lost in the desert."

General Ma's aide was taking notes and he lifted his head to nod slightly at what Henry was saying.

"Now, tell me more about what corporate structure means," General Ma said.

Henry suppressed a smile. He was glad he'd had a dry run with Tang. General Ma might be a more demanding audience.

It took Henry the best part of two hours to explain to Ma what it meant and to answer all her questions. Tang had been a keen learner, but Ma grasped instantly how complex corporate structures could be used to evade legislation and provide anonymity.

"And you can find out which of our citizens hold assets in any of these tax havens?" Ma concluded after Henry had finished answering her queries.

"Perhaps not everyone but a large proportion."

General Ma turned to her aide and asked him to fetch Warden Tang.

She addressed Henry again and stood up. "Warden Tang will provide you with what you need to start the work. I'm expecting swift results." Ma helped herself to some tea.

It was only the two of them and Henry thought he'd risk a question while they were alone. "Why would the army be interested in this?"

Ma stopped pouring and shot him a hard look. "Why would you want to know?"

"It might help me to target the right people more quickly."

"Money is used to counter the interests of the People's Republic of China."

Henry frowned, but then he smiled. "You're interested in money coming in as well as going out?"

Ma gave him a brief smile. "You do learn fast."

There was a knock on the door.

"Enter." Ma answered and returned to the chair she'd used to listen to Henry's presentation. She'd had her aide roll Warden Tang's comfortable armchair to the top of the meeting table they were using.

She sat in it, waiting for Tang's reaction perhaps. There was a glimmer in her eyes that revealed amusement and fierce determination. She was a woman operating in a man's world but tough enough to do just that.

Warden Tang bowed low as he entered.

Her aide gave a brief nod. Satisfied Tang had shown enough respect and knew his place, General Ma invited Warden Tang to take a seat.

Tang cast a look at Henry and for the first time Henry detected some apprehension from the man.

"We have had a lengthy and fruitful conversation with your prisoner, Warden Tang, and we believe that his skills can be used for the benefit of the People's Republic of China."

"I will assist in any way I can to make sure that the prisoner delivers what you have decided he must, General Ma." The right words were used and the tone was flattering enough.

Ma simply nodded and turned again to Henry. "How would you go about identifying China's enemy within, those who exploit these –" she again searched for the word for a moment "– loopholes that allow them to export money illegally?"

Henry had answered the question already and it was highly unlikely Ma had forgotten. She wanted him to speak about this again for a reason.

"I would go to the tax havens where I know I can obtain information and start from there."

"You will need more people to help you." Ma was thinking aloud. "Warden Tang, how many people can be spared from the engineer's drawing room?"

Tang stiffened a little but didn't object. "Perhaps a couple."

"That should do for the time being."

"Respectfully, General Ma, if I may." Henry stood up and bowed to make his request.

Ma waited, making Henry wait to see whether he had overshot the mark.

"A request?"

"A suggestion... I will need fluent English speakers if they are to make enquiries, so it does not raise suspicions."

"Make your choice and let Warden Tang know."

Henry bowed again and glanced at Tang. The warden was giving nothing away. He had sat down on the only chair left available at the table, positioned far away from Ma and her aide.

"How about those who import cash to foster trouble?" Ma's hands rested on the table, tips touching – a resolute yet elegant gesture.

"They will be using the same routes, so once I have a list of companies that have links to Chinese individuals, I can work out which way the flow of cash goes."

"This is good. I expect to see a list in ten days." Ma pushed away from the table.

Her aide peeked at his watch. He stood up and left the room.

"I intend to return and see the results for myself." Ma stood up.

Henry and Tang did the same and bowed deeply.

She continued. "Warden Tang, you too have your orders."

Tang bowed a little deeper as he spoke. "May I be permitted to make an observation?"

Ma picked up her hat from Tang's desk. "Speak."

"Taking three prisoners from the engineer's drawing room will slow our other project."

"Then find more prisoners who can calculate."

Ma placed her hat underneath her left arm. She stopped just as her aide opened the door. "You have ten days, Warden Tang." She walked towards it.

"Certainly, General Ma." Tang's bow deepened further but Henry doubted it was out of respect.

She stopped at the door and spoke over her shoulder. "And Warden Tang, get this man another set of clothes. He stinks."

Ma left without further instructions.

Henry didn't move until he heard Tang stand up and take possession of his desk.

"Ten days to show results – a very tight schedule," Tang said in a bitter and aggressive tone.

"It is." Henry stood up slowly. "Unless I have the right people with me."

"You will choose the American Rob Walker, I imagine?"

"That's right. His accent will help when calling Panama."

"Who else?"

Henry hesitated, but he had nothing to lose by asking. "There is a man that sits next to me in the engineering room. He looks quick."

Tang wasn't happy to concede so easily. "Why him? Anyone in that room has a good enough brain."

"I understand he comes from Hong Kong and –"

Tang cut him off. "Have you been speaking to him?"

"Not particularly."

"How do you know?"

Henry thought fast. "The green armband he wears."

Tang stood at his desk, too proud to roll the armchair back in place himself.

"The quicker I put the team in place, the quicker I can deliver and keep General Ma happy." He wasn't asking for special treatment; Tang had to know that he would also be in the firing line if the task wasn't completed to her satisfaction.

Tang didn't reply. There was a question he wanted to ask, but he seemed to be weighing whether he should.

Henry gave Tang his best professional look. "I know when it is in my interest to be discreet."

152

For the first time since he'd met Warden Tang, Henry saw a flutter of emotion in his eyes: relief. The warden's name hadn't been mentioned in Henry's conversation with Ma.

* * *

The old SUV Genghis was driving was more comfortable than Mattie had expected. They had left Ulaanbaatar at around 7am, with little more than four hours' sleep. She had asked the hotel for a packed breakfast and a large flask of coffee. 6.30am was too early for food but she wasn't skimping on a hot shower. She was certain it would be days before she'd enjoy that luxury again.

The bar Genghis had dragged her to the night before had been a real find. She never knew there was such thing as Russian disco; the music was playing in the background and vinyl was available for purchase. Genghis had bought them a couple of beers and Mattie had been grateful he hadn't insisted on something stronger.

"How're you feeling today?" Genghis asked as she got in the SUV.

Mattie smiled at the Brooklyn accent – lips pitched forward, mouth doing a lot of work.

"I'm fine, although four hours' sleep is a bit on the short side."

"I'm driving, no worries..."

"I'm not worried – not until we reach the border that is."

Genghis gave her a broad smile. "I've done this dozens of times. No worries."

Mattie wondered whether Genghis was old enough to have done this half a dozen times. But she trusted Han and she could always back out at the last minute. It wasn't the first time that she'd had to bail out because of danger.

Mattie dozed off as soon as they hit the motorway and when she woke up, she didn't let Genghis know. Curled up in her seat, she went through the events that had led her there.

This new investigation had fallen in her lap a little too perfectly, she knew that. And yet, all the counterchecks she'd carried out validated the package Han had put together for her. The fake trip she was supposed to have taken through Mongolia was well documented and the hundreds of pictures supporting it looked good and professional. The Chinese approval wasn't a fake, but bribery could buy a lot and she hadn't been too surprised by it.

The papers Han had produced under her pen name looked like real documents. She had seen her fair share of fakes, but she could have sworn those came from the British themselves...

Perhaps they had. The idea unsettled her. Was this incursion so risky that even the great MI6 didn't want to involve one of their own, forced to turn to a journalist whose life was expendable?

Mattie moved around in her seat, attracting Genghis's attention. Her mind drifted to the one person she would want at her side for such a stupidly dangerous trip. She pushed the thought away as pure fantasy. She would never see Henry again. She was not even sure Henry was his real name.

"Are you awake?" Genghis asked.

Mattie stretched and yawned. "Yep... How far are we?"

"Another four and a half hours."

"Fancy breakfast?" Mattie pulled out the breakfast bag the Holiday Inn had organised for them.

"What have you got?"

"Bacon and egg in a bagel?"

Genghis's eyes lit up. "They import their bagels from the US."

Mattie shook her head in disbelief as she handed over a bagel to her travel companion.

She poured two mugs of coffee, placing one in the drinks holder of the SUV, and they chatted about Mongolia. She'd read as much as she could about the country in the past few days, but she could do with first-hand intelligence.

The quality of the roads was much better than Mattie had anticipated, even when they branched away from the motorway, about 100km from the border.

When she queried it, Genghis explained. "It's because of the export of coal. China can never have enough, and lorries drive to the border every day to deliver their cargo across China."

About 10 km from the border Genghis slowed down and their conversation became more focused. They had spoken about what to expect at the checkpoint the evening before and again as they'd left the motorway in the direction of Gashuun Sukhait.

"Not many tourists go through this point. It's mainly goods being exported to China."

"Won't the guards be difficult?"

"They will probably check your documents thoroughly but the good thing about all these lorries going through is that there are a lot of bribes."

"Why?"

"To speed up the checks, to allow a bit of contraband."

"They might let us through because?"

"I've got enough to bribe them well so we should be fine."

Now that they were close Mattie questioned whether bribes would allow a journalist to pass through the border, even with a raft of official papers.

The dry and dusty landscape that had accompanied them thus far turned into a more crater-like environment. A deep gorge had opened along the road on the right-hand side of the vehicle. Barbed wire ran alongside the edge, and on the other side was a large car park, peppered with a few official-looking buildings stretched halfway along its perimeter.

"The bulk of the lorries have been through this morning." Genghis sounded more official and a little nervous. "You'd better prepare your papers."

Mattie took the documents out of a brown envelope and checked them one more time. Genghis slowed the vehicle down to a crawl. The tarmac was about to switch to what looked like a cement slab, the area surrounded by tall and narrow railings on both sides.

Genghis turned to Mattie. "Ready?" He could stop and do a swift U-turn now but in a few metres time they would be committed to entering China.

The boom of a lorry's horn shook them both. A large trailer had moved in behind them, and the driver was becoming impatient.

Mattie nodded with a smile. "I guess I am."

Genghis nodded back and drove the car slowly to a cabin for the checkpoint.

The Mongolian guard looked at their papers with little interest and waved them through towards the Chinese border post.

The border control guard looked more like a soldier. His khaki uniform with red and golden stripes gave him the authority he moved with. The uniform was brand new and so was, it seemed, the young officer wearing it.

Genghis rolled the window of the SUV down and started a conversation in what Mattie knew to be Mongolian. Genghis presented his papers first which the man took time to consider. Mattie recognised her name being spoken and the guard impatiently gestured for Genghis to hand over her papers. The guard opened her passport, looking a few times at the photo and Mattie.

She wore as little expression as possible. It wasn't the first time she'd gone through a checkpoint with guards unwilling to let her through.

The questioning started and Genghis responded amiably. He glanced at Mattie who dared not move a muscle. Something was bothering the young guard.

He took the papers away and disappeared into the guard post.

"What's the problem?" she asked Genghis.

"He says there are not many tribes on this side of the border and wonders why you want to cross here."

"That's not a bad question."

"I told him that we were going through some of the places you visited last time so that you could remind yourself about what you saw."

"That didn't work?"

"Not really..." Genghis's hands were wrapped tight around the wheel and his knuckles had turned white.

The young guard returned and asked for Mattie and Genghis to step out of the vehicle. He waited and then walked around the SUV checking it out. He pointed to the boot and Genghis opened it. There was camping equipment and a couple of light cameras that Genghis would use for filming. He showed them to the guard and the young man looked at them with suspicion.

The slamming of a door interrupted the conversation and a stocky little man started moving towards them. He'd just left the cabin of his lorry, unhappy with the delay, it seemed.

He moved right up to the guard and started addressing him with the certainty of someone who knew the way things were supposed to work. The young guard raised his voice, pointing at the lorry.

156

Mattie didn't need an interpreter to know that the guard was asking the lorry driver to get back in his vehicle. Instead, the driver started shouting and pointing in the other direction. He had a cargo to deliver, and he didn't want any more delays.

Mattie and Genghis moved away from the scene.

"The driver is really pissed... I've never seen someone doing that before," Genghis said.

"Neither have I." Mattie wished she could take her camera out of her rucksack and take photos. The leathery face of the lorry driver, angry and unafraid, was in stark contrast to the smooth and startled face of the young guard.

As Mattie was thinking about the angle, the guard stepped closer to the man to shove him away. The driver pushed the guard first and he stumbled back. The driver started walking towards the guard post without hesitation.

The young man's face had turned red, and he shouted back, without result. The driver was about to reach the post when the guard unsheathed his gun.

Mattie couldn't help but cry *no*.

The lorry driver turned back to check the reason for the cry. He shouted a name at the top of his lungs and the young man hesitated.

Another guard walked out of the post. He too started to shout but not at the driver. Instead he screamed orders to the young officer and started walking towards him at a pace, lorry driver in tow.

"What's happening?" Mattie whispered.

"The young guy has been told to step down," Genghis said.

"That's all?" Mattie didn't believe it was only orders that had been shared.

Genghis shook his head. "The other guard was being really rude."

The young guard replaced his gun in its holder, looking lost. His superior reached him and sent him back to the guard post.

The lorry driver returned to his cabin, grumbling some insults. He opened the door, leaned inside, retrieved a thick envelope, and handed it over to the guard who nodded his thanks.

Genghis moved swiftly to close the boot of the SUV. Mattie climbed into their vehicle and Genghis did the same. He prepared to hand over the papers again to the older guard. The man glanced at them and spotted the envelope Genghis had prepared. He simply opened his hand to receive his due and waved them through.

A minute later the heavy gates opened, letting Mattie and Genghis through. The large trailer was following close, and Genghis drove close to the kerb to let him pass. The driver sounded his horn a couple of times and was on his way.

Genghis took a sharp left into a small street and stopped his car in the car park of the Hua Meng Hong Fa convenient store.

"That was... different," he said, leaning back in his seat.

Mattie shook her head. "I've seen a lot in my time but that was the first time a lorry driver saved my day in such a dramatic way."

"Hey, whatever works." Genghis cracked a smile. "Welcome to China."

CHAPTER SIXTEEN

The backroom had been transformed into a tech enclave once more. Nick had managed to find a replacement desktop that looked as though it had seen better days.

Harris frowned at the sight. What had all this fuss been about spending 100 grand on tech stuff when this equipment, that looked a tad on the second-hand side, would do?

Nick caught Harris's expression. "I know it looks crappy, but it belonged to a gamer who didn't think that cleaning his hardware was a priority. It's good enough for what I want to do." Nick inserted the Radeon card Harris had retrieved in the early hours of that morning and declared himself satisfied that none of his priming work had been lost.

The two Lenovo laptops that had also been saved were positioned around the table in such a way that Nick could wheel himself on the chair from one to the other.

Harris came back from the kitchen with a couple of mugs of coffee. "What's your next step?"

He presented a cup to Nick who took it absentmindedly, until he drank from it. His face lit up and he sighed. "Just what I needed." Nick turned his chair around to face Harris. "Hacking the CIA is not something you do in a few hours. It takes preparation."

"Even I know that." Harris frowned. "I thought you had some previous experience which would make it quicker?"

"Yeah, I do." Nick took another sip of coffee, and a wicked smile crossed his lips. "I already hacked it."

"Really? Before or after Henry?"

Nick cocked his head. "Are you checking on Henry?"

Harris flashed a wicked smile of his own. "I'm always checking on Henry."

"You're gonna be disappointed, then. Before Henry."

"So that was a little while ago?"

"It's a good question," Nick admitted. "I know, none of these big players stay static. They patch their systems all the time and then you need to find a new way in."

"That doesn't fill me with the warm sensation that we're closer to our goal."

"The answer is to outsource." Nick took another sip of coffee and then crossed one arm over his chest, balancing the mug on his limb.

"Like finding other hackers to help?" Harris finished his coffee and felt he almost certainly needed another one. "Because if that's your idea, I'm not sponsoring a bunch of hackers to go and crack open the CIA."

Nick shook his head. "I wouldn't want to sponsor a bunch of hackers, either. Very unwise."

"So the solution is?"

"The dark web." Nick looked at Harris as if this was obvious.

"OK, I admit I'm not Henry Crowne, so you are going to have to explain how the dark web, which I know is full of drug dealers and organ harvesters, is useful to us."

"Because apart from all this, you also can find useful companies whose business it is to sell hacking software or other hacking tools."

Harris took a minute to understand the implications of what Nick was saying.

"You mean that you go to Hackers Limited and ask for software that will help you get into, say, the FBI's fingerprint database?"

Nick grimaced. "I reckon that's probably on offer... But of course, the more protected the agency the more difficult it is to get in straight away. What these guys have is a stash of entry points into the systems of, say the Feds or the CIA, but they don't exploit them."

"Oooh, I see." Harris stretched in his chair. "Then they sell these so-called doors to a client at an exorbitant price?"

Nick gave Harris two thumbs up. "You got it."

"And you have such contacts at the ready, I presume?"

"Been making some soft enquiries. I've got a couple of options, but I need to test that what they're selling is not out of date."

"You mean the weaknesses already discovered in the system?"

"You're almost as fast as Henry."

Harris sighed. "Nah, Crowne would already be on the computer with you to evaluate these bloody entry points."

Nick gave Harris a friendly smile but didn't contradict him.

Harris stood up ready to get more coffee. "What do you need from me?"

"Your credit card."

Harris grumbled and handed it over. "It's not coffee I need. It's a double dose of Valium."

"Don't worry. I'll get us a good price and I'll make sure they can't use it again for anything else."

Harris had moved the coffee machine out to Nick's tech enclave and started brewing a serious amount of the drink. He no longer cared what it tasted like. It just had to keep him awake after two nights with almost no sleep.

The laptop that had all of Nick's attention displayed an ominous image. The background was black and at the top of the page, the Welcome to TOR Browser was still showing. Below it a circle, split into various shades of colours, occupied a large part of the space and at its centre was a skull and crossbones – a user warning.

Without hesitation, Nick clicked on one of the sections of the disk and another page instantly opened.

Nick went to a part of the site that requested sign-in details to advance. He did and called up a chat box in which he asked for a contact to respond. The response came.

- Hey CrackerJack, haven't heard from you for a while.
- Busy, you know... hacking here and there.
- Anything interesting?
- Very but couldn't tell.
- Even to a friend?
- Especially to a friend.
- What can I do for you then if we can't compare notes?

– I need a penetration back door into the CIA email system.

The chat remained silent for a few seconds. Then:

– Whaaaaat? You've gone up in the world since we last spoke.

– Maybe... Can you deal?

– Let me see what I can do. Contact me again at the end of the day.

– Need an answer sooner. Either you've got the product available or I need to go somewhere else.

There was another moment's silence.

– 2pm today. I need to get to the right people first.

The site shut down before Nick could reply.

"CrackerJack, eh..." Harris grinned and stood up to brew some more coffee. "Is that your hacker name?"

"Yup... from way back when I was a geek at school. Can't even remember who came up with it." Nick stretched, looking satisfied.

"So, CrackerJack... Do you think they have something?" Harris topped up Nick's coffee and his own and moved closer to the screen that was blank.

"My contact is good at hacking and he would know, but he needs to discuss that stuff with his boss."

"Like in any good corporate structure."

"I wouldn't know." Nick shrugged. "I've never had a job in a corporate structure."

Harris had to smile. "I'm sure the head of MI6 would love to know that you don't consider us a corporate structure."

"I s'pose we are."

"I know, working with Crowne doesn't feel that way."

Harris checked his watch. It was 11am in Taiwan and 4am in the UK. He had missed his slot to call the Chief at MI6. Harris had spotted a call request from him on his way back from delivering his postcard to Rodriguez. He had conveniently put it to the back of his mind.

He needed a few hours' reprieve before dealing with the man at the top of the corporate structure that employed him.

* * *

The three Humvees that had accompanied General Ma to Zhaga were parked in the front yard, waiting for her imminent departure. Henry wondered whether she was having a few last-minute conversations with other high-profile prisoners.

The same guards who had accompanied Henry after his fight with the Grinning Man were on duty when the warden called. He gave instructions for Henry to be taken to have a shower, and get a change of clothes. They led the way to the shower rooms with Henry in tow.

Henry entered the place that looked basic and reeked of cheap detergent.

The shower room was a rectangular area with a row of shower heads and taps beneath. Henry doubted there would be any hot water, but a wash would be good no matter the temperature.

Opposite the showers, there was a row of benches for inmates to dump their uniform and towels. Henry spotted folded clothes at the far end.

The guards jerked their heads in that direction. They sat heavily on the bench and lit cigarettes.

Henry walked over to the pile and started to unbutton his shirt. He had blocked the smell of it for as long as he could. Now the idea of being able to wash and change made the stench almost unbearable.

He reached the pile of clothes, moved them aside to fetch the towel. He hoped for a bar of soap. Instead, he found a small bag placed between the main fold of the bath towel. Henry inspected it with surprise. He slid the zip back cautiously and looked inside. There was some shower gel, shampoo and a comb. As he reached into the bag to retrieve the items, he felt a hard object hidden in the lining.

Henry immediately knew what this was. His heart pounded at the discovery of a small set of lock picks. He rapidly searched the rest of the bag and discovered two small capsules wrapped in foil and a SIM card.

The guards were looking in his direction. There was no time to wonder who had gotten these to him.

He turned away from the men, pretending he was shy about un-dressing, and kicked off his shoes. He placed them on the bench and grabbed the three items, stuffing them into the pair. Henry finished undressing and walked into the shower with the wash bag in his hand.

When the cold water hit his skin it made him shiver, but it felt good. He lathered up his body with soap, shampooed his hair and fought the desire to linger. His small bag of goodies had already attracted the attention of the guards and he didn't want them getting near his pile of clothes.

Henry rinsed off quickly and wrapped the towel around him. He dried off on his way back to his fresh prison uniform. He dressed fast and arranged the contraband around the toe space in one of his shoes so that he could walk without discomfort.

As he reached the door one of the guards gestured for him to hand over the bag. When Henry frowned, the man moved his hand over his baton. Henry shrugged and handed over the bag of empty bottles. He took the comb out, ran it through his hair and gave it to the guard. The man smiled, looking satisfied to have robbed Henry of these small items of comfort.

The idiot hadn't thought to check Henry's shoes. Perfect. The guards led Henry back to the foundry and the drawing room. A few heads lifted a fraction, but the engineer's hard look around the room returned everyone to their work.

Henry sat down without acknowledging Bo. The engineer was watching his every move, and he looked unhappy. By now, Warden Tang would have told him three of his best people had been recruited for another task. But Henry had an offer for the engineer and Tang that he thought would appease both men. Until then, he resumed his calculations up to the end of the morning shift when the prisoners left for lunch.

As soon as the bell rang, everyone lined up and followed the guards that had come to collect them. Henry slotted in behind Bo and followed him in silence. They reached the canteen, took a tray each and picked up their bowl of noodles, veg and chicken, and mug of tea.

Henry sat at the middle of a free table and Bo sat on the same side a little farther away.

"You got into another fight?" Bo asked whilst slurping his noodles from his bowl.

"No, I got a new job offer... The interview was a little tougher than I'm used to."

Bo smiled. "That's what you get in this place. They squeeze your balls hard first before they start squeezing your brain."

"Talking from experience?"

Bo's head dipped a little. "I'm glad I already have kids is all I will say."

"I've been asked to help on another project."

Bo nodded. "Fresh clothes when yours are not even two weeks old and a shower outside normal showering hours? Management wants you."

"And I need a team that –" Henry stopped talking when he spotted Rob with his tray and food.

Henry focused his attention on Rob long enough for the man to realise someone was looking at him. Their eyes met for a few seconds and then Henry resumed eating.

Bo had slowed down his own meal. He drank some tea and waited a moment before picking up his half empty bowl.

Rob made his way over to their table and sat at the end, on the opposite side to Henry.

"You've been in another fight?" Rob asked, as he took his chopsticks and started mixing noodles, veg and chicken.

Bo bit his lip. Henry supressed a grin. "I'm acquiring a reputation... but no. As I said to Bo, I got a new job, but the interview focused on the parts of my anatomy where a man is supposed to hold his brain."

Rob's eyes lit up with humour. "I know. I got the same interview. You obviously have a lot more brains than I do."

"Nonsense. I just focused on what I'd do to these bastards, if I got the chance. It helped."

Rob started on his food, waiting, it seemed, for what Henry had to say next.

"I've been told to gather a team," Henry murmured.

"Who by?" Bo resumed eating.

"General Ma."

Both men kept eating and for a moment Henry thought they hadn't heard him.

Rob answered first. "This is a one-way ticket. As long as you succeed you're fine. and then..." He trailed off.

Bo added, "That's what this place is about, anyway."

"I'll need to make contact with the outside world to fulfil the terms of this project. I can get a message out," Henry said.

"About this place?" Bo pushed his empty bowl away and brought his mug closer.

"And what's going on." Henry finished his food and turned his attention to his tea as well.

"I find it hard to believe Ma would let you contact the outside that easily. It's a big risk for her if things go bad," Bo said.

Henry agreed. "I'm sure Tang has been told to watch us like boiling milk, but I'll find a way. In the meantime, Tang is to look after the people in the team."

Rob sat back, waited a moment and returned to his food. "It's worth taking the risk," he said before another mouthful.

Henry clasped his hands around his mug, a little tighter than before. He was making progress.

* * *

The car was stocked up with fresh food and water that was to last Mattie and Genghis a week. Genghis insisted he would do the shopping on his own at the Fa convenience store just outside the border checkpoint.

Mattie had resisted the temptation to check out the shop – there was no reason to attract attention at such an early stage in the trip. Fa convenience store was likely the ideal place for the Chinese government to plant observers reporting what and who came in and out of the country.

They drove for twenty minutes down a well-maintained motorway. Lorries driving way over the speed limit passed them on the opposite side of the four-lane highway. Genghis didn't bother to check the GPS. He slowed down the car and turned into what looked like a small funnel road that took them straight into the desert landscape.

The orange colour of the land was unusual, or perhaps Mattie had been expecting the same sandy grey colour she'd got used to seeing while visiting the Middle East. Here the earth and the hill formations had a light orange hue that turned darker in patches. The colour change gave the land a rich glow that she had not noticed the first time she'd visited Mongolia, all those years ago.

Genghis slowed down, turned onto what he'd called a road. "You like it?" He adjusted the SUV's speed to the dirt track.

Mattie smiled at him. "Some people find it strange but I like the desert." She turned back to take in the view.

"I like it too, but then I'm biased."

"Which tribe do you come from if you don't mind me asking?"

166

Genghis grinned. "Not at all. I love to talk about that stuff. My father is a Khalkha Mongol, and my mum is half American, half Oirat."

"So, you are a descendant of Genghis Khan then?" Mattie teased.

"And I'm not the only one. I read in a news magazine a couple of weeks ago that one in two hundred men in the world has DNA from the great man himself."

"I knew he had a reputation for having fathered a lot of kids but that's funny to think that science supports what people thought was a legend."

"How about you, Mattie?"

"I'm boring... a pure Brit product with a splash of Scottish on my mother's side – something my father keeps reminding me is a bad influence."

"I thought the Scots were tough fighters?"

"Ach ay, they arrre." Mattie rolled her rs, putting on what she thought was a good Glaswegian accent.

Genghis laughed. "I like it."

A GPS warning interrupted the conversation.

Genghis grew serious again. "We are approaching the point where we should go off track. If you still want to spend time in the foothills of the desert tonight, that'll be the way to go."

"Let's go and set up camp, like your ancestors did then."

"We're not quite building a yurt." Genghis nodded. "But a modern tent will do."

Mattie took the new burner phone she'd bought in Seoul out of her bag. She switched on the GPS. They were getting close to the place that was the target of her trip.

Han hadn't told Genghis the full story; Mattie had decided she would wait to get better acquainted with the man before telling him more. Now that they were so close she felt a pang of guilt. Finding a secret prison camp in China could well cost them their lives. Genghis had the right to know whether he wanted to be part of that discovery.

"It's already 3pm. We should head for the foothills now and find the place we'd like to settle in. There is always time to change our mind."

Mattie shook her head. "I won't change my mind, Genghis. I've done more rough sleeping than you can imagine."

Genghis took a right turn after a few hundred yards. As far as Mattie could tell they'd left any distinguishable track, but after a few minutes she spotted what looked like a faint path ahead. In the distance, the foothills of Inner Mongolia spread across the horizon and some spectacular ridges lifted higher over them. Mattie let herself get absorbed in the beauty of the bare land until the darker colour of the earth announced the terrain was changing.

Genghis stopped the car and took out a pair of binoculars from his rucksack. He handed them to Mattie, and they left the car.

Mattie stuck the binoculars to her eyes and adjusted the lens. She saw nothing for miles in the direction of the hills, but her compass had already told her the place she was looking for would lie in the desert, away from the hills.

"I think this spot looks incredible. Let's get settled."

She would have a much better view from up high and there would be enough daylight until 6pm. Mattie returned to the car and stood on the front guard of the SUV, a habit she'd picked up back in Syria. She brought the binoculars to her eyes once more.

She assessed the horizon, adjusting the lens as she went, until a shape stopped her. It was too small to be the camp she was looking for and yet far too large to be a house. Mattie closed her eyes to give them a moment's rest. She opened them again and tried to make sense of what she was seeing. It was an odd structure, and it wasn't finished either. The back was missing.

Mattie removed the binoculars. It wasn't possible.

She passed the glasses to Genghis. "Someone is constructing a large ship... in the middle of the desert."

CHAPTER SEVENTEEN

The guards brought Henry into a small room. The desks made it look like a cosy office. Tang had requisitioned a place used as storage space to house Henry's team. Computer desktops were being installed. It looked as though the warden had followed Ma's orders, albeit reluctantly. The desktops looked second-hand and the desks had seen better days, but Henry didn't care. He was exactly where he wanted to be.

"It will have to do," Warden Tang said, entering the room a few moments later.

Henry nodded approvingly. "This is all I need."

The man who was setting up the computers looked up at Tang and took his cue. He mumbled a few words of excuse and disappeared. Tang waited until the door had been shut. He walked over to it and opened it in a dramatic move. But no, the IT man had left, not taking the risk of listening in on Tang's conversation. He closed it again.

"I have asked the engineer to release Rob Walker and Bo Chan from their duties. He is not happy with the decision. This will slow down his work considerably."

"Perhaps we could reach a compromise?" Henry walked over to the desks and sat in one of the chairs.

"What do you have in mind?" Tang moved closer to the desks but remained standing.

"Let us work in the morning on General Ma's project and then we can resume work with the engineer in the afternoon."

"General Ma insists on speedy results." But Tang's expression had shifted a little. He was thinking.

"But I'm sure that whoever wants the engineering project delivered also wants it done yesterday."

"This is true, even the day before yesterday." Tang's eyes glinted as he said it. The warden must have good connections in the business world. Bo had hinted at it, yet Tang remained a mystery.

"I will need to speak to Nick Fox again," Henry said.

"This will be done in my office, and I'll make contact first."

"As you wish."

"You won't be granted email access, either." Tang started to pace.

"That won't be necessary. Very little of my business is done through mail and if I need to use one, I'll use my office one. Nick can forward the documents to whatever account you'd like to use."

Tang stopped abruptly. There was nothing he could sink his teeth into to stop Henry and Ma's project. He added, "I also want a guard in with you at all times."

Henry gave a simple nod. "I don't see a problem with that apart from the fact that we will be exchanging highly confidential information."

"Most guards don't speak English."

"That's not an issue then."

There was a timid knock on the door. Tang barked enter in Mandarin and the IT man reappeared, asking whether he could finish the set-up.

"You start tomorrow," Tang said to Henry.

Tang left. The guards who had accompanied Henry walked into the room. There was no need to order Henry to follow. He walked forward, slotted himself between the two men and waited for them to start walking.

The trio walked out of the building, turned towards the shower rooms and kept going. A handful of inmates were cleaning the space. They looked thin and tired. Henry recognised the green armband of the Hong Kong rebels. Bo's friend was amongst them and yet Henry didn't know which of the men it was.

One of the prisoners dropped what looked like a heavy bucket of dirty water. Two wardens took their batons out and reminded the man that Warden Tang didn't permit mistakes in his camp.

Henry tried to shut out the whimpers of the man on the ground.

The slight discomfort in Henry's right shoe reminded him of what lay there and the likely beating he'd receive if the items were discovered.

Henry hadn't given much time to think about it; securing Rob and Bo's cooperation and trust had been his priority. Dealing with Warden Tang's tenacious suspicion was his next task.

Still, Henry needed to uncover who the supplier of this unexpected bonanza was and what it meant for Henry's escape plan. More importantly, this was almost certainly a clue as to who Dragon was. Henry couldn't quite understand what the purpose of the SIM card was. Why present Henry with something that could put Dragon in danger if the communication it facilitated wasn't of vital importance? Unless there was something worth communicating that was more important than Rob Walker's escape.

The hiss of incandescent metal being poured into a mould interrupted Henry's thoughts. He had reached the foundry and another large piece of ship was being cast. The orange-armband prisoners were busying themselves around the space, manoeuvring the heavy cauldron and making sure it didn't shift position as they poured and risked being hit by 2500F liquid carbon steel.

Henry slowed down to take in the sight. A loud whistle over the noise of the workshop made him look further. A man had jumped on the upper part of the cauldron, balancing dangerously close to its opening.

"Hey, Westerner..." he shouted.

Henry looked up and the man gestured that he and Henry should meet. Henry stopped and faced the pit. The inmates also stopped what they were doing. A slam of a baton on Henry's back reminded them all what they were here for.

Shit, another nutter in need of a good thrashing.

But Henry wasn't so sure he would survive another encounter with one of the Macau gang members. Henry's training had taken the Grinning Man by surprise. His next opponent would be prepared.

* * *

"It is time." Nick cracked his fingers and opened a TOR browser to start his access sequence into the dark web.

It took him a little less than fifteen minutes to access the same hacker site as before and open a chat.

Harris was sitting next to Nick, in front of a second laptop.

"Remember, if they try anything funny, you need to release the virus I prepped." Nick sounded unusually nervous.

"I may not be a tech wizard but I can press a couple of keys in the right order," Harris protested.

"I didn't say you were tech inept."

"Then why did you have me stick this Post-it on the side of the laptop with the key stroke sequence?"

"Insurance policy. And as you said before, you're not Henry."

Harris couldn't argue that.

Nick started typing in the chat box.

- Any news for me?

There was no reply for a couple of minutes. Nick was about to close the chat, concerned that what he'd been asking for was too much, when the chat sprang to life.

- Hello CrackerJack, our common friend tells me you're after something rather special.
- Who am I speaking to?
- Your friend's boss.
- And does my friend's boss have a name?
- So many questions... but yes, call me Pythagoras.
- Do we have a deal?
- Perhaps... It depends how far you'd like to go.
- I need to access the CIA email server for one particular email address, and I can give you details of the server itself but not the name.
- I have a couple of back doors that are dormant and I'm sure one of them will work, but this is an expensive business. These little gems don't come cheap.
- Your price?
- $250,000.
- Too expensive.
- $220,000... My final offer.
- You won't be able to sell these little gems, as you call them, on the hacker markets. Hackers would rather take the time to find these doors themselves. Those who would use your software

belong to government agencies. The risk of being uncovered and taken down is on you.

- Don't worry about my risk. So why are you calling me then?
- I just need a bit of a lift. No time to browse and find the door myself.
- $200,000. I'm not budging.

Harris shook his head at the price. "It's complete theft."

When Nick had announced a heavy budget for what Harris had in mind, this was where the money was going. Nothing to do with hardware but to purchase hacking software.

"Yep... hacking is theft." Nick's attention shifted to a small icon on his screen. "Shit..." He flew his fingers over the keyboard. "Shit... Steve, release the virus."

Harris took a couple of seconds to understand Nick's instructions.

"Steve... the goddamn sequence!" Nick continued on his own laptop to confirm the hack attack.

Harris's mind finally engaged, and his own fingers raced as fast as they could to enter the keystrokes Nick had asked him to.

Nick was still fighting on his side to close the hack.

Harris followed the download bar of the virus Nick had designed as it was reaching into the dark web to invade Pythagoras's site.

"Come on..." Harris glanced at Nick. The download slowed down to a trickle. Perhaps Pythagoras was already fighting back. Harris reported, "It's going really slow and –"

Pythagoras's website froze suddenly; it exploded into a thousand pieces like a handful of confetti, with an ominous message from Nick at the centre of the image. A laughing skull that said: "NEVER CROSS ME AGAIN."

"Bugger, that was intense." Harris ran his fingers through his hair.

"Not as much for us as it was for them." Nick sat back and looked around for his mug of coffee.

"So, what's happening now?"

"It's not because they are hackers that they can't be hacked. If they want to get their site unlocked and not lose face, they'll need to give us what we want."

"I suppose it's not good for your reputation to have a sign showing you've been hacked on a hackers' website." Harris poured some more coffee into his own mug.

"They know that, all right. I'll go into another chat room in a moment and ask for the spyware to be sent to me."

"At a reduced price?"

"For free." Nick found his mug and sipped his coffee. "Teach them a lesson."

"Hey, that's more like it." Harris grinned. "Shame I can't brag about it with the Chief."

"Why not? We've just saved MI6 $200,000."

"And what am I going to say? Sir, we've managed to hack the CIA on the cheap."

"Sounds good to me."

Harris hesitated. "Nah... I'm keeping this little nugget of success between us. We are still keen on maintaining the special relationship – you know, the UK being so pally-wally with the US."

Nick frowned. "That sounds a bit old-fashioned."

"Even if I were to agree, some of the old farts who govern us are dead keen on keeping things as it is."

"Well, I'll do my best to get this CIA hack done in the most civilised way possible. Hunter won't feel a thing."

"Now, that is a great shame."

The light banter was interrupted by Harris's phone ringing. It was not a call but a reminder: time to catch up with London. Harris inhaled deep and released it. "Right... I can't delay the fun."

He walked out of Nick's tech cave, into the living room and then into his bedroom. The safe house had been fitted with enough eavesdropping counter measures that would make any call safe.

Harris sat on his bed, took a moment to rehearse what he would say and dialled the Chief's PA's number.

"Hello, Maggie, this is a reporting call for the Chief. I'm on a secure line." He didn't need to say more. The urgency was always understood.

"He is on the line but it's a conf call. I'll let him know you're on and I'll put you through."

The line clicked. "Harris?"

At eight in the morning, the Chief was already sounding harassed.

"Sir, I'm sorry I couldn't update you beforehand."

"So now that you've found the time in your very busy schedule, perhaps you could tell me where we are at?"

"Things progressed as discussed when our operative was dropped into China."

"You mean he separated from his SEAL team and landed on his own..."

"That's right. And was picked up by the Chinese authorities and driven to the target camp."

"But then...?" the Chief asked with a hint of impatience.

"We haven't had any news."

"Nothing from Hunter and his contact in China?"

"Nothing... and we are already on day four of OP TECH LEO-PARD, sir."

"When did you last try Hunter?"

"Yesterday, sir."

"Any intel from the US army?"

"Radio silence." Harris thought about his latest escapade with the ALPHA team, but this was not HUMIT he was about to release. "But this was expected, sir. They have not been told about phase 2 of the operation."

"So, now we have a renowned tech scientist and one of our best operatives locked in a secret prison camp in the middle of Inner Mongolia and zero intel to assess the situation?"

"Yes, sir."

"Your thoughts on what to do next?" Harris could hear the Chief typing on his keyboard.

"Are you contacting Hunter?"

"You're goddamn right I am," the Chief replied. "He was the one who refused to have more people involved in order to protect his source. Now I want this source of his to deliver."

"I'm not sure Hunter has received any news."

"What makes you say that?"

"A hunch. He may want to play his cards close to his chest, but he could still brag about the quality of the intel and yet tell us very little," Harris said.

"You think Dragon has gone underground?"

"He may be feeling exposed and can't risk communicating."

"You don't think he's been outed?"

The Chief had stopped typing and Harris imagined a well-worded yet rather terse email reminding Hunter he had assured his British Intelligence counterpart Dragon was a reliable source.

"Why? You think we would have been contacted by the Chinese to protest about it?"

Harris shook his head as though his boss could see him. "It may be too soon for that. They would want to interrogate our operative first. But I think we would have heard it from our own network."

"My question therefore stands, Harris. What's your next step?"

"I'm trying to see whether I can get eyes on the camp."

"You're not sending another operative in, I hope?"

"Of course not, sir. I'm looking at alternatives."

"What smugglers, traffickers... journalists?"

"Money can buy a lot in China."

"Money can buy a lot everywhere," the Chief grumbled.

"I have some very good contacts in Seoul with a good network in China."

"As long as this doesn't blow Dragon's cover. This time it will be us who will feel the heat, I can guarantee you."

"It goes without saying, sir."

"Yeah... I've gotten to know you, Harris. Sailing close to the wind is a feeble description of what you're capable of."

Harris wracked his brain for an answer to that, but the Chief spared him the trouble. "I'm about to go live on this call. I want an update in the next twenty-four hours unless there are developments, in which case, I want them as they come."

"Certainly, sir."

"And Harris... I mean any developments."

The phone went dead.

Harris scowled. That might be a little tricky.

* * *

The SUV reached the bottom of the hillside and Genghis found a large mound covered with desert grass. He inspected the depression it created against the foot of the hill.

Genghis nodded. "It's a good place to settle."

Mattie gave him one thumb up and started climbing the hill, holding the binoculars close to her chest. She slipped a few times on the dry gravel covering the slope. She reached the height she judged to be sufficient to inspect her recent discovery.

As her eyes adjusted to the far sight view, she then used the wheel to adjust the focus and trained on the horizon, to spot the ship.

The vessel was almost complete. From their location she could see its profile, the unmistakable shape of a large aircraft carrier. It looked as though its hull had been partially buried in the sand to hold it up. Mattie wondered whether it was done like that so it could mimic the multitude of decks a war ship would have.

She dropped the glasses for a moment and gazed into the distance. The ship was perhaps two or so miles away. She glanced at her watch. It was 3pm. If she walked there, she could reach it in forty-five minutes. There was still plenty of time before nightfall to investigate the structure.

Mattie returned the binoculars to her eyes and pushed the vision as far as it would go without blurring. There was no one around the build, but she spotted what looked like powerful high intensity discharge lamps surrounding the ship, similar to the ones used in sport stadiums.

She hadn't felt Genghis move closer but when she dropped the glasses again he was at her side.

"Are you sure you want to check this thing out?" he asked.

"I'm a journalist. I investigate." Mattie tried to sound cheerful.

"It may not be my place to say this, but this has nothing to do with reporting on tribal life in Inner Mongolia."

"I know." Mattie sat on the ground. "And I think you've got the right to voice your opinion. You're my guide."

Genghis held his hand out and Mattie handed over the binoculars to him. He took his time to scrutinise the horizon.

"There is a faint plume of dust to the southwest." He concentrated on it for a moment. "I think some heavy vehicles are coming towards the ship." He returned the glasses to Mattie.

She checked for herself. "How do you know that? I can see a bit of dirt lifting in the distance but that's it."

"I know how much it takes to create dust in this landscape, and I'm telling you they're on their way."

"How far out?"

"They'll be there before us if that's what you're thinking."

"I was not thinking car. There are a couple of low hills on the way to the ship. It's good terrain to creep up on foot."

Genghis crouched next to Mattie. "This is almost certainly a military operation."

"Look, I know it's not exactly what I came here to do but this could be big."

"Han said you may want to go off-piste a bit."

"That's all he said?"

Genghis nodded. He was looking at the ground, drawing a few circles into the gravel with one finger.

"I can't lie to you, Genghis. I'm going to go where there is something to talk about." Mattie's stomach clenched. She might have organised this trip for nothing if Genghis wasn't willing to help, but she wouldn't push him even if she wouldn't survive five minutes alone in this desert.

"How much danger have you been getting into?"

Genghis's question startled Mattie. "Well... quite a bit."

"And you got away with it?"

"Only because I had great people helping me out."

"So, you really want to talk about what you see in China?"

"Yes..." Mattie wondered why Han had chosen such a young guide for such a risky project. It was stupid. "And it may involve getting close to places people don't want us to find."

"Nasty things happen here, in this country." Genghis sat next to her. "The Chinese are trying to wipe out the Mongol history from this place. They don't want us to remember who we are."

"Why do you think my project was accepted, then?"

Genghis shrugged. "Bribery... and I bet that when we cross the border again, they'll confiscate all film and notes from you."

"Why join me, then?"

Genghis smiled. "I might have been able to smuggle you and your films out."

Mattie returned the smile. Han had been a wise old bird after all.

"How do we get to this ship, then?" Mattie asked.

"We wait for dusk, and we go there on foot."

178

CHAPTER EIGHTEEN

Rob dropped his tray on the canteen table with a small clunk. "When do we start?" He was the last one to join Henry and Bo.

"Tomorrow," Henry said, slurping some noodles. "I've made a deal with Tang."

Bo slowed down his eating and Rob's expression tightened.

"Relax. It's all in our interest otherwise Tang and the engineer are going to have issues." Henry continued eating. "Morning we work on Ma's project and the afternoon on the engineer's drawings."

Bo's eyebrows shot up. "That's a good option. Tang is a devious little shit but he knows the engineer has the ear of the Navy."

"You said he was in business?" Henry asked.

"His father was, and he would have inherited the business had the Chinese government not decided otherwise."

"What sort of business?" Henry looked around; no one was paying attention to them.

"Property. His father owned buildings all over Asia and he also ran a newspaper."

"Now, that's more interesting," Rob butted in. "Political affiliation with pro-democracy?"

Bo nodded. "Exactly, and with the money he had he could fund a campaign or two."

"China pressured him?"

"You could call it that. They deported him and his eldest son to the mainland."

"Let me guess." Henry sipped from his mug of tea. "They were never seen again."

"And Tang cut a deal with the government. He gave intel on the people his father was supporting and got to keep some money." Bo started on his mug of tea. "Or so the rumour goes."

Rob frowned whilst finishing his noodles. "What is he doing here then?"

"It was part of the deal. Be 'retrained' and become part of the regime..."

"Very cultural revolution then." Henry put his mug down. "It's also a perfect way to ensure that Tang can never claim his father's legacy if he ever tries to. No one will ever trust him in Hong Kong again." Henry understood better Tang's interest in money laundering. He needed to get some of his father's money and secure it somewhere untraceable. One day he would escape China and finish his life in style somewhere discreet.

Henry changed subject. "I've agreed with Tang that I needed to make a call to my senior adviser. Tang will be there but that is fine. We are just getting started."

Rob pushed his bowl away and drank his tea. "When is Ma coming back to check results?"

"Why do you think she'll even come back?" Henry asked, surprised at the assumption.

"I wouldn't want this list to circulate on email even if the email *is* encrypted."

"I suppose you're right. So she's not the army official in charge of the construction of the aircraft carrier? I made that assumption and Tang didn't contradict me."

"That's right," Bo said. "Ma is counterintelligence, the only area in the Chinese army that has appointed a woman at the top. The US aircraft carrier construction is the Navy's project, under Admiral Yi."

Henry smiled at Bo's resourcefulness. "How did you come by that intel?"

"I can read upside down and the engineer was too concerned with a letter he had just opened. I sped up my calculation and submitted my work just in time to see who had sent the letter."

Henry nodded. "And what is the plan for the carrier then?"

"Train the Navy to assault and destroy?" Rob finished his mug of tea and placed it in his empty bowl.

"Who does the assembly of the pieces?" Henry asked.

"Another part of the Macau gang," Bo said.

"Does the engineer supervise?"

180

"No, Tang does the supervision," Bo said with a shrug. "I guess they don't need the assembly to be perfect."

Rob pulled his tray over and placed the plate and mug on it. "It still needs to be strong enough to sustain an assault."

Bo nodded. "As soon as a couple of pieces are ready, they assemble a team and off they go."

"I presume they lose a lot of men?" Henry asked.

"There is hardly any protection given, so yes. And then there is the usual retribution: execution, revenge, fight."

"Do they take men other than the Macau gang people?" Henry finished his tea in one large gulp.

Bo finished his tea also. "Very rarely. It doesn't end up well for whoever they take there, though."

"But they do *take* other men," Henry murmured.

Rob glanced at him but said nothing.

Other inmates were leaving the canteen and Henry sensed it was time to leave and let the next lot of prisoners get their food. That was fine with him. He didn't want to find out just yet who the new challenger in the Macau gang was.

The guards directed their group of inmates to one of the exercise yards and the prisoners scattered into small groups. The usual group of players gathered and started to toss balls around the volleyball net.

Henry and Rob chose different teams and the game got going in earnest after ten minutes of warm-up.

It was almost fun, and the teams were doing well, chasing each other on a score board that had been drawn in the dirt. There was a short break and the teams swapped positions.

Time passed without the guards calling the inmates back. It surprised Henry.

"Is this normal?" he asked Rob.

"Never happened before."

He played through another couple of exchanges and threw his hands into the air after missing an obvious ball. His team made amiable fun of him, but a sense that their time in the open had lasted a little too long made the prisoners slow down.

A couple of the players went over to the tap that was dispensing water in the yard and had a drink.

"What do you think this delay means?" Rob murmured as he stood next to Henry waiting for his turn at the tap.

Henry took one guess. "Nothing good, because in a few minutes the nutters from the Macau gangs are about to join us." Henry jerked his head at the canteen.

The players were about to restart their match when a couple of guards banged their batons against the wire of the exercise pen. Everyone fell into line. A few more guards arrived and entered the space; they moved towards the volleyball net and stopped the prisoners from leaving.

"Fuck," Henry said between gritted teeth. "I think the guards and Tang want a show tonight."

Rob understood immediately but it took a moment for the other men to gather what was happening. Two disorderly lines of gang men walked out of the canteen. The guards were using batons and guns to move them. One of the guards opened the door to the exercise yard and six gang men walked in.

Henry had no time to escape before his next gang challenge.

The men trapped inside the pen looked at each other in disbelief. Rob was still at Henry's side. Some players retreated but four stepped forward. Henry had never spoken more than a few words to them in the yard, but going by their muscle tone, they were men who trained regularly in their cells. All of them wore the black armbands of spies.

The gang men walked past and took their place on one side of the net. Henry followed and his team took up position on the opposite side of the net. A game began with a lethal opening ball that was difficult to catch. Rob managed to rescue the situation and returned the ball with some force to the other side.

One of the gang men slammed the return before it could cross the net and it hit one of Henry's teammates square in the face. The man fell backwards, stunned. A roar of laughter came from the assembled gang crowd, who had been allowed to watch the match and have their fun.

"It's a fucking fault," Henry cried. Where had his advice that he needed to lie low gone?

The man who had challenged him in the foundry in the afternoon shrugged and picked up the ball. He gave a decent service, and the ball moved a few times. The last exchange brought another of Henry's team close to the net. He received a kick in the stomach from the gang man who was returning the ball.

Henry walked up to his teammate and helped him to stay upright. There was more laughter from the crowd again. Henry's challenger walked to the net to pick up the ball once more, but Henry lunged, snatched it up from the ground.

"You're just a coward." Henry spoke in Mandarin, as he held the ball out of the man's reach. "You need the protection of your men and the guards."

From the sudden show of anger on the man's face, Henry knew the man had understood him.

"We need neutral grounds... no guards, no men. You and I." Henry spat on the ground not far from his challenger's feet.

The man's eyes flashed with hatred. "Anytime."

"The building site. Get it organised." Henry turned around and threw the ball into the far corner of the playground.

The gang men waited for their boss's reaction. He shouted some insults that Henry dismissed with a shrug. His team followed him to the gate of the exercise pen.

"We're done," Henry said to the guards in Mandarin. When they hesitated, Henry clicked his fingers impatiently. "Do I have to speak to General Ma?"

One of the guards pushed past the others and opened the door before the gang men could lunge at Henry's team.

"I hope you know what you're doing," Rob murmured to Henry.

"So do I."

* * *

Mattie dug her elbows into the sand of the long desert ridges that had been hiding her and brought the binoculars to her eyes.

"They are wearing prison uniforms," Mattie murmured, turning her head to Genghis. "And there are quite a few guards with machine guns surveying the site."

Genghis had slid back down the ridge that was giving them protection and a good view of the ship.

183

"I saw that too. That's strange. There is no official prison camp in this area, although I'd heard rumours."

Mattie slid down the hill. There was no point staying exposed at the top of the ridge for longer than necessary.

"Rumours even in Mongolia?" She would be surprised if this hadn't spread further.

"No, only amongst certain Mongol tribes who live in the area. They've been told to avoid a certain area when they travel with their yurts."

"No one thought to check?"

"If you know what's good for you, you just do what the Chinese government orders."

Mattie checked her watch. The crane that had accompanied the trucks had been moved away and the men were welding the last piece of steel they'd brought with them. The floodlights illuminated the construction, giving it an ominous look.

"They won't be long now finishing the job."

Genghis flipped onto his back. "What then?" Since agreeing to help Mattie, his slight nervousness had been replaced with a focus Mattie had witnessed in some of her best guides.

"We follow their tracks and see where they lead."

"Don't you want to take a closer look at the aircraft carrier?"

"We'll come back at daybreak and then take pictures."

The sound of the men calling to each other as they were finishing the work started to die down. It was replaced by the sound of lorry engines being fired up. Mattie and Genghis slid halfway down the ridge and waited.

The floodlights were switched off, plunging the desert into its natural darkness. The lorries that had brought the men and their handlers departed one after the other and the buzz from the worksite completely died.

Genghis crawled back up and lifted the binoculars to his eyes. He took his time to survey the place and check whether they had left a small team behind to check the perimeter one last time.

"They've all gone," he confirmed.

Genghis and Mattie slid down to the bottom of the ridge and walked back to the SUV they had parked half a mile away. Genghis had convinced Mattie that he knew the terrain well enough to approach in a vehicle without being seen and not to create the same plume of dust the lorries had.

"I'll drive without lights on so our approach will be slow," he said.

"Do you think there is a dirt track they use?"

"Even if there wasn't, the weight of the crane and the steel pieces will have left a distinct trail. Also they'll have to stick to the rocky parts of the land. Sand is out of the question with that load."

Genghis gunned the engine and the SUV slid onto the gravel with a light crunch. They drove in almost silence; the car came close enough to the site that they could see the details of the impressive structure. Genghis stopped.

"This is a full-size replica." Mattie nodded.

"You can tell?"

"I wrote a couple of articles about the relative military strength of the US Navy in the Pacific compared to that of the Chinese Navy. I wouldn't be surprised if this was a US aircraft carrier."

"What is the Chinese Navy doing here, preparing for war?" A frowning Genghis looked more serious than she'd seen him look.

"I'm not sure but the outfit is most certainly targeting the US." Mattie wound the window down and leaned out until her bottom was on the frame. She came back in, took her camera out of her rucksack, and slid out again. She took some photos, moving the camera around, widening the angle to take in as much as she could of the ship and its surroundings. "I don't know how much surveillance the military has around the site, but I'd rather not risk a closer approach," Mattie said, returning to her seat.

"The sun will be up at 6am. We'll get a better view then and detection of ground alarms will be easier."

Genghis stepped out of the SUV but like Mattie he didn't take any chances. He took the binoculars out and scanned the area surrounding the ship.

"They're headed to the southwest. Back the way they came," Genghis said, as he climbed back into the vehicle.

"Is there a small town or a settlement of some kind in that direction?"

"Nothing for miles as far as the GPS and the earth maps are concerned."

"Then southwest we are going."

Mattie almost dozed off while Genghis drove slowly to keep sight of the track. The night's sky was clear and the moon was of great help. Genghis's voice jerked her out of her slumber.

"We've been driving for one hour and still nothing."

"But we're going slow." Mattie yawned. "Let's give it 'til midnight, then we'll turn back."

"I could do with a bit more coffee, then." Genghis sighed.

Mattie smiled and reached between the front seats. She pulled Genghis's rucksack closer, removed a flask from it and poured two mugs of coffee.

"I'm a poor co-pilot who doesn't help keep her pilot awake." She handed a cup to him.

"We are arriving at the border of the desert." Genghis sipped some of his coffee, giving a low groan of satisfaction. "I'll find a ridge or some boulders for shelter if we need it."

Mattie drank some of her own coffee, grateful for the warming effect of the liquid. "Are you worried about patrols?"

"If it is the army we're tracking, they're bound to have surveillance on their camp."

"Is there an elevation we can reach before we enter the desert? We can scan the horizon from there."

"OK, I'll record the coordinates for the spot at which we deviate from the trucks' tracks."

He turned the SUV left and retraced some of their steps before stopping the car. Mattie did what she'd done before, winding the window down and sitting on its frame. She scanned the horizon for signs of any construction.

The camp had to be out there. She was close to the coordinates Han had given her. She opened the car door and stepped onto the front bumper of the SUV and resumed her scanning.

Genghis had parked the SUV at the bottom of the cluster of boulders that topped the small mound. Mattie left the car and climbed onto the boulders next. She sat there for a while, getting accustomed to the landscape – a trick the female Peshmerga she had accompanied for a while during the war against IS had taught her.

Let your eyes know the land you are seeing. You will watch it better then.

Mattie restarted her meticulous scanning of the horizon.

The familiar sound did not register with her immediately. She'd been too busy focusing on a shape that broke the skyline and looked too perfect to be just another set of large rocks. That sound had become almost too familiar while she'd been covering the Syrian war.

Mattie's heart started beating faster before she managed to articulate her fear.

"I think there is a drone in the air," she whispered.

She jumped away from the bumper and dived into the car.

"There is a drone coming!" she repeated.

Genghis shoved his cup into the holder, jumped out of the car. He opened the boot and yanked out a piece of cloth from underneath the boot cover. He threw it over the car roof.

"Spread it out on your side," he commanded.

Mattie took a second to understand, but she finally pulled the cloth towards her.

"Get underneath the car." Genghis had already slid under. "Come on."

Mattie slithered underneath the belly of the SUV and slowed her breathing down, listening for the unmistakable buzz of the drone's propellers.

"Can you hear it?" she whispered.

"Yes, it's coming our way."

"How long have we been here for?"

"Half an hour, why? You think they spotted us and sent a drone out?"

"No. I hope the car engine has cooled down enough, otherwise the drone will pick up its heat signature. The temperature drops a lot at night. That will help." Genghis sounded almost convinced.

"I guess we'll soon find out."

The buzz of the drone was now distinct. It was almost overhead. She recalled how these tiny crafts would return to the area their handlers had spotted unwanted activity in, like wasps waiting for the right moment to deliver their sting.

The sound started to fade and eventually disappeared.

"Which way do you think it went?" Mattie managed to turn her head towards Genghis without swallowing a mouthful of sand.

"I think it was moving west."

"We must be close."

"Drones have a large radius of operation. If I recall from what I've read, we could still be a few miles away."

"Shit..." Mattie banged the ground with her fist. "A couple of miles is not that far."

"But with drone surveillance we can't simply rock up there and hope they won't spot us."

"We've got to find a way."

Genghis nodded. "I read something about hiding heat signatures once. Let me try to find out again. I think I've got an idea."

CHAPTER NINETEEN

"Have you got it?" Harris walked into Nick's tech cave after going out to find them both a takeaway.

"Just arrived a minute ago." Nick stretched his arms over his head.

He was starting to look tired, and Harris calculated that the young man hadn't slept much since he'd arrived in Taiwan, two days ago. "Perhaps a bit of rest might be a good idea." Harris dumped food from the nearby food market on the table.

Nick shook his head. "No can do. Pythagoras was really pissed off when he handed over the software and key to the CIA mail server's back door. He's going to be on my case the minute I send the final instruction to release their site from my virus."

Harris went into the kitchen and opened the small, sealed containers of food. The room filled with an appetising mix of aromas.

Nick swivelled on his chair and wheeled it over to the door of the kitchen. "What did you get?"

"Beef noodle soup, braised pork rice and a large hot pot with some veg. I need to keep you healthy."

"Did I tell you I thought about becoming a vegetarian once?"

Harris rolled his eyes. "Just as well you saw the light."

"It's better for the planet to eat less meat."

"I know and in principle I agree, except that I'm the one doing the shopping. It makes my life much easier that you're delaying your newfound food choice until after we're done with TECH LEOPARD."

Nick stood and walked to the kitchen table, picked up one of the plates Harris had stacked, and helped himself to some food.

"I've had a quick look at what Pythagoras sent me," he said between mouthfuls of braised pork rice. "It's good quality and a good entrance door. I'm almost sorry we didn't pay them anything for it."

"We're not a charity." Harris slurped on some beef noodles. "You're right to be tough. You'll get more respect that way. Pythagoras tried to rumble us. He lost. He pays the price."

"And I've made a mortal enemy."

"Because you showed him up? Don't worry about that. You will have gained reputation. You can't be in the spooks business without ruffling a few feathers."

A mobile ringing interrupted their conversation. Harris glanced at his MI6 device but it wasn't active.

"Shit..." Harris fumbled in the pocket of the light jacket he'd hung on the back of his chair. He retrieved a burner phone from it and pressed the answer button just in time.

"Can you talk?" Hunter sounded more gruff than usual.

Harris's stomach tightened. "I can, sir. News from our operative?"

"Nothing new. But Sir Alex, your boss, has emailed me. So, I can confirm to you and him by the same token that I have no further news."

"And no further contact from China?"

There was a fraction of a second's hesitation in Hunter's reply. "No."

"I'll make sure I'll let him know, but it has been four days. Should we be worried?"

"Dragon won't contact me unless there is something important to report."

Harris bit his tongue. It was not what he'd agreed with Hunter at the outset. "No news is good news, then?"

"I'll contact you again as soon as I hear." Hunter terminated the call and Harris threw the burner phone across the room.

"That was a waste of time, and a waste of yet another burner phone."

"Is he holding back?" Nick had helped himself to some of the hot pot and it looked like most of the veg had ended up in his bowl.

"Quite possibly."

"We'll know soon enough."

"If I were a betting man, I'd say Hunter has been told by Dragon not to contact him."

"But doesn't Dragon have a way of regularly transferring intel?"

"If all was well, yes, he would, but I'd say all may not be well." Harris finished his bowl in a hurry and stood up. "I need to make another call."

He moved to his bedroom, closed the door and retrieved another burner he had stored in the safe of his room. He called the only number in it and waited for a response.

The phone went to voicemail – nothing unusual for Han. Harris dialled again and this time he got an answer.

"You need to contact your man. I need to know how far they've progressed."

"He sent me a text to let me know they are in China."

"Where exactly did his mobile ping and at what time?"

"Twenty miles from the camp and the text came in at 19.00."

"Mattie is getting close."

"And Genghis is resourceful. But then again, we are talking Chinese military."

"Just keep me posted. If you detect anything unusual I need to know."

"Goes without saying, Steve." Han hung up and Harris slumped on his bed in frustration. He still hadn't had any news or sighting of Henry and it was already the end of day four.

Harris returned to the kitchen. Nick had sucked up most of the food. Harris couldn't help but smile; the boy needed the calories for what lay ahead. "Any time frame for this super hack of yours?"

"I'll work for a big part of the night and get a few hours' sleep. I should be ready by early morning. Before I breach the server I'll let you know. It won't be long before the IT team at the CIA detects the hack, so we need to get straight to the info you need."

Harris checked his watch. It was almost 10pm. Time perhaps to buy a beer for Rodriguez and his ALPHA team.

* * *

A light snoring sound made Mattie stir. For a few seconds she wondered where she was, but then remembered she and Genghis had decided to camp in the SUV to wait for sunrise.

They had reclined each seat fully and it made for a comfortable enough bed. The thermal blanket she'd thrown on her body had kept her warm all night, even as the temperature dropped to around 5C. She checked her watch and rolled onto her side to face Genghis.

The young man was sound asleep, his face relaxed and lips slightly apart. He'd taken the challenge in his stride to move them without detection and had found a way. Soon he would implement it.

Mattie sat up and rolled her window down a little. The cold air rushed in, and she inhaled it deeply. The sky's colour was already changing and in an hour the sun would rise.

She heard a yawn and a stir.

"What time is it?" Genghis asked, eyes still closed.

"5am, so time to rock and roll."

He sat up farther, pushed his thermal blanket away and opened his door. "I can't brew us a fresh cup of tea but at least we can have a bite to eat," Genghis said.

Mattie fetched the flask that still had coffee in it from the day before. It was lukewarm, but it would do.

Genghis returned with some flatbread and cheese. "Not a typical Mongolian breakfast but it will do."

He handed some food to Mattie and she handed him a cup of tepid coffee. "Tell me again about thermal crossover?" she asked as she started on her food.

"Well, it's the time of the day when objects adjacent to each other can't be distinguished on an infrared sensor."

"In other words, if we go flat to the ground the drone won't spot us."

"That's right." Genghis shaved off several more slices of cheese and put them on the small napkins he'd spread across the cup holder between the seats.

"Then we have these thermal blankets." Mattie shook hers. "I learnt that from my time in the Middle East. These things don't let infrared through."

"I reckon we have an hour at the most to try to find the camp before we'll need to return." Genghis chewed on his food slowly. "We need to give ourselves a bit of time to get out of here and back to the camp we set up yesterday."

"Sounds like a plan." Mattie sipped some coffee, barely noticing its bitter taste.

If they walked fast, they could cover two miles easily. She needed a little time to take some photos. Still, an hour would be tight.

They finished their breakfast in silence. Genghis put the rest of the bread and cheese away and Mattie stood on the SUV's sturdy front bumper once more. She brought the binoculars up to her eyes. She couldn't see anything in the air, at least for now.

Genghis stood next to her and handed her a thermal blanket. "Let's get our rucksacks on and wrap ourselves in this afterwards. There won't be much sun until an hour after sunrise, so the foil won't reflect the light just yet."

Mattie scoured the horizon rather than the sky. Again, she spotted the shape she'd seen the day before. It seemed too large to be a bolder.

"Let's do this." Mattie jumped from the bumper to the ground, stuffed the binoculars in her rucksack and wrapped the thermal blanket around her. "I would understand if you'd rather stay behind and wait for me," she said as they were about to go.

Genghis gave her a broad smile. "Mongolia is my land whether the Chinese like it or not, and on my land I am your guide."

Mattie hesitated for a moment, but Genghis was already on his way. She caught up with him and walked close behind him.

"This is sand and desert in the west," Genghis said.

"That should make the walk a bit easier as long as we don't encounter any steep dunes."

"Nothing like that at least for a hundred miles."

They rapidly reached the truck tracks they had abandoned the day before. The deep indentation in the ground spoke of how heavy the load they had carried to the ship must have been.

"It's a good sign," Genghis said as he crouched to the ground. "These lorries took exactly the same route in as back."

"And they are headed west."

"In the same direction as the drone that flew over us last night." Genghis stood up again and this time he picked up the pace. He also must have felt there was something worth checking at the end of these tracks.

The colours of dawn were starting to stretch over the horizon; they reflected on the sand, giving it a light orange glow. Genghis had decided to walk not on the tracks but a few metres away from them. He didn't want to leave footprints where they could be seen.

The shape Mattie had spotted the evening before was becoming more distinct in the horizon, but the light of dawn wasn't yet strong enough for the binoculars to distinguish the details of it.

The pair stopped at the same time and listened for the sound of propellers. But there was only silence around them.

"It's odd," Mattie said, as they resumed their walk. "I was expecting more drone activity after what we saw last night."

"Perhaps they were checking out the ship and whether their activity had been noticed."

"That's a point but still."

Genghis stopped again, this time to survey the land. "There is a dip in the ground slightly away from the tracks. It may be a good place to survey what lies ahead. The light is going to grow stronger in ten minutes or so."

Mattie nodded and followed Genghis. She checked her watch; only twenty minutes left before they had to return, but perhaps she could stretch that time out.

Genghis arrived first at the top of the dip. He dropped his rucksack to the ground and, still wrapped in his thermal blanket, crouched to take binoculars out of his bag. Mattie joined him a minute or so later.

What she saw caused her breath to catch in her throat. In the clear distance were the watch towers belonging to what she'd been looking for. The hidden camp stretched over a large area and although she couldn't make out all its size, she knew it was vast.

Genghis waved his hand and Mattie crouched next to him. "It's incredible," she murmured.

"I can't believe it myself. I thought the rumours were only that but now I know."

Mattie lay flat on the ground and shrugged her rucksack off her shoulders. She took out her own set of binoculars and her camera.

"There is already light in some of the buildings." Genghis was sweeping his binoculars across the camp.

"I guess whoever is in there wakes up early."

"If they are prisoners, the Chinese government will work them like dogs."

Mattie focused on the parts of the camp that were already awake. "It's got to be a factory of some sort at the centre of the structure."

"It's the foundry that cast the steel pieces the lorries brought to the building site yesterday. Got to be."

"Do you think we can get closer?"

Genghis shook his head. "If this camp is that secret, they will have buried motion sensors around the outer walls."

Mattie was already taking pictures, but she needed a little more sunlight to get the photos she knew would be irrefutable proof of what was in front of her.

She crawled forward and adjusted her camera accordingly. The rhythmic sound of her clicks reverberated in the silence around them. Genghis was busy inspecting a part of the camp structure Mattie guessed must house the drones.

There were quite a few buildings that had been erected on the periphery of the main construction. Some looked like lived-in quarters, housing for the guards and other support personnel. Then there were hangars of various shapes, that almost certainly were being used for the trucks and cranes they'd seen. The landing track two hundred metres from the camp was big enough for a small aircraft or a helicopter, and certainly a drone, to land.

Genghis turned to Mattie to point out what he'd found. "There is a landing strip, to the far left of the camp."

Mattie stopped shooting pictures and half turned on her elbow towards him. "Where do –"

The soft ground gave way in beneath her arm and shoulder. With a squeal, Mattie slid down the ridge. She grasped at the soft sand unable to stop herself.

Genghis threw his binoculars away and lunged to catch her. Their fingers touched but it was too late.

* * *

The light in Henry's cell came on. He rolled to his other side to avoid the glare. The slam of a baton against the side of his bed told him he was wanted and he was wanted now.

The other inmates were still asleep and the other cells were silent. It must have been just before 6am.

Henry and the guards took what was now a familiar route towards the front yard of the camp. They entered the main building and climbed the stairs to the warden's office.

Tang was sitting at his desk when they entered. A pot of tea and a cup sat on a small tray. The stick Henry had seen him walk with was on his desk, ready to be used as he saw fit. There were signs that Warden Tang had had his breakfast and was enjoying a fresh pot.

He gestured the guards to leave them and waited a moment before addressing Henry. It was fun for him to see this tall westerner bending in front of his master.

"Sit."

Henry sat at the meeting table, the same one he'd been at when General Ma had visited. A new phone and a recording device were on the table.

Tang stood up and walked over to it. "You need to call your assistant in Washington DC." He pushed the phone towards Henry with the tip of his stick. "Today is the day."

"He might be travelling."

"Then you'll leave a message."

Henry went to pull the phone towards him.

Tang slammed his stick on the device to stop Henry from grabbing it. "Before you call, you'll set up the recorder ready to tape what you are saying. I want to record every last word."

"As you wish." Henry grabbed the recording device and moved it around. It was an old Dictaphone, the likes of which he hadn't seen for a very long time. He pushed a couple of buttons and set it on pause.

"Test it," Tang instructed.

His eyes hadn't left Henry since he'd entered the room; an occasional flash of anger showed in them. Last night's confrontation with the new gang's challenger hadn't gone the way he'd expected.

Henry released pause. "One, two, three..."

Henry rewound and played the short message. His voice sounded odd on the audio, but it could be clearly understood.

"Call him and put it on loudspeaker." Tang sat down across the table and Henry joined him.

Henry took his time in dialling the number. He was certain that by now Nick had joined Harris in Taiwan. Nick's mobile rang a few times. Another ring and it would go to voicemail. He pressed the recording button and moved the phone closer to him so that the loudspeaker was easier to reach.

He formulated his short message in his head and as he bent to deliver it, Nick answered.

"Nick Fox." The voice sounded tired and almost unhinged.

"Hey, Nick... it's Henry."

"H... this is a surprise." Nick sounded it, but he still managed to make it natural. "I thought you were still on holiday excavating mammoths."

"It's not mammoths, it's dinosaurs... but yeah, still on holiday."

Tang waved his hand to hurry Henry along.

"Anyway, I was wondering whether you've heard from our prospective Chinese client?"

There was a small pause and he guessed Nick was working out what Henry expected from him.

"Nothing I'm afraid."

"Not to worry. I have another possible new avenue and need some HUMIT for this."

The use of spy jargon would send the right message to Nick: they were being listened to.

"Shoot... I'm very busy but I'll make some time."

"I'm looking for a list of companies in Panama with an ultimate beneficial owner in China."

"Any particular industry?"

"Start with the property sector." Henry focused on the phone whilst speaking; he heard Warden Tang shift on his chair.

"Will do. I'll start by putting together a corporate-flow diagram of how these people stack shell companies, trusts, and nominee accounts and turn that into an opaque corporate structure. Then I'll get to the individuals at the end of the chain."

"Perfect. I'll call you back in three days."

"I'll have something for you by then. But in the meantime, have fun digging out dinos and let's hope the weather holds."

"Weather a bit unpredictable but I can still do plenty of digging."

Tang stopped the recording as soon as Nick ended the call. "Why the property sector?" He spat out his question.

"It felt like the obvious choice." Henry faked surprise. "I can call back and ask for a change?"

Tang sat back. The mask of calm came over his face again.

"Perhaps you're right..." He used his stick to flick the phone away from Henry. "Once the list you present to General Ma is final there won't be any further questions."

Henry nodded. "There shouldn't be."

Tang dismissed Henry with a wave of the hand. It seemed the warden needed to think.

Henry yet again entered the canteen just as everyone had almost finished breakfast. He hurried to get his bowl of sticky rice and his mug of tea.

Rob and Bo had finished their food when he joined their table.

"I thought Tang had changed his mind and sent you to the holding cells for solitary confinement." Bo shook his head, relieved.

"I'm sure he'd love to do that, but I just bought us some time."

"Can you reveal your cunning plan?" Rob sat back in his chair, mug against his chest.

"He got me to call my assistant this morning, which is why I'm late."

Rob and Bo exchanged a quick look.

"I know it didn't bode well, but –" Henry chewed a couple of mouthfuls before continuing "– I asked Nick to delve into the property sector."

Bo frowned. "But this is almost certainly where Tang's got money he needs to hide."

"Not almost certainly, most certainly, judging by his reaction. On the other hand – as he put it – once the list is final any players not listed won't be in trouble."

Bo's eyes lit up. "In other words, you falsify the list for Tang, make sure his name is not on it and he gets away with money laundering."

"And until then he sort of needs us alive to put the list together."

Rob sipped some tea before asking. "How long will it take to put that list together?"

"Weeks." Henry took a gulp of his own drink.

"But Ma asked for it to be delivered..." Bo didn't finish. He smiled, shook his head and said quietly, "You're buying time until you're ready."

When Rob's expression tightened, Henry felt a pinch of anxiety. Had he told Bo too much too soon?

But then Bo nodded. "I'll help you to get out. Just tell me what to do."

Henry grew serious. "I won't leave anybody behind."

"You must, my friend, otherwise your great attempt won't succeed."

CHAPTER TWENTY

Harris couldn't tell if the banging was on his bedroom door or in his head. It had been fun and a good idea to catch up with Rodriguez and the ALPHA team, but Harris no longer had the capacity that these lads did when it came to alcohol consumption.

"Yes, I'm coming," Harris shouted, wincing at the noise.

He opened his bedroom door to a very excited Nick. "I spoke to him. He is alive. He is –"

"Slow... Down..." Harris walked past Nick to the kitchen where he poured himself a large glass of water. "Is there any coffee?" He looked around and Nick gestured at a fresh pot. Harris ran his hands down his face.

"Are you listening to me, Steve? I spoke to Henry."

He pulled them off swiftly at the news. "You mean... you spoke to him?"

Nick rolled his eyes. "I told you three times already."

"Twice only," Harris said, lifting a finger. "But come on. What did he say?" He went to the coffee pot and poured himself a full mug. His head had miraculously cleared at the news.

"He couldn't speak freely, and he was on a loudspeaker. It was very quick, but he asked me to start working on establishing a list of Chinese owned companies that have been incorporated in Panama."

"That's it?"

"He said he would contact me again in three days' time."

"How much progress can you make on this in three days?"

Nick shrugged. "Not a lot. I can start and I now have a good list of contacts that H introduced me to but we're not buddies yet."

"They will want to know why you're asking all these questions."

"For sure, and even if I had fast access to the data, it would take me a while to assemble the list Henry wants."

Harris drank his coffee in silence. He returned to the coffee pot to replenish the contents and offered a mug to Nick. Nick pushed his mug towards Harris.

"Henry knows his timetable is unrealistic, so he is telling us something," Harris said.

"What?"

"He is telling us that he is planning to escape within that timeframe."

"He wants me to start with the property sector."

"Does that make sense to start there?"

"I guess. It's a sector that is used a lot for money laundering."

"So, the Chinese are interested in money laundering one way or another."

Nick shrugged. "Or the particular Chinese man who spoke to me, perhaps."

"That's a good point... I'll get on to GCHQ and see what they can gather on property tycoons from China."

"We finished with a weather thing... apparently the weather is uncertain. He was telling me he still needs to work on the escape plan."

"That pushes the escape out to three days from today." Harris stretched and looked at Nick. "How do you feel?"

The young man looked as though he might have gotten some sleep. "Have prepped everything for the hack. I think we should go this morning, which will be the evening in Langley. It's always good to pick a transition time when the day shift team leaves and the night guys come in. There are fewer eyes on the ball."

Harris checked his watch. 7am. "What time?"

"I'll start at 7.30am, which is 7.30pm in Langley, Virginia, and get into the system at around 8pm their time."

Harris disappeared into the bathroom for a shower that he hoped would help dissipate the lingering effect of last evening's beers.

At 7.20am Harris walked into Nick's tech cave and sat on the chair Nick had pulled over for him.

"Are we ready?" he asked the hacker.

Nick smiled. "This is where the fun starts."

His fingers glided over the ergonomic keyboard. He had switched from a laptop to a more conventional PC as, he explained, the three screens he had arranged around his desk gave him more data control. Nick retraced a path he had trodden in the early hours of the morning, testing again the software and the pathway Pythagoras had given him.

Harris smiled at the focus the young man was displaying. Harris could see why Henry enjoyed working with him and why Henry had given Nick the benefit of the doubt after he'd got himself caught by the Russians, and why he'd been willing to exchange him for someone Henry had grown close to.

"I'm about to start the breach into the CIA systems and start looking around for the server we need."

Harris rolled his chair closer. He was about to have a peek into Hunter's email box and with some luck, at some of his files too.

The lines of codes Nick was tracking, testing and breaking moved across his central screen at an astonishing pace. Harris thought he'd spotted the name Hunter III, but he wasn't sure.

And then, Nick's black screen morphed into something Harris recognised. The inside of an Outlook mailbox.

"It's a large email box..." Nick was scrolling up and down the left-hand bar, looking at the folders Hunter had created to file emails he needed to keep.

"How long have we got?"

"No more than ten minutes. The system already knows there has been an intrusion. Normally the hackers would hoover as much data as they could in a few minutes and close the door so that the breach can't be precisely identified. Or they would release a ransomware virus, but in this attempt we are being surgical." Nick spoke in a distracted way; his focus was on the folders.

Harris toyed with the idea of doing exactly what Nick had suggested hackers did, which was to download Hunter's entire email box, but it would perhaps be pushing his luck too far – assuming he had any luck left. "Does he create folders by continent?" Harris asked.

"No, he goes by years and then... types of operations."

Harris stood and looked over Nick's shoulder. "How about co-operation or joint ops?"

"I thought the word cooperation never entered his vocab?"

"Only when he is in charge."

"Well... it doesn't enter his filing system, either –"

An alarm interrupted Nick. Harris knew what it meant. The CIA's own hackers were onto them.

"I'll do a search by name and date..." Nick's fingers were running over the keyboard again and a long list of emails appeared containing the word Dragon. Nick started speed reading them and shook his head. "It's all about the recruitment process of Dragon, no name..."

"Hunter set up a different way of receiving data from him. Emails are dangerous even if encrypted." Harris tried to think how he would tackle the data download.

Nick was about to comment when a second alarm sounded. "We've got less than five minutes and only two nodes before I drop the hack."

"Voicemails!" Harris pointed at the screen. "Can you find whether voicemails have been sent to email?"

"Good one." Nick's fingers were already flying to find the answer. "Yes... Look at that, a whole host of them."

The third alarm rang and Nick stiffened. "I'm downloading the whole lot."

Nick placed the USB key into the port and the intel sucking started; the tool bar was whizzing up, slowing down and whizzing up again.

The final alarm sounded. Harris took a small gulp of air.

Nick's finger was on the kill button; a continuous alarm shrieked, filling the room. "Fuck... I've got to –"

Harris pushed the kill switch and the screen dissolved into a black hole.

Nick swivelled on his chair to face Harris. "I could have got a bit more!"

"Am I right in thinking that the newest recording would be downloaded first?" Harris retrieved the USB from its slot.

"That's right."

"Then we've got all we need. Let's not be too greedy this time." Harris grinned. They'd just hacked Hunter III, and it felt bloody good.

* * *

Mattie's thermal blanket had fallen off. Her camera had followed her in her fall. She managed to muffle her cry and slow her steady slide towards the bottom of the ridge.

Her boots found some purchase against a piece of rock, and she came to a stop. Genghis heaved himself over the ridge and started a controlled slide on his back to her. He moved away from Mattie, in the direction of the thermal blanket.

He squeezed his own blanket to his chest and managed not to lose it as he reached Mattie's. "Don't move," he whispered. "I'm coming..." Still lying down, Genghis wrapped himself up in his cover again and rapidly folded Mattie's. He turned on his belly and started to crawl towards her, digging his feet in the sand to stop a further slide down. He reached her after a couple of minutes and moved alongside her. "I'm going to anchor myself in the sand and help you to turn on your belly."

"What about my camera?"

Genghis looked around quickly. "We don't have time. We have to get shelter again."

"I can't leave without it." Mattie started to move; her body slid down a little.

"One thing at a time." Genghis's voice had an urgency she recognised; it meant real danger.

"Sorry..." She refocused. "What do I do?"

"Your left foot is on a rock?"

"Yes."

"Dig your heel in as deep as you can in the sand. I'm going to move a little above you and grab your left hand, then you slowly flip over."

Mattie nodded and did as she was told. She felt sand entering her shoe and hoped it meant she had dug deep enough. Extending her arm over her head she felt Genghis's solid grip on her. Closing her eyes, Mattie flipped onto her belly. She started to slide again but Genghis held firm. Finally, she managed to dig the toes of her shoes in the sand and stay put. The sky had become much lighter and soon their bodies, even lying down, would become visible.

"Are you OK? Can I let go?"

"I'm fine, I think –"

The familiar sound of propellers cut her off.

Genghis threw the thermal blanket her way. "We don't have time to climb over the ridge," he said, adjusting the foil over him so that his body and head were completely concealed.

Mattie threw the cover over her, hiding as best she could without making too many sudden moves. She could feel her feet were only partially hidden but there was nothing she could do.

The drone was coming in low and its distinct buzzing noise was growing stronger by the minute.

"It's coming in to land," Genghis whispered.

"Where is the landing strip?"

"300 yards to the left."

"The operator may switch off the camera so he can land the drone safely."

Mattie had seen it done before when she was covering the search for Bin Laden in Pakistan.

The drone moved above their heads and banked left. Its noise increased as it came to land and then all went quiet.

"You move first," Genghis prompted Mattie.

She started to crawl up, focused on making sure her feet were well anchored before she took another step. After what felt like an eternity, her hands reached the ridge and the few blades of grass she'd seen growing here and there.

"Let me go first." Genghis moved past her and rolled in one move over the edge of the slope. He waited a few seconds, shored himself up and heaved Mattie over.

They both stayed silent for a moment, listening for any activity coming from the camp. But there was no sound of cars or trucks rolling out of the gates and being driven in their direction.

Genghis retrieved the binoculars he'd thrown away to help Mattie. He dusted them off and surveyed the perimeter of the construction, where they both anticipated the guards would be coming from.

"Do you see anything?"

"No movement."

Mattie hesitated but she had to ask. "And my camera?"

Genghis shook his head. "Nothing in the sand."

"Shit..." Tears of anger stung her eyes. How could she have been so careless?

"I've got another one in the SUV..."

"Not today."

"I know..."

Thermal crossover that had given them cover would vanish in less than half an hour. Just enough time to reach their vehicle and retreat to their camp.

Genghis tapped Mattie's shoulder and placed a sand-covered item in her hands. "I hope it can be salvaged," he said, sliding down the ridge towards the track they had used to reach the camp.

Mattie widened her eyes as she fingered her camera. "How did you manage to spot it?"

Genghis grinned. "That's why I'm your guide."

Mattie slid down the ridge. Genghis had already started to trace their steps back to the car. They accelerated their pace to begin, dropping back to a slow jog along the flat desert land.

Shortly after 6.30am they reached the SUV. Genghis moved quickly to secure the camouflage netting over the car. Mattie climbed into the car and started to separate out the pieces of her camera to ascertain the damage.

Within a couple of minutes, they were on their way back to the foothills where they had set up camp.

"That was too close." Genghis shook his head.

"I know... but that's sometimes the only way to get to the truth." Mattie put down her half-dismembered camera. "Is this too much for you, Genghis?" She felt she had to ask. She had stupidly expected to do a lot more on her own, but this was not the Middle East, a place she knew so well she could drive to the most dangerous spots alone and still come out alive.

"Remember, most of us in Mongolia have inherited DNA from the Great Khan. I'm not backing down in front of the Chinese military."

Mattie sighed at this chest-beating, Genghis-Khan-inspired speech. "But you don't have the great Mongol Army with you." She smiled.

"I know, but I've got my brain and a deep knowledge of the desert these people will never have."

"Did your father teach you about the nomadic life when you were a kid?"

"You mean pony riding, yurt living and all that good stuff?"

Mattie gave him an intrigued look. "Well, yes."

"Of course, and that was magic, but the best bit was –" Genghis grinned at the thought. "– the cigarette smuggling with my uncle. That taught me a lot."

* * *

Henry slid his tray along the conveyor belt and joined the line of men that had formed, ready to leave the canteen for the factory. A wiry old man hurried to deposit his tray and slid in behind Henry.

One of the guards gave a short whistle and the line started to move forward at a steady pace. The old man came uneasily close to Henry's back and for an instant he worried that he was perhaps carrying a knife.

Instead, the old man whispered a few words in Mandarin. "Tomorrow night... seven o'clock, outside the walls."

"How?" Henry whispered back.

But that was all the old man had been told. When they entered the yard, he retreated to a safe distance from Henry.

Henry raised his head a little to once again take in the security measures of Zhaga: 25-foot-tall concrete walls, watchtowers, guards with dogs walking the inner perimeter at night. The drones were what Henry worried about the most. He'd finally identified the noise he'd heard when one of them had landed in the early hours of the morning.

But Henry was banking on one thing he knew the Asians enjoyed most of all: gambling. The fight would happen. And he was pretty sure that bets were already exchanging hands all around the camp. He wondered whether Warden Tang would be in on the action.

One of the guards picked Rob first out of the line, then Bo and finally Henry. He used his baton for good measure. There was a noticeable ripple of fear amongst the other inmates. The line moved on from the scene more swiftly than usual. The guards started moving them towards the opposite entrance.

Rob lost his calm composure.

"Don't worry, it's the way to the office that has been set up for us," Henry whispered. Yes, that was also the way to the interrogation cells, and Henry hoped Tang hadn't changed his mind.

The room was just the way Henry had left it. The three men entered followed by a guard who picked up the chair he felt was most comfortable, moved it next to the door and plonked himself on it.

"Gentlemen, choose your desk and let me explain what we need to work on," Henry said in a formal tone. Neither Rob nor Bo said a word.

Henry moved to the desk closest to him, sat down and switched on the PC. He bent down and ran his fingers underneath the desk. The recording device he found was barely hidden. He resurfaced swiftly but he needn't have worried. The guard was on his mobile, probably watching porn. "It's easy to switch on the computer. Just *look* underneath your desks."

Both men did and resurfaced a moment later with a nod to Henry. Tang was taking no chances. The devices were crude but would be effective.

Henry spent time explaining what the three of them would be looking for in the realm of corporate structures.

"And all that we discover we record on an Excel spreadsheet. Let me show you."

The two men moved to Henry's desk. He opened an Excel document and started typing.

And this is the way we communicate. Type it, show it and erase it.

"Can I have a try, please?" Rob asked whilst taking Henry's seat.

"Sure."

What did the old guy say?

Henry stood next to him and started typing.

Tomorrow, seven o'clock, outside the perimeter walls.

"Do you mind if I join the tuition?" Bo shuffled closer to Henry's desk. He read briefly and nodded.

"May I suggest we set it up this way? I am a lawyer, after all." Bo typed: *You'll need a match referee and a man to be your coach.*

"That looks much better." Henry moved away from the desk as Bo kept typing.

The guard stood up suddenly and walked over to them without warning. He pushed Henry away from the desk with a vicious shove and plonked himself in front of the screen.

The spreadsheet had columns at the top with engaging titles such as Country of Incorporation, Capital Structure, Number of Directors... One didn't have to speak English to know this was just a boring old document.

CHAPTER TWENTY-ONE

Harris played the message again. The recording Hunter III had received of the last conversation between Dragon and the CIA couldn't be clearer.

The net was closing in fast around Dragon and comms had become too dangerous. So, Dragon had gone underground – or perhaps worse.

This had not surprised Harris as much as the identity of Dragon. He couldn't help but smile at his own assumption. Dragon wasn't a man. And although Harris couldn't be certain yet – as no name had been given and wouldn't be – Harris knew that Dragon could only be one of the few senior women in the military and an equally senior member of the Chinese Communist Party.

After, he had sent a request to Elaine in London for a list of all high-ranking officers in the Chinese Army. Harris didn't specifically ask for a list of female officers. He trusted his team, of course, but the risk of a leak – even an infinitely small one – was just too big to take.

Harris removed his headphones and stood up. Nick had given him access to the downloaded data on a laptop that wasn't linked to the internet. Nick had done a final check of his own system to make sure they hadn't been tracked and then collapsed for a few hours' kip in his bedroom.

The smell of freshly brewed coffee lured Harris to the kitchen after a few minutes.

Now that he knew more about Dragon's identity, Harris felt the heavy burden of that knowledge. To Harris's irritation, he almost sympathised with Hunter's decision to keep the latest developments from him, but not quite. There was no good reason for the silence. Dragon would no longer be communicating any update on the status of

TECH LEOPARD. She wouldn't tell the CIA if Henry was at risk or if he'd even been discovered.

Careful what you wish for...

Henry Crowne was on his own behind enemy lines.

Harris poured another mug of coffee. He reached for the packet of biscuits rather than his cigarettes, and returned to the laptop. He checked again the time stamp of the recording. Exactly forty-eight hours after Henry had arrived in Inner Mongolia.

Harris took a sip of coffee and winced. This brew was not up to his usual standard, but it would have to do. He listened to the recording one more time, focusing on Dragon's voice, her intonations and the emotions, if any, she may be conveying.

There was nothing Harris could hang his hat on but the feeling persisted that there was more to TECH LEOPARD than he'd been told. Dragon didn't sound pressed or worried. She was relaying a pure statement of fact. Her days were almost certainly numbered. Was she confident Rob Walker would be saved?

Harris thought about the type of spy she was, one who turned against her own country. Spies fell into two camps: the greedy or the idealist. Which one was Dragon? He guessed idealist. If greed had been her motive, she would have asked for an exfiltration and even more money to tell all her secrets to the most generous intelligence service in the world.

But Dragon was intending to stick it out 'til the bitter end. Harris wondered whether Hunter knew why.

Harris's MI6 mobile buzzed. Even at 2am his team was willing to produce the intel for him. He opened the file sent by Elaine and scrolled through the names of high-ranking officers in the Chinese Army. There were quite a few and Harris knew he needed to exercise patience. The first names – listed second after the family name, as was the way in China – didn't tell him much about whether the person was male or female.

He decided to change tack and look for officials who had a link with the intelligence community.

And there she was. The president of the National Defence University and a member of the 18th Central Committee of The Chinese Communist Party was also a general of the Chinese People's Liberation Army and a woman.

General Ma's picture was not what he was expecting from an official portrait. She had been photographed during a tour of the forces she oversaw, speaking to a crowd of cadets who looked enthralled by what she was saying. General Ma had charisma, it seemed.

Harris browsed through her biography quickly and it read like the perfect propaganda story. The daughter of a pig farmer, and born during the Cultural Revolution in the late '60s, she had escaped the one-child policy that had been introduced in the 1980s by the Chinese Government. The decision had been made to restrict the growth of the Chinese population that already topped 1 billion people. It had been introduced, however, without taking into account the traditional views that ascribed more value to boys than girls. The policy led to a countrywide cull of baby girls which had continued until 2015, when the policy was withdrawn.

Harris kept reading. Ma's intelligence had been noticed by her teachers. She was sent to university and then selected to enter the realm of National Security. General Ma had spent time in Hong Kong.

On the recording, Ma's accent had been soft and distinct. She used colloquial expressions without hesitation and sounded certain of what she wanted to convey.

Harris finished reading the file. Something important must have happened to convince this highly successful woman, the first to be elevated to the enviable position of General, to betray her country. She was about to throw thirty years of hard work and dedication to the wind.

The thought sent a shiver down Harris's spine. TECH LEOPARD was perhaps more than simply the extraction of a genial technology scientist named Rob Walker out of a mysterious camp in China.

Harris decided to park that thought for later. His immediate priority was to get more intel about Henry's progress and if possible, eyes on Zhaga. Henry had told them he'd found a way to escape the camp and that it would happen in the next three days at most. Harris needed to know whether the rest of their plan still stood firm.

Henry had gone through several permutations of it with Harris. They had focused on one that involved a long trek in the opposite direction to where they hoped the Chinese army would be looking. Then again, two westerners walking the Inner Mongolian desert wouldn't be that difficult to spot. Henry and Rob wouldn't have much time to get out of China once they escaped the camp.

A text pinged on Harris's burner phone. He picked up the phone from the desk. Han was calling for his daily update. Harris dialled Han's number and waited. The call went to voicemail. Harris didn't bother with a message. Han would know Harris was free to talk.

"Just the person I needed to talk to," Harris said, as he answered Han's call back.

"We agreed on a daily call, right?"

"We did indeed. What have you got for me?"

"They spotted the camp."

"And they haven't been spotted themselves, I take it?"

"No." Han sounded as though his question wasn't worth asking but Harris didn't care.

"Anything else? The suspense is killing me."

"They've set up camp and might be returning for another look."

Harris took the news in. Han didn't know about the planned escape, and it would stay that way for the time being.

"They're confident they won't be detected?"

"My guide knows the terrain better than anybody else. He could be ten yards away from the Chinese Army and they wouldn't spot him."

"I'll take your word for it." Harris meant it. Han was one of MI6's top operatives in Asia.

"There is something else." Han paused for a moment. "Both of them think the camp is being used to build a ship."

"A ship... in the middle of the desert?"

"Not any kind of ship. An aircraft carrier, and according to them the replica is very good."

"OK, I'll need to think about that." Harris thanked Han and hung up.

OPERATION TECH LEOPARD was a lot more than just a rescue mission, Harris was now certain of it.

* * *

The tea had just finished brewing and Genghis poured a large mug for Mattie. He had used a small solar kettle instead of the traditional gas

212

camping canister. The other advantage was that solar didn't emit a glow and wasn't detectable the way the old-fashioned gas rings would be.

Mattie had just returned from a call with Han. She'd promised she would get in touch if she made significant progress.

Genghis pulled out a bread different to what they'd eaten for breakfast from the small cooler. This time instead of cheese, he offered Mattie some jam.

She smiled. "This can't be what Mongols used to eat for breakfast either?"

"Course not. It's what I used to eat when I lived in New York. I love blueberry jam."

Genghis opened the pot and placed it on a flat rock between them.

Mattie sat cross-legged on the ground and helped herself to a slice of bread. She grabbed the knife stabbed in the pot and smoothed a thick layer of blueberry preserve on her bread. "I haven't thanked you yet for this morning... so thank you," Mattie said, raising her mug.

Genghis grinned. "All part of the job of being a top guide."

"It's a lot more than that. You've taken a lot of risks and we're not even out of the woods yet."

"We're far enough. I scanned the horizon this morning after we came back and I didn't notice any drone."

"And yet they must be out there."

"I don't think the prison is exploiting the full radius of the drones, so that they don't attract attention."

"That's a good point." Mattie nodded. "They want to protect their military installation and the ship, but they don't want people around asking too many questions."

Genghis bit into his bread and jam and grunted with pleasure. "The Chinese authorities have told people to stay away and they do, because they think it is some military exercise field. But if they knew it was a camp, I think there would be a lot more interest and people would talk."

"Aren't they frightened?"

"Some are but not the nomads. It's in their blood. They still think they are roaming their land and that no one has a right to interfere."

"Aren't the Chinese trying to settle them?" Mattie helped herself to more bread and jam.

"They are making it harder and harder. I think it will soon become illegal to live such a nomadic life but for the time being it's still acceptable here in Inner Mongolia." Genghis finished his tea and stretched. "I'm setting up the tents in the shadow of the hill. We may want to rest before deciding what to do next."

Mattie drank up and followed Genghis to the place where he'd hidden the camping gear the day before. He'd been confident it would still be here on their return. Mattie hadn't been so sure, but she was glad she'd been proven wrong.

They set up the small, single occupancy pop-up tents quickly. Genghis rolled out two thick mats inside, one in each for additional comfort.

"Why don't you take a nap?" Mattie suggested.

"You sure?"

"I'm not sleepy and I'm going to enjoy some more of your excellent tea."

Genghis gave Mattie one thumb up, and he slid into the diminutive space, not bothering to zip up the entrance.

Mattie moved back to where they'd been sitting and helped herself to more tea. She hadn't had much time to think about the events that had led her to where she was now.

True, she'd felt things had moved fast with her project and she had entertained the thought that she might have been played, but the speed suited her. She had briefly wondered whether the Chinese had granted her access because of her MP father, to whom they could issue a demand for ransom. But any prospective kidnapper would have found out that Harold Colmore MP belonged to the side of the Conservative party that advocated zero tolerance towards terrorists. He had already shown no mercy when he'd found out his own daughter had been kidnapped in Syria.

The sun had risen high above the horizon and the autumn season made the daytime temperature bearable. Mattie took time to look at the landscape around her. She liked how the fractured terrain transformed into smoother slopes, which turned into a flat expense that housed the dunes of the desert.

With Genghis now sound asleep, Mattie returned to what was still troubling her. It was almost impossible to believe that Han had obtained enough information from his contacts in China to locate the camp.

214

Genghis had said it. The camp they had found was a vague rumour and the Chinese authorities were protective of it. None of the few settlers in the region had set eyes on it and Mattie could only imagine the fate of the unlucky nomads who came across it.

She poured more tea in her mug and sipped it. There were only two organisations with the means and the incentive to secure her involvement in discovering the camp: MI6 or the CIA.

She smiled at the thought of being part of the great network of undercover agents, and yet also felt irritated. She was a journalist who strived never to take sides and to report the news faithfully. Still, she couldn't help wonder why she'd been chosen from all the other excellent reporters with more experience in China. Or perhaps she'd just struck it lucky.

A low snoring sound had Mattie smiling and shaking her head. Genghis was more than a guide. He had helped her escape the Chinese military and that needed someone with more knowledge than a simple guide would have.

* * *

The work they'd been doing over the past few hours had been tedious. Henry had managed to compile a lot of information he'd committed to memory. He had considered giving Warden Tang a string of red herrings but there was Bo to think about. Henry needed to convince him to join the escape party. It made no difference to the plan and exfiltration route he had discussed with Harris.

But if Bo stayed, perhaps his supply of a credible amount of information to help Tang set up the money laundering structure would spare the man. He was a lawyer after all and would know what to do with it.

Bo had asked for a toilet break and the guard had grumbled, calling someone else to escort Bo out. Rob was busy filling in his spreadsheet.

Henry stopped what he was doing for a moment and glanced at the man he was supposed to rescue. Rob was not letting anyone past his defences. He had a brilliant intellect, and his psychological profile was solid, but he was guarded in a way that was surprising. He must have decided he trusted Henry or at least knew Henry was his only hope.

Henry returned to his document, but was too distracted to resume his activity. There were very few people Henry couldn't get to talk but Rob was one of them. And yet they were about to embark on an escape that needed both men to work together to ensure they were successful.

Bo returned and Rob decided it was his turn to trouble the guard for a trip to the gents. The guard started shouting at him and Rob shrugged his shoulders. Henry exchanged a quick smile with Bo. For a creative scientist Rob was a rather thick-skinned bloke.

"Can I show you something?" Bo waved Henry over to his desk.

Henry nodded and stood up.

The bets are on and you're doing pretty well... the guard told me. A lot of the inmates and the guards think you'll beat the Challenger, Bo had typed on his spreadsheet.

"I suggest you add this." Henry typed a response.

If the guard knows, then Tang must know.

Bo added a line. *I said I had no idea what he was talking about, but he didn't believe me.*

Henry gave Bo a friendly slap on the shoulder. The guard looked at the exchange with suspicion but didn't bother to check the document.

Rob returned and his impassive countenance from before appeared now to be shaken. There was no way of asking directly what had unsettled him.

"Now that you are back, perhaps I could take a quick look at your spreadsheet?" Henry asked the man.

Rob sat down and quickly typed on his spreadsheet: *General Ma has been recalled to Beijing and is doing an interview with the politburo on Tiananmen Square.*

Is it official?

Only on social media according to the guard.

We stick to the timetable, come what may...

Rob hit the keys more firmly. *Don't you get it yet?* His irritation was audible. The guard must have felt it because he raised his head.

Henry pulled back and Rob erased the conversation.

"I'll think about it," Henry said, hiding his shock.

He returned to his desk and idly browsed through a website that advertised cheap, already incorporated companies in the British Virgin Islands. Rob had just confirmed what Henry had guessed: General Ma was Dragon.

216

Why else would she have driven Henry so close to the edge in the torture room and not kept going to drag the information she wanted out of him? And why hand him this project that was an ideal way to get close to Rob and work on his escape? Not to mention the set of tools that had been left for him wrapped in his bath towel. It was she who'd ordered he get cleaned up.

Ma's identity as Dragon didn't surprise Henry as much as Rob knowing the name. Ma was their patron and escaping without her help would be that much more difficult.

Rob returned to his work and nothing in his attitude betrayed his concern. There was some information the scientist was holding back, something more than his vast knowledge of high-grade military semiconductors.

And it was time for Rob to spill.

In the canteen, Bo sat with the Hong Kong crowd to catch up on the latest on the grapevine.

Rob sat at an empty table and Henry joined him. They started eating in silence. Rob seemed lost in his thoughts, weighing perhaps what he might say to Henry and what he would keep to himself.

"Shall we put our cards on the table?" Henry said, as he put his bowl down.

Rob didn't look as surprised as he was expecting.

Henry continued as he ate. "You don't need to say anything but I'm going to ask questions and you can reply with a yes or no. You didn't meet Ma for the first time here at the camp, but you've met her before?"

This time Rob looked taken aback. He nodded.

"And you think she is material in our ability to escape."

He gave another nod.

Henry gathered up the few noodles left at the bottom of his bowl and ate his last mouthful. He continued. "If she came to see us it's because she senses she's on borrowed time. I don't think she would have pushed for the project had she known there was no chance of an escape. Do you agree?"

Another inmate tried to sit at their table, but Henry flashed him a murderous look that made him move on.

"Yes," Rob said.

Henry grabbed his mug and took a long sip of his tea. "What is it she has told you you're protecting so closely?"

This time Rob's eyes opened wide.

Henry flashed him a faint smile. "Don't tell me here. You're facing the room, and someone could read your lips... It happens more than you think, by the way."

Rob gave a slow nod.

"But I want to know before the fight. And just so you know, I mean it when I say cards on the table... MI6 and the CIA sent me here to get you."

CHAPTER TWENTY-TWO

The afternoon's activities had been slow and sluggish. As soon as he had woken up, Genghis had spent time surveying the horizon in the direction of the ship. Mattie had cleaned her camera, unscrewing each part with caution and resting the dismantled object on a cloth spread out on the ground.

"The trucks are coming back," Genghis announced.

Mattie didn't look up from her camera. "Can you tell how many?"

"I'd say either more in numbers or whatever they are carrying is much heavier."

"They looked almost finished yesterday."

"This could be the last part of the deck that was missing."

She stood up. "I'd like to go and take a look again. I can use the spare camera."

"The drones will be flying overhead I would think," Genghis said.

"Even in broad daylight?"

"Possibly not, but I'd rather wait for another thermal crossover."

Mattie was about to object but rushing in again would be a recipe for disaster. She returned to the camera and the burning question that had occupied her since it popped into her head in the morning. Who was trying to manipulate her?

Another pot of tea was brewing by the time Genghis slid down from the sheltered place from where he had chosen to observe the horizon.

Mattie stopped pouring tea and looked at him expectantly.

"They are leaving the site."

"It's almost 5pm, thermal crossover is only an hour away..."

Genghis grinned. "You learn fast."

"I'm probably old enough to be your mum but that doesn't make me a dinosaur."

Genghis chuckled. "Let's have tea first, then we go."

The sky had turned a deep shade of purple and the temperature drop was starting to chill the ground. Mattie and Genghis wrapped themselves up in their thermal blanket once more as they made their way to the aircraft carrier building site.

In a safe spot, Mattie was prone on her elbows, binoculars to her eyes. "They've finished the construction. It's incredible... This aircraft carrier is over 1,000 feet long. I'm sure it's a US Navy ship." She dropped the glasses, took out her camera, and started shooting pictures, moving along on her belly to change the angle of the shots. "Can we get a little closer?" she asked.

Genghis nodded but he stopped her with a gesture of the hand. He would go first and check. He rose slowly to a crouch and moved stealthily through the long grass of the desert.

The silence of dusk was broken by a faint sound. Mattie swapped her camera for her binoculars again. She scanned the skies but couldn't see any drones. The sound became stronger and Mattie recognised it. It was the sound of a vehicle, the sort heavy armoured vehicles make; she'd heard it while working with the army.

Genghis had dropped to the ground and froze. He looked back in her direction and signalled she should drop to the ground too.

A moment later the powerful stadium lights came on and the ship was illuminated. The lights made its bulk look even more impressive. Mattie craned her neck to see a certain part of the ship. To her astonishment, there on the hull in large letters was USS *George H. W. Bush*. Its construction had been completed down to the finest of details.

There were only two vehicles at the site and the first one looked more like a simple jeep than a Humvee. Mattie moved again to see who was in the vehicles. She could feel Genghis's eyes on her, warning her, but she needed to know. A small wiry man dressed in a uniform Mattie didn't recognise got out of the jeep. An aide exited the Humvee and opened the passenger door.

A young man stepped out. He looked almost too young to oversee such a project but here he was strolling through the site accompanying who Mattie guessed was the man in charge of the camp. They were speaking animatedly. The young man was nodding and couldn't help a smile, it appeared. He walked right up to the hull and leaned against it, as though making sure it was real.

He returned to where the camp's warden stood and asked a question. The warden nodded and the young officer must have paid the older man a compliment as the warden bowed to thank his superior.

The ship was ready for whatever purpose it'd been erected. Mattie speculated that the war games were about to begin. The thought sent a shiver down her spine. She looked at the camera next to her. She caught Genghis's look that said *don't even try*.

She hesitated, then grabbed the camera and pressed the shutter button a few times. The clicks sounded deafening. Genghis turned his face towards the men who were still talking and walking alongside the ship's hull. They were far too absorbed in their conversation to take note.

The young officer retraced his steps back to the car and turned one final time to face the warden. The older man once more gave the other a bow. They had almost certainly agreed on what came next. Mattie feared the site and the camp itself would be swarming with military personnel very soon. She didn't have much time to get all the evidence she needed to support the next explosive article she was intending to send to *The Times of London*.

The sound of cars reversing and disappearing in the distance relaxed Mattie a fraction. She didn't move until Genghis told her she could. She had disobeyed him enough for one day.

They belly-crawled away from their observation post and sat at the back of a couple of boulders that were hiding them from view.

Genghis didn't protest. Mattie had gotten away with it and he seemed happy she had a few compromising pictures of the Chinese military standing next to the replica of the USS *George H. W. Bush* aircraft carrier.

"Did you see that? The army is taking possession of the ship." Mattie was scrolling through her pictures, frowning as she went along.

"What does that mean?"

"That they are going to bring troops to train here."

"You mean... train them to lead an assault on an aircraft carrier?" Genghis scratched his head. "Is it at all possible?"

"I know it sounds impossible, but why not? At least they can play war games and although the ship is not moving, they can run simulations."

"But that would mean preparing for war against..."

"The US. China's ambitions for the Pacific have grown significantly. The US is the only power China must truly worry about. Even if war is not happening tomorrow, it's advisable to prepare for any eventuality." Mattie sounded confident in what she was saying. Years as a war reporter had taught her a thing or two about the way power shifted and was retained on the world map.

"What do you want to do?" Genghis asked.

"We need to go back to the camp this evening. I need to take a chance. Troops won't arrive today. After that we don't know."

"The problem will be the car. I'll think about how we can use thermal crossover to our advantage."

Mattie smiled. "And now that I know where the ridge is, next to the camp, I'll make sure I don't slide down it this time."

"And make my job as a guide easy? Boring!"

* * *

"I wish we could have got the lot." Nick had taken his headphones off and was adding data to an Excel spreadsheet he'd built to harvest key details.

"On reflection, so do I, but it was better than getting busted – for now. What makes you say that, anyway?"

"A lot of the conversations between Dragon and her minder relate to an operation they've discussed previously. They only refer to it by its code name. And they only mention Rob Walker later."

"That's a surprise. I thought Rob Walker *was* the operation."

"No, I don't think so." Nick shook his head to emphasise his point. "Rob Walker was picked up by the Chinese because he has the right tech profile, but not only because of that."

"Is that what Dragon says?"

Nick nodded. "It's clear. She calls Rob the carrier of the ultimate data Dragon wants to send the west."

"Are you maybe splitting hairs here? She might have meant techno-logical advancement and used data as a shortcut word."

"She's very precise when she speaks, and the difference between data and tech development would not have escaped her."

"OK." Harris grabbed a chair, dragged it over to Nick's desk and straddled it. "Enlighten me, just the way you would a ten-year-old."

"Some ten-year-olds are pretty geeky."

"I know you were that type of kid. Me, I was more the sort that avoided gang fights or getting clobbered by the police for driving my bike on the wrong side of the road."

"Different places, different fights." Nick shrugged.

"I suppose... It's not easy to be a genius," Harris said, with sympathy, "to be different."

"That's the beauty of being a spook – no one cares as long as you can do the job."

Harris grinned. "Yep, and you can."

Nick clicked on the cells he had highlighted on his spreadsheet. "Well then, do you know anything about neural networks?"

Harris raised his eyebrows. "Should I?"

"Perhaps not – very few people do. Think of how your brain functions, through biological neurons that signal one another. Artificial neural networks mimic that behaviour."

"So, these networks do what – speech and face recognition, image analysis?"

Nick looked impressed. "Yes, exactly, and the tech is used in autonomous robots and aircraft, in particular."

"And yet I haven't heard it mentioned in the wider public."

"It's a bit of a specialised area. The tech makes driverless cars possible, for example. But for us, what matters is that ANNs are capable of learning from what they observe, and can evolve."

Harris frowned. "I guess that's what artificial intelligence is all about?"

"True, but there are many ways to construct AI. ANNs are just one of them. I read an article about it in one of my mags. Really interesting," Nick mused.

"But what has Walker designed that is so amazing, then?"

"Sorry... I should have said. He's found a way to train his ANNs to recognise when a system is being hacked and know how to defend against it."

"So, Rob Walker has found a way to make hacking impossible, then?"

"Not exactly... ANNs of that calibre require a vast amount of computer memory and data storage."

Harris pursed his lips. "In short, it's a great idea but it can't be implemented..."

Nick smiled. "Nope. The genius is in the way Rob has designed the ANNs. He uses nanodevices and processes to improve the AI's training. Man, I'm envious."

Harris gave Nick a blank look.

Nick's smile broadened.. "Sorry, I get all worked up over this stuff... This machine learning stuff can be very powerful if applied to armaments such as autonomous aircraft, missiles or even satellites."

Harris nodded, getting it. "And eighty percent of these nanodevices come out of Taiwan."

He could see why China would want to monopolise the technology, or at least stop it being used by the US Army. Kidnapping the man who designed that technology might have seemed far-fetched before, but Harris wondered how many other countries or rogue organisations would have done the same had they known who Rob Walker was.

"But surely, Rob must have locked his technology someplace other than in his head and worked with a team." Harris checked his mobile. No calls. He put it in his pocket.

"It requires a team effort to build something like that, agreed, but depending on the state of development, he could still be holding a lot of the developmental ideas in his cyber head."

"You mean he's done some development but not shared it yet?"

Nick nodded. He stood up, moved to the table behind him and grabbed a bottle of water. "I have to say, I find that strange. If you want to get this tech guy to produce, you don't lock him up in a prison camp."

"You lock him in a lab, with lots of tech gadgets he can't resist?" Harris agreed.

"Exactly. That would be more tempting and at the end, whoever is after his tech would need him to tell him what next to develop. Very few can verify the accuracy."

"In short he could string them along without them knowing."

"I think so." Nick took a gulp of water.

"On the other hand, torture is an effective way of getting someone to talk. Although again Rob could tell them a fib and they wouldn't be any the wiser."

Nick nodded. "And it would take a while before they realise."

"OK, keep going." Harris stood up. "I need to think about this a bit more and I need to call the Chief."

He moved to his bedroom and changed into an old pair of shorts and a T-shirt that had seen better days. Harris had taken up running to fight off his cigarette addiction and he hoped that a good run now would prevent him from attacking a new pack. He put on his running shoes, told Nick he was off and left the safe house after a short warm-up.

Harris started slowly and decided to follow the road next to the small food market. He didn't want to smoke Nick to death, but the company of a cigarette usually helped him to think. A good run might be an alternative and one that might at least do his health some good.

Harris came to a set of traffic lights and jogged on the spot whilst waiting for the light to turn green. He kept returning to what Nick had uncovered and it still gave him pause for thought.

This was no longer purely a rescue mission. Rob Walker certainly needed to be extracted from Zhaga, but not only for the knowledge he had about tech and for the research he was conducting, or the tech tools he was developing. Harris was convinced Rob had access to intelligence that outweighed his tech expertise. What could be more valuable than a technology that made weapons technology impossible to hack?

Harris crossed the street and cleared his mind to find his rhythm. He would return to this thought a little later. The area in which the safe house was located was a mix of residential and small office buildings, a mix of more traditional constructions and modern buildings.

Harris noticed that since cutting back on his cigarette consumption, his lungs were doing a decent job of keeping up with his pace. He turned into a smaller street, the likes of which were common in East Asia; lots of stalls selling street food that smelt delicious; residential houses, the ground floor of which had been turned into shops, were gathered around inner courtyards that provided a community hub for the people living in the area.

Harris's mind had quietened to a low buzz and his breathing was now in rhythm with his running. He glanced at his watch. He'd been running for fifteen minutes. He would keep going for another ten before he made his way back.

The small food market near the safe house was straight in front of him. Even in the middle of the afternoon the place was busy. Harris decided to avoid the flow of shoppers and banked left towards a larger street that led to the main road.

He was stopped by another set of traffic lights. He jogged on the spot again and scanned his surroundings. Nothing looked suspicious but Harris couldn't shake the feeling that someone was following him.

Harris crossed the street as soon as the lights turned green; he retraced his steps on the other side of the street and decided to risk crossing against oncoming traffic. A couple of cars beeped in protest but Harris ignored them. He increased his speed to reach the food market again.

Unlike on the way in, he dived into the crowd and kept running. It was hard to avoid people and Harris almost bumped into a young couple. He muttered an apology and kept moving towards the centre of the market. There he turned right and right again, into a small alley. Harris found himself in the lane he'd left a few moments ago and caught sight of a man wearing a familiar cap turning the corner.

"Got you."

Harris sped up to lose the man who was tailing him. He turned into some smaller lanes and was convinced he'd succeeded in shaking the shadow off until someone's meaty hand stopped him in his tracks.

"Hey, Harris. How long does it take for an English spook to find out he's being followed?" Rodriguez whispered as he stood in front of Harris.

Harris couldn't hide his surprise and Rodriguez didn't leave him time to ask why he was following at all.

Rodriguez said, "Let's do a bit of running together."

Harris followed him and they jogged out of the market. He came to Rodriguez's side. "It's a new assassination method of yours: find a really unhealthy target and run with him 'til he drops?"

"No, I want to keep you alive because I've been thinking about the spot of bother you and H are in."

"I'm listening."

"We are about to receive our marching orders back to the US."

Harris faked surprise.

"But the team and I may decide on a holiday..."

Harris smiled. "I hear autumn is rather pleasant in Taiwan."

"And it's the perfect season to visit the Gobi Desert in Mongolia, too." Rodriguez nodded, still looking ahead.

"Let me see whether I can get you some tickets." Harris thought about slapping Rodriguez on the back, but he wasn't sure he could handle the return compliment.

*　*　*

Both exercise yards were occupied by inmates. Henry's group had been allowed into the first one after dinner but some of the Macau gang had exited the factory early and they'd been allowed to exercise in the pen next door.

Unsurprisingly Henry's challenger was there. He'd set up court next to the mesh wire that separated the two areas. His own gang was around him and the man who acted as his coach was taking his role seriously.

The challenger wolf-whistled at Henry, but Henry didn't acknowledge the taunt.

"Still happy to be my coach?" Henry asked Rob, as he was taking in the posturing of the gang men.

"Fine by me, although I doubt you're going to listen to any advice I have for you." Rob smiled.

"You never know, I might surprise you."

"I've seen a few of these so-called challenges since I've been here."

One of the volleyball balls rolled close to Henry. He started playing with it.

Rob nodded. "The winner and loser are chosen in advance."

Bo appeared at Henry's side. "Rob's right. People gamble of course, but the game is rigged before it starts."

"Just like in real life – how boring. And I thought we were going to have a fair competition in the middle of this prison camp that seeks to reform characters?"

Rob shook his head. "I said you wouldn't listen."

"Why come with me and risk being caught, then?"

"Because time is running out and I've got to escape."

"Bo, still happy to be my interpreter?"

Bo nodded. "I said I would."

"There is room for one more, Bo. Three is a good number in China."

"You've said and I appreciate it, but I've got family in Hong Kong still..." Bo's voice trailed off and Henry knew he was torn. "You've just got to make it look as though I'm being dragged out against my will."

"You can change your mind right up to the last minute." Henry waited a moment to see whether Bo might waver, but he didn't. "Whatever you decide, I'll tell you both what I have in mind at breakfast."

Henry turned towards the volleyball pit. No one was playing. The inmates' attention seemed to be focused on Henry. "Let's play." Henry moved into the pit and a few inmates volunteered to join. "Are they frightened they'll be associated with a loser?"

"Something like that." Bo moved to Henry's left.

"What are the odds against me?"

"Three to one..."

Henry grinned. "As much as that?"

Others joined and Henry moved to the back to open the match with a wrist serve. The ball flew over the net at a difficult angle and the opposite team moaned when they missed it.

Henry was a little kinder with his next serve and the ball was returned. Henry moved in for a savage slam that cleared the ball over the net at speed and landed on the other side.

"Is this the tone of the game?" Rob asked, wiping sweat from his face.

"No... it's the tone of the next fight."

Rob nodded in understanding. A lot of posturing told the opposition in the exercise yard next door that he was not scared. Rob moved to the back of the pit to deliver a serve of his own that didn't disappoint.

After a couple of games, the other team threw their hands up in defeat.

Henry gave Rob a fist bump. "My question still stands," Henry said as they were walking towards the tap to get water. "What is it that you need to get out so urgently?"

Rob ran the bottom of his shirt over his face to wipe the sweat again and murmured whilst the material was hiding his face. "The Chinese army is preparing to move and I can access intel on how they plan to do so."

CHAPTER TWENTY-THREE

"How many blankets have you got?" Mattie had the window of the passenger seat rolled down and was firing her camera at the broader landscape that surrounded them.

"Four. Thermal blankets pack nicely and are really handy."

"Although you never thought you might be using one over the bonnet of your car to hide its heat signature?"

"I'm known to be a resourceful kinda guy." Genghis gave Mattie his best Khan-the-conqueror grin.

"So, Mr Resourceful Man, how long have we got this time?"

"I looked at the map of the area I brought with me, and spotted another hill. It's a little nearer the desert but it should give us a better view of the camp. Perhaps even a look over the walls."

Mattie stopped her incessant photo-taking and turned towards Genghis with a frown. "I wasn't able to locate the camp on Google maps. How did you manage?"

"Who says I used Google maps? I'm trying to keep the use of my smart phone to a minimum."

"Come on, then, how?"

"I bought a set of old maps of Mongolia and Inner Mongolia a few years ago. People don't want them because they think they're unreliable. But it's crap; the land doesn't change that quickly here." Genghis swept his hand over the horizon. "It's taken millions of years to make this, so an old map is still very reliable."

Mattie gave Genghis a teasing look. "You are a resourceful kinda guy!"

"I hope you will still share my views when I tell you we have until 8pm. After that we need to be on our way."

"Even with the cool trick of the thermal blanket?"

"Yeah, we need an hour to get back and hide the car safely."

Mattie checked her watch. That gave her an hour around the camp, and she knew she could do a lot in that hour.

They dumped the car near a ridge that gave the vehicle some protection and made it look like a part of the landscape. They walked the rest of the way to the small hill that Genghis had seen on his old map. It was not as close to the camp as they had been the night before, but the extra elevation gave Mattie a better view beyond the walls.

The buzzing sound of a drone stopped them before they reached the top of the hill. They hid underneath a thermal blanket each and waited for the noise to disappear.

"Let's go," Genghis said when the noise disappeared. He crouched before he stood. "It's almost 7pm. We should see some activity in the camp."

Mattie felt a slight prickle in her hands, a mix of anxiety and excitement that often manifested when she was about to make a major discovery.

Genghis stopped a few yards before the top. He dropped on his belly and slithered to the peak. He nodded and Mattie dropped on her belly also. This time she would take care to secure her position before shooting photos.

She settled her camera next to her, slid her rucksack off her back and took the binoculars out. The hilltop provided her with a better angle to see the shape of the buildings. There was a large factory and Mattie guessed it was where the pieces for the aircraft carrier had been cast.

She spotted a long and thin building immediately in front of the foundry and then rows of smaller buildings that she guessed must be the dorms. Between the long building and the dorms, she saw a couple of exercise yards that looked as though they were being used.

Between the main entrance and the dorms was a building a little taller than all the rest. There was a bridge that communicated with one of the dorms.

Finally, her eyes fell on a couple of squat constructions between the entrance and the tallest building and Mattie knew from experience what those places were. She felt a familiar pang in her stomach that she hadn't for a while. The days of her kidnapping in Syria were in the past but the fear the experience still elicited would take time to disappear.

"More prisoners are arriving," Genghis murmured, surveying the site and the activity of the guards with his binoculars.

Mattie moved her own binoculars back to the two exercise pens. One of them was now full and the second one was welcoming new inmates.

She switched her binoculars for her camera and started taking photos, of the men in the yards, the walls of the camp, the buildings. She returned her camera to the prisoners just as the second pen filled up.

There was something different about the energy of the two groups. The first lot looked calmer, people who didn't seem to manifest their anger at being incarcerated through challenge and scuffles. They weren't subdued either; there were friendly exchanges between them.

The second lot were more aggressive. As the newest inmates entered the other yard, they started shouting and pushing each other around, some of it playful, but a lot of it violent – a show of power and dominance to secure a pecking order.

A small group of men approached the mesh wire that separated the two enclosures. Mattie guessed they were calling some of the prisoners to the divide.

A tall man who didn't look Asian took a few steps towards the fence and then turned around, ignoring them.

Mattie stopped for an instant to adjust her camera. She hadn't anticipated there would be any westerners at the camp; she needed the shots to prove it. She zoomed in to get better photos of the tall man.

The same anxiety she'd felt a moment ago returned. She pushed it away to concentrate on the people in the yard. The man turned fully towards her this time, and she could almost make out his face.

He was walking away from the fence towards a volleyball pit. There was something assured and attractive about the way he moved. Mattie felt like she knew him, but it was impossible.

She watched him head to the back of the pit and deliver his first serve. It was focused, uncompromising and lethal, dispatched by someone who knew what it took to challenge and win, by someone who was a fighter, by someone she now recognised.

Mattie let out a cry and dropped her camera. She closed her eyes so tight they hurt. She muffled another cry with her hand and willed herself not to shake.

"What is it?" Genghis slid closer to her.

She shook her head, not able to speak.

Genghis brought his own binoculars to his eyes and scanned the camp. "Have they killed someone?"

Mattie shook her head again and rolled onto her back, cradling her camera to her chest. "I know... one of the prisoners," she managed after a moment.

"What? Are you sure?" Genghis moved his binoculars up and down, then stopped and focused on a point.

"Westerner..." Mattie's voice croaked.

"Which one? There are two of them."

Mattie's mind was in turmoil. Old memories of her kidnapping in Syria fought to resurface. Fragments of conversations with the enslaved women she'd met reminded her of the savagery of the men who'd held them. But above all, she remembered the man who had risked his own infiltration into the heartland of Islamic State to help her escape, and yet she didn't even know Henry's real name.

"Mattie... Mattie!" Genghis sounded worried. He shook her shoulder gently. "Are you OK?"

"Yes... I'm fine. It's impossible and yet –" Mattie rolled onto her side and faced Genghis. She recalled what he'd said. "You said there were two westerners?"

"Yes, two playing volleyball."

She hesitated, picked up her binoculars and checked.

Genghis returned to his own glasses and nodded. "Two of them, and they are quite good, too!"

Mattie mustered the courage to check for herself. She adjusted the binoculars one more time and the sight of Henry caged behind the walls of the camp took her breath away. "The man serving the ball, I know."

"And what about the other guy?" Genghis asked.

"No idea."

It took all her willpower to keep still and take photos. She snapped as many shots as she could of the buildings and the landscape around them, returning regularly to the exercise grounds where Henry was playing.

Genghis looked at his watch. "We should get moving." He showed it to Mattie.

"I'd like to see what happens next."

"They're going to be sent back to their dorms."

She disagreed. "Something is going on between these two groups and the man I know is somehow involved."

"How can you tell?"

"Some of the prisoners were calling him and he ignored them, very obviously."

Genghis scanned the two exercise pens again. "It's true that a lot of the prisoners have gathered to watch the match."

"If Henry is here, it's for a reason." Mattie kept firing shots at the camp with her camera.

"His team is winning, by the way." Genghis appeared interested in the match.

"I'm not surprised. He is that sort of guy. Likes to win."

While Henry was displaying his best serves and ball slams, Mattie kept firing with her camera. The match stopped and the other team declared defeat. It all looked amicable but the prisoners on the other side of the fence seemed to think otherwise.

Some of them were shouting and even at a distance, Mattie could hear the clamour. Some were now shaking the mesh wire that separated the two yards. The other inmates did their best to ignore the riot as they formed a line to leave the exercise enclosure.

Mattie focused on Henry. He looked relaxed, not moving to acknowledge the havoc his team had created. He would be last to leave the pen and he was taking his time.

One of the prisoners started climbing the fence and the yelling raised an octave.

The crack of a rifle firing and the fall of a body to the ground seemed to remind everyone that this was a high security prison not a sports stadium. Silence descended over the yards; some inmates weren't ready to submit, but the sound of a second gun discharged convinced them.

The first pen was now empty, and the line of prisoners was slowly disappearing into one of the buildings.

Mattie followed Henry until he too disappeared. He hadn't even shown surprise at the incident. He was working on a plan.

* * *

The moon was still bright when Henry woke up. He had never needed an alarm in the morning when he was working in banking, and today was just the same. He had planned to wake up at 11pm and by the angle of the moon in the sky it was exactly that time.

Henry drew the lock-picking kit out of his shoe, making sure that the SIM card and the one sleeping pill he had left remained well-hidden.

He had used one of the pills on the guards on the nightshift. Henry had taken advantage of their routine.

Each night they'd make strong tea which they'd start drinking as soon as their shift started. They were usually vigilant with the first inmates that came in but not so much with the last few, eager to start watching a film on their smartphone whilst occasionally checking the surveillance monitors. A little commotion towards the back of the line had distracted them enough and allowed Henry to drop the drug in their tea.

Bo had pretended to feel unwell. The guards had showed their sympathy by using their batons. The first guard started to prod then ram the baton into Bo's back; when he hadn't got up the second guard joined in. It had given Henry just enough time to leave the line, move in two long steps to the guards' small room and drop the drug into their drink.

Rob, who'd been in front of Henry, had slowed down to give him a little more time and cover.

Bo had stood up after a couple of minutes and started hobbling to his cell. A bad beating for a letter delivery to his family in Hong Kong... This was an expensive price to pay.

Now, Henry stood at the door to his cell, listening for signs of activity outside. He fingered the lock in the dark to find the best angle of attack. The lock-picking kit was good and might open doors other than to the cells. He tested a couple of picks before choosing one and slowly proceeded to lift the pin of the lock. It gave way in one loud click.

Henry held his breath for a few seconds and pushed the door open. He placed a small stone from the yard into the latch bolt space to prevent the door from closing again and he walked a few paces along the corridor. If the sleeping pill hadn't worked, he was now in full view of the guards.

There was no point waiting. He needed to know if the men were asleep. Henry reached the larger door that led to the entrance hallway. There was complete silence and Henry felt a surge of hope.

He used the pick again to release the bolt on the next door and moved quickly to the guards' room. Both men were sound asleep; one had collapsed on the table face down. The other must have tried to check the monitors when the drug sent him to sleep. His head was at a strange angle, his mouth open with a little drool dripping from its side.

Henry shook the man on the table gently – no reaction. He removed the guard's jacket and put it on. It was a little tight but he only needed to look credible from afar. He took the baton and the gun still in its holder and fastened both around his waist. The keys to the outside steel door were hanging on a hook on a board in the guards' room. Henry grabbed the set and moved to the steel entrance door.

Now the hard work was starting.

The door opened without a sound and Henry left it ajar, waiting to hear the first round of guards with their dogs. Bo had told him the guards moved around every fifteen minutes, so he estimated he had less than ten minutes to reach the factory.

Henry counted for a couple of minutes and left the building, following the wall and turning to the left while the guards went right. He moved against the walls of the dorms. Stopping and starting, he listened for sounds. He remembered that not everyone in the camp was asleep at night and that Warden Tang may have decided to interrogate an inmate to alleviate his boredom.

The most open part of the journey was the walk along the edge of the exercise yards.

Henry dropped to the ground and started crawling alongside the pens. He was counting the seconds in his mind and had now reached six minutes to get to that point. Standing, Henry moved quickly along the outside wall of the canteen. There was another yard to cross to reach the factory, this one much smaller.

If he crawled again, he might be too slow to make it. Henry looked around and in the direction of the surveillance towers. There was no light shining his way and the floodlights, moving rhythmically, hadn't yet reached the yard. He bent and moved forward in an awkward run. With a couple of minutes to spare Henry reached the factory's entrance.

There was no door or lock to pick, and Henry walked cautiously into the pit. He had never been down there before, only seeing it from above.

Henry had spotted a few surveillance cameras but hoped that those would only be used during the day rather than at night. He moved farther in, skirting the walls again and passed into the part of the pit that was a mystery still to him. It was the space that received the finished pieces of steel and where those same pieces were loaded to be transported to the assembly site.

The vast hangar was almost empty. A few crates had been stacked ready for delivery. Bo had assured Henry that those crates were why some of the gang men would be heading out to the aircraft carrier the next day. Their role was to help with the finishing touches and to test some of the equipment installed on the site, making it ready for use.

Henry moved slowly towards the stack of crates. He reached it and tried to read the words on each box. If he was going to leave a loaded gun in one of them, he needed to recognise which one and fast when the time came.

A faint noise stopped his search. He looked around and dived into a recess in the wall. The noise grew louder until the sound of voices speaking in a low tone announced that two men were coming.

Henry recognised the bulky body of his challenger. The other man was one of the guards, but he couldn't make out which one in the darkness. They moved fast and with confidence to the crates, opened one that had been set aside and placed some items into it. Henry couldn't see what. They exchanged a few words and moved out as quickly as they had come.

Henry waited a short moment, then rushed over to the check what the men had dropped in the crate. He smiled at his discovery. A handgun was sitting on top of electronic devices.

He wasn't the only one who was preparing to play dirty, but in his case luck had favoured him – and quite right too. He didn't have a guard helping him to access the building.

Henry removed the gun, checked that it was loaded and chose another crate, one with a sign in Mandarin that said RADIO EQUIPMENT.

He wouldn't need to relieve the guard of his gun after all. He'd weighed the risk that a missing gun would trigger a lockdown and a full search, as well as result in the fight he was relying on to escape being cancelled. But now, he could rely on the one the challenger had unwittingly let him have.

Henry took a few more moments to check the radio equipment and realised it too could be used to his advantage. This was an unexpected bonus.

He rushed back to the entrance of the factory. He stopped to check whether he could see the two men, but they had already disappeared beyond the canteen's walls.

Still, with an inmate out in the open the dogs would be restless, yet the guards might assume Henry was only one of the gang men and keep their dogs calm.

Henry took his chance.

Stooped over, Henry half ran to the canteen's wall without a problem. He followed it and came to the exercise yard. The challenger and the guard were just about to disappear inside one of the dorms. Their route meant Henry had to make a detour, but he thought it worth taking the longer way back. This time he wouldn't need to crawl on his belly.

As steadily as he could, he walked across the empty space. He had almost reached the shadow of the dorms when a dog barking made him freeze. Henry listened for a couple of seconds. It was coming from behind him.

The bark turned more vicious; any moment the guard would release his dog.

Henry started running towards his building, trying to keep to the shadows of the other dorms. The guard was now shouting something Henry couldn't understand, perhaps checking where the gang man and guard were.

There was no response and the fevered barking that followed told Henry that the dog had been released. Henry accelerated, reached the door of his building and opened the steel door frantically. He shut it as softly as he could.

Removing the guard's jacket, he walked back into the guards' room. He left the jacket on the chair next to the sleeping men. Henry placed the holster with the baton and the borrowed gun on top of it. Next, he threw the guard's tea down the small sink. He did not have time to rinse the teapot. It would have to do.

The dog was lunging at the door to his dorm. His master would arrive at any moment and call the guards to access the building.

Henry replaced the set of keys on the board and moved to the CCTV camera control panel.

The crackling of the guards' walkie talkies made him almost lose his nerve. He clenched his jaw and rewound the tape of the camera that had been tracking his moves. He erased the clip and paused the camera, delaying the recording by three minutes. Someone was now banging on the door and the guard that had collapsed on the table began to stir.

Henry ran to the inner door. He didn't have time to use the pick to relock it. The banging on the door became louder and soon it would wake up the inmates.

Henry reached his cell. The pebble had kept the door open. He clawed the stone out, closed the door behind him and used the pick to lock his door properly.

Someone must have finally opened the entrance door because Henry could hear loud voices in the dorm's hallway.

Henry replaced the lock-picking tools in his shoe and lay on his bed, heart pounding. A few minutes elapsed; they turned into fifteen minutes and then an hour.

Henry smiled in the dark. A gun was waiting for him ahead of his fight and escape.

CHAPTER TWENTY-FOUR

The drive back to their camp had almost been in silence. As soon as they had reached the SUV, Mattie had sunk into an unusual stillness. Perhaps this time she had overestimated her ability to control a difficult and risky situation.

The irony of her thought didn't escape her. Her father would have been delighted to remind her that the last time she'd made a similar mistake she had ended up in the hands of Islamic State fighters. She hadn't told the Right Honourable Harold Colmore MP much about her rescue and nothing about the man who had saved her.

Mattie started scrolling through the dozens of photos on her camera. Seeing Henry in the yard amongst inmates she suspected were political prisoners or dissidents had deeply shaken her. But she had also witnessed what Henry was capable of and by his demeanour, she believed he was there because he had chosen to be.

She stopped on a picture of Henry leaving the volleyball pitch. His face was to the camera. He had turned to speak to someone else behind him. She couldn't help but smile at the memory of seeing his clean-shaven face for the first time when they'd both reached safety and were waiting for a transfer from the Akrotiri military base in Cyprus.

She had been going back to London and had no idea where Henry was being transferred to. The few spare hours they had spent in each other's company had been wonderful; Mattie's smile broadened at the memory. There had been no expectation or words about tomorrow. Mattie's smile softened. She had regretted their parting and she thought he had too.

Genghis was unusually quiet, only making a comment as they were approaching their camp.

"I'll make some dinner," he said.

Mattie pulled herself from her reverie. "And I need to make a call."

"I thought we agreed to only make calls when absolutely necessary?" Genghis's harsh tone wasn't very convincing.

Mattie shook her head. "This is an emergency. Han owes me an explanation and I'm jolly well going to have it. Otherwise, we are packing up and going back to Ulaanbaatar." Mattie wasn't prepared to leave Henry behind, but no one knew enough about their connection to guess as much.

"You need to head to the top of the hill where –"

"– we relieve ourselves. I'm aware."

Mattie wasn't an idiot and Genghis might as well know she knew he'd been speaking to Han on the sly. She picked up her mobile, slotted the SIM card back in and, as soon as the car stopped, started to move uphill.

She progressed quickly to a place where she managed to receive a signal. It wasn't very strong, but she would be in the open if she progressed any farther. At least she had the advantage of being protected by a few large rocks.

She dialled Han's latest burner phone and waited only a couple of rings before he picked up. "Don't tell me you are surprised to hear from me? I don't want to stay long on this call, so I'll get straight to the point. Why am I in China and who sent me?"

"What's happened?" Han sounded surprised and a little less distant than usual.

"Answering a question by asking a question is not going to work. Just give me a straight answer."

"It's not as easy as –"

"Fine, you need to get your cues from your master – I get it. I'm calling back in one hour and if I don't like the answer, we'll be back in Mongolia tomorrow." Mattie killed the call; the rush of adrenaline made her fingers tingle. "Fuck... who do these guys think they are?"

She rushed down the mountain and reached the part of the camp where Genghis was making dinner. He'd plugged an electrical ring to a solar battery. Genghis looked at Mattie but didn't ask any questions.

240

"I'll call back after we've had something to eat," she said.

"I made soup. Out of a can. I'm sorry, but we still have some cheese and some flatbread."

Mattie sat cross-legged on the ground. Genghis handed her a bowl and she helped herself to soup. She finished her food and nodded her thank you. "And I'm sorry I dragged you into this." Mattie helped herself to some bread and cheese. "I know that Han chose you because you're a little more than just a guide but I'm not sure he told you how dangerous this journey could become."

"Han never quite tells me the whole story." Genghis sat down on the ground as well. "He assumes I'll go along with most of his crazy ideas."

"Aren't you annoyed with him?"

"Not really. I like to improvise." Genghis grinned. "And I know I can say no whenever I feel like it, despite what Han thinks."

"Did he talk about a camp then?"

"No. I told you before he only mentioned that things could be a bit more complicated than we'd planned."

Mattie gave Genghis a hard look. She wasn't completely convinced by his answer yet but Genghis was the resourceful type and had been honest so far. Perhaps it would be OK; spending time with smugglers had taught him a thing or two.

She had just accepted a cup of tea when her phone pinged. Someone was trying to get through. She grabbed her mug and moved up the hill again to get better reception.

The caller's number wasn't Han's, and she didn't recognise the prefix either. It wasn't China and it wasn't South Korea.

She took a deep breath and braced herself for what could be an uncomfortable conversation. She wouldn't be played and yet, how could she walk away from the man who saved her life.

"Whoever this little bastard is, he knows it," she murmured. Mattie pressed the recall button and waited for someone to pick up.

"Good evening, Ms Brook."

Mattie hadn't expected to be called by her pen name. She took a moment to respond. The man sounded English, with a slight East End accent that made him a Londoner.

"Who are you and what do you want from me?" she demanded.

"By now I think we probably want the same thing, to help a friend who is in trouble."

"You still haven't told me who you are, and I'm not budging until you do."

"The only thing you need to know is that I'm here to facilitate."

"Not good enough."

"I'm afraid it will have to do. And before you tell me I'm being unduly difficult let me simply add, it is for your protection as well as the young man's who is with you that you do not know."

"You lead me to a place in the middle of the desert in China no less. I discover a high security prison camp tasked with building a perfect replica of a US aircraft carrier. I also spot that someone –" Mattie almost faltered "– that someone who saved me from IS is being held prisoner there and you're telling me you are looking after my interests?" Mattie couldn't disguise her anger.

"I didn't say that exactly. I said the less you know about who's behind this operation the better. Your story that you're a journalist writing an article on the Mongol tribes of China is still credible."

"Not if I get involved in your operation."

"Who says I want you involved? I'm after intelligence of what is happening to our common friend."

"What sort of intelligence?"

"I assume you've seen him otherwise you wouldn't be calling, so as much detail of what you saw would be helpful."

"And then?"

"Depending on what you tell me this might be enough."

Mattie was taken aback by the apparent simplicity of the request. This couldn't be the whole story. "I don't believe you. I'm the only eyes you have on this op? What sort of shambolic arrangement is that?"

There was a little intake of breath and Mattie was satisfied to have unsettled her caller a little. "I'm afraid the business we are in is a risky one," the man said. "Not everything always goes to plan."

"Let's assume I tell you all I have seen. You are telling me this is it, that I don't need to be doing more?"

"Again, it will depend on what it is you tell me."

Mattie inwardly cursed. She didn't want to be simply relaying the information she had gathered, she wanted in. "You know I can't just leave this place without knowing –"

"– our common friend is safe?" The man had spared her asking to become involved. "Of course – and quite frankly, I was hoping you might say that – we also have to consider the possibility that our common friend may not accept it."

She hadn't thought about the possibility Henry may not want to see her again or want her involved in any of his work.

"Well then, what?" she asked.

"I need to know what you know, all the details of what you've witnessed in the past twenty-four hours, then I'll tell you how you can help."

The man sounded genuine, and she had little option but to tell him what she'd seen. Even if she left China and got to the British Embassy in Ulaanbaatar, there would be denial Henry was where he was, and any mention of her sighting would probably endanger his life rather than save it.

"This is what I have seen, and I have photos to back it up."

Mattie sat down on a flat rock and told MI6 her story.

* * *

Rodriguez and Fergus were already at the Hot Pot restaurant and bar along the edge of the Tamsui River when Harris arrived. Harris had spotted the Hot Pot along the Zhongzheng Road on one of his previous safe house recces. It was close to the mouth of the river and off the main road, away from their current safe house.

Harris had suggested they discuss what plan B would look like – if there was going to be a plan B. Rodriguez's performance at the food market had irritated Harris at first, but he was grateful the man had taken the time to let him know the ALPHA team were being recalled to the US.

As soon as he spotted Harris, Rodriguez stood up and ordered a beer at the counter. He handed one to Harris.

They clinked bottles and Harris settled down before recapping. "When are you officially leaving?"

"Tomorrow night," Rodriguez said with a frown. "We've had zero intel from the CIA, by the way, nothing."

"I guess Hunter is going to ask for a fresh team to be used if he needs it." Fergus took a swig of beer.

"He knows his op is unravelling but he can't own up to it." Rodriguez's eyes darkened and Harris felt unease at his admission.

"I think you're right." Harris took a long pull of beer. "But I've managed to get eyes on the camp where H and the other man are being kept."

Rodriguez slapped his back and Fergus gave Harris a fist bump. It was all good stuff amongst brothers in arms and Harris almost felt part of the team.

"I'd say H is mounting an escape in the next couple of days. We've had one call from him, just long enough to give us a timeframe and a sighting that tells me he is getting ready."

Rodriguez leaned forward. "What will he do next?"

"As soon as he has escaped, follow the original plan, get more inland, rather than attempt to cross the border with Mongolia. There is not enough time to cross and then be picked up, as you know. The Chinese won't be stopped by a border, a line that is arbitrary as far as they are concerned. They'll send search parties to get them back, so the idea is to cross the border with Mongolia where it's the most difficult."

"Is the guy travelling with him trained?"

"No, but he is a keen mountaineer."

Fergus shook his head. "The desert is a completely different animal."

Harris agreed. "I know and that's where they will need some help."

"I'm still pissed at the thought we weren't told about this plan." Rodriguez finished his beer in one long pull. "No point in recriminations, though. Let's do what we weren't meant to do –" Rodriguez smiled "–but what we should have been asked to do and get these guys out of China."

"To state the obvious." Harris stood up to buy a second round of beers at the counter. "Officially, you won't be anywhere near Mongolia."

Rodriguez and Fergus exchanged a *we know* look and Harris shook his head. "Why am I trying to tell grandma how to suck eggs?"

Rodriguez crossed his thick arms over his chest. "Just tell me where you need the ALPHA team to be and leave the logistics to my guys. I want to get H out of this mess just so we can have a good solid chat about him going off the plan."

"Don't damage him too much, will you? He's one of my best operatives." Harris joked, half serious.

"I'll think about it."

Harris returned with three beers and placed them in the middle of the table. "I'll do location once we are in a more secure place, but the steps are simple. The execution will, as ever, be the tough part."

Rodriguez grunted and Harris took it to mean it was obvious.

Harris continued. "H has buried his equipment not far from the camp. He will seek to retrieve it, then move inland to the nearest city to find the motorway that runs parallel to the border, towards the west."

"Counterintuitive," Fergus said with an approving nod. "That will give H and the other guy some extra time but not much before they are spotted."

"I think H will try to escape. Whether he can secure transportation or not for the first few hours of the journey is another matter." Harris looked from one man to the other. "A car would be better of course. The escape can be done on foot but with some significant disadvantages H will have to factor in."

"You mean he won't have time to retrieve the buried equipment and will need to head for the town straight away," Rodriguez said.

"Spot on. There is a petrol station that is used by a lot of lorry drivers for food etcetera. That's where H plus one can get a ride in the direction of the town I spoke about."

Fergus nodded. "Then repeat the process with another lorry, or better still, a car, and drive down to the point, then dump the vehicle near the crossing."

Harris shook his head. "That's not going to be easy. You've seen the land. Any abandoned vehicle will look suspicious if the authorities are already on high alert, so they will need to hitch a ride along the G7 motorway."

"Assuming they do that, how long will it take?" asked Rodriguez.

"Six to seven hours."

"Then what?" Fergus swirled the untouched beer in his bottle.

"Leave the lorry as close as possible to the shortest point between the motorway and the border, then walk to the foot of the hills that cross the border with Mongolia. It should take them three hours to reach the hills."

"Then the crossing is another matter," Rodriguez said.

Harris gave a small nod. "Another matter as you would say."

Rodriguez dropped his head to his chest for a moment. Neither Harris nor Fergus interrupted, both men quietly concentrating on their beer.

"All told, to the foot of the hills should take fourteen hours if all works well, which it never does, of course." Rodriguez rested his arms on the table. "Let's assume H doesn't get a car. From what you've said, he has given you a timeframe and that means he needs out by then for whatever reason."

"I agree with you, he needs out within the next couple of days," Harris said.

Fergus raised an eyebrow. "Still, the car, is it a realistic option?"

"It's a possibility."

"Then it'll shave off a few hours, but I presume he'll want to dump the car at the first petrol station," Rodriguez added.

"H will save perhaps three hours – which is a lot when you're a fugitive."

Both Rodriguez and Fergus nodded.

"On the other hand –" Fergus was taking his time "– a suspect car that looks as if it's driving away from the place where an escape has happened is a good decoy."

"That's a good point." Harris had to admit.

"Can you suggest this to whoever might be sourcing the car?" Fergus said.

"I should be able to get the message out."

"H will know whether it's worth his while doing it." Rodriguez sounded confident enough, but it was what he did that mattered – make sure an op happened even when it was almost impossible to succeed.

"I'll need a reception team for a rendezvous at the hills to get them over the border," Harris added.

Rodriguez nodded. "I'll see how to best get the team to the Mongolian side of the border. As I said, a bit of time off for me and my guys is overdue."

Harris chuckled. "No better way to relax than a trip to the Gobi Desert and an under-the-radar op."

Fergus pushed his beer bottle to the middle of the table. "I would drink to that, but I finished my beer."

Harris glanced at his watch. "It's 10.30pm. Let me get more details of location for when we reconvene tomorrow at the safe house."

"That's a plan."

Rodriguez and Harris clicked their bottles and drank up. Time to do some organising on both sides.

Harris walked away from the harbour wondering whether he was mad for going off-piste as much as he was. He now was involving an entire team of highly respected US SEALs. It was one thing to wreck his career but another to ask others to do the same.

Harris shook his head and smiled, imagining what Rodriguez would say if he shared his concern with him. The response would be unequivocal and no doubt full of expletives.

He jumped on a crowded bus and went through a routine designed to spot any shadow following him: changing buses and retracing his steps several times.

Harris felt his mobile ping in his jacket pocket. He checked the time. It was 3.30pm in London and the Chief's PA was giving Harris a not-so-gentle reminder that he was expected to give an update.

The timing couldn't have been better. He was only five minutes from the safe house. There was not much point delaying. He just needed to gain a little more time to organise the op beyond the point of no return. Once Henry was on the run, MI6 would have no choice but to get their agent out of China and let Harris implement his plan B. Or at least that was what Harris hoped.

He walked into the flat, checked that Nick was fine. The young man was sprawled on his bed, still fully dressed, catching up on sleep.

Harris retreated to his own bedroom, sat on an old armchair and dialled the Chief's number.

"Do I need to worry, Harris?" the Chief asked after the briefest of hellos.

"Perhaps, sir. I still haven't received any news from Hunter."

"And you are telling me that you have been waiting for news, sitting on your hands like a good boy?"

"I wouldn't be a good boy if I were sitting on my hands, sir." Harris silently swore. This was not the right answer.

But it made the Chief laugh. "I guess not... So now that you've volunteered you haven't been idle, would you care to enlighten me?"

"I'm trying to find alternatives to get eyes on the camp."

"So you said earlier... Any success?" The Chief sounded a little irritated. Did he have to pull the information out of Harris the hard way?

"I have found contacts that are on their way to Inner Mongolia, through one of our operatives in Seoul," he lied.

"Is Inner Mongolia that popular?"

"No, but there are some issues regarding minorities that draw outside interest."

"And that means getting who involved?" the Chief asked. "A member of the press?"

"Possibly..." Harris was at a fork in the road; he waited for a verdict. Whether he would go with the Chief's recommendation was another matter.

"Not a bad idea. As long as the person you chose can hold their own."

Harris didn't realise he'd been holding his breath and let it go. "Goes without saying, sir."

"Excellent. When you find the lucky candidate, make sure you run that name past me."

Harris groaned. There was no peace for the wicked.

CHAPTER TWENTY-FIVE

The day dragged on. Henry had woken up before the prison bell rang. He'd done two sets of a hundred press-ups, some weightlifting using his bed, and a series of sit-ups. He'd started the routine as soon as he'd been told of the existence of the Macau gang and was glad he had.

At breakfast, he joined Rob and Bo. There was not a lot he had to add, simply that he was ready and hoped they were too. Their small group was picked up by the guards and led to the room where they gathered more useless information for the warden. Henry had nothing more to communicate to the other two men through the Excel spreadsheet. They should now remain as invisible as possible until the evening, where they would be picked up and brought to the site of the fight.

Towards the end of the afternoon, a Macau gang inmate Henry didn't know came to the engineer with a request on paper. The work had been slack as it appeared the current project was at an end, but another project was taking shape. The engineer was about to suggest some names, but the man pointed at Henry and his small team. The engineer looked surprised, but he knew better than to refuse.

As soon as the gang man had arrived, Bo turned to Henry and slid a small piece of paper towards him; it was so well folded that Henry almost missed it.

"This is the address in Hong Kong..." Bo murmured.

"Why don't you deliver it yourself?"

"Too risky for my family."

"Too risky for you if you stay."

Bo looked straight ahead, and Henry hoped he was hesitating. Staying behind was suicide.

"Too risky for them."

The engineer called their names and Rob was the first to stand up. The other two followed. They were led down the same walkway they took every day, but this time instead of walking out the gang man turned left into the pit.

The three men slowed down and the gang man turned around, shouting insults at them in Mandarin. They walked past the large steel frames that were used to cast the pieces of metal, and Henry couldn't forget how brutally one of the men had been cast into boiling water.

They walked through the pit and into the back of the factory. Henry noticed that the crates he'd seen the night before were no longer there. He hoped no one had checked their content.

Two army trucks were there, ready to depart. The gang men working on the ship had already boarded the trucks. Henry couldn't tell where the challenger was. The gang man who had collected them jerked his head towards one of the lorries.

Henry walked up to it and lifted the tarp cover. Gang members sat on benches on one side; the other bench was empty.

Five against his team. Henry didn't show any concern. The men sniggered when Henry climbed into the truck. Rob was subjected to the same treatment, but when Bo got in the insults really started pouring. Henry hesitated and Bo shook his head softly. He was right, all part of the tactic to unhinge the team.

The gang man fastened the tarp to the frame of the lorry and shouted instructions to the driver. The truck shuddered and started to move. Henry was surprised that no one had searched them before they boarded. Whether by complacency or by design, Henry couldn't tell.

The gang men started to chatter among themselves. There was no need for a translation to know who they were commenting on.

"Is that Cantonese?" Henry whispered to Bo.

"It is," Bo murmured.

"Do you understand it?"

"Most of Hong Kong speaks it."

One of the men stood up and started shouting a mix of words in English and Cantonese ... *no speaking* was the only thing Henry understood. He shrugged and stopped talking.

We'll see who doesn't speak when I get hold of the gun.

The gang man looked satisfied.

Henry leaned against the side of the truck. He turned his head slightly and glanced at Rob. The man looked anxious and yet there was a quiet determination about him.

Henry turned his attention to the journey. He tried to figure out whether they'd left the camp. He hadn't felt the lorry slow down to cross a gate. The gates to Zhaga must have been opened already.

Warden Tang was sending them out of the camp for them never to return.

Henry half closed his eyes, resting his head against the side of the truck. For the rest of the journey, he studied his opponents. The five men were lean yet muscular from working in the pit, but they weren't fast or had much coordination. Simple foot soldiers, expendable and easy to replace, as they probably would be for having witnessed the fight.

The lorry sped along a track that felt smoother than Henry expected and after what he estimated to be half an hour, the truck started to slow down.

The men's banter had quietened down during the journey but resumed now that they were approaching. A display to intimidate Henry and his team but also to make sure the men's taskmaster was satisfied when he opened the back tarp.

The lorry stopped and the sound of doors opening and banging closed told Henry that the first truck had arrived at almost the same time as theirs.

Men started shouting and the cover on Henry's vehicle was lifted in one swift gesture. Henry's challenger stood there, flanked by one of his men. The gang men in Henry's truck jumped out without being asked. They knew what their job was.

The challenger grinned. "Are you ready to fight?"

"Are you ready to fight?" Henry grinned back, replying in Mandarin.

The challenger's eyes flashed with amusement. He didn't seem to care that Henry spoke his language or that he had defeated the Grinning Man. He was there to win.

Rob and Bo jumped out of the truck before Henry and the challenger whistled to one of the men who had sat in the lorry with them. He came running and was told to take Henry's team away.

Before he jumped out, Henry tried to locate the crates, but he couldn't see any of them. He didn't want to give the impression he was looking for something. When he stepped away from the truck, he was greeted by two guards with rifles. Two more armed guards appeared from behind the first truck. Warden Tang wasn't taking any chances.

The buzz of a drone overhead confirmed what Henry suspected. Someone would be watching the fight live.

Rob and Bo had slowed down to an almost stop and Henry understood why. The trucks were only a few yards away from the stern of the aircraft carrier they had helped to build. The size and mass of the construction was astonishing.

Two of the guards took over, pushing Henry and his team along the hull. They passed underneath the second landing strip that would be devoted to helicopters and a second lot of fighter jets.

Henry stopped. He turned to Bo and Rob who did the same.

The guards hadn't expected this. They moved fast, rifles aimed at the men, giving them instructions to keep moving.

"No." Henry faced them without budging. "We are warming up here," he said in Mandarin.

Farther along the hull were the stack of crates he was looking for. Three of the gang men from their truck were stacking some of the crates near a thick metal door – an access opening to the interior of the ship.

Henry's defiance made the guards hesitate. They probably would have used the baton or perhaps killed them on the spot had there not been a fight due. They didn't want to interfere with instructions to keep Henry alive, before the fight had even begun.

One of the guards called one of the gang men over. He spoke to the man briefly. The gang man glanced at Henry and scuttled off. The challenger would be overseeing the fight's preparations, and he would decide whether to indulge Henry and his team in their choice of training ground.

Henry turned his attention to the area around the ship. There was nowhere to hide. The land had been cleared so that the approach to the ship was unencumbered. Henry could see boulders in the far distance, but he estimated they were a quarter of a mile away.

The gang men had stopped stacking the crates against the door and were now moving some of them into the open, setting out the perimeter of the ring inside which the fight would take place.

The challenger's deputy appeared, grabbed Bo by the arm, and shook him. "Why here?"

Henry shoved the man away from Bo. "It's not his decision. It's mine."

The challenger's deputy tried to grab Bo again but Henry stepped between them once more. Rob came to his side and together, the 6 foot 2 tall men made for an impressive duo.

The man spat, pointing at the extended deck over them. "Only cowards need a roof over their heads."

Henry shrugged. He didn't care. He was not relocating. He had a little freedom as a designated loser and future victim. Henry needed to use this to the full.

The deputy hesitated, swore at them again for good measure, but then left. The stack of crates had been organised as intended. Henry noticed that the men were debating among themselves over something that appeared important.

The two guards in charge of surveying Henry moved into the ring, still keeping an eye on their prisoners. One of them took his walkie talkie out and exchanged a few words. He walked around the ring and inspected the way the crates had been set up. He called back and spoke a few words again, nodding as he listened intently at what he was being told.

"Let's get you warmed up," Rob said, turning away from the scene.

Henry's mind refocused on what he needed to do to get ready.

Bo moved closer to Henry. "You know what's going to happen next?"

"To us or to them?" Henry jerked his head at the gang men who had just completed their task of assembling the ring.

Before Bo could answer the discharge of a rifle crackled in the air. The men the bullets hit didn't even make a noise. Their bodies hit the ground with a thud.

The sound of another discharge in the distance told the same story. Those who were redundant had been discarded the way a dirty cloth would.

Henry clenched his fists. He needed to get to the gun before the fight started.

* * *

"I saw him again this morning." Mattie had insisted she wanted another debrief with the man she didn't yet know was Harris. She'd agreed not to use Henry's name over the phone, and this was fine by her. It still felt odd that Henry was there, in China, and that now she was the one who could help him.

"It's got to happen either tonight or tomorrow night." Harris sounded certain and she assumed he had other intelligence to confirm that.

"We had to leave the camp an hour after we'd arrived, but I don't think there was anything to gain by staying put. Henry and the other inmates were being sent back to their dorms when we left."

"It's a good call. I presume you are using thermal crossover for part of your cover?"

Mattie nodded as though Harris could see her. "And some thermal foil blankets."

"How far are you from Zhaga?"

"Forty miles or so."

"You're within their drone range."

"That's right. But I got the impression that the drones are focused on the approach to the camp and on the site of the ship."

"Have you investigated the terrain more towards the west?" Harris asked.

"I'm a journalist, not a military scout."

"You're doing pretty well so far." Harris sounded impressed but Mattie didn't care.

"What have you got in mind?" she asked.

"There is some equipment that he may need, and the use of a car would be good."

"Is he supposed to escape on foot? With drones and Humvees chasing him across the desert?"

"He is resourceful chappie and one of the scenarios contemplates an escape on foot as you say."

254

Mattie bit her lip. She still couldn't understand why Henry was pushing himself so hard. Was Harris exploiting Henry's resourcefulness and willingness to go the extra mile?

"Getting to the equipment he buried saves time, I get that. A car is a must, but I can't see him safely attempting a crossing near to the border checkpoint I came through."

Harris stayed silent for a moment. "You understand I can't fully comment −"

"It's a bit late for that, don't you think?" Mattie interrupted angrily.

"I know you think it would be easier if you had the full picture, but trust me, I don't either. I can only tell you what I think is certain."

"So, apart from asking me to play sniffer dog and retrieve Henry's pack buried somewhere in the middle of a vast desert, what else can you tell me?"

"That a decoy would be good."

"What do you mean? We get caught so that he can walk free?" Mattie would have gladly agreed if it meant Henry could walk, but she had Genghis to worry about. He wasn't spending time in a crappy Chinese dungeon.

"You and your guide are perfectly entitled to be in Inner Mongolia," Harris said.

"But we are supposed to be moving to the west to meet with local tribes."

"Exactly right and you could even decide to cross into Mongolia again, because the tribe you wish to interview has crossed as well."

It was Mattie's time to take a moment. "I'll think about how this could work. Still, for all I know he could try to escape today or tomorrow, and I could miss him altogether."

"This is not the sort of camp you escape from by digging a tunnel with a spoon. There is no time for that, and he was clear that he would be found out if he overstayed his welcome."

"Fine, Genghis and I will get the pack and return to survey the camp tonight. When it comes to the decoy, I need to make sure my guide is safe."

"And so should you be, if you don't mind. I will not have a repeat bust-up with the Right Honourable Harold Colmore MP."

"You knew about..." Mattie's throat tightened at the thought of the failed first rescue mission to save her.

"A story for another time. Let's make sure everyone comes out of this in one piece."

"That goes without saying," Mattie grumbled.

"You'll need the approximate coordinate for the drop: 40.8073°N, 111.7052°E. Good luck," Harris added.

Mattie killed the call and removed the SIM card from her phone. She was talking too much to a man she assumed was MI6 and sooner or later her phone would likely ping on the radar of the authorities.

She returned to her bivouac. Genghis was resting, stretched out on an old sleeping bag he had laid on the ground. An old book was open on his chest, the title of which was in Mongolian.

"We've got to find a buried pack." She was not going to dither about telling Genghis what the next task was.

He opened his eyes. "Cool... Where is it?"

Mattie's eyebrows shot up. "Does anything faze you?"

Genghis scratched his chin, giving the question some thought. "No." He stood up, folded the bag and threw it into his small tent. "I'll get my bearings first with the GPS and then I'll do the rest by sight."

Mattie looked at the time. It was 4.30pm and thermal crossover was about to start. "Let's get going. I presume we're back observing the camp this evening?"

"We are taking a lot of risks, you know."

"Exactly... It's the *we* that makes me more comfortable. You're taking the risks, too."

They drove in silence. Mattie was scouring the skies in search of a drone. Genghis had turned off the GPS early on to avoid an unwanted trace. He stopped the SUV as they were approaching some more rugged terrain and got out. The softer landscape had given way to much taller hills that morphed into low mountains. Sharp ridges in the same orange hue as the lowland looked on fire.

He took his binoculars out of his rucksack and moved them around, looking for areas of disturbed dirt.

"Spot anything?" Mattie asked.

"Nothing." Genghis kept moving methodically over new ground. "Spot anything?" he teased back.

Mattie smiled. "Nothing. Brilliant result on my side, not so much so on yours."

"Don't speak too soon..." Genghis adjusted his binoculars again. "There is something farther up the hill." He returned to the SUV and drove the car up a slope that soon became steep.

Mattie moved the field of her glasses in the direction they were driving. "I see something..."

"In the sky?"

"No, on the ground." Mattie smiled. "OK, back to my drone watch. For a guy so young, you're such a stickler for rules."

"Yeah... can't help it."

Genghis stopped the car and got out. "I'll check."

Mattie was about to protest, but she still needed to watch for drones. No point in letting her guard down if there was nothing to uncover.

Genghis walked steadily towards the disturbance in the earth. Something made him slow down and finally stop.

Mattie didn't wait for his call and caught up with him. The smell of rotting flesh told her all she needed to know. They hadn't found a pack with a gun and ammo, they'd found a shallow grave and a body.

"The animals have had a go at it," Genghis said, covering his nose with his elbow and getting closer. "He's been shot dead." He pulled back and moved past Mattie to take a gulp of air.

"There was a car... Look, tyre track marks." Mattie pointed.

Genghis moved closer to inspect them. He crouched and took a moment to inspect the ground. "And some people walked around the car to another car." Genghis moved a few paces around still crouching. "Except these tracks here... Someone came on foot from that direction." He stood up and pointed in the direction they'd come from.

"But we've gone over that terrain."

"Then we have missed something."

Genghis and Mattie jumped back in the car.

"Should we do something?" Mattie asked, looking back at the remains of the dead man.

"Let nature take charge of this. Whatever we do, the animals will still finish him off."

The drive back to retrace the steps of the walker was laborious. Time was running out, and Mattie couldn't miss an evening's watch of the camp for the sake of a pack.

"Let's get to Zhaga. We can't arrive there after 7pm," Mattie insisted.

"I'm nearly there," Genghis said. "I think I spotted something. If it's not the pack, we'll go."

Genghis stopped the car and walked downhill this time. He crouched again to the ground. "It's an unusual skid mark... I don't know." Genghis looked around and stood up, then walked over to a couple of boulders farther down.

He pulled on something but stopped and let it go. "Mattie, it's a parachute."

She ran to him and fingered the material. "You're right, someone landed here."

They both looked around frantically. The pack had to be here. Mattie returned to the parachute, tearing a piece from it whilst checking what lay underneath. But she couldn't find anything.

Genghis moved across the ground methodically and shouted. "I've got something!"

He pulled a rucksack from underneath some stones in triumph. Mattie ran over to him only to see his face drop. The bag went limp and when he opened it, it was empty.

"Shit..." Mattie stamped the ground with her foot. "Shit."

They both remained still for a moment.

"Let's go," Mattie said, wiping a tear of frustration from her eyes. "We still can make a difference at Zhaga."

CHAPTER TWENTY-SIX

Henry removed his shirt and so did Rob. Rob rolled both shirts around his hands to pad them up and nodded: it would work. He started shadow boxing, walking at the same time as he moved his fists, delivering imaginary hooks to a not-so-imaginary adversary.

Henry arrived at the crates that the now dead men had lined up along the hull of the ship. He spotted the one with the writing he was looking for only two boxes away from where he was exercising.

One of the guards had sat down on the other set of crates being used for the perimeter of the ring. His eyes were on Henry, assessing his potential to win, and almost certainly deciding whether he should alter his bet.

Henry moved back to Rob and started some squats and lunges.

"You need to start warming up the larger muscle groups." Rob unravelled the shirts from his hands. Henry was not ready for a sparring game yet.

"Great idea..." Henry turned to the crates. "Why don't we use these for sit-ups?"

"Which crate are we looking for?"

"Second nearest the door."

Rob followed Henry and sat next to the box marked RADIO EQUIPMENT.

Henry lay down on the ground, the top of his head pointed at the guards. He brought his feet up so that Rob could hold them, and he started his repetitions.

Henry stopped for a short moment. "Where is Bo?"

"He's asking for water."

"Forever optimistic."

Henry went through a second round of repetitions. "The crate next to you should be open." Henry fell heavily to the ground.

Rob slid his hand around the rim of the cover and gave Henry a small nod.

He started his third round of sit-ups.

"How many guards in the ring?" Henry asked.

"Two."

"Let's wait 'til Bo is back before creating a diversion."

Henry did a series of press-ups so that he could see better what was happening in the ring. The second guard had taken a seat also. They were clearly absorbed in what Henry was doing and Henry sensed the outcome of the fight mattered to them.

The clunk of a heavy bucket stopped Henry. Bo had returned with water.

"How did you manage it?"

"The challenger and his deputy are a little preoccupied. They didn't seem to notice that I was taking water from the tank of the truck."

Henry smiled. "They've just lost an important item and they won't find out until the end of the fight." He started walking up and down the hull, doing arm and shoulder circles, making a good show of his training.

To Bo he said, "I need you to create a diversion, so that Rob can retrieve what's in one of the crates."

Bo didn't reply. He lifted the bucket and walked over to the guards, with a look of anxiety on his face. "Which corner is Henry going to sit in?"

Henry kept moving as before. Bo was in deep conversation about where he was going to set his bucket of water. Rob lifted the lid of the crate marked RADIO EQUIPMENT and stuck his hand in. Henry hoped the item would still be there. Rob pulled out the gun and let it fall to the ground. The sand muffled the noise.

One of the guards started to raise his voice at Bo.

Henry took a couple of steps towards Bo and the guards. "What is the problem?" he said in Mandarin.

"The guards say that the far corner has been reserved for your challenger. I said we should toss a coin, but they don't agree," Bo said.

Henry looked menacing enough, muscles pumped up and his torso covered in sweat. The guards tightened their grips on their rifles.

Henry shrugged. "I don't care... any corner is good for me."

The guards didn't need a translation to see he wasn't going to give them trouble. They sat down again. Bo shrugged and plonked the bucket in the corner nearest to the ship.

Henry moved back to where Rob was now standing. "Where is the gun?"

"Between the first and second crate from the door."

Henry couldn't stop a brief smile. "Are you ready?"

"Whenever you are."

Rob lifted his shirt-covered hands and Henry started throwing some punches into them. His sparring partner didn't budge as much as Henry thought he might. It was good to see that Rob's mountaineering had toughened him up.

The two guards rose to their feet and Henry and Rob knew the training session had come to an end. The buzzing sound of a drone made everyone look up at the noise.

"The radio equipment is easy to get to as well, " Rob murmured while everyone was looking up. "Give them a good spectacle and I'll jam the drone with it."

Henry rolled his head like a boxer. "Right, whatever you say, partner."

The Challenger and his deputy entered the ring and moved straight to the spot reserved for them. The other two guards that had driven the challenger's truck arrived too. One of them was putting his phone back in his pocket, after getting instructions, it seemed, to start the fight.

Henry moved slowly towards the corner he'd been given by default. The four guards were now grouped around the ring where the spectacle was taking place. Rob and Bo had agreed they would sit on the ground and be ready as soon as Henry gave them the signal. In this bare-knuckle fight, Henry needed to last long enough to execute his plan.

The Challenger removed his shirt, rolled his shoulders, and jerked his head at Henry.

"Are you ready to lose?" he shouted.

"Are *you* ready to lose?" Henry shouted back.

Both men started to move towards the centre of the ring. Without warning the Challenger sped across and lunged at Henry with a vicious right hook. Henry didn't manage to avoid the blow completely and got clipped on the side of the jaw. He moved his body sideways and delivered a left hook to the Challenger's stomach that made the man heave.

Henry took a couple of steps away, fists raised. He didn't want to attack yet, just observe. His opponent was fast, and Henry had just felt the power of his fullest blow.

Both men were now circling each other, deciding on the most opportune moment to strike. Again the Challenger moved first, sliding to the ground and delivering a low kick, aimed at Henry's knees. Henry jumped in the air to avoid being toppled but a second kick as he was landing threw him on his back. The shock almost winded him, but he managed to roll on his side, avoiding a stomach kick. Missing his aim threw the Challenger off balance and he fell, instantly rolling sideways to get back to his feet.

So far Henry hadn't engaged the Challenger, banking on the effect his weakness would have on the audience. By now Warden Tang should be a little less interested and if Henry managed to evade the Challenger for long enough he should get bored, and the drone jamming might only be seen as an annoying malfunction.

The circling resumed but this time the Challenger grew bolder. He threw a couple of well-aimed punches that caught Henry on the cheek and in the chest. Henry absorbed the shock, pulling back to a safer distance. This time the Challenger went on the attack straight away. He tried to deliver another couple of right-left hooks, but Henry evaded them easily and was able to move out of the Challenger's reach for a few rounds.

Exasperated, the Challenger lunged at Henry like a bull to a red rag and Henry let him slam into him. Both men collapsed to the ground. The Challenger tried to force Henry on his back but a head-butt stopped him. The man was dazed for a few seconds, and blood started to pour out of his nostrils. Henry delivered a couple of side blows that pushed the Challenger to one side.

The guards' attention had been rekindled. It was Rob's cue to slide away from the ringside and over to the crates. He moved fast and silently, opening the box to find the radio he needed. In the semi-darkness, Rob switched it on by touch. He hid its glow with his body and tuned into what he knew would be a jamming frequency. Rob slowly closed the lid again. He then retrieved the gun from between the crates, sliding it into the back of his waistband and returned to his place next to Bo.

The fight had taken a different turn. Both men were now bleeding from the head, Henry from a blow to the jaw and the Challenger from a fresh open wound to his brow ridge.

The guards had started to cheer now that the fight had become a lot more ferocious. The Challenger had spent a lot of energy at the beginning of the encounter and Henry sensed his focus had dropped a fraction.

Henry went on the attack with a high double kick that threw the Challenger from right to left and made him look like a rag doll for a moment. The guards clamoured and Henry stepped away to let the other man recover.

The guards had congregated as close as they could to the ring. Two of them had left their original place and moved to a spot where the stadium light made it easier to watch the fight.

The Challenger glanced at his deputy and Henry noticed him shrug. The gun was still nowhere to be found.

"So, are *you* ready to lose?" Henry shouted.

* * *

Their car was hidden at the bottom of a ridge. Genghis and Mattie had moved a few yards away from it on foot so that Genghis could scan the sky.

"Drones?"

"I see one hovering above the camp."

"We'd better wrap the thermal blanket around the bonnet of the car." Genghis nodded but didn't move.

"Anything else?" Mattie glanced at her watch. They were losing time.

"It seems to be changing course... going in the direction of the site of the aircraft carrier."

"Then we need to move..."

Genghis and Mattie returned to the car. Mattie was already unfolding the thermal blanket from the back seat. She and Genghis placed the blanket on the SUV hood and sat inside again.

While Genghis drove slowly to keep the blanket in place, Mattie started to get restless. Something was happening at the camp and she was missing out on it. When they arrived on the flats of the desert Genghis stopped the car again. He grabbed his binoculars and started scanning the horizon once more. Mattie bit her lip so as not to say something impatient.

"There are trucks on the move," Genghis said after a moment.

Mattie closed her eyes for an instant. What did it mean for Henry? "In which direction?"

"Again, I think they are going to the ship site."

"Perhaps another military guy wanting a visit?"

"I don't know."

Her stomach tightened. MI6 had said the next couple of days but perhaps they were wrong. She thought for a moment and remembered the other westerner. She had scanned the yard before they'd decided to move away from the camp. The other foreigner wasn't in the exercise yard either.

"Shit, I've made a mistake. The man I know is no longer at the camp and I think he is in one of these trucks."

Genghis didn't reply. He started the engine and sped off in the direction of the site.

"I'd say the camp guards have half an hour on us."

"But we need to be wary of the drone... I know." Genghis nodded and drove a little closer north to avoid being directly under the flight path of the drone, adding more time to their journey.

Mattie spotted the drone with her binoculars, but it was almost impossible to track at speed. She dropped the glasses into her lap and stopped herself from fretting. She couldn't make the journey safer or quicker. But what she could do was work out how to identify herself to Henry so that he would let the SUV come close.

Genghis slowed the car to a crawl. He stopped at the bottom of a small hill. "We can't get any nearer."

"OK... I'll go on my own and try to get as close as I can."

"Since when are you playing things solo?" Genghis stepped out of the car and slung his binoculars around his neck.

"There is not much point in both of us getting caught."

"Why? Do you intend on getting caught?"

"Don't be silly... You know I'm right."

"And you know nothing of the terrain so I'm coming with you, and that's that."

264

Mattie considered Genghis for a moment. "You're pig-headed, you know."

Genghis grinned. "Look who's talking?" He moved cautiously up towards the ridge and Mattie followed, still unhappy about his decision and yet admiring his grit. The great Khan would have approved.

They moved silently from a couple of boulders to another ridge to the site perimeter, where it became impossible to advance without being seen. They lay down and started scanning their surroundings.

"Two lorries... and a couple of guards," Mattie whispered.

"I think there are some prisoners with them carrying crates."

Mattie moved her view from the guards to the left of the ship's hull. "I see that..."

"The prisoners have just disappeared farther down towards the bow."

"Did you see anyone else go that way, other guards, perhaps?"

"No, but with two trucks this can't be all the guards."

The prisoners Genghis had spotted did not return, whereas the two other inmates looked strangely comfortable with the guards. They were chatting and Mattie could have sworn the bulkiest of the pair was giving them orders. One of the prisoners started to remove his shirt and the other inmate took some sparring pads out of one of the trucks.

"He's warming up for a fight." Mattie's mind raced to understand the impact of this.

The discharge of a rifle startled both Mattie and Genghis. A prisoner had just returned from the bow of the ship. He stopped at the sound of the gun; his eyes widened when the guard took aim at him. He collapsed before he could attempt to flee.

"I've got to see what's at the bow of the ship..." Mattie whispered. She almost moved but Genghis gripped her arm.

"We have to wait." She tried to fight him off, but he held firm. "Mattie, they'll see you."

The bulky man, who had been sparring with his trainer without pausing for the summary execution of the other prisoners, stopped. He rolled his head around a few times, wiped the sweat from his face and spoke to the guards. He and his trainer started walking along the hull of the ship.

He disappeared and Mattie relaxed a little. One of the guards was now on his mobile and they too were moving towards the bow. In a moment both she and Genghis could follow.

Genghis started to move slowly around the perimeter, advancing in a quick belly-crawl which Mattie found hard to imitate. He put his hand down to tell her to stop and after a moment, gestured she could join him.

When Mattie arrived at his side, Genghis was focusing hard. Mattie brought her binoculars to her eyes and fought a cry.

The fight had started and Henry was standing in the ring, his face bloody. She had no weapon and no other way to help. All she could do was pray this fight was all part of his plan.

Genghis turned to her and whispered, "He's gonna win."

* * *

"So, are *you* ready to lose?" Henry shouted.

The Challenger shouted back something Henry couldn't understand and came at him with fists raised. Henry couldn't avoid the blow to the head that forced him a step back, but he managed to duck and avoid a lethal uppercut.

Missing his aim destabilised the Challenger again and Henry took advantage, throwing a knee into the man's kidney and repeating the knee blow to his stomach. The Challenger bent over. Lifting his right arm and folding his left for cantilever, Henry delivered a hammer fist to the back of the man's head.

Henry repeated the move relentlessly until the Challenger collapsed into a heap at his feet.

The guards were stunned and so was the Challenger's deputy. It was impossible.

In three fast steps, Henry reached the corner of the ring where Rob and Bo were sitting. He bent down, took something from Rob, then turned around to face the ring, this time with a gun in his hand.

One of the guards went for his rifle. The two bullets that Henry delivered hit him in the head and chest, throwing him to the ground.

"Anybody else tries anything and I will finish them off, too," Henry shouted in Mandarin.

Everybody lifted their hands and the remaining guards dropped their rifles to the desert sand.

"Step away from them," Henry said, waving to one of the guns.

The guards took a few steps back and Rob went to collect the rifles.

"Get some ropes..." Henry ordered Bo who had also lifted his hands, an agreed gesture that was aimed at distancing himself from Henry and Rob.

"Jackets off and watches as well," Henry shouted at them.

Bo returned with some electrical wires and Rob went around tying the men's hands and feet. He grabbed the shirt that the Challenger had dropped on the side of the ring and tore strips to tie over the guards' eyes.

Each guard had done as they were told. Rob collected the garments and watches and handed one watch to Henry and one to Bo.

"Sorry, but the fun stops here for me." Bo shook his head.

"What...? You can't stay..." Rob turned to Henry with genuine fear in his voice. "Tell him he can't stay."

"Rob's right, you can still change your mind." Henry threw some water over his face and was putting his shirt back on.

"It's too big a risk for my family."

"But why help in the first place?" Rob's gaze shifted from Bo to Henry.

"I needed to get a letter out to them and also... I just like to know I can still raise a middle finger at the Chinese government." Bo managed a brave smile.

"We've got to go," Henry said to Bo, a last attempt to convince him. "Assuming the jamming works for a little longer, it won't be long before Tang sends people to find out what's happening at the site."

Bo nodded. "Then, you'd better give me one of your best goodbye punches."

Rob shook his head. He hesitated and for a moment Henry wondered whether he would threaten to stay. But for Rob, it seemed that the information he was helping to deliver was too important for him not to follow Henry.

Henry stretched his hand out and Bo shook it warmly. "Get my message to my family."

"I will," Henry said through clenched teeth. He didn't want to leave Bo behind either.

Rob shook hands with Bo and moved away, head hanging in sorrow.

Bo turned to Henry. "I'm ready."

Henry slammed his fist near Bo's temple, knocking him out in one go. He caught Bo's body before it hit the ground and made sure he was breathing all right. Henry tied his hands and left him where he'd fallen.

Rob watched from inside one of the trucks where he'd taken a seat. "I hope you haven't killed him," he said, as Henry joined him.

"I might as well have. I don't think Tang will want any witnesses to this debacle." Henry slammed the door of the truck closed, gunned the engine, and drove away from underneath the shadow of USS *George H. W. Bush*'s aircraft carrier.

CHAPTER TWENTY-SEVEN

Their drive to the drop site where Henry had left his equipment would take twenty minutes at the most. Rob hadn't checked that the jammer was still working but it was fast becoming irrelevant. Warden Tang would by now have sent some of his most trusted men to check the site. He might even have decided to join himself. This didn't give Henry much margin for error, but nothing in OPERATION TECH LEOPARD did.

Rob hadn't said a word since they left the site. Leaving Bo behind still rankled with him and Henry couldn't blame him. Rob turned sharply towards the window and his body tensed.

"Problem?" Henry's hands tightened on the steering wheel of the truck.

"I think there's a car coming our way."

"A car or a truck?"

"A car... SUV."

"Shit... we can't outrun them in this piece of junk."

Henry hadn't switched the lights on and neither had the SUV driver.

"They must have been waiting for us..." Rob sounded more puzzled than scared.

"Almost certainly."

Henry turned the steering wheel in a fast, determined move. The back wheels slid sideways, sending sand and gravel into the air. He was now on a direct collision course with the SUV.

Rob braced against his seat. "It's a tough game of chicken you're playing."

"I know, but I need to find out who we're dealing with."

The SUV didn't change course but slowed down, and then altered its direction in a broad U-turn. The SUV accelerated enough to be pursued but not caught.

"Are they leading us into a trap?" Henry grabbed the gun he had stuffed in the side pocket of the truck door. He was losing valuable time to find out but there was no option. Henry dropped the gun into his lap, wound down the window and accelerated hard. He was still a little too far to shoot.

The ground had become rockier. Soon, it would be almost impossible to shoot at the SUV whilst driving. Henry suspected the driver knew this and yet his speed had not increased by much, preferring to choose a difficult terrain for its means of evasion.

Henry floored the accelerator and the truck lurched forward. "Help me hold the steering wheel," he said to Rob, dropping his right hand from the wheel to hold the gun and take aim.

Rob grabbed the wheel and Henry decided to aim at the wheels rather than the passengers. His gun was trained on the front right tyre when a piece of cloth appeared out the open window of the SUV.

Its white colour stopped Henry. The cloth was then spread out, helped by a pair of hands. There was something written on it which Henry couldn't make out. He raised the gun again. If they wanted to talk, he'd rather it be on his own terms.

"Wait!" Rob shouted, jerking the wheel. "It's a Union Jack."

"What the fuck are you doing? I was –"

"It's a Union Jack... Stop." Rob sounded half hopeful, half angry.

The SUV slammed on the brakes and their truck overtook them. Henry slammed on the brakes too and swerved the vehicle around in a semi-circle. The SUV had stopped, and the passenger door was opening slowly. The cloth flapped in the air again but there was no other movement.

Henry stopped the truck. He waited for a moment, but nothing else happened – just the floating makeshift flag being held up. Opening his door cautiously he slid to the ground using the door as protection.

"Move to the side so that I can see you... I won't shoot. You have my word," Henry shouted out in Mandarin.

The flag moved down; whoever was holding it was leaving the car. Henry frowned at the bearer of the flag but he was sure... It was a woman.

His stomach tightened as she took a few steps forward, then stopped. She was cautious but unafraid. She reminded him of someone, but he didn't have time to let his mind recall who it was. His gun was still trained on the woman who was carefully advancing towards him, but he felt uncomfortable taking aim at her.

"We are here to help." The voice was English, educated, assured without sounding overly so.

"Why?" Henry, his senses on high alert, couldn't make an enemy of that voice.

"Because we know each other…" The woman sounded hesitant, but continued. "Henry, we are here to help."

His grip on the gun loosened and Henry had to work not to drop it. It felt impossible that, here, in yet another desert, they should meet again.

"Mattie?" The name tripped over his lips, almost inaudible. She had stopped and Henry repeated the name louder. "Mattie?"

She started moving again but this time without restraint.

The last bastion of resistance warned Henry this could still be a trap, but he had to know whether it was her. Henry lowered his gun and moved away from the door, exposed.

Mattie accelerated her pace and then he was in no doubt.

He jammed the gun in the small of his back, choked up at the idea of having drawn a gun on her. There was a short moment of hesitation. As they neared, they recognised each other. Henry's breath grew short and he wished they were alone; even the vast desert had become too crowded.

Instead of taking her in his arms, Henry grabbed her hands and squeezed them tight. "Mattie… How?"

"Doesn't matter." She squeezed his hands in return.

"It does, I need to understand… it's too much risk –"

But there was no reproach in his voice and Mattie simply placed a finger on his lips. "We don't have time. The drop site has been raided. There is nothing left there. I got a piece of your parachute to show you." Mattie removed one hand and showed him the piece of cloth.

Henry inhaled deep. He had to get his mind to focus again on the escape. "Everything's gone?"

Mattie nodded. "You can use our vehicle to get to the motorway."

Henry received the information like a cold shower. "How do you know where we're headed?" Anger flared in his voice.

"I promise to tell you, but we need to dump the truck first."

"Who is with you?"

"Genghis, my guide... He is Mongolian. We crossed the border together."

"Genghis... you mean like?"

"The great Khan and he carries it well." Mattie gave Henry a brief smile that softened his hardened heart.

Henry ran his thumb along the tops of her fingers. "Does he know why I'm here?"

"Nothing fazes this guy as long as it is aimed at the Chinese government." She hadn't answered him. Mattie squeezed his hands hard. She too knew what she was doing.

"Fine... I'm not on my own. I have another prisoner with me."

Mattie nodded again. They both hesitated, and then released each other at the same time.

Henry was about to call Rob when he noticed a small figure at the side of the SUV. Mattie turned back and gestured to Genghis.

The young man moved forward quickly. "If you follow me, we can dump the truck somewhere more remote. That'll delay them finding it."

Henry considered Genghis for a few seconds, bright eyes, high cheekbones and the pigment of a man who, like his ancestors, had spent his time in the outside. There was something jovial and fearless about him and the name Genghis appeared to suit him perfectly.

"You lead the way." Henry turned back and jumped into the truck.

They drove less than ten minutes before arriving at a ridge, the drop side of which looked steep.

The four of them got out and Henry introduced Rob to Mattie and Genghis as another political prisoner.

"The plan is for me and Rob to reach the motorway to Bayannur, find a large enough trailer stopped at one of the petrol stations and hitch a ride to the city."

"You're not crossing now?" Genghis sounded puzzled.

Henry shook his head. "The border will not stop the warden looking for us."

"But they are looking for two men on the run, right?" Mattie had moved next to Henry.

"That's right." Genghis looked in the direction of the aircraft carrier's site. "What you need is a diversion."

"What I need is for you to drop me and Rob to the nearest station so we can get out of this country as soon as possible."

"Henry is right." Rob said, looking in the same direction as Genghis. "We don't need more people to get caught."

"I disagree with that." Mattie was standing firm. "The warden is looking for two men not two men and a woman."

"And I can cross the border on my own. If they follow or even stop the SUV they'll only find me," Genghis added.

This was not the plan.

"I need to chat with you." Henry grabbed Mattie by the upper arm and pulled her away from the others. "What are you playing at? I'm not having you join this trek across the Gobi Desert."

"First, the Gobi is in Mongolia barely crossing into China and second this won't be the first desert I trek, as you might recall."

"Syria is a picnic in comparison to this place. And anyway, we had no other choice to get you out safe of Islamic State." Henry squeezed her arm a little harder.

"Henry, you're hurting me."

He let go of her immediately. "I'm sorry..." Henry rubbed her arm. "I don't want you to get involved anymore that you have already. You are not putting your life in danger. I won't have it."

"Why would MI6 get me involved if they thought I couldn't be of help?"

Anger flared in his gut and he clenched his fist. It had to be a mistake. "This is impossible – how do you know they did?"

But Henry didn't need to wait for the answer; Mattie was right. She would never have found Zhaga even with the best sources a well-known journalist like her would have nurtured over the years. She would certainly not have known what his plan was and what the timing of it could be.

"Who did you speak to?" Henry said before she could answer his first question.

"British, with a slight East End accent... I now realise I met him before, remember two years ago."

"How did you get hold of him?" The hint that Mattie had recognised Harris darkened Henry's mood.

"He called me through one of my sources in Seoul."

The noise of a vehicle rolling out of control interrupted their argument. Genghis and Rob had pushed the truck over the ridge and into the ditch. It would take time to discover it.

"I don't care what MI6 or even the CIA says, you're not coming."

"You should know me better than that." Mattie smiled. "I'm here to help and to gather enough evidence for the article I'm going to write about this godforsaken place. You're not stopping me."

Genghis drove the SUV over to Henry and Mattie. Rob was sitting in the back.

"We're losing a lot of valuable time." Mattie turned around and got into the back of the car.

"And this is not the end of the conversation," Henry replied, whilst climbing in the front.

Genghis drove the SUV over the ridge slowly, the vehicle tilted forward at an uncomfortable angle until it reached the bottom of the hill. Genghis then drove in the shade of the steep terrain towards the east and the motorway they were trying to reach.

What the fuck was Harris playing at?

It took Henry a few minutes to dampen the flame of anger. Harris wasn't an idiot, and he was good at pushing people just that extra bit to achieve his goal.

But Harris wouldn't have asked an outsider to interfere unless OPERATION TECH LEOPARD had been compromised in some way.

"Rob..." Henry turned around in his seat. "When are you due to get in touch with your contact?"

Rob looked surprised by the question. "It depends..."

Henry nodded and faced the road. OPERATION TECH LEOPARD had another layer Henry needed to peel back. The Chinese Army was perhaps not simply preparing to move.

* * *

The wall of the lounge in the safe house had been transformed into a planning board. The air was thick with the smell of takeaways, the empty boxes of which were spread out on the coffee table that had been moved to one side.

"I can't get the whole of the ALPHA team to Mongolia in one go." Rodriguez was standing next to the part of the wall that had been pinned with a list of names.

Harris stood up from the settee he was sharing with Nick. "Can you operate with a smaller unit?"

"Not ideal, but we can get away with being two men down."

Fergus had opted to straddle a chair next to the couch. He shook his head, unhappy. "This is putting a lot of pressure on the team that will cross the border to get H plus one. And we won't have eyes in the sky to support us."

"You will," Nick said, finishing off his smoked pork noodles in one mouthful. "I've been working on hacking one of the geostationary satellites that covers the area. I'll relay progress in real time and give you intel on movements on the ground and in the air."

Rodriguez pursed his lips, clearly impressed by the young's man confidence.

"Uninterrupted coverage?" Fergus sounded more cautious.

"Uninterrupted." Nick nodded. "I'll have several feeds open so that if one comes down, I don't lose the image altogether. And I'll have an assistant."

All eyes turned to Harris who was momentarily taken aback. "Blimey! I have come up in the world. CrackerJack trusts me with his computer."

"'Ure all righ', mate... you can press a bu-hon." Nick's impersonation of an East End lad ended with him wiping his nose on his sleeve. The puzzled look on Rodriguez's and Fergus's faces made Harris burst into laughter.

"It's part of the education you're receiving from Henry?" Harris quipped.

"Yey, that's cool..." Nick stretched. "But going back to surveillance, I can start as soon as tomorrow morning, I think. I'm tapping into Landsat 8, one of the satellites used by Google Earth maps."

"That would be good. Fergus and Hulk are officially on holiday as of –" Rodriguez checked his watch "– now. They'll be catching a flight to Seoul first thing in the morning, then Mongolia."

"How are you getting organised once landed in Ulaanbaatar?" Harris asked.

"We've made friends with an old marine who's in charge of security at the embassy," Fergus replied.

"I will then follow with a flight to Japan and then Mongolia," Rodriguez added. "My leave starts tomorrow at lunch. I've booked a late-morning flight to Osaka, then on to Ulaanbaatar."

"Hulk and I will be getting organised, then we pick up Rod as he arrives from Osaka," Fergus said.

"You'll be on your way by the end of that afternoon." Harris stood up and went to the part of the wall where a large map had been projected, thanks to Nick's genius idea to do so, and to outline the part of Mongolia and China the team needed to reach.

Harris started to log dates and times of the arrival of people on site. Everyone was designated by their initials and Harris added Fergus, Hulk and Rodriguez to the timeline. He stood next to it for a moment. He still had Henry and Rob in Zhaga and Mattie and Genghis to the north of the US aircraft carrier site. He added the details of the ALPHA team members who were travelling.

"How easy is it going to be for the other two guys in your team...?" Harris prompted for Rodriguez to give him their names.

"Don and Ray."

"...Don and Ray to join?"

"They'll have to go a bit further afield not to arouse suspicions. They'll be going to the Philippines, then making their way from there to Mongolia."

"Realistically, they won't make it until the day after we arrive." Fergus got up and headed to the small kitchen to make some coffee.

Rodriguez leaned against the wall for a moment. "I think that's right but there is no other way. So, we'll have to perform the initial rendezvous with H plus one with a slimmed down team."

Harris wrote the initials of the other two members of the ALPHA team on the wall and proposed an ETA. He stared at the data. Harris felt all eyes on him; feeling uncomfortable, he walked back to the couch to take a seat.

Fergus arrived with a pot of coffee in one hand and a bunch of mugs in the other. He set everything down on the coffee table.

Rodriguez helped himself to coffee. "Doubt is good," he said softly to Harris, while Nick and Fergus were pouring themselves a mug.

"I can't recall who said 'When there is doubt there is no doubt', but I'd rather not have any at the moment," Harris volunteered.

"What is the alternative? Wait for Hunter to admit he's wrong and then organise a rescue party after it's too late?"

"Perhaps... but even you've got to admit we are a bit slim on the ground for such an operation." Harris almost regretted his words.

But then Rodriguez slapped his back. "But none of us are new to this rodeo, right?"

Fergus and Nick were chatting about what the ALPHA team would need and when. Harris could see that Fergus was at ease with the youngest member of the team. Then again, when it came to tech and hacking Nick was no amateur.

"In any case you're right," Harris said. "Hunter doesn't have the finger on the pulse because he has shut himself away from other routes of communications."

"And whether it was right at the time or not, we have to cope with the current situation." Rodriguez poured himself another mug and gestured to Harris with the pot of coffee.

Harris chose a mug and presented it. Rodriguez filled it. "Agreed," Harris said. "Who said I wanted to retire at sixty-five from MI6 after a distinguished career? I might as well go out with a bang. Early retirement here we come."

Rodriguez toasted Harris with his mug. "Let's go back to plan and rehearse our timeline after we land in Mongolia."

Harris moved to the wall whilst Rodriguez sat down. Nick joined him on the settee and Fergus resumed his position, straddling the chair next to the couch.

"Let's recall the steps of what was the original plan... at the moment I have no indication that H has decided to alter it so let's expect movement on his part as early as tonight, at the latest tomorrow night," Harris stated.

"He'll be seeking exfiltration the day after tomorrow, in the evening, I presume." Fergus crossed his arms over the back of the chair.

"At the earliest and this will happen under the cover of darkness, as you say. Twilight starts at 6.30pm and by 8pm night has fallen. H will start moving around at 7pm and reach the bottom of the hills by 10pm."

"Does he have night vision?" Rodriguez frowned.

"If he manages to retrieve his night goggles from his buried rucksack, then yes."

Fergus shook his head. "They can't cross the border in the dark. Even if he has equipment, the other guy doesn't, and the terrain is too treacherous."

"Agreed," Harris said. "But they'll be ready to cross as soon as the sun rises again the following day, with nautical twilight at around 5.30am."

"By the time I arrive in Ulaanbaatar and the boys pick me up it'll be 3pm. We'll have a seven-hour journey to reach the border," Rodriguez said.

"ALPHA team and H plus one should arrive at the same time on opposite sides of the border." Harris finished the timeline of projected outcome.

"I'll give you a visual," Nick said. "And let me see whether I can find a satellite that carries night vision capability."

Rodriguez and Fergus nodded at the same time. "We know just the one."

CHAPTER TWENTY-EIGHT

The buzz of drones in the distance caused everyone to go quiet in the car. Genghis slowed down to avoid the thermal blanket, still wrapped up around the hood, from flapping or worse, blowing away.

"How far are we from the motorway?" Henry craned his neck to see where the drones were.

"Normally twenty minutes. But as I need to slow down, I'd say half an hour."

Henry checked the watch he'd stolen from one of the guards and made a mental calculation of how much lead they had on their pursuers.

Warden Tang would have sent a small detachment of guards to the site of the US aircraft carrier not long after the drone had been jammed. By the time they'd arrived and called Tang about the disaster there, forty minutes would have elapsed. The second drone prepping and launch would take thirty minutes at most. Henry suspected Tang would not have wanted to send the men he trusted out on a wild goose chase without the drones sending back some images that warranted a move. The desert of Inner Mongolia was a large place to scour.

"I don't think the drones are above us. They still have a way to go before they start circling away from the perimeter of the ship." Henry sat back in his seat.

"Why the noise, then?" Mattie was also trying to spot the small aircraft.

"There's quite a bit of wind tonight and it carries their sound," Rob said without looking up, more interested in what lay ahead.

"That's right," Genghis confirmed, firmly holding the steering wheel and keeping the car from sliding over the sand and gravel. "This is an unusual thing at this time of the year, but it may mean a dust storm is coming."

Henry looked at Genghis. "I thought dust storms were most common in the spring?"

"As I said, not usual in the autumn but the Gobi is one of the world's most abundant sources of dust in the world."

"I have been caught in a couple of haboobs in Syria and Kuwait," Mattie said. "The first time my cameraman and I thought we wouldn't make it."

"And the second?" Genghis asked, glancing into the rear-view mirror.

"I was with a bunch of locals. They knew it was coming and they immediately found shelter. We simply sat it out."

"Good one... you just don't fight a dust storm otherwise it will take you with it. Just lie low and wait." Genghis nodded approvingly.

Everyone fell into silence once more, listening for the sound of the drones.

Henry heard their buzz fade away and he focused his mind on his next task: make sure that Mattie crossed the border with Genghis as soon as they could. Seeing her again had been more of a shock than he wanted to admit. The memories of the last time they'd met made his pulse race. It had been more than simple physical attraction with Mattie; the chemistry between them was complex and powerful, perhaps too powerful for a man like Henry. It was all about fate and attachment. He wouldn't lose another person he cared for.

"We're about to hit the motorway." Genghis slowed the vehicle to a stop. "I'll remove the thermal blanket and we can get to the next petrol station on the way to Bayannur."

"Is there a petrol station in the other direction, near the border?" Henry asked before Genghis left the car.

Genghis looked puzzled. "There is."

"Then, that is where we are going."

Genghis nodded and stepped out.

"Why?" Mattie and Rob asked as one.

"Because if we are using this car as a decoy, it can't be spotted heading towards Bayannur."

"That's a good point." Rob pursed his lips.

"And because it gives both Mattie and Genghis a greater chance to reach the border before Warden Tang tracks the car and puts out a warning at the border checkpoint."

"I'm not going back with Genghis. I'm your next decoy." Mattie didn't sound annoyed. She was making a statement of fact.

"No." Henry turned around fully and they glared at each other for a few seconds.

"MI6 thinks it's a good idea and I'm going with it."

"MI6 is not on the ground, I am." Henry pushed away the thought of calling Harris here and now to give him a piece of his mind. He was sure Mattie and Genghis had a mobile, but it wasn't yet the time to call.

"Mattie may have a point," Rob ventured.

"Don't get involved," Henry snapped.

"You know I can hold my own... I've spent months with the Peshmergas in Iraq and that wasn't a picnic." Mattie's voice rose.

"I know and the answer is still no."

"What have I missed?" a returning Genghis asked with a wry smile.

Henry faced the front. "Nothing of importance. Just get us to the petrol station near the border."

"Aye aye, sir."

Genghis put the car into gear and accelerated to a less comfortable speed. He soon found the motorway and turned left towards the border.

The road wasn't empty as Henry had worried it might be. Lorries and a few cars travelling at high speed were headed for the crossing between China and Mongolia. Business was strong, and goods needed to be delivered at any time, day or night.

"Is there a reason why there is so much traffic on the road today?" Henry counted at least six lorries that had overtaken them and as many coming in the opposite direction.

"It's easier to smuggle at night." Genghis nodded. "You pay your money and the guards go back to dozing off in their shacks. They don't even want to see your official papers most of the time."

"And the authorities don't care?"

"They do but the Ganqi Maodu border check is a long way from Beijing."

A stream of red lights started to show in the distance and Henry braced a little. The petrol station was getting close and lorries were slowing down to turn into it.

"Genghis, you'll need to do a quick recce of the place. I need to know how many drivers there are and whether they are resting, having food, etcetera..."

"OK, sure. How do you want to go about choosing the lorry that will get you to Bayannur?"

"It's got to accommodate two of us and be easy to get out of, so a lorry with a tarp cover or similar is the best."

Genghis slowed the car and crossed the dual carriageway to reach the petrol station on the other side of the road. The lorry car park was a third full and the restaurant that stretched behind the pumps looked busy.

Genghis parked the car at the end of a row of heavy lorries, two of which were clad with the requisite cover. He left the car and walked straight to the restaurant.

Mattie wriggled in the back of the car. "I need the ladies."

Henry looked into the rear-view mirror and smiled. "I don't think you'll find one of those in this place."

"Oh, yes, I will. See that trailer on the edge of the car park?"

"What about it?"

"I bet your bottom dollar that it's a little entertainment place."

"How do you know that?" Rob sounded shocked.

"Because it's my job to notice these things. Things that speak volumes about how people live their life."

Henry was about to mention that there was no one around the trailer when a podgy guy walked out. He finished zipping up his fly and hoisted his trousers up a bit more. A scantily clad woman stood in the doorway and waved at him. A returning customer it seemed.

"See what I mean?" Mattie said.

"And how do you think a westerner will fare walking into that place, in the middle of China?" Henry said, straightening up.

"Perfectly fine. I'm a journalist and I have authorisation to cross the border." Mattie opened the door before Henry could pull her back. "Anyway, we're not in the middle of China; we're near the border with Mongolia."

Henry opened the SUV door to go after her, but a couple of drivers were on their way back from the restaurant. Mattie was already in the open and walking towards them. The men slowed down to a stop and turned around to check where she was going.

"Fuck..." Henry slammed the dashboard.

Rob stuck his head between the two front seats. "You're not going to shake her off, you know that, right?"

"We'll see about that."

Henry turned and cast a dark look at Rob, then asked him a question. "Since it is only the two of us, you can now answer my question more fully. When are you due to get in touch with Dragon, in other words General Ma?"

* * *

Warden Tang lashed at Bo as soon as he saw the man bound and kneeling on the ground.

"What – do – you – know?" Tang screamed, hitting Bo with his stick, one for each word.

"Nothing... nothing!" Bo covered his face with his bound hands. "They threatened me with a gun."

Tang stopped suddenly. He wasn't getting much luck with Bo and was losing precious time. He would revisit the issue of whether Bo was involved with the escape in the confines of the camp and the torture rooms.

Tang turned to one of the men he had brought with him. "Are the drones in the air?"

"The second one has just been launched, sir." The guard added a small bow.

"You found the source of the jamming?"

"Yes, sir. It's been disabled."

Warden Tang walked past the guard, back to where they'd found the first lot of guards who had been gagged and bound. Henry's challenger hadn't recovered yet from his beating and his deputy looked as pathetic as the guards did.

"Get rid of them," Tang instructed. He turned around, oblivious to the screams for mercy of those he had just sentenced to death.

Another of his men came running up to him, looking eager. "We found the tracks belonging to the missing truck. They headed towards the hills."

Tang slapped his stick against the side of one of the crates. "Get the drones to move over the area."

The man bowed and moved away to carry out Tang's instructions. It was obvious that the escaped prisoners would want to cross the border as soon as possible. Tang pondered the question as to how. What he had seen of Henry and Rob told him these were not simple fugitives trying to reach safety in another country.

"We found the truck, sir." The same guard interrupted Tang's thoughts and was rewarded with a nasty glare.

"Show me."

Tang leapt into one of the Humvees they had driven to the site. They followed the tracks for about fifteen minutes and came to a steep ridge. Tang walked to the edge of the drop and looked down at the truck nose-deep in the sand.

Two other guards descended into the dip and began inspecting the wreckage and the ground around it.

"Do you see any footsteps?" Tang shouted.

"Nothing, sir, but we're still looking."

"Any evidence to indicate they've cleaned their tracks?"

"No, sir."

Tang stood up and took a few steps back. The moon was strong enough to give him a good view of the landscape as it stretched for miles around him.

"Where are you, you little shits?" Tang half closed his eyes. In the distance, he could make out the hills that crossed into Mongolia. Tang bit his lip a few times. It wasn't this porous frontier that would prevent him from getting the fugitives back. He returned to the ridge. "Still nothing?"

"No, sir."

Tang returned to the Humvee. The fugitives had pushed the truck down the slope to gain time and yet they were not on foot.

"Retrace the tracks of the truck." He jumped into the vehicle and the driver drove towards the west. He stopped the car ten minutes later.

"This is where they turned back, sir."

Why lose time unless there was something valuable at the end of that journey?

Tang left the Humvee and, equipped with a torch, inspected the tracks the truck had left. He walked around in increasing circles until he found what he'd been looking for. A fresh set of tyre tracks from a lighter vehicle.

"Call the camp and redirect the drones towards the motorway."

The driver took Tang back to the accident site. He asked his driver to bypass it and move along the ridge. The sand looked barely touched, that was until they drove another hundred yards or so. The marks of a vehicle driving down the ridge were clearly etched in the sand.

"Drive down the slope." Tang opened his window and shone his torch on the sand. The driver stopped and Tang recognised the same tracks he'd seen a few minutes ago. "You may be crossing the border in a car, but I'm still going to get you." Tang picked his mobile out of his uniform pocket. He hesitated for a second or so. Once he made the call the story of the escape would be more difficult to contain. But the man he was about to call owed him a favour and Tang had enough on him to send him to Zhaga for a very long stretch.

The mobile rang a few times, and a sleepy voice finally answered.

"I have been handed some vital intelligence and informed that two westerners are attempting to cross the border illegally at Ganqi Maodu. I want the border guards on high alert."

The man at the end of the line didn't ask any questions, simply assuring Tang that the guards would be told straight away.

Tang sat back in his seat, satisfied that one of the escape routes had been closed.

The Humvee crawled back up the ridge and returned Tang to the ship site. The guards were lugging the bodies of the dead men onto the truck that had brought them to the site alive. They would be disposed of in the pit like all the other men and prisoners who had opposed Tang and the other wardens before him.

Tang reflected that the pit had been filling up, perhaps more rapidly, under his tenure. He shrugged. When this one was full, they'd dig another one.

He took a moment to think about which other routes were open to the escapees. They could perhaps still attempt to cross on foot, being dropped off by the mysterious friendly car near the border. Tang indulged for a short moment in the fantasy of catching the driver of that car and what the torture chambers would mean for him. But he shook the thought away; the driver wasn't worth hunting as much as the prisoners were.

Tang used his mobile again and called Zhaga, asking to redirect one of the drones to the border away from the motorway.

There was no point in staying at the site. He needed more information on the fugitives' plans and the only way to get it was to interrogate Bo.

Tang got out and walked back to the spot where he'd left Bo. The place was now empty and instead a large bloodstain had seeped into the sand. Tang swore and speed-walked to the truck. The last body had just been thrown into the back of the truck.

Warden Tang shoved the guards aside who'd just finished moving the dead men. Tang recognised Bo's body. He was face up, eyes wide open, and his lips were set in an ironic smile. He would be taking his secrets to the grave.

Tang screamed; the guards stepped back, not understanding what they'd done wrong. Tang slammed his stick against the side of the truck a few times and disappeared back into the Humvee.

He would have to figure out the westerners' plans on his own.

* * *

Genghis and Mattie walked back to the SUV and Henry knew she'd won her bet to stay.

"I found a nice lorry driver who doesn't mind giving a lift to a journalist and her crew," she said, as she sat back into the car.

Genghis added, "He's Mongolian and we come from the same tribe."

"Just like one in two hundred men share in Genghis Khan's DNA," Henry shot back.

"You know that?" Genghis sounded genuinely impressed.

"I know many things, and I know this idea that sounds so smart now will bite us in the butt later."

"Then we'd better get moving before it does bite us in the butt." Mattie dragged her rucksack out from underneath her seat. She moved to the boot and retrieved a smaller camera.

286

The same podgy guy they'd seen leaving the trailer after spending a good time with his favourite madame waved at them. He was ready to leave and if they wanted a ride, it had to be now.

Rob and Mattie left the SUV.

Henry yanked Genghis's rucksack out of the footwell. "I need this to hide my gun. Do you mind?"

"No worries. There is a compass and a GPS. That might be helpful. Plus other bits and bobs, including my mobile."

"Are you sure?" Henry frowned, but Genghis looked at ease with the idea of losing his phone.

"My passport and money are in my jacket. That's all I need. I'll get a burner phone as soon as I can."

Henry nodded his thanks. He rolled the jacket he'd stolen from the guard and stuffed it into the bag.

Genghis jerked his head towards the truck that was waiting for Henry. "The lorry is ready to go with both your people waiting for you."

"You're right. Not much point in arguing with her now... You need to get going, too, Mr Decoy. Thanks for your help." Henry extended a hand and they shook.

Genghis smiled. "I'll see you in Mongolia soon." He jumped back into the SUV and drove off at speed.

Mattie and Rob were already settled in the back of the truck by the time Henry arrived. The podgy man was speaking a little English to Mattie.

"Thank you for giving us a ride," Henry said, as he took his seat inside the lorry.

The man's face dropped. and Henry realised that speaking Mandarin wasn't an endearing feature to a Mongolian.

"Translator," Henry said in English, pointing towards his chest, hoping his lie had worked.

The man took a moment to process.

Then his eyes brightened, and he repeated, "Tran-sle-ator." He laughed and repeated the word. Henry grinned and jumped into the back of the truck.

Rob had moved to a corner next to a pile of cardboard boxes. Mattie had taken the opposite side of the truck and Henry chose Rob's side.

"What does the driver say about timing?" he asked Rob.

"Three hours to the suburbs of Bayannur." Rob took a bottle of water out of his rucksack.

Mattie didn't add anything, but simply took a fresh water bottle from a plastic bag that was covered in Chinese characters.

She threw it to Henry. "I bought a few bits after I used the ladies. The convenience store at the back of the restaurant is well stocked."

"Did they have video cameras?" Henry asked, opening the bottle.

"Thank you, Mattie, for thinking about food and drinks..." With a huff, she took an energy bar out of the same bag and threw it at Rob.

"You haven't answered my question." Henry took a swig and shoved the bottle into his rucksack.

"There was, near the till. I made sure I showed the camera as little of me as possible. In any case, I don't think it was recording anything. The red button was flashing constantly and that's what you get when you start a recording, not when the CCTV is rolling."

Henry's stomach grumbled and he considered asking her nicely for a cereal bar.

Mattie gave him a quick look, to see whether he was ready to make peace. Henry crossed his arms over his chest, rested against the side of the truck and closed his eyes.

He wasn't that hungry after all.

CHAPTER TWENTY-NINE

Tang stood behind the two men who were manning the drones. He checked the images one more time, but the stretch of motorway only showed a steady stream of lorries of different sizes and shapes. No car had been spotted yet.

One of the men who was manning the drones turned to Tang. "May I make a suggestion, sir?"

"Speak."

"Perhaps the car hasn't taken the motorway. If it's been going down a ditch –"

"It's an SUV and SUVs can go off road!" Tang interrupted. "Widen the search and direct the drone straight to the border checkpoint, then work your way back inland."

The operator acknowledged Warden Tang and flew the drone towards the Ganqi Maodu border crossing. There was some distance to cover. Tang checked his watch. It was almost 11pm and the fugitives had escaped over three hours ago.

The drone would take another few minutes to start transmitting images of the border crossing cabins and the road that led to them. Tang walked to the back of the room, checking on whatever might be available to drink. He boiled some water and made himself a cup of tea.

"Sir, we have something."

He rushed back to the control panel for the drone.

A dark SUV was approaching a road close to the border station. It meandered through the back streets, then drove into a large car park where cars and lorries were waiting to head through the first border checks which Chinese guards were manning. The SUV reached the car park, crawled slowly towards the first gates and stopped.

Tang set his cup down on the desk and dialled the same contact he'd called before.

This time the man picked up the phone immediately. "Warden Tang?"

"The man I am looking for is attempting to cross the border right now." His eyes did not leave the screen for one instant. "Call your people and report back." Tang killed the call.

The driver of the SUV was now speaking to the guard at the checkpoint.

"Can you magnify the image?"

The operator nodded and the image grew larger. An arm was stuck out of the window. The driver was holding what looked like papers. The gates were still closed and the guard and driver were still in conversation.

"What are you doing, morons? Get them!" Tang was about to call his contact back when his phone rang.

"I've just given instructions –" the caller said.

"– which appears to be having no effect. Call them back." Tang hung up.

The guard had just returned the papers to the SUV driver. He released the heavy doors of the gate. They slid back to let the vehicle through.

Tang leaned on the operator's desk. "Can you crash the drone on his car?"

"Sir?" The operator turned towards Tang, not certain he had heard correctly.

"Do it!"

Impatient, Tang shoved the man off his seat and took control of the drone. He checked the altitude and made a quick mental calculation. If he pushed the small aircraft to its speed limit, it would take a couple of minutes to reach the SUV.

The SUV had passed through Chinese border control, and was now moving towards the Mongolian one, less than fifteen yards away.

Tang increased the speed of the drone, forcing it into a steep dive towards the earth. The drone instruments started to flash, and a warning sound filled the room.

"The car is being stopped, sir..." the operator said, next to Tang. He was pointing desperately at the image on screen.

Tang took a few seconds to decide and, in one swoop, brought the drone up then levelled it out. He stood up and allowed the operator take control again.

Four border guards had jumped over the barrier and were surrounding the SUV, rifles trained on the vehicle. One of the guards was ordering the driver to get out. He moved closer and pointed his rifle in through the driver's window.

The car door opened slowly. An old man slid out of the car with raised hands. He looked more like the great-grandfather of a Mongolian family than a risk taker who trafficked people across the border.

Warden Tang carefully watched the scene. The old man hobbled to one side and the guard who'd asked him to step out opened the doors one after the other. He finished with the boot. The SUV was empty.

The border guards on the Mongolian side had come out of their hut and were watching the scene. The SUV had a Mongolian registration plate and Tang could see their tension by the way the men were holding themselves on the small strip of land between the two checkpoints.

The Chinese guards ignored their Mongolian colleagues. One of them turned away from the scene and started asking questions. The old man was shaking his head and the guards got closer.

Tang picked up his mobile again and called his contact. "Call off your dogs... This is not the right person, and I don't want a diplomatic incident at the border."

Within seconds, the phone of the guard who was speaking to the old man rang. He picked up and pulled back immediately. The old man climbed back into his SUV and drove through Gashuun Sujkait, also known as Ganqi Maodu border station.

Warden Tang ordered the drone operators to keep scanning the border and left the room. He returned to his quarters where he lashed an old leather chair with his stick.

The fugitives were well-organised and inventive. He no longer wondered why General Ma had insisted on this stupid exercise for the wealthy Chinese keen to hide money. Tang suspected she knew who these people were. She had just been placed under house arrest and Tang needed to decide how much he would contribute to the accusations of treason against her.

Tang walked over to a small cabinet in the corner of a room that served as lounge/dining area. The space that was his home for the duration of his tenure wasn't large but it was well conceived, making his stay in Zhaga just about bearable.

He pulled a bottle of Cognac out of the cabinet and read the label. Hennessy XO Cognac – seventy years old. He'd managed to sneak the expensive drink out of his father's house without anyone noticing. His father would almost certainly have given him the pricey bottle if he'd asked, but that had not been the point.

Tang poured himself a glass in a proper cognac short-stemmed tulip glass he kept for special occasions, and sat down slowly. The clock on the wall indicated 12am. He raged inside at the thought of having been outsmarted by the westerners. Bo might be dead but Tang could still get revenge on his family.

He took another sip and closed his eyes. The priority was still to recover the fugitives, even if they managed to cross the border. His drone operators would be up all night and if the men had gone to ground to wait it out, he would be there to pick them up when they next emerged.

He glanced at an old box that he hadn't touched for a while. Tang set his glass carefully on a side table and picked up the box. It was a very old Mahjong game set. Tang recalled his father calling Mahjong a game of skill, strategy and luck.

Warden Tang opened the box and spread the pieces out next to him on the settee. Skill and strategy he had. What he needed now was a little luck.

* * *

"We need to take a rest but also take it in turn to watch out for problems." Henry opened his eyes after a few minutes.

Rob had finished his food and volunteered, "I'll take the first hour."

"And I'll take the second," Mattie jumped in.

"Sounds fine. Just wake me when you switch shifts. I'll want to check where we are."

"Do you have a compass?" Rob asked, intrigued.

"Genghis left me his. Otherwise I would have got it from the position of the stars in the sky."

Rob looked impressed. "Navigation the old-fashioned way..."

Mattie smiled, closed her eyes, and managed to find a position that looked cosy enough against the cardboard boxes the truck was carrying.

"Old-fashioned is the operative word," she murmured.

Henry chose to ignore her remark. It was a little unfair of her and she would know that. She clearly wasn't going to let her anger go until he accepted she was a worthy contributor to the operation.

He and Rob changed places. Henry moved to a part of the truck that was stacked with larger wooden boxes. He shifted a couple around and sat down at the back of the truck. He took his gun out of the rucksack and placed it underneath the bag. He closed his eyes and rested his head against one crate.

But his mind was too active and sleep wouldn't come. Harris had been right in a way that now surprised Henry. Harris had involved Mattie, judging she would not only jump at the opportunity for a scoop but that she'd put her life in danger for Henry. Henry knew why but it angered him that Harris had read them both so well and guessed there were still feelings between them.

Henry hadn't tried to see Mattie again after the Middle Eastern operation ended. The mission had been his first one after joining MI6 and it had pushed him to the limit. Saving Mattie from certain rape, and perhaps death, had made it more dangerous, and yet so much more worthwhile. He found it ironic that the part of the operation he'd been secretly most proud of had been that, and he knew he would have felt the same had his feelings for Mattie not developed.

The smooth vibrations of the truck on a surprisingly smooth motorway lulled Henry into a more relaxed state. He was on the edge of sleep and yet the question as to why Harris had sent Mattie to China kept him out of it. Rob had read with pessimism news of Dragon, received from the guards at Zhaga. She was under house arrest, yet it wasn't unusual for high-profile figures to be questioned. If she kept her cool she might get out of this tight spot – unless Harris knew otherwise. His handler might have received some fresh intel that confirmed this.

Henry shifted a little to find a better position. He'd landed in China seven days ago and he wondered why Dragon's position had deteriorated so quickly. Or perhaps, that had been the goal. Hunter might have known it would and yet had not said as much to Harris.

No matter how valuable a scientist Rob was, the intelligence he was to receive from Dragon would surpass this.

Sleep hit suddenly, and Henry only realised he'd drifted into it when someone squeezed his arm. His hand slid automatically for the gun underneath the rucksack, but he released his grip on it as soon as he heard Rob's voice.

"It's time to wake up," Rob murmured.

"Anything noticeable?" Henry sat up.

"No, apart from the fact that this motorway is very busy even at 1am."

"That's good for us. This truck doesn't stick out like a sore thumb." Rob sounded hesitant and Henry caught it. "Something else troubling you?"

"I should try to get in touch with..." Rob sounded uncertain again.

"I've been thinking about that since you mentioned it. The SIM card that was left for me in the prison might be the means to get to her, but we only have one shot at it. If she's been outed then her comms will be monitored. We can't reveal our position until we're ready to leave China."

"And you're confident we don't need her guidance to get out?"

"If she's been outed, she won't be able to help in any case."

"That was a silly question." Rob shook his head. "I'm sorry."

The men's conversation had disturbed Mattie. She yawned and stretched. "What did I miss?" She picked up her water bottle, drank from it and stood up.

Rob came to snuggle in the spot she had vacated. Mattie sat at the opening at the back of the truck, a place where she could survey the road.

Henry closed his eyes again but Mattie's presence just a couple of feet away from him made it harder to fall back asleep. The lull from the lorry's motion did its trick again and he fell asleep for an hour.

He woke up before the due time for his shift. The lorry had swerved a few times and he had registered the change of direction. He sat and checked that Mattie was still awake. She was sitting in the same corner of the lorry and was very much awake.

"Why the swerve?" Henry murmured.

"We're going through the road that crosses the low mountain ridge before Bayannur. I guess the road won't straighten out again until we are over the mountain."

Henry nodded and waited a moment to stand up. He had hoped Mattie would exchange places with him without being asked, but she wasn't moving.

"I'll take over now. Why don't you go sleep for a stretch?"

Mattie gave a short, sharp exhale. "How long are you going to sulk for?"

"That's an unfair question."

"It's not. I know you're unhappy but now that I'm here, we've got to work together."

"I'm not denying that we do."

"But you're not trusting my judgement."

"I don't trust that easily, Mattie..." Henry trailed off. This was becoming too personal, and this was not where he wanted the conversation to go.

"I gathered that in the Middle East, but I also know you can trust when people deliver."

She was right but he wasn't going to say so just yet.

"I delivered a car and secured a driver to Bannayur." Mattie stood up and retrieved an energy bar from the shopping bag without waking Rob up. She handed the bar to Henry. "And food. Not bad for someone who's just been back in your life for two days."

Henry peeled the wrapper and took a bite. "Not bad, as you say. I'm talking about the energy bar, of course."

"That's a relief... I thought you were going to complain it was too sweet."

Mattie moved to Henry's old corner. He stood up to let her have his place and there was an awkward moment where they circled each other. Mattie snuggled in and he sat at the watching post Mattie had just left.

The landscape they'd encountered near the petrol station had disappeared, replaced by dark rock that created a wall on each side of the road. If there was to be an ambush, this would be the ideal place. There was no way to move sideways.

They were inside a lorry that certainly wasn't equipped to take evasive manoeuvres, whatever the surroundings.

He glanced at his watch. They had another thirty minutes before they reached the outskirts of the city. It would be 4am, giving them plenty of time to cross the city and find a new mode of transportation.

The lorry slowed and the downward slope grew steeper. It eased off after fifteen minutes and Henry peeked through the thick tarp.

The countryside couldn't look more different. Sand and rocks had been switched to fields organised around clusters of houses. The Yellow River, the second-longest river in China, ran through Bayannur. Henry recalled reading that when preparing for the operation. The pocket of lush culture and green space was caught between the river and the mountain, giving Bayannur the feel of a small haven.

The lorry slowed down again and this time it felt as though the driver was looking for the right place to stop. Henry took the gun from under the rucksack and slid it in the small of his back. He called Mattie's name and then woke Rob up.

The driver veered the truck to the right and stopped. Mattie stretched, moved to the back opening of the truck and lifted part of the cover. Henry and Rob sat down again, ready to make a move.

They heard the driver open the door and get out. He yawned and took a few steps away from the road. He relieved himself and yawned again.

Mattie waited for a moment longer to avoid embarrassing him, and called out softly. "Have we arrived in Bayannur?"

The podgy man stuck his face through the opening and smiled at them. "Fifetee minute..." he said, counting out to fifteen with his fingers.

Mattie bowed a few times, thanking him. He smiled again and they were back on the road.

The pockets of houses and small buildings turned into denser clusters, but still everywhere there were fields and agriculture. The town itself was small and the motorway they were headed to did not lead straight into it. Small pickup trucks and 4x4s were parked everywhere.

Henry wondered whether he could ask the driver to stop just before they reached town, but it was impossible. Genghis had told the driver the three travellers had booked a guest house in the centre of the city but would be waiting 'til the sun was up, out of courtesy to their host.

The lorry picked up speed again on the flatter land and there was an air of impatience in the way he was now driving. They entered the suburbs. The truck turned, left, right and left, and stopped abruptly.

The driver appeared again, looking happy. He threw the tarp up and back to let his passengers step out. He pointed to a neon sign and a place that looked as though it never closed.

"Food…" he said, indicating they should follow.

Mattie tried to communicate that perhaps they should be on their way. The face of the man dropped.

Henry came forward and nodded with a smile and a bow. "Food… very good."

The smile returned to the man's face, and he moved towards the small restaurant, to choose the best table for him and his guests.

"Won't this put us behind schedule?" Mattie asked.

"Perhaps, but better that than have a suspicious driver who alerts the authorities. What else can we do but eat breakfast? We're waiting for the so-called guest house to open." Henry jumped out of the truck.

The driver stood at the door of the restaurant, waving them in.

"Let's just hope it's not too crowded." Henry waved back and started walking.

* * *

Rodriguez and Fergus had gone, leaving Harris with the feeling that for once he did not have the support he needed to get his man back home.

ALPHA team would be there to extract Henry and Rob, but they too were putting themselves at risk. Harris wished he had done a stint in the army. He might be of some help.

Nick had returned to his tech cave. He'd started speaking to himself and threatening the computer with retribution. This did not concern Harris. Nick was a genius and geniuses were meant to behave strangely.

Nick had explained that in the treasure trove of voicemails he had pilfered from Hunter and the CIA, one remained mysterious.

Only one word had been spoken: Flamingo.

So far none of the other voicemails Nick had gone through had given him a clue, and he had tried several methods but failed to decrypt the word. The code had been agreed in advance, Nick had concluded, and the word chosen at random.

Harris checked his email on his encrypted mobile. There was nothing that needed immediate attention and thankfully nothing from the Chief, and sadly nothing from Hunter.

"I've got something..."

Nick calling to him stopped Harris's scrolling; he pocketed his phone.

"Steve..." Nick called out again. "I've got it."

Harris crossed the lounge and arrived at Nick's side. The young man was typing away and there was no hesitation from him. He had solved the word puzzle and was simply going through counterchecks.

"I've picked up another single word... another bird name: Parrot. Then a conversation between Dragon and her minder that refers to the sequence of words that she'll use in case she can't say much and that will enable her minder to know what is happening to her."

"OK, so Parrot means that, say, she's all right and Eagle means she's about to be discovered?"

"That's the gist," Nick said, still facing his screen. "Then I found another conversation that is four months old. The conversations back then are lengthier and there is the occasional joke. Then she says, 'Pink is my favourite colour, let's hope I won't refer to it in that way'." Nick turned to Harris, waiting for him to draw his conclusion.

"Flamingos are pink, and you think that using this bird's name means she's giving a negative signal?"

"The last conversation is only a few sentences, and the communication stops then picks up a day after Henry lands in China. She sends one word to her minder."

Harris washed a hand over his face. "I think you're right, we've established she's already on a slippery slope, but I think she now knows it's only a matter of time before they come for her."

"Why has Hunter not said a thing?"

"He has cornered himself and he also hopes she can pull it off. My interpretation is that she knows she's finished, and yet we don't know for sure what Flamingo means."

"Perhaps we should put our cards on the table?" Nick's bold suggestion surprised Harris.

Harris's burner phone rang. He moved out of the room and towards his bedroom. "Han? What's up?"

"I've just had a conversation with Genghis. He's back from China and tells me he and Mattie picked up two fugitives from Zagha."

Harris's tight gut relaxed. "That's the news I was waiting for." Henry and Rob had escaped. Now he needed to deliver their exfiltration.

"And before you ask, yes, the decoy worked fine. Genghis got one of his relatives to drive the car through the checkpoint. He himself got a lift from a smuggling contact."

"You only mention your guy. What about Mattie Colmore?"

"Were you not expecting Mattie to stay with them?" Han's voice sounded neutral. He hadn't been told of the detail of the operation and was only relaying facts.

"What do you mean? She's still in China?"

"That's what I just said. She's on her way to Bayannur with the two fugitives."

Harris exercised enough control not to swear, and yet he should have seen it coming. What had attracted Mattie to cross into China and find out about the Zhaga camp was exactly what would keep her with Henry and Rob.

"Fine. Just one more person to extract."

Han didn't reply. He'd done what he was meant to do, and Harris knew he wouldn't care what came next. His own contact had come out of China intact. The rest was up to Harris.

Harris terminated the call and sat slowly on his bed. The sense of déjà vu forced him to stand up again. He knew what would be coming next. Mattie's father would need to be informed. The last time Harold Colmore MP had learned that his daughter was in a foreign country he had gone to great extremes to get her back. It was not so much out of concern for her welfare but because it wouldn't do to have the daughter of a prominent Conservative MP being used to blackmail the British government.

Strangely, Harris had never bought the concerned father angle. Colmore just didn't want his daughter to become a bargaining chip in Islamic State hands. He sure wouldn't want her to be one for the Chinese government.

"Fuck…" Harris slammed his hand on the wall. "Fuck… I need to call London." The time difference was giving him no excuse to delay. It was 4pm in the UK and the Chief would be reachable.

Harris called the Chief's PA and braced himself.

CHAPTER THIRTY

Breakfast had not disappointed. The lorry driver even made an effort to speak to the waitresses in Mandarin. Henry, Rob and Mattie admired the spread. At least they would be fed for the next twenty-four hours.

The restaurant was almost empty apart from another driver who'd finished his meal and left almost as soon as they'd arrived. A couple arrived quickly after and Henry suspected that the driver had other things on his mind than to take note of who was having food and who they were.

An hour and a half later, the driver dropped Henry and his team near the North Ring Road residential district of Bayannur. After much posturing and refusing the lorry driver finally accepted Mattie's offer to pay for the food. Women had a voice in traditional Mongolian society and Mattie seemed to convince the man despite her poor grasp of his language.

The driver drove off and the three fugitives moved farther inside the residential district.

"It's not what I expected." Mattie was looking around with interest.

"We don't have time for a photo shoot." Henry sped up his walk, leaving the main road and moving deeper into the smaller streets.

"Why not? We are supposed to be a bunch of journalists, after all."

Rob just smiled. He seemed to find the tit for tat amusing and Henry shot him a look.

"We need a car or a small pick-up truck. Something that will not attract attention on the road." Henry looked at the sky. Dawn was breaking and people would soon be going to work.

They passed a few tall modern and unappealing buildings, then came upon low individual houses that made the district look more like a village than a modern city.

Houses backed onto one another with small gardens separating them, and the small streets alongside the buildings felt more like alleyways. The fugitives walked even deeper into the maze of small lanes until they came to a larger road that seemed to encircle the entire neighbourhood. There were a few different styles of cars parked along it and Henry asked for the others to wait in the shadow of one of the houses.

The vehicle that had attracted his interest looked to be the oldest on the street. It seemed well enough maintained, but one wing had been replaced; the attempt to match the paint colour to the car was not so successful. Still, it wasn't so bad that it would make the small pick-up truck stand out.

"I found what we need," Henry said, returning to them.

"Are you going to hotwire it?" Mattie asked.

"No. I'm going to ask the owner for the keys."

Mattie shrugged. "I can hotwire a car, too. I just thought I would offer my services."

Henry simply nodded. "Rob, can you pull a registration plate off one of the other vehicles on the street?"

Rob raised an eyebrow. "I'm sure I can, but why?"

"We're doing a swap. If we do get spotted at least it won't be the right registration they see."

The light came on in one of the houses and the three fugitives moved deeper into the alleyway. After a few minutes the house went dark again.

"Let's get going..." Henry jerked his head at the pick-up truck. To Mattie he said, "We'll call you when we're ready."

Both men walked over to the small truck Henry had in mind.

"Perhaps you two could bury the hatchet?" Rob murmured, as Henry leaned against the door and used the lock-picking kit he still had on him.

"Nope... I don't want her to feel she's on a reporting trip, writing her next scoop. I know what she's like when she is."

The lock gave way and Henry handed over the kit to Rob. It would help with unscrewing the plates of the next car.

Henry got into the pick-up and Rob crouched down, busying himself with his task. Henry checked the inside of the vehicle. It was suitably dirty and had been used for transporting grains, going by the mess. Some empty sacks lay on the passenger seat and Henry could see more of them in the open back of the truck, through the rear window.

He shifted a little and slid his hands underneath the steering wheel. He felt the wires sticking out and smiled. It would take no time at all to start the small truck. Rob had moved around the second car. He was doing well with the plates; another couple of minutes and they would be off.

The sound of voices stopped Henry dead. He glanced in the side mirrors and saw a woman on the doorstep of her house, carrying a bucket. She was speaking to someone inside her home, but Henry couldn't tell who.

She turned towards Henry and Rob. In a few seconds she would be upon them. Henry slid over to the passenger side and opened the door gently.

"Rob... someone's coming," Henry called in a low voice.

Rob took a moment to understand.

The sound of another voice had Henry checking the rear-view mirror. Mattie had walked out of the shadows and was asking the woman something. There was a lot of sign language and much bowing. Then the two women walked past the pick-up just as Rob moved to the side of the vehicle. Mattie disappeared into a building on the corner of the small street. The woman followed her and reappeared before Mattie did. She returned to her house, and glanced back at the building. As Mattie re-emerged, she gave the woman a wave from a distance; the woman waved back and disappeared inside her home.

Rob returned to swapping the plates and Henry pulled the wires, ready to strike as soon as Mattie reached them. She jumped into the cabin of the truck and Rob followed. The pick-up started immediately, and they were off.

"What was that about?" Rob asked, not hiding his amazement.

"She was going to empty her chamber pot into the nearest public toilet. Some of these houses still don't have inside toilets."

Henry drove the car at speed out of the residential district. "Wasn't she surprised to see you there?"

"I learned a few helpful words in Mongolian... One of them is aid worker, the other one is toilets. That seemed to convince her when I pretended to look desperate for a pee."

"At least that gave me enough time to take cover." Rob nodded.

"That was the idea." Mattie smiled and shuffled a little more towards the middle of the seats. "How are we getting to the motorway?"

"I'm going back to the place the lorry driver dropped us off. I can find the G7 from there. It should take no more than fifteen minutes." Henry's hands tightened on the wheel.

They found themselves back on the main street and headed for the motorway just as the sun was appearing on the horizon. There were quite a few cars on the roads already. Henry hoped there wouldn't be too many police cars around now as he was not intent on respecting the speed limit or the traffic lights. He sped out of Bayannur much more quickly than he'd anticipated.

"We'll be leaving the G7 in seventy miles. From there, we'll take a smaller road that is a shortcut route to the next petrol station, where we change vehicles again." Henry glanced at Mattie. She'd done well so far. Perhaps it was time he gave her a break, as Rob had suggested.

The lull from the movement of the pick-up on the even road surface sent both his passengers to sleep. Rob had his arms crossed over his chest and was leaning against the passenger door.

Mattie's camera was resting on her lap, and she too had succumbed to sleep. She had taken some pictures as soon as the light was good enough, but when the landscape switched from the lush greens of Bayannur to the usual desert emptiness, she had stopped bothering.

Her head had tilted ever so slightly towards him, and he suddenly wished it could rest on his shoulder. He shook his head to dispel the idea. It was neither the time nor the place.

The smell of something hot and acrid focused Henry's attention. They had left the main motorway half an hour earlier and were the only ones driving on a smaller road. If the smell was coming from anywhere it had to be the pick-up.

The smell grew stronger. Henry checked in the rear-view mirror and saw a plume of white smoke that was thickening by the second.

"Shit..." The car ground to a halt. His passengers woke up from their sleep.

"You're stopping?" Rob yawned.

"No... the pick-up is stopping, and I don't think it's going to start again."

* * *

The call from London came as Harris was about to go to sleep. He'd spent the night waiting for it and at 5am he had finally dozed off.

"Is it urgent?" The Chief sounded tired yet alert.

"I'm afraid so, sir." Harris allowed himself a quick sip of water before continuing. "The good news is that my operative and his target are out of the camp and on their way."

Harris waited for a second for the positive news to sink in.

"The not-so-good news is that they are now accompanied by a third person."

"And that third person is an issue because...?" The Chief exhaled sharply.

"She is the journalist I used to get eyes on the camp and she has decided to travel with them."

"Her name is?" The Chief sounded more alert.

"Mattie Colmore." Harris closed his eyes as he said her name.

"As in the daughter of Harold Colmore MP?"

"Yes, sir."

"The very same person who your operative rescued and who almost cost him his life and us the operation?"

"Yes, sir."

"Are you out of your bloody mind?"

"It's a fair question, sir."

There was a heavy silence on the line that lasted for too long.

"I know Hunter has been uncooperative and that you are worried about your asset, but something else has pushed you to take that risk and I want to know what that is," the Chief finally said.

Harris gnawed on his bottom lip a few times. Would the Chief pull the operation if he knew to what extent Harris had gone to get the information he needed? He just wanted enough time to get Henry and his team out of China. After that, he'd take whatever was coming to him.

"I'm concerned Hunter is not being transparent about the status of his Chinese asset," Harris said.

"You think Hunter is not communicating with us because his asset is no longer in contact?"

"That's right, sir."

"Hunter might simply be protecting his source... As long as the operation is on track," the Chief said.

"But the only reason MI6 knows the operation is on track is because of our eyes on the ground. This was not the deal we had with the CIA."

"I hear you." The Chief was moving around his office. "The only way to know for sure is to ID Hunter's source and perhaps to find out whether we have credible HUMIT on that person also."

Harris was thinking about how to best respond to the Chief's latest insightful suggestion.

He must have waited too long because the Chief barked, "My God, Harris... You've already found who that person is, haven't you?"

"I have credible HUMIT and think –"

"Don't bullshit me. I may no longer be on the ground, but I know how this business works. You used whatever resources you have in Taipei to get the information."

Harris hesitated. "I just knew what I was looking for."

"Do I want to know how you looked for the intel?"

"Probably not..."

There was another interminable pause from the Chief that was excruciating. "You are lucky that you have one operative and now two British nationals who need you focused on getting them out, otherwise you would be on your way back to London as we speak."

"I'm sorry, sir, but I couldn't see any other way out for my man and his rescue."

"But you could have discussed it with me. Instead we are backed in a corner and obliged to go ahead with your plan B – whatever that plan is."

"What chance do I have at being successful with plan A if Hunter doesn't feed back any intel, even to you?"

"I made one call..." The chief trailed off. Perhaps he too was assessing the likelihood of Hunter responding to the demand for more information, even with a more forceful request. "Anyway, we are where we are. What is the timeframe of the extraction?" the Chief added.

"Next twenty-four hours."

"How is it going to happen if Hunter has lost contact with Dragon?"

"I'll be organising this, sir. ALPHA team is ready to follow the initial plan."

There was no point hiding his plan B. It was the only one that could work, and perhaps the involvement of Mattie Colmore was a good thing after all.

"And how does ALPHA team know..." Another loaded silence followed. "You told them and they agreed to help?"

"That's right, sir."

"I'm sure you know how deep you're in it and how deep the service is in it too if – no, when this comes out."

Harris shrugged as though the Chief could see him. "I won't leave an operative behind."

"Neither will I." His response was rushed, but both Harris and the Chief knew better. Sometimes sacrifices needed to be made and they would be. Harris was grateful it wouldn't be him making them.

"I will try Hunter again and see whether I can drum some sense into him..." the Chief said.

"And I'll keep going at my end, sir."

"I don't need to tell you that OPERATION TECH LEOPARD is no longer a joint MI6-CIA approved op..."

"I'm aware, sir."

"However, let's take it that you and I haven't had this conversation yet."

"Thank you, sir." Harris hesitated and the Chief picked up on it.

"I don't want to know who Dragon is. I don't want this intel to navigate on any comms written or oral, no matter how good we think our encryption is. This is the one element that gives us an advantage at the moment, so let's keep it that way."

"Next update, sir?"

"When your operative is in touch or if there is any setback, no matter how small. It's damage limitation from now on, and I trust you will at least allow me to do that."

The Chief hung up and Harris felt doubt creeping in. It was up to him, Nick and the ALPHA team to get the fugitives out.

* * *

A call at 5.30am woke Warden Tang. He listened to the summary of last night's search without uttering a word and hung up.

There had been no sightings, not at border control, not along the border itself, not in the desert, whether on the Chinese side or the Mongolian side. Anger propelled him out of bed. He moved to the small bathroom that felt like luxury in a place so devoid of comfort. He showered, shaved, and got dressed in a mechanical and precise way that helped him control his rage.

Tang ignored the breakfast that had been served in his dining room and walked straight to the drone control room.

The two operators looked drained and worried, but he didn't care.

"Show me the area you have covered."

The young man who had called him brought up a map on his screen and he showed the area that had so far been canvassed. It had been a comprehensive sweep and extended deep into Mongolia, far beyond what men on foot or in a car could possibly cover since escaping.

"Call in the next team and hand over," Tang said, still scrutinising the zone covered by the two drones.

The young man made a call and assured Tang a fresh team was on their way. Tang hardly acknowledged him, still focused on the land that had yielded nothing so far.

The new team presented themselves and Tang asked them to scan the same area again. Perhaps the fugitives were hiding and waiting, to emerge and attempt a crossing.

But Tang didn't buy the idea. Henry was a rather clever man and a trained man too. Once more Tang's anger rose at not having seen through Henry's ruse quickly enough. He could at least blame his lack of judgement on the untimely intervention of General Ma. Although his preferred solution was still to capture the fugitives and get the situation under control before he had to find excuses for his lack of insight.

Tang moved to his office and called up a map of the area on his computer screen. He zoomed in and analysed the border zone. It was a succession of rugged hills and steep canyons that softened heavily towards the west.

He called for some tea and food, stood up when it was brought to him and ordered it to be laid out on his office meeting table. He remembered the initial interrogation with Henry. The story about Henry straying into China from Mongolia had sounded so far-fetched that it had made it credible. Plus, Henry's knowledge of banking was real, of that Tang was certain. Tang started pouring tea into a cup but then stopped.

He stepped back to the screen and zoomed out of the area he'd been focusing on to give himself a broader map to consult. He and his team had initially picked Henry up closer to the west where a car could, as he had claimed, get lost across the border.

The men who had killed the smuggler Zu had been interrogated. It was the usual story of greed amongst smugglers. But perhaps Zu had not simply spotted a foreigner worth kidnapping for ransom as he had told Tang. Unfortunately for him Zu was dead, and so too were the men who had killed him.

Tang returned to his tea and finished pouring. There was something he was missing. He looked at the map, sensing there was a clue there eluding him. He drank some tea and pursed his lips. It had been prepared to his liking. Finally, the kitchen staff had learned.

The rice and vegetables that had been brought in didn't appeal as much. He took a few mouthfuls and pushed the food away.

What would he do if he wanted to escape Zhaga?

Go underground was the obvious solution but in the westerners' case, it was more complicated. They couldn't mix easily with an Asian crowd, and it would take someone with nerves to provide them with cover for a long period of time.

Tang picked up his mobile phone and dialled his contact again. "Find out whether any westerners have been spotted in the area."

If the man was surprised by Tang's request, he didn't sound it. "How far shall I look?"

Tang was about to respond when he thought for a moment. "Include Bayannur." Why not? It was no harm to cast the net wider. Tang returned to his ruminations. He finished his tea and poured another cup.

The other way would be to cross the border at the least expected point, but that could be anywhere. He checked his watch and calculated that the fugitives had escaped nine hours ago. Tang returned to his desk, cup in hand, and sat again in front of his screen. He called the drone operators with new instructions. "Broaden the search to the west and the east along the border."

On foot they could not have gotten far, if what they had done was follow the border and avoid the crossing. The drones would not have picked them up yet. But it would be different if they had a car...

Tang called again. "Look for people or cars along the border."

But if they had chosen to drive on the road and not the dirt tracks along the border their vehicle wouldn't be picked up.

Tang fingered his walking stick and hoped he would have the occasion to use it soon. For a moment he indulged in the fantasy of bringing Henry and Rob back to the interrogation rooms.

Tang's mobile rang. His contact was calling back already – perhaps he might indulge in his fantasy after all. He picked up with an eagerness he disliked showing. "Speak."

"Two men and a woman have been spotted in a Bayannur restaurant."

"Find out more."

It was perhaps unlikely, but his contact would soon know whether these people were expected tourists visiting the area.

CHAPTER THIRTY-ONE

The pick-up spurted for a few extra yards then came to a sudden stop, giving a loud sigh. Henry had steered it to the side of the road, close to the rock face that rose above it. The desert flats had been gradually replaced by hills of hard rock and the road was now winding around them.

Rob opened the bonnet, and a belch of smoke blew up into his face. He waved it away and shook his head. "I'm not sure the engine can be repaired."

Henry joined him and both men surveyed the disaster. "It's a miracle it got us this far," Henry grumbled.

Mattie joined them. More adventurously than the two men, she pulled at the piston part of the engine, grimaced as though the part was still too hot to handle and shook her head. "Piston's fried."

"The pick-up won't start again," Henry said, pulling Mattie away from the bonnet before closing it.

The sound of an approaching lorry startled them, and they moved back inside the vehicle wondering whether the driver might stop. But the truck was travelling at speed and the driver clearly keen to meet his delivery schedule. It sped past and disappeared around the next bend in the road.

"By my estimate we are about half an hour's drive from the next petrol station." Henry looked in the side mirror, hoping the next lorry or car was just around the corner, but nothing came.

"Is walking along the road an option?" Rob asked.

"Not really." Henry shook his head. "Unless we can cover our heads with a hat or cap that shields us enough from view."

Henry glanced into the side mirror again and left the car. He walked over to the rock face and explored it with his hand. It was firm with grooves and small crevasses. The slope was steep, but it could be climbed. The process would be slow going and they would be as exposed to prying eyes as they would on the road.

Henry returned to the truck and heard a car coming from the opposite direction. His watch indicated 9.30am and traffic volume was building. "We could climb to the top of the hill and get to the next station that way, but this still leaves us exposed during the climb."

Mattie nodded. "We need a new car."

Henry stopped himself from making a flippant remark.

"Except that they are all driving at speed and they will almost certainly not stop." Rob shook his head.

"We have to make them stop." Henry considered the distance between the two sharp bends at either end that hid their truck from view. "But if we roll the car into the middle of the road, there won't be enough distance for a vehicle to stop. They'll simply crash into us."

Mattie turned to Henry. "What's the plan after a vehicle stops? Bundle up the driver in the back of his car or truck and take over?"

"Something like that." Henry left the vehicle again as soon as the road was clear. He walked to the next bend and returned at a jog. He got in. "We could push the pick-up to the next corner and let it freewheel for a while."

"But that still doesn't get us to the petrol station," Rob said.

"No, but it gets us closer to a flatter part of the road. We can then push our pick-up into a section of the road that will give vehicles enough space to stop."

"Or... we could draw the driver's attention to someone they may stop for." Mattie gave the two men a grin.

Henry picked up on her idea first.

"Oh no you're not."

"Why? This is the perfect trap." Mattie looked innocently at him. "I play the demoiselle in distress, and I bet you that the first driver that comes along will stop."

"I'm not sure this is the right place to call upon the chivalrous side of men." Rob frowned.

"Who says I'm talking chivalry? I'm pretty sure that this will be the last thing on the driver's mind but if he thinks I'm on my own, there is a good chance he'll try it on."

"That's a good point." Rob nodded.

Henry slammed his hand on the wheel and the other two stopped talking.

"That's enough! We are not using anybody as bait." He turned to Mattie, angry. "Do I need to jog your memory about the last time I got you out of a tight spot?"

Mattie's face dropped and Rob looked stunned at the revelation Henry had just made.

"You're driving the pick-up and Rob and I will push it to the next bend in the road."

Henry got out of the truck, slamming the door. The memories of the Islamic State's treatment of female hostages had brought back too much anger. He'd saved Mattie but so many others hadn't been so lucky.

He heard the door on the passenger side open and Rob appeared at his side.

"Don't ask," Henry shot to Rob.

"I wasn't going to."

"That's wise."

The sound of yet another lorry drove the two men to the rock face where they flattened themselves against it. They waited until the sound of the truck disappeared. Both men returned and leaned into the back of the vehicle.

"Release the brakes," Henry shouted.

The weight of the pick-up made them buck but they made a concerted effort to push, and it started moving up the slope.

It took them a couple of attempts that were interrupted by more cars coming their way before they reached the top of the small hill. Both Henry and Rob returned to the pick-up to take their seats.

Henry took a sip of water and a moment to recover. The muscles of his legs were shaking and his back was in pain. He glanced at Rob whose face looked drained. Mr Tech Genius sure didn't fit the nerdy profile generally associated with his kind.

Henry released the brakes and the pick-up started to roll downhill, gathering some speed down the slope. The terrain and the sides of the road levelled out to become increasingly flatter on both sides. When the car slowed considerably, Henry jerked it into the middle of the road, before it stopped.

"Let's get out and wait for the next car to turn up."

They jumped out of the pick-up and walked far enough away that they wouldn't be identified but close enough that they could run to the new vehicle as soon as their target had stopped.

A lorry came around the corner of the hill and Henry turned to the other two.

"I'll grab the driver as soon as he is out of his truck." Henry's hand went mechanically to the gun in the small of his back. The lorry was approaching fast, and Henry readied himself to move.

"He's got to start braking now otherwise he's going to hit the car." Rob was following the truck with his eyes as he spoke. His body tensed as though he was preparing for impact.

"Shit..." Henry half rose from his seated position. "He's not going to stop..."

The realisation froze the three of them. They watched helpless as the truck continued to drive towards the pick-up. The driver didn't even bother to sound his horn. The vehicle started to swerve to the left and the wheels bit the side of the road throwing dust and small stones around.

The lorry clipped the pick-up truck and pushed it to the other side of the road. The pick-up stopped after a few yards. The truck was already in the distance.

"Fuck... this is not happening." Henry ran to the pick-up to inspect the damage. The wing had been badly dented and the tyre torn by a piece of metal that had lodged into it.

Mattie and Rob arrived, and he felt Mattie stand close.

"OK, you win..." he said to her. "That's the only way these bastards are going to stop."

Mattie simply nodded and Henry turned to Rob.

"We need to bury ourselves in the ground so that whoever stops, thinks Mattie is alone." Henry took a shovel from the back of the truck and the two men hurried, digging a hole for themselves in the sand. The next truck had to stop. They'd already lost over an hour.

* * *

313

In the past twenty-four hours Rodriguez had sent just two words to Harris's burner phone.

Arrived and *Boarding*.

Harris had updated the timeline on the wall of the safe house. Fergus and Hulk had also arrived in Ulaanbaatar as expected.

He checked his watch. It was 2pm and Rodriguez was on his way to Mongolia, departing from Osaka in Japan. Rodriguez would be out of touch for the next three hours. When he landed in Ulaanbaatar, Harris would update him with details from the various satellite hacks Nick was performing.

Just has he stepped back from the wall to consider progress on OP TECH LEOPARD's timelines, Nick walked out of the room he'd turned into the new command and control centre.

"I'm done." Nick plucked the pen from Harris's grip and wrote on another part of the wall. He ticked a box next to his name and the list of deliverables became shorter.

"Just finished establishing a good hack of the Google Earth satellite and I'm there with the BlackSky next-generation satellite used by the US Army Tactical Geospatial Intelligence prototype program, known as TACGEO." Nick grinned.

"Is this the satellite carrying night vison capability?"

"The very same... Fergus was right. It's a bit tricky to hack but well worth it when you do."

"How likely are we to get rumbled by TACGEO?"

"More likely than by Google Earth, although Google is a serious player when it comes to tech, of course. I won't stay connected to BlackSky as much as I'm going to stay connected to Google Earth to limit the risk of getting caught."

"Rodriguez is on his way and on time."

Nick checked the time on his Luminox watch. "I'm ready when they are. Rodriguez said he was landing at 3pm. Fergus and Hulk are with their embassy contact getting some gear. If they leave Ulaanbaatar in the evening, I'll get night vision images to cover the journey the ALPHA team will travel after sunset, and also check for activity on the Chinese side of the border."

Harris nodded and couldn't suppress a smile. Nick was going native with army vocabulary and he looked at ease with it.

Nick smiled in return. "I guess I'm more suited to the job than I thought I was."

"As long as you don't sign up to join the Army Corps, I like the emerging Nick."

"No chance, I still owe Henry."

"You're doing well at repaying your debt. I'm sure he would agree with me."

"Let's hope I hear that from him directly."

Harris and Nick fell silent for a moment. A buzzing sound reminded Nick he was on call for the ALPHA team, and he ran back to his tech cave.

Nick picked up his headset and responded to a video call. "Are you guys all set up?" Fergus's image materialised on screen. He was still wearing his civvies and would only change when the time came to cross the border with China.

Harris moved to Nick's side, picked up another headset, and listened to Fergus's update.

"We have found some gear, good enough stuff that we can operate with."

"At least the radio sounds clear," said Nick. "I presume you need me to find a frequency we can work with and that won't be picked up by the Chinese?"

"That right... and we managed to find some Bittium Tough SDR Handheld."

"That's great news. Can you confirm the range is a wide 30-2500 MHz?"

Harris frowned and Nick picked up on it.

"Bittium is the next-generation software defined tactical radios for squad or platoon leaders," Nick answered Harris whilst listening to Fergus's answer.

"Correct..." Fergus replied. "And I managed to find enough for all of us."

"I'm on it. I'll establish a frequency rotation so that we maximise our chances of evading attempts to eavesdrop."

Harris moved closer to Nick's computer screen, leaned in and asked his question. "Will you be leaving Ulaanbaatar as soon as you pick up Viper One-Zero?"

Code names had been agreed again for the members of the ALPHA team and Harris thought it was time to start using them. It was easy to remember who Rodriguez was.

"We're all set," Fergus said. "We're picking up Viper One-Zero and we are on our way."

"How about the other guys?"

"We sourced a car and have left some gear for them. It'll be ready for collection when they arrive tomorrow."

"What are you missing that could jeopardise this mission?" Harris felt obliged to ask but Fergus didn't seem to mind.

"Better guns, better protective vests, better detection systems, better –"

"OK, I get it," Harris interrupted.

"But as long as Nick can get us proper satellite intel day and night, we'll be good."

"I'm ready when you are," Nick said.

Fergus gave the thumbs up. "You have a map of the route we are proposing to take. A quick look at what's happening there would be good."

"I'll scan the route right down to the meeting point and will take a peek into China."

"Good man…" Fergus hesitated, then asked another question. "Any contact with H?"

Harris shook his head. "I'm afraid nothing yet."

"What was the agreed call timeframe?"

Harris forced himself to answer without hesitating. "11am to 1pm."

Fergus looked at his watch. "You've still got thirty minutes."

* * *

The roar of an approaching truck made Henry and Rob flatten lower in their shallow graves. Henry pulled the slide of his gun back and lay on his side ready to kneel and shoot. He would be guided by the sound of the lorry stopping and the driver's door opening.

Mattie had pulled her shirt out of her trousers and tied it around her midriff, exposing part of her tanned belly.

Henry had tried not to look, but Rob had smiled at her. "That should do it."

Mattie had smiled back. "I could tear up my shirt but that might be a bit too obvious for the rest of the trip."

Now, she was waving frantically at the incoming truck driver, as agreed.

The screeching of brakes and the loud grunt of an engine told Henry the truck had stopped. He could now hear Mattie speaking and a door opening. Henry was about to kneel up and take aim when a second door opened and shut. He stopped and waited. He had to be sure the other man had joined his colleague on Mattie's side of the lorry so that he had a clear aim.

Mattie screamed suddenly and Henry bit his lip. The voices of the men rose at the same time, one laughing, the other one shouting.

Henry waited a few more seconds and sprang from his hole, taking aim at the men. One had already taken a knife out and was threatening Mattie with it. She'd run for cover behind the stranded pick-up, but the other man was circling around to reach her.

Henry didn't bother to call the men. He shot the man with the knife in a two-touch shot to the chest and head. The man collapsed after a small recoil. The second assailant turned and started running.

Henry shouted, "Stop or I'll shoot you down!" in Mandarin. He discharged his gun only a foot away from where the man was, letting him know he was still in range. The man stopped and held his hands up. As he turned around to face Henry his eyes glittered with a mix of fear and anger.

Rob had run to check on Mattie. She shook her head, mumbling a few inaudible words.

"Can you two check the back of the lorry to see what it is we are transporting?" Henry said, as he waved his gun at the man to come closer. "I'll drive until we reach the petrol station and you two can hide in the back of the truck."

Rob unbuckled the heavy tarp and started lifting it. Henry saw the face of the man he was ready to shoot drop as fear took over.

"Shit…" Rob froze.

Mattie moved to his side. "Oh, my God."

She put her hand to her throat and Henry guessed there were people in the back of the lorry.

"A lot of money…" the man was saying. "We can share… a lot of money," he repeated, whilst bowing in hope.

"I bet it is." Henry took aim and pressed the trigger, hitting the man in the knee.

The man dropped to the ground with a scream. Henry slotted the gun into his waistband and grabbed one of the man's arms. His screaming intensified but Henry didn't care; he dragged him to the shallow grave he'd just dug and threw him in it.

"Shut up or I finish you off."

The man nodded with a grimace of pain.

Henry left him there and returned to the truck. Mattie and Rob had disappeared into the back. Henry climbed in and dropped the tarp down.

Five children and two women had been chained together and gagged. They looked dirty, exhausted, and terrified. Mattie was kneeling next to them, speaking in a soothing voice, and although she used English her words seemed to comfort.

Rob had kneeled down too, his face white. He looked helpless and yet keen to reassure.

"You are not in any harm," Henry said, his voice trembling with anger. "My friend here is going to undo your gags. Do you understand?"

One of the women nodded and Henry was grateful she understood Mandarin.

"Mattie, I've just told her you're going to remove the gags."

Mattie smiled and moved closer. She slowly reached behind the woman's head and managed to untie the grimy piece of cloth the men had used.

"Water..." the woman mumbled in Mandarin.

Rob didn't need a translation. He took a bottle out of his rucksack and handed it to her. Mattie moved to the next woman and then to the children. The water bottle circulated so that all got a turn to drink.

"We need to remove your chains too. Do you know where the key is?" Henry asked.

"The big man... he has it around his neck."

Henry jumped out of the truck and walked to the side of the pick-up where the first man had fallen. He turned him around, reached for a chain around his neck and snapped it clean off. The sound of a car approaching made Henry push the man underneath the stranded truck. He then opened the door and hid in the back, waiting for the car to drive past.

The engine sound told him the car was slowing down.

"Go away..." Henry mumbled through gritted teeth. He didn't want to have to gun down more people.

318

The engine of the car revved and it continued on its way. Henry thought there was urgency in the way the driver had sped off. Perhaps he was going to alert the authorities.

"We need to make a move. A car just drove past. We don't want someone else stopping," Henry said, as he climbed back into the truck to hand the keys to Mattie.

Rob moved to the pick-up to retrieve a bag containing all the food they had, then swiftly returned to the truck. Henry jumped into the driver's seat and slowly manoeuvred the lorry back onto the road.

The small hatch between the driver's cabin and the rear of the truck opened. Mattie's face poked through. "The woman I untied first is called Batu and she speaks a little English."

"You're going to have a good conversation, then. You can talk to people even when you don't know their language, so you'll likely know everything about her before our next stop."

"That's the idea."

"By the way..." Henry hesitated, as he looked ahead with more focus than needed. "You did well out there."

Mattie moved her hand though the hatch and squeezed his shoulder. "As long as you've got my back, I know I'll pull through."

Henry gripped the steering wheel a little harder, to stop from squeezing her hand in return.

CHAPTER THIRTY-TWO

Henry was pushing the lorry hard. Unlike the pick-up, this vehicle was well maintained. It wouldn't do to break down and need a tow-truck with human trafficking victims in the back.

It turned out his driving wasn't out of place against other lorries that were barrelling down the road, some of them almost out of control.

Mattie appeared at the hatch. She handed a bottle of water to Henry.

Henry grabbed the bottle with thanks and took a couple of sips.

"I found out that none of the women and children are related," Mattie said. "They were picked up from different parts of Inner Mongolia. Batu is a medical student, but she was visiting family when she was abducted. She comes from one of the tribes that live in the area. The other woman is Chinese from a little hamlet near Bayannur and the children are from different families. Same story of being kidnapped from small villages in the area."

"I've read there is a fair bit of kidnapping in China. I got the impression that this was linked to the one-child policy. There is a shortage of women, and some people resort to this tactic to find workers for positions normally only held by female or even brides."

"The one-child policy has just been relaxed to two children last year, so yes, women are in short supply."

"So, these girls were kidnapped to join a community that needs more women?" Henry glanced back at Mattie.

"That's right. There are remote places in China that have been so harsh in selecting boys only and aborting female children or abandoning them that there aren't any women left for all the men that are reaching marrying age."

"And I presume looking after a house and doing chores has also got to be done by women not men."

"I'm afraid the old patriarchal society is strong in this country. It's the man who looks after his parents in their old age, so families also prioritise boys for that reason."

Henry glanced again at Mattie. She had squeezed her head, arm and shoulder through the hatch and rested her hand on the top of his seat. "It's strange to think how current Confucius's thinking sounds when applied to matters of the state or even people's psychology but how backward it is when applied to women," he said.

"What are we going to do with them?" Mattie's voice broke a little and Henry knew that meeting these women and children had brought her back to the Middle East.

"Does the woman who speaks English have a phone number she can call?"

"I haven't asked, but I will. Why?"

"I need to make one call and that will cost me one of the mobile phones we carry. After that I'll have to dump it. She can use it to make a call too and ask to be picked up. I trust she'll help the others."

"But what if the rest of the gang catches up with them? We can't leave them in this truck."

"We can leave them at one of the resting areas we'll find on the road. I'm going to dump this truck. By now, it's been probably been flagged with the authorities, so I'll dump it as soon as we hit the junction between this road and the G7 motorway. There is a small town with plenty of restaurants and car parks for truckers around the entry point. We'll switch vehicles there."

"We don't know how safe they will be if we leave them on their own, Henry. It could take hours for them to be picked up."

"Then you'd better find out whether Batu's tribe can help."

Mattie disappeared into the back. Henry cursed. His latest plan had flaws. He also didn't want to leave the women and children in a remote place that might be teeming with similar traffickers. But he had to get Rob, and now Mattie, to safety.

Low-rise buildings appeared in the distance and Henry recognised the rising slope of a motorway junction. According to the intel he had received from MI6 and the CIA, the motorway had recently been completed. It provided a direct route to the shortest distance between the G7 motorway and the border.

Henry slowed down. He would drive past the junction to check access to the motorway, and then move to the small town and find a new vehicle.

Signs with Chinese characters on them told him they were 214km from Bayannur in the east and 257km from Ejin Banner in the west. The additional symbol on the panel caused Henry to slow down further. Ahead, a man in a booth was waving cars forward.

"Shit..." Henry bent his neck to get a better look. "Shit. It's a toll booth."

Mattie appeared through the hatch again, eyebrows knitted tight. "Problem?"

"There's a toll booth at the entrance to the motorway."

"Is it working?"

Henry slowed down to a crawl. Another truck sounded its horn as it overtook them. It hardly slowed down in its approach. Its brakes screamed as it got closer.

"I guess the answer is yes. It is working." He drove past a couple of makeshift car parks where lorries of various sizes had parked and chose the largest one on the outskirts of town. He pulled into it and stopped the truck.

"Batu says her tribe lives to the west, so it'll take two to three hours for them to get to her," Mattie said.

Henry turned to her with a question. "What are they using – horses or camels?" He hadn't meant it to sound flippant.

"SUVs." Batu spoke loud and clear from the back of the truck.

Mattie couldn't help a smile. Henry shot her an angry look. Batu's English was better than simply a few words. He fell silent for a moment and then turned towards the hatch and leaned against it, forcing Mattie to pull back.

"Batu, can you drive a lorry?" he asked.

Batu moved towards the hatch, her soft brown eyes intrigued by the question. "Lorry?"

"Truck, I mean... Could you drive this truck?"

Batu looked around and then her head popped through the hatch. Henry pulled back to let her take a look.

"I can drive this..."

"You said your family would take a few hours to get here?"

She nodded. "To here two, three on other roads."

"Two hours on the motorway?"

"Two hours."

Henry glanced at his watch. "This is what we are going to do."

Batu drove the lorry slowly towards the toll booth. It stopped with a small jerk and Batu lowered the driver's window. The clerk lifted a surprised eyebrow but said nothing. It wasn't uncommon for large trucks to be driven by women in Inner Mongolia, something that may have been less common in other parts of China.

He looked inside the truck cabin with suspicion. Someone was sleeping in the passenger's seat. Definitely a man, with a jacket covering his body and a cap over his face. Somehow this seemed to reassure the clerk.

"All the way to Ejin Banner," Batu said before he could ask where to. "Yuan 130."

"I make it 127.50," Batu replied.

"That's the price to use the motorway. Otherwise use the other road." The clerk didn't budge.

Henry shifted slightly to remind Batu that they had a meeting in two hours' time."

She shrugged and took money out of an old bag, counted the notes twice and handed over the bunch to the clerk. He repeated the same process of counting the notes twice and then opened the barrier. Batu moved the truck into gear and drove on steadily.

As soon as they were out of the feeding lanes and on the motorway, Henry sat up, removed the old cap he'd found in the truck, and took the mobile phone Batu had used to call her father out of his jacket pocket.

Harris's phone rang only once.

"I'm on my way to the crossing point," was all Henry said after Harris's hello.

"How late are you?" Harris asked.

"A couple of hours, perhaps more by the time I change vehicle again."

"I'll feed this to the team. They'll know to expect one more person."

Henry clenched his fist and relaxed it. He would have a conversation with Harris about involving Mattie in Taiwan and even if it got personal, he didn't care.

"Do we have the full ALPHA team extracting us?"

"No, our friends from across the pond are not playing ball..." Henry heard the frustration in Harris's voice.

"How many of them?"

"Three for sure... The other two will be arriving twenty-four hours later."

Henry lowered his voice. "Dragon has been put under house arrest." Harris seemed to take his time to absorb the information. "I don't want to give you a name over this phone but –"

"Nick and I figured it out... Don't ask me how. I don't want to talk about it over the phone, either."

A surprised Henry took a few seconds to return to the call. If Nick had found out, a serious hack had been initiated.

"Have we stunned you into silence?" Harris sounded amused.

"Not yet."

"I suspected as much, but when did you come across the intel about Dragon?"

"Two days ago."

"As long as we get you and Rob out, we shouldn't need her input any longer."

"I don't think it is as clear-cut as you think, Steve."

"You think she'll talk to save her skin?"

"That's not the worry. Rob is not only the man we need to get out. There is some intelligence that he was supposed to receive from Dragon. He hasn't been able to collect it yet."

Harris didn't sound as surprised as Henry had expected. "I'm sorry if I sound like a broken record but –"

"– you figured that one out, too." Henry finished his thought. "Anyway, you're right and we have one crack at getting this intel out before we leave China."

"How do you propose to do this, H? You only have twelve hours left in the country and I presume Dragon is back in Beijing if we are talking house arrest."

"I don't think it's a question of location. I think the intel needs to be transferred to a place where we can pick it up digitally."

"You mean like a cache somewhere on the net?"

"Something like that, and that's why she picked up Rob."

"To make sure he could find it... But why not get the intel to him in the first place, avoid the kidnapping?" Harris sounded dubious.

"I think his kidnapping was proof to someone that she could be trusted with high-grade military intelligence."

"You still haven't answered my question... How?"

"I have one mobile phone left that is not registered in China, and she got a SIM card to me, which I plan to use before we cross the border."

"The more you delay the call the less likely she'll be able to take it."

Henry nodded. "I thought about that but if the Chinese authorities are on the lookout for mobile activity next to the border, this mobile will ping loud and clear. Same thing if they are tracking mobile activity at Dragon's address. I can't call now; we are still too far from the crossing point. I will call when we are about to cross. This gives us a fighting chance to have advanced into Mongolian territory before they can get to us."

"OK... What else do you need from us?"

"The warden at the camp has been using drones to track us. Get Nick to deal with them."

"Two little drones shouldn't be a problem for him."

"You're impressed?" Henry smiled.

Harris grunted. "Reluctantly, yes."

"And...?"

Harris sighed. "You were right to recruit him and persist."

Henry glanced in the side mirror. "I've got to go... I think we have company."

* * *

"Journalists, you say?" Tang had received snippets of information on the westerners' whereabouts that hadn't amounted to much – that was until a call from his contact.

"Two of my men have gone to check with the restaurant owner. He wasn't around at the time as it was very early so, he had to –"

"I don't care what he had to do to get the information. Who saw them and how do they know they are journalists?"

"The waitress who does the early morning shift saw them with a regular client. He is a trucker, a Mongolian leaving in Bayannur. He turns up regularly at 5am on his way back from the border. The waitress –"

"Stop... go back. You said the border. I presume he drives lorries across that border, and this is where he was coming from when he stopped at the restaurant?"

"I think so."

Tang exhaled, exasperated. "Find out. Who is the trucker?"

"He doesn't seem to be employed by any of the big companies." The man hesitated.

"Who told you that?"

"The restaurant owner."

"Do I have to do all the thinking myself? Don't rely on what the wretched restaurant owner says, find out yourself. His truck has necessarily passed the border. I want an answer before 2pm today."

"Fine."

The resentment coming from his contact was palpable but Tang didn't care.

"How do you know they are journalists?" Tang asked again.

"It's what the trucker said to the waitress when he chose a table for his guests," the man answered gruffly.

"That's what they told the trucker." Tang wouldn't share any more of his thoughts. Journalists could be many things other than people reporting the news. He'd seen this in Hong Kong, where a large part of that community took sides in the battle for a free and democratic Hong Kong.

"Who paid for the meal?" Tang asked instead.

"The woman."

"In Yuan?" Tang spared his contact from saying he didn't know and added, "Find out."

Tang hung up. He had been standing at his desk for the entire conversation and his frustration hadn't abated with the call. Instead of calling the operators like he usually did, he walked out of his office and to the drone control room. His presence would galvanise the new team, of that he was certain.

The two operators were staring at their screens when he entered. The cups of teas and snacks of those manning the drones were almost consumed. Tang liked the effect his regular visits were having on his people. Fear was an essential ingredient of running Zhaga, whether it was the inmates or the staff.

Tang walked silently to their desks, but didn't manage to surprise them. They spotted him.

"Progress?" he asked.

"Nothing, sir. We've flown the drones along the edge of the border and covered eight hundred miles. We're just bringing them back."

Tang reluctantly agreed this was the right thing to do.

He left the control room and headed for the steel factory. A new piece of the US Navy's arsenal was under construction. This time a replica of a US Ohio-class submarine would turn Zhaga camp into the top site for military assault and counter-attack exercises for the Chinese Navy. If the Chinese ambitions expressed by President Xi were to be realised, all factions of the Chinese Navy needed intense and realistic training.

Tang couldn't remember who had said "an army is only as good as its last victory" but the army for the People's Republic of China had never been tested, or at least not yet in battle.

Tang arrived at the main doors to the foundry. The sound of heavy pieces of metal being cast and moved around bolstered Tang's progress in at least one area. The production was going well and it was ahead of schedule.

The engineer hadn't asked questions about the absence of his three best workers. Tang winced at the thought of having to replace at least one of them. Bo Chan wouldn't be coming back. Tang needed to contact Hong Kong again and check if they were willing to send over men who had been arrested on political activism charges. Hong Kong was becoming much less tolerant of dissent and the current Chief Executive of Hong Kong would soon be replaced by someone Tang suspected would be more to President Xi's liking.

Tang walked inside the factory. The guards were looking anxiously in his direction and the workers had also noticed. The yelling of instructions gave way to commands that were less controlled. Tang walked slowly around the factory, satisfied with the impact his visit was having.

He spent almost an hour there making the life of the prisoners that much less bearable. He smiled. As he was observing the production line for the replica submarine, an idea had popped into his head.

He would ask his contact to check who had crossed the border at Ganqimaodu. Journalists travelling to China would often begin their trip in Beijing or Shanghai, but perhaps these people, whoever they were, had started in Mongolia, hence the ride with the Mongolian trucker.

Tang walked back to his office, satisfied that this was an avenue worth pursuing.

* * *

A highway patrol car was following them. The driver started flashing the car's lights at them. It overtook the truck to drive alongside it.

Batu pushed Henry back into his seat and opened the driver's window. She smiled without slowing down. "Hello, officers. How are you?"

A woman driver was clearly not what the officer had been expecting. He was momentarily taken aback but managed to ask his question. "One of your lights is broken..."

"I'm so sorry, Officer. I'm on my way to the next petrol station. I will stop to carry out the repair there."

The two officers had a quick chat and the second officer asked him something which the first officer relayed.

"Are you authorised to drive this truck?"

"Of course. I have a full licence for large vehicles." She glanced at him, giving him another innocent smile.

The officer strained to look inside the cabin. He noticed the man sleeping in the passenger seat.

"My father is travelling with me." Batu nodded with respect in her voice.

"Change your light and be more careful next time."

The patrol car pulled away.

Henry couldn't believe their luck. He waited for a moment before lifting his cap from his eyes, and turned to Batu. "How did you know about licences for large vehicles?" he asked in Mandarin.

"My brother, he drives a truck."

"And when you travel with him, he lets you drive the truck?"

"Occasionally..." Batu smiled. "We're not far from the petrol station."

Henry smiled back. "Then I'm happy for you to take us there."

Henry removed the SIM card from the mobile phone he had used to call Harris, and threw it out of the window. The mobile followed a few seconds later and a metallic crushing sound told Henry the device had been caught under one of the wheels of the truck.

Batu was right. Less than ten minutes later, a couple of buildings appeared in the distance. She started to slow down. Henry turned towards the hatch to call the others and let them know. "We are approaching the station. Whatever happens, get ready to move fast."

"What do we do if Batu's contact is not there?" Rob asked from the back.

"I'll find another vehicle and we'll switch anyway."

"Are we leaving them on their own?" Mattie asked.

"Mattie, I don't like this either, but we have no choice."

Mattie didn't reply and he knew this wouldn't be the end of their discussion on it.

Two large buildings drew nearer. The bright neon billboard advertised outstanding food and drinks, as well as a bed for the weary trucker. The other building looked like a minimart with a row of petrol pumps outside.

Batu entered the car park.

"Can you park it at the far end?" Henry pointed in one direction.

She nodded, moving slowly to avoid the other trucks that had been parked badly and without consideration for other drivers.

The lorry came to a stop and Batu pulled the handbrake. She looked around the area and Henry did the same. There were a couple of vehicles parked next to the minimart, none of which were SUVs. But one of the cars both Henry and Batu recognised.

The police patrol car was tucked near the entrance of the shop, waiting.

CHAPTER THIRTY-THREE

At 1.55pm Tang's phone rang. He had braced for some delay in getting feedback from his contact, but the man was obviously keen to please the warden.

"A car went through border control, entering from Mongolia the day before yesterday. It was carrying a female journalist and her guide, and it left China last night with another driver at the wheel."

Tang sat up straight in his office chair. "The car I asked you to stop?"

"Exactly."

The pang of pleasure coursed through Tang's body, reminding him of what it felt like to track and hunt someone rather than something. "What else?"

"She paid for the meal at the restaurant, in Yuan. The notes looked well used according to the waitress, and she left a nice tip."

"Keen to use notes that won't make her stand out," Tang mused.

"My men have located the trucker. He is hired by transport companies; he is freelance."

"Bring him to me."

"I could try to get some information out of him first. My men are good at that."

"No doubt, but I'd like to hear his story for myself." Tang hesitated. "Bring him to one of the sites in the desert. I don't want him at the camp." The location may delay the start of interrogation for a few hours, but Tang felt it was necessary to hide the existence of a witness to the escape.

"What now, Warden?"

"I'll tell you which site in a short while. Just bring him there as soon as I decide."

Tang hung up and slapped the table with a victorious hand. He moved the mouse of his computer to wake up his screen and consulted the map of the border again.

He was now almost certain that the two men accompanying the woman were Henry and Rob. Tang went to one of the filing cabinets behind his desk and pulled two files from it. Henry's mugshot looked puffy from the beating he had received but his features were still easy to recognise. Rob's mugshot showed no injuries. Tang put the two files on his desk.

He was about to call his contact again when an email flashed up on screen. Tang thought about ignoring it but the storm gathering around General Ma's deception meant that Military High Command was becoming more interested in the trip she'd taken to Zhaga.

Tang opened the mail and scanned it, but when the topic became clearer, he sat down and took his time reading it.

As he had suspected, a series of detailed questions had been put together regarding her visit. The questions had moved away from the factual – who had she interrogated or spoken with, including staff, what had she learned and what had she asked Warden Tang to do next – to the more subjective: did Tang notice a change in her attitude? Was General Ma making remarks that questioned or criticised the purpose of the camp? Had she shown weakness or been accommodating to the prisoners?

The last question made Tang uncomfortable. He had indulged Ma's idea on the basis that it might serve him to have Henry help with hiding the money Tang still owned in a couple of bank accounts in Hong Kong. He would have to tread carefully when answering.

Tang read the long list of queries again and sat back for a moment. Ma was under intense scrutiny, the likes of which Tang knew would be difficult for her to come back from. Whether she was a defector or not – as the questions seemed to imply she was – she would never survive the ordeal of interrogation and suspicion. There were too many people, too many men who wanted to prove a woman wasn't fit to hold such high office.

The email was long and would take time to review, and yet an answer would be expected soon. High Command wouldn't take kindly to a slow response. Even worse, they may infer Tang was in cahoots with her.

Tang ignored the email and returned to the map on screen. He studied Bayannur's position in relation to the border. The move inland had been a judicious one by the prisoners. It had sent Tang's team off track, but as he had predicted, to stay hidden as a westerner in Inner Mongolia would be hard. Tang considered next the grid of roads that departed from Bayannur. The one going east would lead them deeper inland and towards Beijing.

The motorway to the west hugged the edge of the border for a few miles. Tang tapped his finger on the map and grinned. "I know where you're going, and I know where you'll cross." Tang picked up the phone and called the drone control room. "Concentrate both drones to West Zhaga."

The operator confirmed the order and Tang hung up.

He then called his contact. "Deliver the trucker to Zhaga. I've changed my mind."

Tang had no time to lose. He first needed to carefully answer the email about Ma. After, he would concentrate on capturing the fugitives, although the fall of General Ma had made Henry's capture far less appealing. Perhaps a hunt that finished with a kill was what the next twenty-four hours would bring.

Warden Tang pushed away the fantasy. He needed a clear mind if he was to convince High Command he was just an honest warden doing an excellent job.

* * *

Batu's confidence evaporated as soon as she saw the highway patrol car. "What do we do?"

"I presume these petrol stations have a phone box?" Henry asked.

Batu frowned. "I don't know. I haven't seen a phone box for a long time... since I was a child."

"Everyone owns a mobile phone?"

"Even my grandmother has one."

Henry dug into his rucksack and drew some cash out of it. "Where are the ladies' toilets?" he asked. Batu looked at Henry, puzzled. "I have a plan to get you into the place without using the front door. If we find the ladies' toilets windows, I'll get you through them."

Rob stuck his head through the hatch. "Can we help?"

"Not yet. We don't need two westerners out in the car park when there is only one hat. Just stay put."

Rob grumbled an OK.

Batu and Henry slid out the passenger side of the lorry cabin. It was more sheltered from the view of the patrol car and would give them time to figure out their next move.

"I need to know if there is a window to the outside in the ladies, assuming the toilets are inside the minimart."

Batu nodded. She removed the band from her hair and shook her hair loose. She took off her jean jacket and handed it to Henry. The move made him smile. Her appearance was rather different to how she'd looked whilst driving the lorry. Shame she wouldn't be easy to recruit; she would have learned the spook's trade quickly.

She darted towards the building and disappeared behind it.

Henry felt at his back for his gun. He had spent six rounds already and had another fourteen. He'd seen the typical sidearm the Chinese military carried before, and recognised it in the gun holsters of the Zhaga guards. Henry was glad that the Norinco QSZ-92 he'd stolen was the 5.8mm form which carried up to twenty rounds of ammunition rather than the 9mm version that only carried fifteen.

Batu took an eternity to come back, and Henry wondered whether it had been such a good idea to send her. She was just a nurse who happened to know how to drive a heavy truck. The report Henry had read about Mongolia emphasised the difference in how Mongolian society treated women – more respectful, much freer to do things that were deemed a male preserve in other countries. And yet, in this car park, this was China.

Batu appeared a few seconds later. She walked back to the lorry as quickly and calmly as she could.

"Two windows, close to the –" she searched for the word "– packet doors?"

"You mean delivery doors?"

"Yes… Had to wait, otherwise noticed."

"OK. That's good to know. How high up are the windows?" Henry mimicked height with his hand.

"Much higher –" Batu smiled "– but good for you to reach."

"How do you know they're the right ones?"

"One window open and I hear women voices."

Henry nodded and moved to the side of the lorry, nearing the front. He could see the building only a few yards away. He glanced at the patrol car. The windows were rolled up and he couldn't see inside. No one had come to investigate the truck yet, so either they hadn't recognised it or the men were inside the minimart getting food and drinks.

"I'll go first, and I'll wave to you to come across."

Henry drew the cap down over his face and walked the few steps fast, the way a man might if he needed to relieve himself urgently. As soon as he reached the building, he stopped to survey the layout of the outside. Batu was right: the two toilet windows were high up but not so high he couldn't reach them. Farther along, a large opening gave access to the back of the minimart where supplies would be delivered.

A couple of men came out of the door. Henry dashed over to the side of two containers that were being used as trash cans. They were smoking a cigarette each and chatting. Henry waited, praying neither of them needed a pee. By the smell of it, the back of the containers was a favourite spot of theirs.

The men disappeared back inside, and Henry went to the toilet windows to investigate their layout. He gripped the window ledge and lifted himself up slowly, mindful not to be noticed by the women who may be inside. One of the windows was situated just below a washbasin. There was no one inside the toilets and Henry pushed the window open further.

It would be difficult for a man to get in, but Batu would be small enough to climb through the opening. Henry returned to normal height and waited a moment to make sure he was still alone. He retraced his steps and waved Batu to him.

She walked over.

"You should be able to get in. I'll tell you how."

She nodded and they both stopped next to the containers to check no one was coming.

"I'll give you a lift up. You see this gutter above the window? Test it and hang from it if you can. Then get in feet first. The ledge will give you better purchase that way." Henry presented his locked hands and Batu placed one boot in them. He lifted her as high as he could and gave her a push. She managed to grab the gutter and her feet found the window ledge. She stayed there for a few seconds and slid in through the windows. She glanced down at Henry and then nodded, before disappearing through the opening.

He heard her land on the other side, safe. Now she needed to get a burner phone and call her father. Henry crouched until he heard the toilet door slam shut. He stood up, covered his eyes with the cap, and returned to the truck.

The patrol car hadn't moved. A few lorries had departed, making the car park look more sparse. Henry checked his watch. It was already 3pm and the SUV hadn't arrived yet. He would give Batu ten more minutes and then try to enter the minimart through the delivery doors.

The sound of a commotion made Henry jump. He got out of the truck and ran to the back of the building.

Batu was standing on the window ledge and one of the men who Henry had seen smoking a cigarette had grabbed one of her ankles. He was trying to bring her down.

"Hey you!" His call in English startled the man.

Henry reached him in a couple of steps and slammed his fist into his gut. The force of the blow bent the man over, exposing the back of his neck. Henry punched him a couple of times at the base of the skull until the man collapsed.

Batu was holding back a cry. Henry stretched his arms out for her. "Come on, jump..."

She did and he caught her easily. They both ran to the edge of the building.

"You go first."

Batu walked to the lorry shaking. As soon as she was inside Henry followed. The man on the ground would be out for some time but they needed to get a move on.

"Speak to my father," Batu said, as soon as Henry got in.

"Where are they?"

"Fifteen minutes only... coming from other side of motorway. Difficult to cross..." She was looking for a word.

"Because of the central reservation?" Henry mimicked a stretch.

Batu nodded. "Yes."

"They have to find a point to cross farther down the motorway so that they can double back and access the petrol station." Henry slowed down to make sure she understood.

"Yes, did not want attention."

"Very wise..."

Henry wondered how long they had before the patrol officers recognised their vehicle or before the man he had knocked out woke up. He turned to the hatch and called Mattie and Rob.

"We've been lucky so far, but I won't count on it lasting," he said to them. "The patrol car is still here and there is a guy at the back of the building who will recover in a little while."

"There is nowhere to go," Rob said, irritated. "Look around, Henry, it's the desert."

"This is not quite true." Henry shook his head. "The terrain drops at the back of the restaurant, enough to hide there if we lie flat."

Rob shrugged. "So what, we make a run for it, all of us together?"

"We don't need to be that obvious. We can go one after the other..."

"I'm not sure we're going anywhere," Mattie said with a jerk of her head at the buildings.

Henry and Batu faced forward. The two patrol officers were leaving the minimart and walking in the direction of their car.

Batu called her contact's number again. The conversation between them was fraught. She hung up just as one of the patrol officers, standing at the door of their car, looked in their direction.

"Two minutes..." Batu said in English.

"Let's change places." Henry slid across to the driver's seat and pulled his gun out.

The two officers were now chatting, perhaps debating whether this was the same truck or whether to bother at all. Henry could tell from their body language that one was keen but the other wasn't. The driver got into the patrol car, but the other shook his head, making a move in the truck's direction.

Two SUVs cut across his route to the lorry and parked alongside it. Four men got out, and Batu gave a small cry of joy. One of the men was taller than the others. His short beard was well trimmed and greying. His hair was thick and long, reaching his shoulders.

Batu got out, and ran to him. He opened his arms and the joy of their reunion made Henry smile, despite the situation. The patrol officer had stopped, taken aback by the scene.

"Get ready... We won't have much time to do the switch," Henry said, as he turned to Mattie and Rob. "And yes, I think the women and children will be safe."

Mattie looked at them and the uncertainly on their faces didn't seem to convince her.

"We've got to go." Henry laid his hand on her shoulder and squeezed it gently.

One of the men who had driven one of the SUVs knocked on the window. Henry wound it down. The patrol officer continued to observe the situation from afar.

"The second car is for you." The man's Mandarin was heavily accentuated, and Henry took a moment to understand.

Batu spoke rapidly to her father. His eyes met Henry's for a short moment and the gratitude in them was genuine. Then he turned towards the patrol car. He spoke to the men who had accompanied him and the three of them walked towards the patrol car with assurance, but without looking threatening.

"Come on..." Henry slid out of the passenger side, away from everybody's view.

Rob and Mattie joined him. The man who'd spoken to Henry moved the SUV closer to the back, out of view of the patrol officers. He handed the car keys to Henry with a nod and extended a hand. This didn't feel like a gesture the man was used to but rather something he thought he ought to do to show his respect.

Henry responded with a nod of his own and shook his hand. There was little time for anything else. Mattie and Rob were already in the SUV. Henry grabbed the keys, moved to the driver's seat, and started the car. It purred into action.

Henry reversed slowly and drove towards the back of the building. He cast a quick glance over at Batu before the SUV disappeared behind the minimart. Batu was looking in their direction and her father and the two other men had pulled the officer's attention away from the truck.

Henry drove around the petrol station and reached the road quickly on the other side. He pressed the accelerator; the engine responded with a smooth forward motion.

"We should be able to make up some lost time with this car," he said.

"I might even be allowed to drive," Rob said from the back.

"What about you, Mattie?" Henry teased.

"Nope... You boys can knock yourselves out driving this brand new SUV. I'll simply recline my seat and go for a sleep."

"Very wise." Henry nodded. "And I'll do the same when Rob takes over."

Henry drove for another couple of miles and as soon as there was less incoming traffic, Henry pulled over and they swapped.

Henry reclined the passenger seat and dropped his cap over his face. "Wake me up in an hour and a half, Rob. You'll need some sleep before we start our crossing."

"You got it." Rob returned the SUV to the road and within seconds Henry was asleep.

Rob's voice woke him up with a jerk. "It's been an hour and a half, as you requested."

Henry stretched before opening his eyes. He pulled the cap away from his face and looked around. "What time is it?" he asked, staring at his watch.

"5pm. The light has faded much quicker than I expected. Night time is meant to come at 8pm not before."

"When did dusk start?" Henry asked.

"About an hour ago."

Henry brought up the back of his seat and looked into the rear. Mattie was still asleep. They had another hour to go, or perhaps less if Henry pushed the SUV a little harder.

Rob slowed the vehicle down to a stop and both men waited until the road was almost empty before switching again.

When Henry drove on, Mattie started to stir. "Are we there yet?" she said in a sleepy voice.

"No, we have another hour, maybe less."

Through the rear-view mirror, Henry glanced at Mattie's dishevelled head. Even with it so messy, he found her attractive. Rob had reclined the passenger seat and was already asleep, a discreet snore coming from underneath the jacket he'd used to cover his face.

Mattie poked her head through the gap between the seats. "Those children are safe, right?"

"You know they are, otherwise you wouldn't have left them." Henry shook his head.

"I sometimes make mistakes..." Mattie gulped down some water and handed the bottle to Henry. She looked out the window. "It's very dark and it's only –" Mattie pushed the sleeve of her shirt up to check the time "– 5pm."

"I know, both Rob and I remarked on it. The sky started to darken an hour ago according to him."

Henry took a few mouthfuls of water and returned the bottle to Mattie. She squeezed his fingers for a moment, and he returned the gesture.

The sky abruptly darkening further caught their attention.

Henry frowned. "What's going on?"

Mattie wound the window down a little and slid her hand through the gap. She pulled it back after a few seconds and her face had lost its colour. "Shit... the wind is picking up a lot."

"I noticed it was a little windier when I switched with Rob."

"If it's a thunderstorm that will be bad enough... as long as it doesn't bring a dust storm with it."

"Haboob..." Henry said.

"Exactly and the Gobi, like the Sahara, is one of the worst places for these."

"Any warning signs?"

"None, other than seeing a wall of dust moving at speed towards you."

CHAPTER THIRTY-FOUR

Harris brewed more coffee and brought a mug to Nick. The young man nodded, absentmindedly grabbing his cup. He was conducting a thorough review of the route the ALPHA team would be taking as well as the topography they'd be crossing to extract Henry, Rob and Mattie. Harris left him to it without asking for an update.

He returned to the timeline on the wall, took a chair and sat for a moment to consider progress. In a couple of hours' time, he would get in touch with Rodriguez for a briefing. Nick was building an accurate picture of the terrain, including any hostile activity. The drones Henry had mentioned worried Harris, but Nick had assured him that he would deal with them if they ventured too close to the crossing point.

Harris finally took a sip and winced. His drink had cooled down a little too much for his liking, but it was coffee and he needed plenty of it. He took another sip and went over the call between him and Henry a few hours ago. It had been two hours late, but at least Henry had sounded like himself, in control and focused.

Henry hadn't said a word about Mattie. Harris knew him well enough to be certain they would be having an almighty argument about her inclusion as soon as Henry found the right occasion. Harris usually only indulged his operatives and their tantrums if necessary to the success of an op. This time he wouldn't mind and might even find it justified.

Henry ran his hand through his hair. He still needed to tell Rodriguez that ALPHA team would be extracting one more person: Mattie.

Someone calling his name made Harris snap back. "What?" He turned his head towards the source of the sound.

Nick had left his desk and was looking worried. "You've got to come and see this."

Harris sprang up from the chair and moved over to Nick's screen. "Show me."

"I have been surveying the terrain from Ulaanbaatar to the designated crossing point. So far nothing was showing on the Mongolian side, but I came across this on the Chinese side."

Harris squinted. "It's a cloud formation."

"More precisely, it's a thundercloud formation. I've checked the atmospheric pressure around the area and it's dropping fast."

"How fast is fast?"

"At the moment I register 29.2 inches. To give you an idea, 29 inches is indicative of stormy weather and 28 inches is a hurricane."

"And how quickly will this storm happen?"

"I'm not a meteorologist but could be in the next twelve hours, or it could be a little less or a little more. But there are freak events, too."

"So, you can't tell." Harris leaned against Nick's desk.

"Not really..."

"We need to get hold of Rodriguez and tell them. I saw a couple of these desert storms when I was in Iraq. They were scary."

"Iraq?" Nick looked intrigued and eager to ask questions.

"A story for another time. Connect me to Rodriguez if you don't mind."

Nick sat back at his desk and dialled the tactical radio frequency both he and Fergus had agreed upon.

Harris put a headset on and waited for the team to pick up. The line opened and Harris took over. "This is base calling Viper One-Zero."

"This is Viper One-Zero, over," Rodriguez answered immediately.

"We have identified a weather event you need to be aware of."

Nick had put his headset on also and gave Rodriguez the details of what he'd spotted.

"A storm will obviously slow us down, but we have good equipment that will help us as long as the storm is not too severe."

"I thought one of your Vipers didn't like the gear he was given?" Harris asked.

"This Viper is an old moaner. What we have is good enough."

Harris heard protesting close by and he imagined Fergus listing the issues he'd found with their gear. He was a meticulous man, one of the reasons why he was still alive and so were the members of his team.

"Good to hear – not about the moan but about the gear," Harris said. "On the positive side, I've had contact with the extraction target and the exfiltration has been delayed by two hours."

"Roger that... Are they aware of the storm coming their way?"

"I can't imagine them not noticing," Nick said. "It's a long weather front and the gathering storm clouds are stretching over a large area."

"Good to know they can see what is brewing, but I'm not sure it will change anything," Rodriguez said.

"Please clarify." Harris frowned.

"They don't have the luxury to wait it out. They'll need to keep moving until they can't anymore. H will know that. He'll be ready for all eventualities."

"He is not on his own, though."

"They still need to keep going, and so will we until we absolutely can't." There was no doubt in Rodriguez's voice. "The trick is to know when to quit."

"What do you need from me?" Nick was gathering more weather reports and data to share.

"Let's have another briefing in one hour, sooner if the situation deteriorates fast. We'll be two hours away from the border and will need to assess our next move."

"Roger that Viper One-Zero."

"One more piece of information that you need to factor in." Harris jumped in as Rodriguez was about to kill the call.

"Go ahead."

"There is one more person to extract." Harris winced at the thought of springing the information on Rodriguez so late in the day.

"How many more is this operation going to goddamn collect before it's over?"

"I think this is it." Harris sensed the anger in Rodriguez's tone.

"You think or you know?"

"I know... She's the journalist who is helping us get eyes on the camp and H." Harris did his best to sound confident.

"Shit, Harris... Don't spring another surprise like this on me."

"I won't."

"Viper One-Zero out."

Rodriguez hung up, leaving Harris uncertain about how he could help Henry and his team of fugitives, and hoping Rodriguez would have simmered down by the time he reached the border.

"I need to call London." Harris had never spoken to Nick about his interaction with the London office, but he felt the young man had qualified for inclusion. "I may need to wheel you in. Are you up for it?"

"If it's about tech stuff, yeah... I'm good."

"I'm not asking you to bare all, OK?" Nick looked puzzled. "Your little foray into Hunter's files and emails–?"

"– is better kept among ourselves. I may be a good hacker, but I don't brag."

Harris nodded. "Then we understand each other."

He left Nick at his desk and moved to his bedroom to make his call. Harris sat on his bed and briefly rehearsed was he was going to say. He dialled the chief's number on his MI6 mobile.

The Chief's PA answered. Harris apologised for making an un-scheduled call.

"This is fine. I will see whether I can transfer you now."

Harris got a glimpse of how deep in trouble he was. The Chief was taking a call from him on the spot, and this never happened – well, almost never.

"Any issues?" The Chief didn't opt for a smooth introduction. He just needed the facts.

"I've heard from my operative and they are on their way, with a short delay."

"Does that compromise the rendezvous with the... other team?"

The Chief's pause for the right word caused Harris to sit up. OP TECH LEOPARD had gone over to the illegal side.

"No, but a developing weather condition might."

"Explain, please."

Harris told the Chief what he and Nick knew about the developing storm. The Chief remained silent for a moment after Harris finished.

"Your man is not an idiot so let's trust he will make the right decision. He won't lose the advantage on the people pursing him unless he makes the wrong choice. His pursuers will endure the same as he does but will they know when to stop the chase." The Chief paused again. "Will Henry know when to stop running?"

* * *

Henry parked the SUV in the car park of a small motel he'd spotted. What was meant to be yet another resting area turned out to have a couple of motels and a restaurant on site. The motel backed onto the desert. The steep hills in the distance that Henry and his people were aiming for jutted up from the horizon.

"We have two and a half hours of daylight left for the crossing, even though the light is not as good as I hoped it would be," Henry said. "We won't be using torches; too dangerous and obvious to spot, especially with drones in the air."

"Unless the storm that is brewing catches up with us," Rob said, frowning.

"The storm could break at any time but spending the night waiting to see whether it does isn't an option."

"Why not?" Rob asked.

"We can't do the crossing during the day and waiting around in the car park or anywhere else is out of the question. We'll be spotted."

"What are the chances of us surviving a thunderstorm in the open, the likes of which you only encounter in the Gobi?" Rob rubbed his face with both hands. "Slim, I'd say."

"Not if we are prepared."

Henry turned around to face Rob.

"What – crawling on our bellies all the way to the hills to avoid being struck by lightning? That's your plan?" Rob shook his head and fetched a bottle of water from the side pocket of the door.

Henry and Mattie exchanged glances in the mirror. Thunderstorms might be the least of their worries if what followed was a dust storm.

"We'll eat first and then we need to get going."

Mattie handed Henry the bag of food.

"Why can't we use the SUV?" Mattie said. "It hasn't been stolen and it will provide some shelter if the storm comes."

"We're back to the same issue. People on foot are less visible than a car and dumping it near the place where we plan to cross the border is a no-go."

Henry's words were measured. He opened the bag of provisions and took out three energy bars and a large bag of nuts. Not a feast but it would have to do.

"What do you propose?" Mattie said. "We start crossing then sit it out without protection if, or rather when it breaks?"

"Exactly that." Henry nodded at the food. "Take your pick."

Rob gestured to Mattie. "Ladies first. Perhaps I should make that call now?"

Henry stiffened. This was not the time to call Dragon, just as it wasn't the time to stop running. They had to stick to the plan of calling her as they crossed the border.

"What call is that?" Mattie poked her head between the front seats.

"Not the time to discuss this." Henry's harsh tone surprised Rob and Mattie.

"And why not?" Rob shot back.

"Seriously, Rob?" Henry glanced at Mattie.

Rob took some food, but simply stared at it.

"We are losing time, here." Henry grabbed an energy bar, opened the packet of nuts, poured out a handful and held it out to Mattie.

"Trying to silence me with food?" she said, grabbing some nuts.

"I'm not trying to silence anyone, unlike the warden of Zhaga if he catches up with us."

The remark hit the spot and silenced the complaints. Although Mattie still shot Henry a dark look.

Rob ate half of his bar and stuck the rest in his pocket. Henry noticed his hands were trembling a little.

"Let's go." Henry said, after he and Mattie had finished. He checked there wasn't anyone around and opened the door.

Mattie followed, getting out discreetly. Rob grabbed the door handle but didn't exit.

Henry turned around and gripped Rob's shoulder. "There's nothing wrong with being frightened of a lightning storm, but you're going to have to trust me and let me lead you through it."

Rob gripped his thigh with his free hand and inhaled deeply. "It's ridiculous, I know."

"Don't worry about what's ridiculous or not."

Rob nodded slowly and opened the door. He stepped out but kept hold of the frame. Henry left the car too. There were a few people around but with his cap set low over his eyes, no one should notice he was a foreigner. At least Rob was out of sight.

Henry circled the car and grabbed Rob by the arm. "When we start moving it'll be all right."

Rob hesitated for a few seconds then let go of the car door. "OK... OK, let's do this."

Henry glanced around the motel car park. A few truckers had arrived and were making their way to reception. When it appeared no one seemed interested in them, Henry turned back to Rob and Mattie.

"I'm moving first to scout out what's happening at the back of the motel. When I signal, Rob comes first, then Mattie."

Henry faced ahead, hoping he wouldn't have to drag Rob out of there. Henry fingered the car keys he had pocketed earlier. A brand new SUV wouldn't be so easy to hotwire, but Rob might be just the guy who knew how to do that.

Henry moved fast towards the back of the motel and stopped. He listened out, only hearing the buzz of electrical equipment. He rounded the corner to discover a jumble of old furniture, boxes of various sizes and rubbish that had been standing around for so long, it was impossible to know what it once was. A couple of cats had taken residence amongst the furniture. They raised their heads, curious at the new arrival on their territory.

Beyond the rubbish, there was a slope that dropped steeply towards the desert. Henry retraced his steps to the corner. He saw Mattie talking to Rob. Rob was nodding.

Henry couldn't help but smile. Whatever she was saying to him seemed to convince him to keep moving.

When he waved at them, Mattie noticed Henry's signal first. Rob took a moment to gather himself and walked towards Henry. The sky hadn't changed colour for a while but it hadn't gotten darker. Perhaps the storm would land somewhere else after all.

Rob reached him.

"Wait on the other side of the rubbish tip. We can get to the desert flats that way," Henry instructed.

Rob barely acknowledged Henry's orders, but he did as he was told. Henry waved to Mattie next; she made her way over in her relaxed yet determined way Henry admired so much.

"The sky colour hasn't changed," he said as she reached him.

"Don't hold your breath. This storm is going to hit us. It's a question of how hard."

Henry didn't argue. She had spent more time in the desert than he had.

Rob had crouched to the ground. He was surveying the slope when Henry and Mattie reached him.

"There are a few grooves on this side." Rob pointed to dents that had been made in the wall of the slope. "I think people must use them regularly to get to the lower level."

"Sounds good." Henry walked to the spot where the deep indentations showed in the compacted earth. "Rob, you're the mountaineer. Do you want to go first?"

"Sure."

Rob kneeled on the ground and placed his foot in the first dent. He tested it to see whether it could take his weight, then descended slowly towards the desert.

"Mattie, you're next."

She followed after Rob as soon as he touched the lower ground. Rob grabbed her before she reached him and made sure she landed safely. Henry noticed the brief contact between the pair and wished he'd been the one down there to catch her.

The two were now looking up at him; he pulled himself together. As he reached the ground, a gust of wind flew a little sand over his feet. Rob didn't seem to have noticed, or perhaps he was trying to ignore it as best he could.

Henry took out the compass Genghis had left him. He checked his watch. They had another two hours of bad daylight in which to walk.

"This way." Henry walked due north, an eye still on the west where the sky was turning a little darker.

The only sound Henry heard was the regular crushing their shoes made on the rocks and sand. The gust of wind had steadily increased. A few times Henry had turned to check on Mattie and Rob. Both were concentrating on where they were putting their feet – each for different reasons. Rob was avoiding looking at the sky and seeing what was happening there. Mattie had spent too much time in war zones where the next step could cost you your life, if you were unlucky enough to step on an IED.

The first flash of lightning came as the sky turned a black inky colour. Henry lifted his head to check but didn't stop. He was expecting a rumble of thunder to follow but nothing came.

"It's more than five miles away. We would have heard it otherwise." Rob had increased his pace.

"We have another thirty minutes or so before we reach the foot of the hills," Henry replied, accelerating his pace also.

"OK," Rob said, still staring at the ground.

He glanced back and saw that Mattie had dropped back a little. She lifted her head, aware that he was looking at her.

"I'm all right. I can keep up."

The wind picked up a little more and this time the sand that came with it engulfed them.

Henry turned around again. "Let's stop and cover our faces."

Rob hadn't heard. He seemed in a trance, just walking and blocking everything else around. The clap of thunder that followed shortly after the next lightning strike stopped him dead. Mattie had almost caught up with them, but she too stopped and looked around, to check where the lightning was striking.

"Rob, you need to protect your face." Henry plucked out a T-shirt Genghis had left in his rucksack. He tore the piece of cloth in half, doused it with water and presented one piece to Rob.

"This won't be enough," Rob said.

"It'll do for the time being." Henry gestured again and Rob reluctantly tied it over his face.

Mattie had an old scarf, which she used to do the same to her face. Henry tied the other half of the T-shirt over his face, took the compass out of his pocket and oriented himself once more. The hills were clear in the distance and despite the dying light, their location looked to be just a few moments away.

The next rumble of thunder made Henry look up. Rob had dropped to the ground, a look of dread on his face. Another flash gave Henry the opportunity to count the time to the next clap of thunder.

"By my count it's moving away," Henry said when it came.

"The thunder is but not the storm." Mattie reached the two men and stood next to Henry, pointing in another direction where the lightning could be seen.

Henry couldn't make it out to start with. In the distance it looked like a haze; the lack of natural light made it even less distinct. But he had seen pictures of it and his training in the camps of Syria had warned him against them.

"Is it a dust storm?"

"Yes, and it's big."

Henry moved quickly to Rob. "How long have we got?"

A fresh gust of wind, much fiercer than anything they'd encountered so far, gave him the answer.

"Minutes rather than hours." Mattie pressed her scarf against her face. She'd put her sunglasses on and although they looked odd, they would at least protect her eyes.

Henry yanked Rob up from the ground. "Come on. We need to move towards higher grounds if we can."

Rob tried to stand up, but his legs buckled underneath him. Henry slid his hands under his arm and started to walk with him. "Come on. You can do this."

Rob held onto Henry and both men advanced together, steadily increasing their pace. Henry looked over his shoulder. Mattie was keeping close to them. Lightning lit up the sky again and Rob almost stopped, but Henry kept him going. The dust flying around them wasn't obscuring the horizon just yet. Henry kept his eyes on a point in the hills that he could still distinguish and was giving him guidance.

The ground started to feel a little more resistant and sloppier underneath his feet. The next clap of thunder sounded much stronger, as its sound bounced off the hills they were approaching. The dust that was engulfing him now made Henry hesitate.

He'd just lost the feature in the hills that was helping him to orientate. The wind whipped around them; he would need to shout over it to give his instructions.

He stopped walking and shouted, "We need to drop to the ground!"

Rob shook his head. "No! We're almost there."

Rob pushed Henry away and started running. In seconds he would disappear in the swirling dust. Henry lunged and rugby tackled him. They rolled together into the sand. Rob threw a badly aimed punch and Henry replied with a punch of his own that dazed Rob.

Kneeling on the ground Henry turned around. Dust and sand were engulfing him, and he couldn't see Mattie. The howling wind muffled his voice when he cried her name.

Despite his efforts, there was no answer to his calls.

CHAPTER THIRTY-FIVE

Tang meticulously washed the blood splatters from his hands. The trucker had proven much more resilient than he had anticipated. He must have guessed that once inside Zhaga he wouldn't be getting out alive.

Still, Tang had got what he wanted out of him. The two men that had accompanied the woman journalist were Henry and Rob. Whatever story they'd fed the trucker was of no interest to Tang, but they had disappeared near an area in Bayannnur that was mainly residential. Tang suspected they were after a car they could steal. He didn't need to investigate which car. He needed to survey the border at the narrowest crossing point and not give up the chase.

One of Tang's men arrived just as Tang was about to leave the interrogation room for his office. The trucker's body had been disposed of. It hadn't been thrown into the pit but into the cremation oven that the camp used for inmates who died a natural death.

The clock on Tang's wall indicated 7.30pm. He'd lost more than two hours responding to the email regarding General Ma, sent to him by Military High Command, but it had to be done. Tang sent the man to finish the job of disposing of the trucker's ashes. He then walked out of the building towards the drone control centre.

The two young men there were concentrating on their screens. They didn't move when Tang entered.

"Anything?"

"No activity yet along the western border, sir," one of the controllers replied.

Tang frowned. It was getting late and attempting to cross at night would be more than foolish.

The second controller turned to deliver his news to Tang. "There is a weather alert, sir. A thunderstorm is developing close to the area we are surveying and high winds, as well as lightning, could damage the drones."

"What are you suggesting? That we call off the chase and call back the drones?"

"We might have to."

"No."

Tang's flat reply was met with a nod from both men and a resounding *yes, sir.*

Warden Tang moved to the computer screen with a permanent display of the map of the area. He zoomed on the part of the map showing the G7 motorway where it neared the border and spotted a cluster of buildings.

"Bring one of the drones over this part of the motorway."

"Yes, sir."

Tang stood behind the operator. "We are still over the desert," Tang said impatiently.

"The drone was completing one of its rounds. It'll take me twenty minutes to redirect it, sir."

Tang thumped the back of the operator's chair with his fist. "What about the other one?"

"Moving away from the storm, sir."

"Bring it back immediately."

Tang stepped away from the operators for a moment. The storm would slow the fugitives down, but as long as he kept the drones in the air, he would be able to spot them as soon as the storm had passed.

He stepped outside the room and called the drone hangar from his mobile. "Prepare the helicopter to depart. I want a pilot on standby."

When he entered the control room again, Tang noted the slight hunch of one of the controllers. The man was concentrating on the image the drone was transmitting.

"What do you see?"

The operator picked up a pen and pointed to a few dots that appeared to be moving on the ground.

"People, near the hills that are close to the building complex you asked us to survey."

"How many?" Warden Tang leaned in to look at the image more closely.

"Three."

"Can they hear the drone?"

"No, sir. The drone is too high, and the wind has strengthened significantly."

Tang straightened up and squeezed his stick so hard, it made a cracking noise. "I'm coming for you…"

He was about to step out of the room to order the helicopter take off when the other operator called him back. "The storm is moving fast towards the east, sir and it's now morphing into a dust storm."

Tang returned to the screen and watched powerless as the dust wall rose steadily. He had spent enough time at Zhaga to know what a dust storm could do. The helicopter wouldn't be allowed to take off until the storm had passed. "Keep following the people you identified."

"I'm sorry, sir but we do need to fly the drones out of the storm and back to base."

Tang dismissed his request with a wave of his hand. "Not until I say so."

One of the drone images froze a couple of times and the picture, when it returned, was hazy.

"We're at the edge of the dust storm, sir. I must insist. I'm already having difficulties with the drone controls." The operator turned to Tang; even Tang's glare didn't deter him. "We are about to lose this –" The operator didn't finish his sentence. The screen changed to a static image of dancing grey dots. The operator didn't need to elaborate.

"Call back the other drone," Tang said, as he turned around to leave.

The storm would take hours to move through the land and over Zhaga. Tang would have to wait a little longer to launch the hunting party he had assembled.

* * *

"Are you sure?" Harris was standing over Nick's shoulder. It had become his default position in the last few hours.

353

In lieu of an answer, Nick used the zoom function on the Google Earth satellite he had control over and showed Harris. One of the three figures that was walking through the desert looked immediately familiar. Harris nodded and leaned against Nick's chair.

"Henry Crowne, you're the business..."

"They're not out of the woods yet, though." Nick zoomed out and redirected the camera over another portion of the terrain the three fugitives were crossing. "There is a drone closing in on them and I'd be surprised if it doesn't spot them soon."

"I thought you were taking care of it."

Nick pushed back, irritated. "I am but there are two drones, so I need to deal with them one after the other. I've identified the make and the model. I can hack into their control software but not both at the same time."

"Got it." Harris picked up Nick's cup. He wondered whether it was wise to ply the young man with more coffee.

"Yes, please... and something a bit stronger than the cat pee you made last time."

Harris went to the kitchen and returned with a fresh cup.

Nick grabbed it without looking at Steve. "That's more like it," he said after taking a sip.

Harris pointed at something on the screen. "What is this?"

Nick zoomed in. "Talk about being caught between a rock and a hard place... The storm is turning into a dust storm and it's big."

"And there is nothing we can do for them..." Harris got angry.

"Disagree. I'm going to use the storm to our advantage and steer the drone towards it. The drone won't stand a chance." Nick had already loaded his hacking program and was facing another computer screen. His fingers were running over his keyboard and his focus had become absolute.

"Is it responding?" Harris felt like a kid on a long journey asking the are-we-there-yet question. He chewed on his lip and waited for a response.

Nick was too focused on steering the drone towards the dust and lightning storm to reply. He returned to the first screen, checking an image that was becoming increasingly blurry. The second screen gave a warning signal and Harris anticipated Nick would act.

But instead, the young man leaned back and grabbed his cup of coffee. "Bye, bye little drone..." he sang with satisfaction.

354

"Is it dead?"

"Yup... One down, another one to go." Nick took a sip and sighed. "Although no rush. The operator at the camp has recalled the other drone. The storm is moving their way and it will take a few hours before they can launch again."

"You mean the storm is moving east?"

"That's right, and sweeping across the border, too."

"Call ALPHA team now. We need to give them the heads-up."

A concerned Nick made the call to the team using the frequency band they had agreed upon.

The call went through after the third attempt and Harris put on his headset to speak to Rodriguez. "We've had a sighting... They're approaching the crossing as we speak."

Harris waited for Rodriguez to relay the news. He heard cheers down the line.

"The issue though is that there is a dust storm over them at the moment and it's coming your way."

"How big is this thing?" Rodriguez's cheery tone changed instantly.

"Several miles across and it's headed east."

"We're only a couple of hours away from the border. We left the main road half an hour ago and there is nothing we can use to shelter the car. We'll have to stop, close the SUV vents and protect the engine before the storm arrives."

"That's going to delay you." Harris wondered whether they would reach the border before it was too dark.

"Some storms pass quickly but if this one doesn't it will prevent us from reaching the hills before nightfall. It will be impossible to drive without lights on," Rodriguez said.

"At least one of the drones we had spotted is down, courtesy of Nick and the storm."

"I presume the camp has recalled the second one?"

"Yes."

"Storms like the one you're describing move at around thirty miles an hour," Rodriguez said. "It'll take ten hours to sweep the land and reach Zhaga but it still means that by morning, the search for H and the other two can resume."

Harris followed with, "And if you are delayed, H and the others will have to cross on their own."

"That's true." Rodriguez fell silent for a moment then said, "I'll contact you as soon as we arrive at the base of the hills on the Mongolian side and if the storm delays us, they'll have to start on their own as you say... Waiting for us is not an option. I reckon their friendly search party will land a couple of hours after sunrise."

* * *

The dust stung Henry's eyes when he tried to open them. He rose on one elbow and searched for his rucksack buried underneath a heap of sand. He fumbled around to find the opening, eyes still shut tight to avoid more grit getting in.

He pulled out a bottle and drenched his eyes with the water, then opened his eyes cautiously. They still hurt but he could see. Henry had protected Rob with his body; only Rob's legs were covered in sand. His face looked a little dusty, but the makeshift mask had worked.

Rob rolled onto his back with a groan. He would feel the effects from Henry's punch for a while, but Henry had no regrets.

Henry tore the mask from his face, wiped his mouth with the clean inner cloth and tried to shout. His throat was dry and only a croak came out.

He stood up, took a couple of sips of water, and tried again. He called Mattie's name several times but got no reply. The moon had reappeared in the sky, and it was surprisingly clear. Sand had collected at the bottom of rocks and boulders, hiding the ground so that everything looked shapeless.

"Where is she?" Rob managed to ask between two coughing fits.

"I don't know..." Henry's mind started racing and he had to steel himself before once more scanning the horizon.

So many shapes looked like a collapsed body. He didn't know which one he should run to. Henry handed the water to Rob and he heard him drink from it.

Henry called to Mattie again but there was still no response. They hadn't been that far apart when he'd stopped Rob from running and the dust storm had engulfed them. Perhaps she'd tried to reach them and passed them by without noticing.

356

The silence around them was almost surreal. A panic, the likes of which he had seldom endured, assailed Henry. He couldn't lose Mattie, not after Syria and not after Russia.

His cries for her sounded more desperate. Rob joined in.

A slight movement to his left caught his eye and Henry froze. He needed to make sure he was right. When the slight movement happened again, he started moving towards it. He ran to the place a hundred yards away and knelt in the sand. He heard a low moan. Henry scooped the sand away, struggling to keep his movements slow and controlled.

Mattie's back appeared first. She had assumed a protective position, knees to her chin and arms around her head. Henry moved faster to free her face. The scarf was still tight around her mouth and nose and she dropped her hands from the top of her head.

Henry search in the sand for her rucksack. He found it and frantically pulled a water bottle from it. He slid his arm around her shoulders and lifted her towards him. Her head rested against his chest and her arms dropped slowly to her side. She moaned again and Henry removed the scarf from her face.

"Don't open your eyes and don't speak yet. You need to drink and then I'll clean your eyes."

He used the inside of the scarf to wipe the dust from her mouth. The movement was gentle and caring. He brought the water bottle to her lips and she started to drink. She grabbed the bottle, but instead of taking it, she closed her fingers tightly around Henry's hand.

She pulled away slightly after a few sips and he bathed her eyes with some of the water that was left.

Mattie's eyes batted open. She used the back of her hand to rub her eyes gently then rested her head against Henry's chest again. "I thought I was lost..."

"I will always come looking for you." Henry closed his arms around her, and she nestled into him.

"You didn't three years ago."

"You were no longer in danger."

"And you were preparing for another operation... I know."

"It wasn't as simple as that, Mattie –"

The sound of heavy footsteps got closer, and they reluctantly let go of each other.

Rob crouched. "Are you OK, Mattie?"

She nodded.

To them both he said, "I'm sorry I took off like that." He sounded remorseful and concerned.

"Don't worry... These storms can scare even the locals," Mattie said. She started to shake free from the rest of the sand, then took another sip and stuffed the bottle back into her bag.

Henry didn't reply, not ready yet to be so forgiving.

When Rob glanced at him, Henry stood up slowly and turned towards the hills. "The sky is clear enough to keep walking to the foot of the hills."

Mattie stood up and leaned against him for a moment.

He looked at her with concern. "Do you think you can make it?"

"Perhaps you guys could carry me?"

Rob nodded. "I'm sure we can take it in turn."

Mattie slapped his back a couple of times and smiled. "Just kidding."

With a smile of his own, Henry shook his head.

She slid the rucksack on her back. Both men picked up their own bags and they started walking towards the hills.

The walk was smoother than he had anticipated and within twenty minutes they had reached their destination. Henry let the other two settle down for the night while he walked a little farther up. There was a faint plume of smoke in the distance. It could have been destruction from the storm, but Henry thought otherwise.

He had heard a faint sound just before the wind had engulfed them. It had sounded like a drone. Zhaga was three hundred miles away but a drone could easily cover the distance and back to the camp. He was now certain that one of Zhaga's drones had been destroyed. Whether it was the storm or Nick's good work, it didn't matter. But Warden Tang still had one drone left and he'd be back to investigate.

Henry returned to where the other two had created a place to settle. He picked up the packet of nuts and helped himself to some.

"We will move as early as we can tomorrow towards a meeting point higher up and then to the border."

"Are we not waiting for the extraction team?" Rob asked. "I don't mind the climb, but we don't want to miss them."

"We won't. We've mapped several points of contact along the terrain where we can meet with the extraction team. We can make good progress and speed up our arrival."

Mattie lay down, one arm underneath her head. "I'm good with the idea. I don't want to be a sitting duck."

She had almost certainly heard the drone too and knew what it was. They had been a permanent feature of the war in Afghanistan and Mattie would have known when to take cover.

Henry lay down and when he heard Rob snore, he reached out to grip Mattie's shoulder. She turned slightly and grabbed his hand, squeezing it hard. They held hands until they both fell asleep.

CHAPTER THIRTY-SIX

The storm had left a trail of debris in its path. The helicopter rotors were throwing more sand around than usual, but Warden Tang didn't care. He'd woken up at 5am after a restless night, waiting for the storm to pass. In the early hours of the morning the winds had started to die down and Tang knew he would be allowed to take off.

His mercenaries were already on board. Tang didn't mind keeping them waiting; it felt like keeping wild animals on leashes. The helicopter was raring to go and his men were keen on the hunt. He would join them soon.

Tang entered the drone control room. The operators looked refreshed after a night's sleep, and they too were keen on his next orders. The lost drone needed to be found, but this was secondary to Tang's renewed need to find the fugitives.

Beijing had sent another email, asking for yet more details about General Ma's visit, and Tang needed to use this request to mount a credible explanation as to why he had to shoot one prisoner and capture the other. He would fabricate a story that linked the prisoners' evasion, his pursuit and the shooting.

"Launch the drone now. I want it flying ahead of us before we take off."

Tang stood at the back of the young operator's chair. His screen was showing a picture of the airstrip, captured by the drone camera. The sun was still below the horizon but the twilight was good enough to see the runway ahead.

The operator executed Tang's instructions and the drone engine fired up. It taxied to the top of the airstrip, acquired speed, and lifted off within seconds.

Tang saw the drone rising and the camp move away.

"Same direction, sir – to the west, following the border?"

"Correct."

Tang left the room. He reached the helicopter and climbed inside.

The Z-20 was large enough to accommodate the twelve mercenaries he had selected. Tang had been granted the right to use the latest helicopter model that had been flying for the People's Liberation Army Air Force.

The Z-20 had been developed after the PLAAF was no longer allowed to purchase US Black Hawk helicopters. Tang had asked for the stealth version. He knew from a source in the Chinese Air Force that the Pakistani Army had allowed the Chinese to examine the wreckage from the US special forces Black Hawk, abandoned during the assassination of Osama bin Laden in 2011. The blueprints for the stealth version of the Z-20 had been drawn up after that inspection. And here it was, made available to him to test and use as he saw fit.

Tang explained to his men what he wanted. The two fugitives should be captured alive. He alone reserved the right to the kill.

One of the pilots checked Tang had buckled up and the Z-20 slowly took off, gaining altitude fast. It banked to the left and was soon high enough that Tang could see the line of hills and canyons that stretched in the far distance, right along the border with Mongolia.

Fifteen minutes into the flight Tang put on the headset dangling to the side of his seat. He asked to be put through to the drone control room and a few seconds later he was speaking to the operator.

"News?" he asked.

"We are experiencing issues with the drone functions, sir." The young man sounded scared. He wouldn't have told Tang unless it was serious, and he couldn't find a solution to the problem he was having.

Tang's anger flared up with no way to let it out. "Explain."

"The drone is flying erratically. I have checked the controls and asked the camp engineer for help, but so far we have not found the answer." Tang heard the young man swallow hard. "But we are still working on it."

"Find a solution." Tang hung up and switched to the flight deck channel. "How much faster can we go?"

"We've reached cruising speed, sir. 180mph. We could go to 220mph but that might mean running short on fuel for the trip home," one of the pilots answered, half turning to face Tang.

"Do it. We'll sort out refuelling if we need to. I want to reach the target as soon as possible."

* * *

The three fugitives had been walking since before sunrise. Henry had been woken up by Mattie. Her hand was on his chest when he opened his eyes and sat up with a jerk.

"Everything's OK. I just need a comfort break," she'd said. "I didn't want you running after me thinking I'd lost my way."

Henry had smiled. "And here I was thinking you didn't object me running after you?"

Mattie glanced at where Rob was lying. She pressed a quick kiss to Henry's lips and stood up before he could respond.

He ran a hand over his face and shook his head. This wasn't the time or the place. He'd better remember the last time he'd thought all was well with the woman he tried to save.

After Rob had woken up a few moments later, they'd shared the last of the nuts and were on the move. They walked now through the hills that straddled the border with Mongolia.

Henry stopped, took the compass out and checked they were headed in the right direction. He'd opted to walk to the first meeting point. The plan he'd discussed with Harris before his departure was to follow the canyons that carved a passage through the hills. There was very little risk of flash flooding there and the canyons would be easy enough to navigate. The arduous part would be on the Mongolian side.

Rob moved to Henry's side and looked towards the far end of the gorge. "How far is the border?"

"We've walked almost three miles so far. Another couple of miles and we'll be at the border."

"How about the call to Dragon?"

"I'd like to be either across the border or have met with the ALPHA team before you call her."

Rob rubbed his jaw, still swollen from Henry's punch.

Henry added, "I agree that the longer we wait the more difficult it is for her to reply, but my priority is to get you out of China alive."

"It might not matter if I can't get the information to the US government that she wants to give me." Rob shrugged.

Henry took a set of binoculars out of his bag and brought them to his eyes. It was the first time Rob had been so open about what he expected to find in General Ma's file.

"You think there is a credible threat of war?"

"Yes, and I think I know where the strike will happen. What if China invades Taiwan and gets its hands on the semiconductor industry that feeds more than eighty per cent of all the high-tech armament in the US and Europe?"

Henry dropped the binoculars for a moment. Hunter must have known what the ultimate threat was all about, and he'd been trying to protect that knowledge accordingly.

Henry resumed his check of the hills. "I understood that Taiwan has positioned its semiconductor production industry along its coastline to prevent their coast being pounded by artillery?"

"This is one line of resistance, but perhaps the Chinese have found a way to invade Taiwan without destroying the entire production. All they need to preserve is enough to sustain their own consumption needs."

Henry dropped his binoculars down again and considered Rob's point. "Still, if we get caught by Tang, there will be no message delivery. Perhaps it's time to explain how that delivery is meant to take place."

Rob hesitated but Henry's mix of impatience and expectancy seemed to convince him.

"I have created a webpage only accessible by her and me. She just needs to dump the electronic file there. But of course, the idea is that I'm online too as she does so that I can retrieve the file immediately."

"You need to agree a time with Dragon and then have access to a computer?"

Mattie had moved ahead a little and came back, putting an end to the conversation. "It's still easy going ahead, but we'd better be out before midday," she said. "The heat gets trapped by the rocks and the temperature soars. It'll be like an oven down there."

Henry nodded. "OK, let's get going..."

ALPHA team wasn't at the first rendezvous point and Henry started to wonder whether they had made it at all. He wouldn't share this with the others. The walk across the border would be child's play compared to their steep climb over the next set of hills on the Mongolian side.

They began to move again and came to a fork in the canyon. Henry turned right, walking along the shady part of the cliff.

When they had reached yet another fork in the road Henry stopped abruptly. He held his breath for a moment and listened, thinking he heard something.

"I heard it, too," Mattie ventured after a moment.

"What is it?" Rob strained to listen.

"I'm not sure... I can't hear it now."

Henry took another turn, this time to the left, and they started to walk again. The next rendezvous point was only fifteen minutes away. He had hoped to identify the sound as human but what he thought he heard had sounded more mechanical.

The sound of rotors in the distance hit them with a sudden clarity.

Henry signalled for the other two to copy him and flatten against the rock face. He hadn't recalled seeing a helicopter at Zhaga but it was likely Warden Tang had not displayed all his military equipment. It was difficult to determine the chopper's position precisely, but if it was coming from Zhaga then it would be coming from the east.

"Let's go." Henry slid along the wall of the gorge, getting closer to the meeting point where he hoped the ALPHA team would be.

The sound of the blades intensified. A brief shadow passed overhead farther along the path.

"How did they find us?" Mattie asked. "We were being careful."

"Our steps must be visible in the fresh sand that's been moved following the storm," Rob said.

The discharge of a machine gun forced them to slam against the rock. There was little cover, but it was better than nothing.

"Don't move," Henry shouted. "They are trying to scare us into running." Henry drew his gun out of his bag. As long as the helicopter was over him for long enough, he could aim for the tail rotor and send the helicopter into a spin. "I'm going to draw them out and fire. Stay put."

Mattie shook her head and pleaded with her eyes, but she bit her lip instead of arguing. Rob was about to protest too but there was no more time.

Henry ran in a zigzag pattern across the gorge for a few hundred yards and then flattened against the rock face. The pilot or someone in the cockpit must have noticed movement because the craft banked sharply for a return pass over the canyon.

Henry pointed his gun at the sky, unsure if the helicopter would be flying across or head-on. The machine gun discharge began way before the helicopter reached the canyon path. Henry stood his ground, checking the direction the bullets were flying as they rebounded off the rock face.

The sound of a competing machine gun volley confused him for a few seconds. The discharge came again, but this time differing sounds told him there were two weapons that were returning fire.

The helicopter pulled away with the energy of a horse rearing backwards.

"Aren't you happy to see us?" Fergus shouted from farther along the path.

"You're late," Henry shouted back.

"You're such an ungrateful bastard." This time it was Rodriguez who answered.

"Part of my British charm."

Henry heard the men running towards him.

"You're lucky we have this motherfucker up our ass or I'd have decked you." Fergus was the first to appear at his side.

Rodriguez and Hulk followed within seconds but there was no time for more banter.

"I left my people farther down the gorge," Henry told Rodriguez.

"Hulk..." Rodriquez instructed.

Hulk ran across the canyon just the way Henry had but this time he was being covered by Rodriguez and Fergus.

"The border is only ten minutes away. After that, we've got ropes for the climb and an SUV waiting."

Henry nodded, watching Hulk's progress. Mattie and Rob were following their rescuer along the rock face and they now only had to cross the same open area. Hulk took Mattie by the arm and shielded her with his body. Henry clenched his fist as they raced across. Hulk returned to fetch Rob and brought him across too.

"Where did the chopper go?" Henry looked at the sky. Even the sound of rotors had vanished.

"Whoever is in there is rethinking his approach," Rodriguez said. "They didn't expect us, and it was our good luck. Now they are looking at the terrain and deciding on the best place to attack again." He looked at his watch and shook his head.

Henry gathered it was the four of them now against the men in the helicopter. No time for reinforcements. "Whoever is in the Z-20 is going to land and those morons are going to come after us," Fergus said.

"They aren't army trained but more mercenary types," Henry said. "Zhaga's warden has his own small army, and he won't hesitate to sacrifice many of them if it means getting Rob and me back."

"Understood," Rodriguez said. "H, you're behind me. Rob and Mattie, you follow."

Rodriguez made it clear who he was there to rescue, and he certainly didn't need to tell Hulk and Fergus their position. Henry appreciated the professionalism and courage of the team.

They walked for ten minutes and came to the end of the canyon. There was an expanse of sand in front of them that led to the foot of another hill. There, they would be in Mongolia.

The sound of rotor blades told the team that the helicopter was on its way back. It was close. Henry turned his head to locate its sound.

"The chopper likely dropped the hostiles farther downhill," Fergus said.

Henry considered the climb ahead of them. "We need to intercept them before they can get to the edge of the cliff, otherwise they'll shoot us like rabbits."

Rodriguez glanced at his men. "That's right. Fergus, do you fancy a climb?"

"He always gets the best jobs," Hulk complained.

"I'll go with him." Henry moved closer to the wall. "And don't tell me I'm not trained for it."

"Never said that." Rodriguez shook his head. "But you're a bit light on equipment." He took his Glock 19 out of his holder and handed it to Henry, along with a couple of spare clips.

Henry and Fergus moved to the part of the cliff that looked the most accessible and they started the climb. Hulk moved across too to give them cover.

The helicopter announced itself with another volley of gunshots. Rodriguez blocked Mattie and Rob with his arm. Hulk didn't budge. Fergus and Henry continued their rapid climb to the top of the cliff.

Fergus reached the top first and rolled onto his belly fast. He found a boulder that would shelter him until he was ready to move. Henry followed swiftly, joining Fergus and waiting to hear Rodriguez and Hulk return fire on the helicopter.

"What's the plan?" Henry had the Glock out and was scouring the terrain. Fergus took out a couple of hand grenades from one of his pockets and handed one to Henry.

"Only when they are close."

"How about the helicopter?"

"Only if they spot us. The boys down there are going to keep them busy until we can engage their people."

Movement across the terrain told them that Warden Tang's men were approaching. There was no tactical thinking in the way they were spread out, it appeared. They didn't look particularly cautious, either.

Both Fergus and Henry released the safety pins on their grenades. Henry spotted four men advancing on his side and he imagined that Fergus could see as many on his side too. They waited for another interminable minute and Fergus nodded. They both released the safety lever at the same time and launched their grenades in a perfect arc into the middle of the advancing men.

The explosion was vicious and resounded around the hills. The cries of the injured followed, as well as the disorganised reply of machine gun chatter from a couple of retreating men. The gunfire ceased. Henry and Fergus waited for a couple of minutes until the sound of the rotor could be heard again.

Fergus took his MP5 submachine gun out and rested it on his shoulder, ready to shoot. But the helicopter moved away and disappeared into one of the canyons.

"They're looping around to sneak up without us seeing them." Fergus slid back next to Henry. "Let's check who's still alive and determine whether they are coming back."

Both men crawled to the site of the carnage. Henry shuddered at the first body he encountered. He stilled himself and followed Fergus past the other dead men. Six of the warden's mercenaries had been killed and the others had fled.

"It's not worth pursuing them." Fergus crouched next to a large boulder. "Let's return to the cliff edge. This spot is where the action's going to be." They walked backwards, protecting each other in turn, and returned to the lip of the cliff.

The sound of the helicopter grew steadily again and could now be heard coming from below. Fergus was right: the pilot had decided to follow the canyons and come at them from the Mongolian side. Warden Tang didn't seem to mind a quick incursion into another country's airspace.

Fergus waited again, MP5 at the ready. Henry pointed his gun. The sound of machine gun bullets whipping the ground was met with a similar response from Rodriguez and Hulk. Fergus moved a little closer to the edge of the cliff, ready to target the helicopter tail rotors.

A fresh volley of gunshots behind them forced the pair to dive to the ground.

"Fuck... You deal with the helicopter," Fergus said sliding backwards. "I'll terminate these sons of bitches."

Henry slid closer to the edge. The machine gun exchange was fierce and soon Rodriguez and Hulk would be out of ammunition.

The helicopter was coming around for another pass. Henry could see the pilot was focused on the entrance to the gorge and at the front, where the co-pilot should be, was Tang, directing the pilot.

Henry lifted his gun higher. The helicopter banked hard to position itself once more over the entrance of the gorge. Henry took aim and, as the helicopter's machine gun started firing, he discharged the Glock's entire clip into the tail. The first shot didn't hit the rotor but the last few went through the fibre glass, shattering the tail.

When the helicopter started wavering, neither the pilot nor Tang seemed to understand what was happening. They hadn't heard his gunshots. Henry saw the look of panic on the pilot's face and the anger on Tang's. It was too late to stabilise the craft and a well-targeted round of shots from Fergus and Rodriguez finished the job. The helicopter drifted towards the ground, spinning out of control and crashed, creating a ball of fire on the border.

Fergus kept firing, but Henry heard no return fire. They both waited for a moment. The helicopter crash must have told the few remaining men that the battle was no longer worth fighting.

Fergus slid back to where Henry was. He fist-bumped Henry with a grin. "That was classic..."

"Let's get down and re-join the others."

They belly-crawled back to the place they'd emerged from after climbing the rock face.

Fergus took out a small spyglass and gave the terrain a final check. He jerked his head. "You first..."

Henry thought about protesting, but didn't see the point. Henry might have been a temporary part of the ALPHA team but he was still a newbie as far as Fergus was concerned. He slid the Glock into the small of his back, swung his legs over the edge and found purchase with his right foot. It felt solid and he started his descent.

Fergus checked on Henry's progress. When he was more than halfway down, Fergus swung his legs over the edge and followed.

Henry jumped to the ground and Rodriguez slapped his back. "Good shot."

Henry joined Rob and Mattie in the shade of the cliff. Rob imitated Rodriguez with a slap on the back of his own. Mattie was for once lost for words, or perhaps the words she wanted to speak were for Henry's ears only.

A single gunshot reverberated through the gorge. Rodriguez lifted his MP5, scouring the terrain systematically. Henry lifted his head in fear.

Fergus jerked back, as a shot hit him in the arm. He lost grip of the rock. His other hand was not quick enough to find a hold. His body fell backward.

With a desperate cry, Henry lunged forward to try to catch his mate.

CHAPTER THIRTY-SEVEN

"No... No!" Nick zoomed in on the hacked satellite image of the rescue scene.

Harris who was sitting next to him stood up.

"Who's down?" He leaned in, desperate to know.

"It's one of Rodriguez's men."

Hulk had sprung into action, delivering a volley of shots that had silenced the hostile gunman.

"Is he dead?"

"I don't know, Steve." Nick had zoomed in as much as he could. Rodriguez and Henry were obstructing the view of the fallen soldier.

"Call the rest of the team, Don and Ray. Tell them what's happened. The last we checked they were very close. Confirm coordinates again."

Harris watched Nick dial in on the agreed frequency. He hoped the second SUV would be helping with the rescue of an injured man rather than ferrying a dead body.

He walked out of Nick's tech cave and to his bedroom. His encrypted phone hadn't left his pocket; he wouldn't have the conversation needed with the Chief in front of Nick.

Harris sat on the end of his bed the same way he did every time he called the head of MI6. It was 1am in London and Harris needed to make sure he'd correctly measured the need to call the Chief in the small hours of the morning. The major incident at the border of China and Mongolia might be a good enough reason and so was the shooting of one man on the ALPHA team, but Harris wanted something else from the Chief.

Henry had told him that Rob had been keeping his knowledge of what Ma wanted to disclose close to his chest. Harris couldn't figure out why, but he suspected that the top-secret information Ma had would be so explosive, it would only be believed if supported by credible evidence.

Whatever the next steps were in the TECH LEOPARD operation, Harris wanted them to be worked out with the Chief beforehand.

Harris shook his head. He was finally calling on his superior, not because he had to but because he could no longer advance the operation on his own.

"A man has got to know his limitations," Harris mumbled, in a poor imitation of Clint Eastwood.

He brought up the Chief's number, hesitated for a second or two and pressed the call button. It took only three rings for the Chief to answer.

"Wait…" was all the Chief said at first. Harris heard him walking around and closing two doors. "Are they alive?"

The Chief's alertness threw Harris off for a second. He had prepared the customary *I am very sorry to disturb you* line, but the Chief clearly hadn't gone to sleep yet. "Yes, sir. They are about to cross the border…" Harris paused long enough for the Chief to pick up on it.

"But…?"

"A helicopter from the Zhaga camp went in pursuit of the fugitives and caught up with them at the border. Our own people were lucky to escape the onslaught but one of the members of the rescue team was not so lucky."

"I presume you're referring to a member of the SEAL team that was working on extracting our people?"

"I'm afraid so."

"Is he dead?" the Chief asked.

"I don't know. I'm making sure the second SUV on its way knows the exact coordinates and the urgency."

The Chief fell silent for a moment. "You need me to inform Hunter?"

"We may need a little more than that, sir."

"How so?"

"The next step is for Crowne to call me and confirm Rob's extraction. Then we need an exfil from Mongolia, which we can organise through our embassy. However, I'm still unclear what the impact of the intel will be that Rob is to collect from the Chinese source."

"And the US embassy has a much larger operation than our own in Mongolia?" the Chief added.

"That's correct, sir."

"Are we really in a position to make demands on Hunter after we shafted him and discovered the name of his source, Harris? Sorry to be blunt..."

"If the intel is as good as I think it will be, without question."

"Fine, call me when you've spoken to Crowne again – whatever the time. I'll get hold of Hunter and put him on standby." There was mischief in the Chief's voice that Harris didn't expect.

Harris thanked the man and remained seated for a moment. He had to go back to the makeshift control room, and he wasn't looking forward to hearing the outcome of the shooting.

* * *

Fergus's helmet had protected his head but the large rock on which he had landed smashed his back. Fergus's eyes were open and he was responding slowly to Henry calling his name.

"Stay with us, buddy..." Rodriguez was kneeling next to his man whilst Hulk was still surveying the edge of the cliff above them.

"We need a stretcher." Rob looked around as he spoke. He was about to break cover when Hulk stopped him. "Let me go. We might be able to use pieces of the helicopter that have broken away from the main frame."

Henry stood up, loaded a new clip into his Glock. "I'll go with Rob."

Both men walked cautiously into the open, towards the helicopter wreckage. The plume of dark smoke was blowing with the wind; they gave the site a wide circle to avoid the toxic fumes and the stench of burnt metal and flesh.

A part of the tail had detached on impact. It was dented but otherwise in one piece. Rob kicked it with his foot and the tail rolled onto its side. He pressed a careful hand on it and nodded. "It's OK to handle."

"What do you suggest?" Henry was scouring the area, concentrating on his surroundings and the possibility of another shooter appearing.

"We slide him on top of the flat part." Rob started kicking the remnants of the small rotor and dislodged it from the top part of the tail. "This is fibreglass, it's light." Rob dragged the piece back towards the gorge.

Henry followed close, gun at the ready. When they returned, Rodriguez had moved Fergus, pressing hard on one of his legs.

"Doesn't hurt..." Fergus mumbled.

Rodriguez looked up at the returning pair and smiled. "We just found a stretcher. We're getting you out of here."

Fergus nodded.

Henry and Rob placed the makeshift stretcher on the ground.

When Henry caught Rodriguez looking at him, the smile had vanished and he shook his head. Knowing that Fergus would never walk again tore Henry up.

Both men heaved Fergus onto the stretcher. Rob offered to help carry the wounded man whilst Rodriguez and Hulk checked their surroundings for hostiles.

The border crossing happened without joy. Mattie had taken Fergus's hand in a simple, kind gesture. The climb to the SUV location was as silent as the crossing, apart from the basic instructions given to make sure everyone was ready for the climb.

"Rob and I will go first, if you don't mind," Henry said, addressing Rodriguez. "We'll find Ray and Don and figure out how to move Fergus to the top of the cliff."

Rodriguez nodded. "You both do a quick climb and we'll keep an eye for more hostiles from down here."

The roar of a car engine at the top of the cliff made everyone freeze. Rodriguez signalled for all to drop to the ground.

Hulk moved sideways to get a better firing angle. The vehicle broke hard, and Rodriguez's handheld radio crackled.

"One man down," came through.

Ray and Don appeared, looked over the edge of the cliff. They spotted the team below them and disappeared again. More engine noise told them that the SUV had moved close and was ready to lift the stretcher and their teammate.

Henry and Rob used the ropes that Rodriguez and his team had ready for the climb. They reached the top of the cliff after fifteen minutes.

There were no greetings, just an efficient and rapid assessment of what to do next. Don and Ray were now keeping watch at the edge of the cliff.

Rodriguez and Hulk strapped Fergus in with more ropes, making sure he wouldn't slip out of the stretcher when the SUV slowly pulled it up the cliff. Hulk started the climb and guided the ropes, to make sure they didn't get tangled or snapped. When the stretcher reached the top of the cliff, Henry and Rob helped lift Fergus to safety.

Fergus was responding to his mates, but all knew that his condition would soon deteriorate.

Mattie and Rodriguez appeared next, and Don and Ray moved back from the edge of the cliff to their own SUV where Fergus had just been loaded.

"I think I should go with him," Mattie said, as she came close to Henry.

Henry simply nodded and for a moment they faced each other, incapable of moving away. The sound of two doors shutting told them that Don and Ray were ready to go. Mattie gripped his shoulder then moved to take her seat next to Fergus. Within a few seconds the SUV left.

"Come on, our own SUV is waiting," Rodriguez said.

The team reached the top of the hill where the first SUV had been hidden. Rodriguez checked the vehicle and called Hulk. The two men removed some of their combat gear and stashed it in the boot.

Henry left them to it. When they were almost done, he walked over to Rodriguez before the man could ask them to take a seat.

"Rob and I need to make a call."

"I can't imagine us without company for long. The smoke from the crashed helo is visible for miles."

"I know, but we need to do this now. It's perhaps one of the most important calls we'll make in this operation."

Rodriguez locked eyes with Henry for a few seconds. Then he got into the driver seat. "You have five minutes and then we're off."

"Rob?" Henry called out whilst fishing out the mobile from his rucksack. He took a small piece of paper he'd hidden in his trouser pocket and unfolded it, revealing the SIM card Ma had given him back in Zhaga. "Let's make the call."

Rob and Henry moved away from the vehicle and Henry placed the SIM card into the phone Genghis had given him.

"I have cranked up the volume. I want to hear what she's got to say without switching on the loudspeaker."

374

Now that they were about to speak to Dragon, Rob looked nervous. He took the mobile from Henry, cleared his throat and selected the only number that was stored on the SIM card.

He hesitated over the green call button, then pressed it and held the phone close to his ear. He counted the ring tones. He hung up and looked at the time display on the screen. One minute later he called again.

"Where are you?" Ma's voice sounded muffled.

Rob looked at Henry and Henry nodded. "Mongolia."

"I'm glad you're out, and I'm sorry I couldn't give you the information we agreed I would."

"Can you upload it to the website I created in case we needed it?"

"All my equipment has been confiscated. I have no access to the internet and it's a miracle they haven't found this phone yet."

"How come you can speak at all?"

"I'm in a small walk-in wardrobe and only have a few more minutes before I arouse their suspicious."

"Has the intelligence been deleted?" Rob's face had turned ashen.

"I have it on a USB key but will soon have to get rid of that, too," Ma replied.

Rob looked again at Henry, at a loss.

Henry hesitated then grabbed the phone from Rob. "Henry Newborn here. Are you able to leave your house?"

Ma gave a small laugh. "Ah, the MI6 Brit. I'm afraid the purpose of a house arrest is to prevent me from leaving my home."

"Can you get me into your property?"

It was Ma's turn to hesitate. "You propose to get in and collect the USB key?"

"That's right."

"Assuming you can get to Beijing – which is a big assumption – I don't think you'll be able to get close enough. A westerner will arouse suspicion and the surveillance here at night doubles."

Henry would make it happen. He owed it to Fergus. "I will be in Beijing tomorrow."

There was a short silence before Ma replied. "Find the Military General Hospital in Beijing. Door 21, emergency entrance, 8pm. Wait for thirty minutes, after that leave. It means I've been caught trying to get to you."

The phone went dead, and Henry removed the SIM card from the mobile. He stamped on the phone and the metallic sound put Hulk on the alert. Henry lifted a hand to show there was no issue. Henry and Rob walked to the SUV and climbed in.

"Let's get to Ulaanbaatar." Henry slammed the door and dived for the handheld radio that lay between the front seats of the SUV. "I have a flight to catch."

* * *

Harris had returned to Nick's computer set-up and followed the injured man's transfer to the second SUV, as well as the call Henry and Rob had made. Although he couldn't hear what was said, Harris knew they were talking to Dragon.

He wasn't surprised when the radio link Nick had established with the ALPHA team got activated.

"Crowne?" Harris said. "What did she say?"

"She has no way of transferring the files anywhere. She is under house arrest and has no way of accessing the internet."

"Do you know what's in these files?"

"Yes... Taiwan is your answer."

"You mean China's plan to invade Taiwan?"

"Correct... and although it's something that has been on the West's radar for a long time, I reckon this is not a vague plan but an actionable one that may be more current than we think."

Harris took a moment to absorb the information. "I hear you but what good is it to us if we can't have the details? I mean I can go to the Chief and tell him this is what we think or that's what she said, but for all we know she could be feeding us a load of garbage."

"Agreed, and that's why we need to get hold of the intel," Henry said. "It's stored on a USB key."

"Don't tell me... You're going to go to Beijing, walk into her house that's teeming with military guards and retrieve the thing?" Harris grumbled.

There was a short silence from Henry and Harris slumped in his seat.

"Wait... You are going to go to Beijing, walk into her house that is –"

376

"– Steve, I'm not walking into her bloody house. It would be suicide."

"And flying to Beijing isn't?"

"Not without the right legend I won't be, and I need Hunter to play ball. Dragon and I have a meeting arrangement at 8pm tomorrow night."

It was Harris's turn to take a pause. "I need to speak to the Chief."

"No, we need to speak to the Chief."

"This is highly unconventional –"

"Nothing about this operation is conventional," Henry said. "In fact, I wonder how many of us who have partaken in OPERATION TECH LEOPARD will still be in employment when we're done."

"Fine... I'll call you back from another device and patch you in." Harris stood up to retreat to his bedroom.

Nick turned around before he could walk out. "I'm in all the way, Steve, even if that means my career at MI6 is the shortest one ever."

Harris drew his MI6 mobile out of his pocket and handed it to Nick. "Can you download an app that can pick up the radio signal so that we can connect with Henry again?"

"I'll set it up right away and make sure it's got the same Frequency Hopping Spread Spectrum as we've been using with the ALPHA team to avoid eavesdropping."

Harris left Nick to it and headed to the kitchen to check what was left in the fridge. The place looked like a tip; empty cardboard boxes that once contained items of food were stacked on the table. Cups, plates and cutlery had been piled in the sink. Harris picked out a couple of Diet Cokes from the fridge and returned to their makeshift control room.

Nick handed Harris back his mobile. Harris gave Nick a can of Coke. He sat down and dialled the Chief's number in front of Nick instead of in his bedroom.

"They are out and on their way," Harris said.

The Chief replied almost immediately. "And the fallen man?"

"On his way to Ulaanbaatar, but I don't know more."

"Dragon?"

"Dragon has made contact, but the information is difficult to extract."

"Dragon has been outed?"

"Not yet but it's only a matter of time, a few days, perhaps less."

"I presume you're only calling me to tell me we missed an opportunity?" The Chief was moving around. He sat down again, Harris assumed, going by the sigh of a leather cushion that seemed to indicate it.

"No, sir, In fact I'd like to patch in our operative on the ground." There was no point in delaying mentioning the highly unconventional call.

"This is very –" The Chief interrupted himself. "But you know that. Is this worth us taking the risk?"

"Yes, sir, it is."

"And our operative thinks so, too." This wasn't a question from the Chief, more a conclusion he'd just drawn. "You're using radio contact, I presume?"

"That's right, sir."

"Give me a moment." The Chief was moving around again, and this time Harris could hear him typing on a keyboard. "What's the frequency you're using?"

Harris gave the Chief the information. He waited until his boss confirmed the Frequency Hopping Spread Spectrum had been activated on his device. Harris then proceeded to call Henry.

"The three of us are now connected," Harris said by way of introduction.

"I understand you have a plan to retrieve the information we expected from Dragon?" the Chief said flatly to Henry.

"I have agreed a meeting with Dragon, tomorrow night in Beijing. I intend to be there, sir." Henry sounded equally calm and detached. It could have been any old operation they were discussing.

"Why do you think it is worth taking the risk?"

"Any insight into the imminent invasion of Taiwan is, in my opinion, worth having, sir."

There was a short pause before the Chief responded.

"It no doubt is, but how credible is this intel?"

"Because of the identity of Dragon, a person who is in prime position to access that intelligence. We'll then assess the data's merit, but the risks Dragon has taken are real. I don't think Dragon is faking her imminent outing to the authorities."

There was another short silence from the Chief.

"What do you need from me?" he finally said.

"I need a credible legend and the documents to go with it. I doubt the UK embassy in Ulaanbaatar is equipped for that, but the US embassy is."

"Ah... I see we need a conversation with our cousins from across the pond and need to be reassured that our special relationship is as strong as ever." The Chief's teasing tone reassured Harris a fraction.

"We may also want to remind the CIA's Head of Operations, Hunter III, that the new President of the United States would take any opportunity to wage war against China. Delaying a Taiwanese invasion might be a good way to avert World War Three."

Henry had not minced his words. Harris would have cheered him for that had they been in the same room.

"I'll speak to Hunter now. Stay put." The Chief disconnected from the radio call.

Harris and Henry waited in silence for a moment.

"Is Nick around?" Henry asked.

"How else would I have got this call organised?" Harris shrugged. He handed over his mobile to the young man.

"Have you been kicking butt in cyber space?" Henry asked. The volume was loud enough that Harris could hear.

"Yup... they didn't know what hit them."

"How bad is it to hack an airport security?"

"Control tower or passport control?"

"Passport control."

"Chinese, I presume?" Nick asked.

"Don't worry, not North Korea. At least not yet."

"That's all right, then. I'll work on it and let Steve know."

Nick handed Harris back his phone. There was a slight crackle on the line and the Chief came back on.

"Gentleman, we are joined by our American colleague who is very keen to support us in any way he can in retrieving the information from China."

Harris punched the air, and he imagined Henry doing the same. They were going to enjoy hearing Hunter III grovel.

CHAPTER THIRTY-EIGHT

Hulk swerved the SUV into the airport drop-off area. Hulk had taken over driving a couple of hours before they'd reached Ulaanbaatar.

Rodriguez was to board the flight on which Fergus was to travel. The medical team from the US embassy had arranged for the wounded man to be transferred to a Japanese airline flight to Tokyo, from there an army medical aircraft from Gham would take over.

Rodriguez shook hands with each of the men in the car; Henry squeezed his hand a bit harder than usual. "You'll know what to tell Fergus. I'm not sure I can find the words just now."

Rodriguez nodded and got out of the car.

Hulk drove off, on their way to the US embassy.

Henry's mind drifted back to the fight in the gorge. He pushed the images away. It was not the time to wonder whether things could have been done differently. There was still much to do to get to Beijing and back. He thought of Mattie; this time it was impossible to get her out of his mind.

He had let her go after they'd reached safety after the Middle East and spent a few hours together. He had known it was more than just sex that had drawn them to each other. But he had already been assigned to his next operation and he was reluctant to let anyone grow close to him. There were good reasons for it. Henry needed to remind himself of those and draw the same conclusion he had drawn so many times: that it wasn't a good idea to become involved with Henry Crowne.

The US embassy compound was surrounded by an impressive wall that made access to the main building impossible except through the main entrance. Hulk presented his passport and gave the names of his guests. One of the guards radioed in and opened the heavy gate. Hulk drove Henry and Rob through and parked the SUV at the back of the compound, where he'd been told to go.

Two more guards walked out of the low-rise building and escorted the three men to a suite of rooms. A tall man with grey hair and a beard was waiting for them. He introduced himself as the CIA chief of station. He shook hands with Hulk and Rob with respect, but when it came to Henry's turn, his eyes locked hard onto Henry's.

The CIA man said to all three, "We've organised tickets for you all to leave Mongolia on friendly airlines as soon as possible. You'll be joining your teammate, Ray, on a different flight to Japan this evening." He handed a ticket to Osaka to Hulk. Ray had not travelled on the same flight as Fergus. "You'll be flying to Seoul," the chief of station said to Rob. "One of our contacts will make sure you're flown on to Taiwan as soon as you arrive there."

Rob nodded, looking unsure that he had truly escaped. Henry guessed the information he was meant to have received from Ma was still on his mind.

"We are still working on yours," the chief of station said to Henry without elaborating further.

Henry moved over to a plate of sandwiches that had been prepared for them. He hadn't realised how famished he was until he started eating. "What about the rest of the documents?"

"Working on those, too."

Rob lifted his brows at Henry.

There was someone missing off the list and Henry gave him a quick smile. "What about Mattie Colmore?"

"Apologies, I should have said... There is a flight to London tonight, but Ms Colmore is not entirely sure she needs to be on it. We can't force anyone, of course."

Henry closed his eyes for the briefest of moments. "I'll speak to her."

The chief of station smirked. "Good luck with that."

It seemed Mattie had already made a reputation for herself.

Hulk disappeared into the next room with his ticket. Rob sat down and helped himself to sandwiches. Both of them were grateful for the food.

"I should apologise to Mattie. She was almost lost to us." Rob shook his head at the memory of his thunderstorm panic.

"I can't imagine Mattie needing an apology, but if it makes you feel better, then perhaps you should."

Rob stood up, poured himself a cup of coffee and returned to his seat. "I don't know whether we would have made it without her – or Genghis for that matter."

"We will never know..." Henry grimaced.

"It's unfair not to recognise how much she helped."

"Fairness has sometimes got nothing to do with it."

Rob frowned and Henry stood up, keen to stop it there. He didn't want to say more.

"I'll tell her you want a chat," Henry said, walking out of the room.

He headed for the end of the corridor where bedrooms had been allocated to each member of the team so that they could shower, change and rest. Listening through the door he could hear Mattie was having a conversation. There was no other voice so Henry assumed she must be on the phone. He hesitated for a moment. They hadn't been alone together since meeting again. Shaking his head he knocked a couple of times.

Mattie cut her conversation short and walked to the door. She opened without checking first who it was.

She froze, and they both stood there awkwardly.

Henry looked past her to make sure she really was free. "May I come in?"

"You may..." Mattie walked to the bed and sat cross-legged on it. There was a chair in the corner of the room, but it looked a little too remote and official, so Henry sat at the bottom of the bed.

"I was told about the camp, which is why I entered China in the first place – just in case you thought I was part of this rescue mission from the start," Mattie said. She took a sip of water from a bottle.

"I never said you were part of it, but whoever put you on it knew you would help."

"Ask your MI6 minder, then."

"I intend to. Look, Mattie, I didn't come here to argue about you being involved with this operation."

"But you'd like me to leave tonight for the UK." Mattie suddenly looked tired. She'd followed the gruelling pace of their escape without complaining, even when she'd almost been buried alive in the sandstorm.

"I am grateful..." Henry bit his bottom lip. That was not what he wanted to say.

A flash of anger and pain crossed Mattie's eyes. Why had she bothered? She stood up in one jump and moved to the door. "I have spoken to Genghis. He's fine and I'm going to meet him for a drink tonight. After that, I will be on my way home to the UK." She rested her hand on the door handle indicating it was time for Henry to leave.

"I want you to leave Mongolia because I want you safe, not because I don't care about you."

"I can look after myself perfectly well, Henry Crowne."

He didn't care if she knew his real name. He cared about what danger it put her in.

"Not if the Chinese military or Secret Service decides they want to question you." Henry's voice sounded more concerned than angry. He stood up slowly and moved to where Mattie stood. Gently he stroked the side of her face. "It's not a good idea to get close to me, Mattie. People who do get hurt."

The anger faded from her expression. She smiled and shook her head. "You don't believe that, surely?" she asked, searching his eyes.

She laid her hands on his chest. Her touch made Henry recoil a little.

"You do believe it." Mattie gripped his shoulder to stop him from moving away. "You're a risk taker, Henry Crowne, and it's not that you bring bad luck to people you care for. It's that you're attracted to people who are like you – who take risks." She slid her arms around his neck and brought his face to hers for a long, slow kiss.

He pulled her close for a moment. "I wish I could believe that," he murmured.

"You're not going back to the UK yourself, so where are you going?"

Perhaps he could explain a little...

A knock on the door startled them both.

"I've got something to discuss with you Mr Newborn," the chief of station said through the wood.

"I'm coming...!" He heard the man moving away from her door.

"Please take that flight, Mattie. Invite Genghis to London. You can chat to your heart's content there." Henry squeezed her tightly and let go.

"Do you think the chief of station could find a ticket for another person on tonight's flight?" Mattie asked candidly.

Henry couldn't help but laugh. "If you threatened to stay here another week, I'm sure he could."

"And what about you? How will I find you?"

"I'll find you."

* * *

Henry ran a hand over his bald head. He had never experienced this before. His thick hair was gone. It lay in a heap in the sink. Henry quickly gathered what hadn't gone down the plug hole and disposed of it in the toilet. He didn't want to leave evidence of him being here.

He dried himself off and proceeded to dye his eyebrows, lashes and beard blond. The end result looked impressive. Even Mattie would have needed a second look to recognise him.

The phone in his room rang. The chief of station was calling him for a photo shoot. His passport, driving licence and credit cards were ready. They just needed to affix a picture of Henry in his new guise to his documents.

Henry's entrance into the small office the embassy used as a studio had the desired effect. The chief of station was about to call security when Henry came in. It was only Henry's voice that saved the Chief some embarrassment.

"I have to say... this is good." The chief of station grinned.

"I'm glad their face recognition software is not up to the task, otherwise I would need to do a lot more than change my hair style."

"You have a flight at 3pm, arriving at 5pm. By the time you get to the centre of Beijing, it'll be 6pm. Your return flight leaves for Seoul at 11pm. It's the last flight we could get the same day into a friendly country. From there, a military plane will pick you up and fly you to Taiwan."

Henry stood still for a moment so that the photographer could do his job. The chief of station then carried on.

"You have two burner phones, and a SIM card that is hidden inside one of your cufflinks. Your glasses-cleaning spray is a powerful pepper

384

spray that will disable any opponent for a while. I can't offer anything else at short notice, I'm afraid."

"That will do. I don't intend to make a fuss when I'm in Beijing. Just a quick meeting and I'm out."

"I also made sure you'll have a tablet with all information loaded on it. And details of your new legend have been printed out and are in here." The chief handed a thick manila file to Henry.

"Thank God I have the day to read it," Henry said, opening the file.

"I hear you're a quick learner. Anyway, I'm not going anywhere. I live on the compound. Let me know if you need anything else."

Henry thanked the chief of station, surprised by the change of attitude and returned to his bedroom. Hunter must have had a word, asking the chief of station to be accommodating, and it made Henry smile.

Henry dropped the file on the bed and returned to the small reception room they had arrived in a few hours ago.

Rob was sitting on one of the chairs, still looking anxious.

"You'll be fine when you're in the air," Henry said as he sat down next to him.

Rob's eyebrows shot up. "It's impressive, your hairstyle."

"Let's hope the Chinese buy it."

"Anyway, I'll feel better when you're back from Beijing with the intelligence we need."

Henry stretched his legs out. "How did you get involved with Dragon?" He wasn't going anywhere yet and Rob had an hour before departing for the airport.

"At a tech conference in Singapore. She came alone and got hold of me after I spoke. I'm rather cautious about Chinese contacts approaching me, but she was willing to share some insight. Then I found that what she told me about had been confirmed by my research team back in Taiwan."

"She was credible?"

"Very. We met a few times after that at other conferences over the span of a year... She was always alone. Then one day she gave me a USB key with data on it that mapped Chinese progress in high-grade semiconductors."

"You mean the ones used in heavy military warfare?"

Rob nodded. "That's right."

"Did you know you would be kidnapped?"

"No, and that was a shock... but then I had to go with the flow."

Henry was surprised. "You sound very philosophical about it."

"I'm about to leave for Seoul then back to Taiwan. She's about to lose her freedom and perhaps more. The Chinese don't take acts of treason lightly."

Both men fell silent, Rob's thoughts caught in what he'd just been through, and Henry's in what lay ahead.

Henry thought of Fergus on his way to Gham for what he hoped would be treatment that may save him from paralysis. Anger flared up inside him; the need to bring back information the West needed was overwhelming. Fergus would get his revenge.

One of Henry's burner phones pinged; it was Nick with a quick text message update.

Ready when you are.

Henry inhaled deeply. He was all set for his trip to Beijing and had less than twenty-four hours to slide into the skin of his legend and make him credible.

* * *

The red seatbelt button started flashing as the pilot announced they'd started their descent to Beijing Capital Airport. Henry pushed his thick glasses back up his nose. The lenses were plain glass only, but they completed his legend's look.

His legend, a professor of medicine specialising in brain surgery, sounded obscure and high-profile enough to impress. Henry's passport was from New Zealand, a country that didn't have a history of open disagreement with China. Henry had spent most of his time the day before learning about his new trade and was comfortable he could fool even a simple GP.

The plane landed with only a five-minute delay. Henry closed the medical journal he'd been reading and waited for the plane to dock at the gate before getting up. His suitcase was hand luggage size and he wheeled it behind him as he left the aircraft. The stewardess gave him an affable goodbye. Henry followed the stream of passengers disembarking and moved with them to passport control.

Nick had managed to find some images of what Henry would be met with. The security at arrivals was tight and the visa control even tighter. The chief of station had assured him that his people were skilled at faking a Chinese visa. Henry had inspected the result when he'd been given his legend's passport. It did look the business but only the next hour would tell if it passed.

The queue moved steadily. Business class had disembarked first and Henry joined the crowd that moved fast and efficiently though passport control. He watched the men who travelled regularly and observed the routine between officer and passenger: standing close to the booth window, bowing a few times when the officer asked questions, replying quickly and with utmost respect.

Henry took his passport out of his small satchel. His palms were sweaty and he wiped them quickly on his trousers.

The passenger in front of him had been with the officer for only a minute or so; his passport was stamped and off he went.

He waited a fraction of a second, then moved forward as the officer was readying himself for the next passenger. Henry briefly met the eyes of the officer, and he could tell the officer was intrigued.

The officer went methodically through Henry's passport to check if any of the visas might be the source of an argument. But there was nothing confrontational in there. Henry had also presented his immigration card. The hotel he would be staying at was the most used by foreigners.

"You stay here for five days?" The officer's accent was strong but the words distinct.

"Yes, I'm meeting other colleagues who are also surgeons."

The officer nodded a few times. "What is your profession?"

"I am a brain surgeon."

The man nodded again and kept going through the document, page by page. "When are you leaving?"

The question was strange as the officer had just confirmed it, but Henry answered amiably. "In five days' time."

The passport was inspected again, and the officer looked at Henry for a short moment. He turned around and called a colleague in who was walking past.

The second officer snuggled into the border control booth with his colleague and was given Henry's passport. He took a long look at Henry's picture.

"What is your profession?" the second officer asked.

Henry gave a forced smile with his response. "I am a brain surgeon."

Beads of sweat collected at the back of his neck. Perhaps his photo had already been distributed to border control and the extreme disguise hadn't fooled them.

The second officer returned the passport to his colleague and with a straight face, commented in Mandarin. "This big nose is really ugly."

"I know... I thought you'd like to check him out."

"Do you think he's scared?"

"I hope so."

Henry resisted the desire to answer back in Mandarin.

After a few more minutes of dithering the officer stamped Henry's passport and let him through. Henry forced himself to walk at a steady pace. He reached the taxi rank where green and grey cars were waiting in organised rows. Passengers were not so disciplined, and Henry managed to spot what he was looking for. The chief of station had given him the plate number of a cab that would take him to whatever destination he needed.

He'd also been told that the minute he arrived Henry would be followed, as most western businessmen were. He now had to shake his tail to get to his rendezvous point.

The young man driving the booked taxi greeted him with enthusiasm. It would take less than an hour to get to the Hilton in Central Beijing, he told him. Henry nodded and settled into the cab for the first part of his journey into town.

The offer of a bottle of water was welcomed and Henry took a few sips. He finally smiled at what he'd just gone through. It wasn't his ugly face the border officers should have noticed, it was that his passport and visa were both fakes. Ulaanbaatar's chief of station had been right. His people were the business.

Henry's driver moved swiftly through traffic and they arrived at the hotel at 6.30pm. Henry asked the young man to wait as Henry went to check in. It was 7pm by the time he got back in the car.

Henry asked to be dropped off next to one of Beijing's old quarters. Many of the courtyard houses had been destroyed to make way for modern buildings, but the Dongsi Quarter was holding strong and resisting destruction. Henry's driver was a little concerned that Henry may get lost, but he reassured him he would be fine.

Henry disappeared into the small alleyways, preparing for a game of hide and seek with the man who'd been shadowing him since he'd left the Hilton. It took less than fifteen minutes for Henry to shake him. The quality of the tail who'd been allocated to follow him encouraged Henry. If he could lose him that easily, he had likely been identified as another businessman, nothing more.

An old rickshaw-type bike was waiting for a customer to use. He climbed into it and gave the man directions in Mandarin. The driver was stunned by Henry's fluency but recovered quickly when Henry showed him the amount of Yuan he was prepared to pay for a swift ride.

At 7.50pm Henry was dropped off three streets away from the Military Hospital of Beijing. Henry took a dark cap out of his rucksack, put it on and walked fast towards the back of the hospital.

At 8pm Henry walked past Entrance 21, one of the two emergency entrances the hospital had. The place was empty.

Ma had another thirty minutes to make her appearance.

CHAPTER THIRTY-NINE

Ma had been clear. "If I'm not here at 8.30pm, assume I've been caught."

Henry had walked past Entrance 21 three times already. He sat on a bench in the small garden square opposite the hospital, but his loitering would soon be noticed. A westerner, even in Beijing, didn't walk the streets without attracting attention.

Entrance 21 had remained quiet since he'd started his watch. Henry frowned. Would that be normal for a hospital in the middle of a busy city like Beijing?

Henry stood up from his observation post and looked around. Traffic had hardly died down and the streets were still busy. It didn't have the vibrancy of Hong Kong, but Beijing was a city still very much awake at 8.25pm in the evening.

Henry crossed the street and joined a stream of people who seemed caught up in their own little worlds. No one noticed him and he used their distraction to walk decisively towards the emergency entrance. This time he wouldn't walk past, he would walk straight up to it.

Heavy translucent plastic sheets covered the entrance. The doors behind it looked locked.

"Shit..."

Henry looked around and then at the walls near the emergency doors. One camera was angled at the doors but there was no other form of security. Entrance 21 looked shut. Ma would not be arriving or leaving through this door any time soon.

Henry moved away from the door and glanced at his watch. It was 8.28pm. He had to find if there was another emergency door.

He returned to the concourse that surrounded the hospital and started to walk towards the public entrance. People were still arriving and leaving the hospital. Visits didn't appear to be curtailed as they were in Europe. Or perhaps the Military Hospital was more flexible with its patients than other hospitals were. The People's Liberation Army was a force to be reckoned with in China.

The size of the building was impressive, and Henry suspected that finding Ma would be almost impossible in the minutes that were left before he had to leave for the airport. Henry walked past the main doors again. This time his presence attracted the attention of some visitors.

He walked past with confidence and turned right towards the back of the hospital, as he had done to find Entrance 21. As he came round the corner, a series of flashing lights forced him to quicken his pace. Another emergency entrance was in front of him, and two ambulances were queuing up, ready to deliver their patients.

Henry sped up. The back of the ambulance opened, medics pushed a stretcher out and wheeled the patient into the hospital at speed. The rattle of the trolley and the shouts from the medics told Henry the man was in critical condition.

The second ambulance delivered its patient – a heavily pregnant woman who was being pushed in a wheelchair.

Henry arrived at the doors of the ambulance that had brought in the dying man. A second stretcher had been left unattended. Henry heard the driver's door open. He hid to the side of the vehicle. Even if he managed to find a uniform, his disguise wouldn't be credible. But Henry remembered he hadn't seen a husband with the pregnant woman.

He turned back and started running. He met one of the ambulance drivers and stopped him getting back into his vehicle. "My wife... it's an emergency. She's having our baby boy..."

The ambulance driver looked lost for words. But Henry's distraught face and command of Mandarin did the trick.

The man sprang into action. "Follow me..."

He pushed the doors open and pointed down one corridor. Henry bowed a few times and started running. The couple of nurses who saw him enter didn't think to ask why, probably because he'd been shown in by an ambulance driver. He was clearly looking for someone.

Henry slowed down a fraction to reorient himself. He reached the corridor that led to the emergency rooms where patients were being looked after. One of the doors opened to his left. Someone had just been prepped for the operating theatre and he was currently being wheeled in by two male nurses.

Henry chose to turn right. For Ma to be brought in here, she must have feigned being unwell so as to be treated as critical. Henry walked along the corridor, peeking through the viewing windows that allowed the nurses to check on patients. Most of the patients were men. Henry kept going. The corridor was about to fork again and Henry slowed down.

Two nurses walked past him and looked back. Henry ignored them. He spotted the gents and made for them as someone in urgent need would. He walked into the first cubicle and locked the door. A couple of men walked in and did their business. Henry waited until all was quiet again. He had one last chance to find Ma.

He left the toilets and chose to walk along the shortest corridor this time. He spotted a guard sitting on a chair, looking straight ahead.

How many patients would need guards?

Henry walked around as before, looking lost and in need of direction. The guard stood up and took one step forward. Henry smiled at the man and walked towards the guard with deference.

"I am looking for General Ma."

The guard's face dropped. This westerner who spoke fluent Mandarin was asking for the very person he was guarding but whose presence should have been secret.

Henry pulled out the fake glass cleaner spray, placed a handkerchief over his face and pepper-sprayed the guard's face. His thick glasses protected his own eyes from the mist. The man dropped to the floor with a cry. Convulsions started to shake his body and Henry cried out for help.

A nurse came running and called for more assistance. Henry retreated to the door of the guarded room and slipped inside without being noticed.

Ma was lying on the bed, one hand handcuffed to the bed railing. She propped herself up on one elbow and couldn't hide her surprise. "I didn't expect you to make it."

"Neither did I." Henry crossed the room in two long strides. He inspected the cuffs, pulled the small lock-picking tool Ma had given him in Zhaga and got to work on freeing her.

"Is it the same tool?"

"I'm sure you never thought it would become this useful?"

Ma managed a smile. The cuff clicked open; she quickly rubbed her wrist and jumped out of bed.

"I need to get you out," Henry said.

"No, I need to deliver the USB and you need to get out." Ma locked eyes with Henry. She was not here to escape but to fulfil her mission.

She moved to the cupboard where her clothes had been stored and found her shoes. She removed the sole of one of them and extracted a thin USB key from the inside. She turned to Henry and handed it over without hesitation.

"This is the latest military plan for the invasion of Taiwan, strategy for air, sea and land assault and capabilities to be deployed. The attack is imminent."

Henry took the device from her. It looked so insignificant for something containing so much value.

Voices in the corridor made him pocket the USB and move to the viewing window. Outside, a doctor was speaking to the nurse who'd first come to help, no doubt trying to ascertain what had happened. Ma was supposed to be guarded and he needed to inform his superiors there was an issue.

"You're not going to get out without help," Ma said, putting her civilian clothes on.

Henry nodded. "Any help gratefully received." The place would soon be crawling with military personnel. He had a few more minutes at most to get out of the hospital.

A fully dressed Ma glanced through the small viewing window. "Let's call in the doctor who's outside my room. I need her coat."

The doctor had finished with the nurse and had taken her mobile out of her pocket.

Ma opened the door. "I need help."

The doctor stopped and was about to reply when she realised General Ma was no longer tied to her bed. It was too late, though. Ma grabbed her by the arm and pulled her into the room.

Henry got the doctor in an arm lock and pushed her against the wall. "You open your mouth and I break your neck."

The doctor moaned in pain but she nodded.

Ma removed the doctor's white coat. She then used the handcuff to tie her to the bed just the way she had been. She stuffed a piece of cloth in her mouth and tore a strip from a hand towel to complete the gag. She put the coat on, pocketed the mobile.

"What now?" Henry asked.

"We leave through the main doors and find a car."

Ma had already opened the door of her room and was walking away hastily.

"Why the main doors?" Henry murmured.

"The military will not want to arrive all guns blazing that way. It's a major loss of face to have to admit you've lost a prisoner. They'll come through the side entrances."

"And the car?"

The sounds of voices and the thudding of boots told them reinforcements had just arrived.

Ma moved to the lifts and pressed the call button. They entered the lift. Ma pressed the ground floor and closing door buttons. The few staff in the lift stared at Henry.

"I'm certain your friend will recover," Ma said. "It was good of you to pop by."

"I couldn't have come to Beijing and not pay him a visit."

The people in the lift seemed reassured by the conversation. Henry and Ma walked out, slowing down their pace considerably. Just a doctor and a patient's friend exchanging information.

They reached the outside just as more military vehicles were arriving. Ma unbuttoned the white coat slowly. When they reached the end of the concourse, she took it off quickly and threw it in a bin.

Henry removed his cap and dug a light windbreaker jacket from his rucksack that he put on. They walked on the road for a bit then Ma turned into a side street. She had a plan, it seemed. She stopped next to a battered car that looked out of place amid the sea of expensive cars that were parked along the street.

"Can you get into this car?" Ma leaned against it.

"It's like asking a nurse whether she can stick a plaster on a cut."

"Some nurses are better at it than others..." Ma nodded towards the driver's door. "The lock is easy on this one."

There was no time for Henry to be surprised. He used the lock-picking tool and the door sprang open within seconds. Ma got into the driver's seat. Henry had just enough time to reach the passenger seat before the car engine was started.

"Is this what they teach you in the military?" he asked her.

"No, it is what a woman in the military needs to know."

"What, hotwiring a car?"

"Be better at everything than all of the men put together."

Ma joined the traffic and drove past a police van that had stopped and was erecting a barricade. "It'll take us forty minutes to reach the airport. When is your flight?"

"Less than two hours."

Ma didn't reply. She was focused on the next task at hand and would suffer no distraction.

They had diverted from the main roads. Ma was weaving through the side streets of Beijing, to avoid any encounter with military or police.

"We've got to cross one of the bridges," she said. "That's the only place where the authorities will have set up a road block to stop us from accessing the airport." Ma stopped at a crossroad and turned into a larger street.

"Any way around it?"

"Yes, but it'll take hours. You haven't got the time."

"What about you? Do you have anyone who can help you?"

Ma gave Henry a brief smile. "This is not the way. I'm not part of the opposition and I have no network. And even if I did, I wouldn't want to endanger them."

Henry shook his head. Ma was telling him with cool detachment she would be caught and almost certainly executed. He could not accept it. She must have sensed his desire to find a way.

"I have made my choice," she said. "It is the way it will unfold."

Henry fell silent for a moment. He could see the bridge in the distance. He had to know. "May I ask why?" he said, turning towards Ma.

She slowed down to match the speed of the traffic and glanced at Henry. "Do you know about the one-child policy?"

"Of course. Couples were allowed only one child until a year or so ago."

Ma nodded. "That's right. But do you know about the impact on baby girls?"

"I heard." Henry recalled what Mattie had told him. Abortions, murder of babies or infants and the widespread abandonment of girls who then ended up in orphanages.

Ma gripped the steering wheel tighter. "My first child was a girl. I married young into a family of military officers. My husband and I met when we both joined the force. I came from rural China. He already had a pedigree through his family's history." Ma stopped speaking and checked the rear-view mirror, giving herself a few seconds before continuing. "Only a boy would do for such an esteemed family. They arranged for my daughter to be adopted. I had no say in the matter. One day she was in her cot, the next she was gone."

"I'm very sorry, General." Henry couldn't think of anything else to say.

"I trained hard to be in this wretched army and I got results. ... but no other children came." There was another long pause from Ma. "I think my husband regretted giving up our daughter, although he never said so. Instead, he let me pursue my career. And then, as I gained seniority, I heard about these people who had been able to trace their lost children. It took me years, but I managed to find my daughter."

The traffic had slowed to a crawl.

Ma wound down her window to check what was happening farther along. "She lives in America, was adopted by a couple in California. The mother is Chinese from Hong Kong and the father American, a lecturer at MIT. She has become a wonderful musician. I saw her in concert once."

The memory of his own father filled Henry's mind – the bond between two people who love each other unconditionally.

"You don't want the US to start a war with China over Taiwan, do you?" Henry asked.

"That's right. I don't want this wonderful girl to die because of two narrow-minded, bigoted men who are fanning the flames of nationalism and dogmatism."

"Did you approach her?"

396

"What good would it do? She has a successful life. What would an American citizen do with the knowledge that their mother was a General in the People's Liberation Army?" Ma managed a wry smile.

Henry shook his head. "It shouldn't matter but I see your point." He hesitated and Ma picked up on it.

"Even now, she doesn't need to know. What matters is I know why I've betrayed my country."

The imposing structure of the bridge became clearer as they approached.

Ma lowered her window again. "Traffic is moving better farther up. No roadblock yet. We're in luck."

As Ma predicted, traffic had eased off and the airport glittered in the distance, thanks to the regular flashing of aircraft lights blinking as they landed or took off.

"By the time I drop you at the departure gates, a rough description of you and me will be circulating."

"I have someone who can help with that," Henry said.

"Good, use it for you but not for me."

Henry turned to look at Ma better. "I don't need a decoy."

"You do. I'm not going anywhere. I might as well make myself useful."

"Negative. My team will erase our profiles from the airport security systems as soon as I call them."

Ma smiled. "Do I then have to run around the airport and shout that I am wanted to attract attention?"

Henry wondered whether she would, but he was in no doubt that General Ma had made up her mind as to the way in which she wanted to be captured and perhaps die.

Ma glanced at Henry. She laid her hand on his shoulder and squeezed it quickly. "You don't like leaving people behind and that's why you got Rob out. But the USB key you are carrying is bigger than one person."

Henry said nothing, his way of reluctantly agreeing.

The traffic in the various lanes that led to the airport departure gates was flowing easily.

"I'm going to drop you at the far end, park the car and enter the airport at the opposite end," Ma said.

"Thank you."

Henry extended his hand; Ma smiled when she shook it. "No, thank you, and keep the world safe."

Henry grabbed his rucksack, took one of the burner phones out and got out of the car.

Ma sped off as soon as he had shut the door, rushing towards the far end of the terminal building.

He called the only number he had saved on the phone. "Are you ready?"

"Just say the word." Nick sounded a little tired but focused. "They are looking for you both."

"Only one name to be replaced: mine." When Nick hesitated, Henry added, "Do it, Nick. Only one." Henry hung up and dropped the phone into the first dustbin he encountered.

The terminal was spacious and less noisy than he had anticipated. Henry checked his watch and saw he had less than forty-five minutes to board his flight. Korean Air was calling its passengers for the flight to Seoul and Henry sped up. There was only one passenger in the business class lane and Henry found himself in front of the airline staff almost immediately.

"No luggage, Mr Brown?" the young man asked amiably.

"I like to travel light." Henry gave his best I-am-a-business-customer-don't-get-on-my-nerves smile. It didn't produce the result he'd hoped. Travelling with only a rucksack must seem a little odd.

"Gate 5A. Boarding starts in ten minutes, but the gate is very close to passport control."

Henry thanked the young man, knowing his name would be flagged with border control.

The queues to passport control were moving fast. There was a lane dedicated to business customers, and Henry considered the flag might have only been raised with them. It was worth losing a few minutes to increase his chances of getting through.

Korean Airline was calling its passengers once more and the next call would be the final one. There was now only a young couple in front of Henry. The officer looked at their passports with complete disinterest but made a show of stamping them.

Henry presented his document and the man immediately straightened up. Finally, a passenger worthy of his attention. The officer went through the document thoroughly and called on screen the list of people wanted by either the police or the army. He was about to ask a question when shouts interrupted him.

There was commotion in the main hall and some of the passengers who were queuing turned around to check what the issue was. Henry thought of Ma. Her timing was perfect.

The gunshot sound that followed forced people to dive to the ground and scream. Henry jerked back to the glass partitioning, trying to look as scared as he could. The officer had dropped down to hide. He returned Henry's passport unstamped and moved him through in a hurry. More gunshots resounded around the main hall and this time the return fire came from a machine gun.

Henry ran to the security checkpoint. The officers were worried but there had been no instructions given to stop processing passengers. Henry's rucksack went through without issue and so did he.

Korean Airline called out to the last of the passengers. Henry sprinted towards gate 5A. He heard the long rattle of a machine gun. One of the airport staff was about to hook the chain that closed the gate door. Henry waved that he was coming in. She held the chain back and radioed in.

The staff member started running down the jet bridge with Henry in tow. The plane door had just closed. Henry stopped dead at the sight. The young woman approached the door and knocked a couple of times. A few seconds later the door opened. A steward held the door open for Henry.

Henry smiled to them both. "Thank you. You saved my life."

They smiled back and Henry moved through the cabin to take his seat. The aircraft was pushed back from the gate. Whatever was happening in the main hall didn't seem to be delaying take-off. The captain made his announcement, and the flight attendants did their safety demonstration. The plane stopped. From what he could see through his window, Henry judged they were at the top of the runway.

Henry thought of Ma and her story and the USB key, slotted in his running shoes.

The pilots unleashed the full force of the engines and the plane started picking up speed along the runway. The nose lifted into the air and the aircraft started to steadily rise. Another twenty-five minutes and the plane would reach its cruising altitude. Another thirty minutes after that and the plane would be out of Chinese airspace.

CHAPTER FORTY

Henry checked his watch as the US C-40 that had picked him up from Seoul airport was about to land in Taiwan. He had only slept a few hours. The first hour had been the most restorative after his second burner phone had pinged with a message from Nick.

Welcome to the free world...

Henry had let his head sink into the soft cushion tucked over his headrest and felt almost dizzy with relief. The Korean plane that was on its way to Seoul had just entered international airspace. The rest of the trip had been executed quickly, with a transfer at Seoul airport to the US aircraft that was about to land at Taichung Airport.

The touchdown was impeccable, and Henry unbuckled his seatbelt before the plane had stopped. The military staff that was travelling with him did the same and got ready to disembark. The door opened and the early morning breeze that rushed through the aircraft made Henry shiver.

When he stood on top of the stairs that had been rolled in, Henry spotted Harris standing on the tarmac. He walked a few steps towards the aircraft and waited for Henry there.

"We've prepped a room with all the necessary equipment," Harris said by way of welcome when Henry reached him.

"Who's around?"

"For the time being it's Rob and Nick and us."

"The CIA is pulling back?"

"It's you who brought back the intel, so I'm afraid we have a first bite at that particular cherry."

"I presume Hunter has had no news from Dragon?" Henry had hoped she might have been spared but he knew better.

"None. The CIA picked up chatter about a disturbance at the airport in Beijing but there is an information blackout on this. We'll find out what happened, but it will take a bit of time to filter down."

"She knew what she was doing." Henry was angry at the thought of her losing her final battle.

Harris led Henry through a couple of doors, where military staff had been posted. He handed Henry a pass and they walked through without being stopped.

"Did you get to ask why she did it?"

"To avoid World War Three."

"That's a good reason." Harris glanced at Henry. "I'm sure everyone will be convinced by the data without needing more evidence."

Henry nodded. It was the one thing about Harris that both irritated and impressed him. He always knew when an answer wasn't complete.

Harris entered a room and the two people in it turned around at the same time. Nick looked shocked and Rob nodded at Henry.

"What happened to you?" Nick looked both shocked and amused.

"The art of disguises," Henry said, as he ran a hand over his bald head.

Nick shook his head. "That sure worked. And glad you're back, by the way."

"Not as glad as I am." Henry dropped his rucksack to the floor, took his light jacket off and sat on a chair. He removed one of his trainers. He peeled the inner sole back, took out the small USB key and handed it to Rob. "All yours."

The three men held their breath and Rob hesitated for a few seconds. "Let's see what's on this." Rob sat at the desk that had been made ready for the USB's arrival. Two large monitors were ready to display the data. A child could have opened the file. There was no password protection. General Ma hadn't bothered making the information difficult to extract.

The file was in Chinese, but Rob and Henry knew more than enough to translate for the others.

"The file is marked TOP SECRET, OPERATION UNITY." Rob scrolled down and provided commentary as he went through the

145-page document. "The document covers the stages of planning for the People's Liberation's Army's invasion of Taiwan. Timeline six to nine months."

The timeframe made everyone recoil for a moment.

Henry stood by Rob's shoulder and took over. "Stage one consists of a systematic intimidation campaign. Intrusion into the Taiwanese maritime and air space using either the navy or the air force, with an emphasis on using drones."

Rob continued. "They will also increase their cognitive warfare by spreading more disinformation in and about Taiwan."

Henry said, "Stage one is already approved and yielding results. Then stage two will involve the positioning of military assets in key locations."

Harris moved closer to the screen. "What assets and where?"

"Navy ships patrolling along the median line in the Taiwan Strait, and deployment of their nuclear submarines," Rob said.

"Stage three is the blockade of Taiwan through the dissuasion of ships delivering merchandise to the island..." Henry kept reading. "...by any means that are plausibly deniable. That means new explosives that leave hardly any traces."

"Stage four, massive air strike to disable the Taiwanese air defence, bringing down comms, followed by personnel landing on the far side of the island." Rob shook his head. "That is unexpected."

"A leaf out of the history books ... this is why the World War Two landing in Normandy succeeded... use the least expected of landing terrain." Harris clasped his neck and held it for a moment, as though the information was making his head so heavy it needed support.

"They still don't know how good their plan is." Nick had been listening, arms crossed over his chest.

Harris frowned. "What do you mean?"

"The Chinese military has no warfare experience," Nick said, "unlike the US, the UK and quite a lot of the other NATO countries."

Rob shook his head. "But they have numbers on their side –"

Henry stopped the conversation in mid flow. "We can discuss the plan as much as we like but what really matters is the implementation timeline and how we release the intel."

"Henry is right," Harris said. "The timeline is what matters. We need to alert the right people in the right order. This time I'm going to do it by the book and call the Chief in London."

"Are you trying to make amends?" Henry couldn't resist the tease.

"It's too late for that, mate. I'll be glad to have a job sweeping the floor when I return to London." Harris sounded serious.

"Then what? We transfer the information to MI6 and the CIA and leave it to them to inform their governments? I want to help find a way to stop China." Rob sounded indignant.

Nick nodded. "I'd say we offer our help and make sure we're heard."

Henry mused. "I can think of a few ways to impose some pretty tough economic sanctions that would bite China hard... They may not be enough but it's a start."

"Such as?" Nick's mind was already at work.

"Shutting them out of SWIFT for a start, the world's international banking system. Can't buy anything without it."

"Taiwan will need a large armament package and they'll need a lot of equipment to deter China at least for a while. Imposing sanctions on China may work as a deterrent but only until they find a way to circumvent them." Rob closed the file and removed the USB key from the computer port. "At the end Taiwan need the US to back the island, too, otherwise it'll be game over."

Silence fell over everyone in the room. Rob handed the USB key to Harris. "I'll call the Chief and let you know what's next for us." Harris disappeared to make his call.

Rob turned to Henry. "Do you think Ma's still alive?"

"I don't know, Rob. I want to believe she's made it, but what then? I don't think she wanted to escape in the first place."

"She could have tried to defect."

"I think her priority was to get the information released and her own survival came last. She also wants to make sure the Chinese government knows their plan is out there."

Rob rubbed his hands over his tired face. "This is suicide."

"Yes, it is." Henry smiled sadly.

"Why did she do it?" Nick also looked dejected. "The obvious is to avoid a war, but she was a general in the Chinese Army, not a peace activist."

404

Rob glanced at Henry quickly, an answer in his eyes. Henry explained, "World War Three means invoking nuclear power. I'm sure generals on both sides want to avoid that."

Harris returned quicker than Henry had expected. "MI6 and the CIA are cutting a deal as we speak for the use of the information. Taiwan's president will be briefed but don't ask me when or how." Harris slumped into a chair. "Both agencies will want to speak to you as well, Rob."

"I hope I won't end up in one of their black op sites." Rob was only half joking.

"I'll come to rescue you." Henry was only half joking, too.

"I don't know about you, but I need a shower and a good night's sleep." Harris stood up wearily. "We've been put up by the UK rep office in Taipei. A car is waiting for us."

Rob stood up, followed by Nick.

Henry picked up his rucksack and made for the door that Harris was holding open for them. He let the other two men go ahead.

When he reached Harris, he asked Henry, "Did you make a copy?"

"What do you take me for?" Henry murmured.

Harris exhaled deeply and grinned. "Good man."

* * *

The terrace was in full sunlight and even in February, it felt pleasant enough to be sitting outside.

Harris was sporting his old leather jacket. He looked relaxed for a man who could be out of a job soon.

Henry handed him a mug of coffee. "How long will you have to wait before they tell you?"

"Not long. I received the latest OP TECH LEOPARD review. I think it'll be the final one and then..." Harris made a vague gesture.

"What does the Chief say?" Henry sat in a lounger that faced the sea. It was almost impossible to think the worst could happen in such tranquil surroundings.

"He knows he can't let the way I handled the operation slip. Hunter got a serious roasting, and the army wasn't best pleased about ALPHA team, either."

"I know. I spoke to Rodriguez. Fergus is to get a ground-breaking surgery, but there will be months of recovery." Henry couldn't bring himself to say that Fergus would never go on an op with the ALPHA team again.

"At least Taiwan is still holding firm," said Harris.

"The Chinese plans were well thought through. They'll try one day." Harris didn't need to agree. They had both seen the plan.

"I received a message from Bo's family in Hong Kong." Harris blew on his coffee and took a sip. "They appreciated me delivering his letter to them."

"You gave them an email address?" Henry was surprised.

"Yep, under another alias name, nothing the authorities can trace."

"What is Bo's family saying? They are getting organised to move to the UK." Henry finished his coffee and offered Harris a refill.

Harris grinned. "I should get going. I'm sure you've got better things to do than speak to what could soon be your former handler." He grew serious again. "I'll be in touch as soon as I know my fate."

"Perhaps we could offer to quit together – Nick, James Radlett to cover military intelligence contacts and me."

"Perhaps..." Harris stood up, slung his rucksack over his shoulder and gave Henry a quick nod. "I know the way, don't get up."

Harris walked through the open French doors. He slowed down when he stepped into the lounge. "Say hello to Mattie for me, will you?"

Henry turned around on his lounger to reply, but Harris was already gone. Henry had planned to speak to Harris about getting Mattie involved but it would have been disingenuous after everything they'd been through.

Henry picked up his mobile and dialled the last number he had called that day. "He's gone, but guess what?"

"He asked for me?" Mattie teased over the phone.

"Almost, he says hello."

Henry walked to the edge of the terrace. From there he could see the bay and the small lane that led to a private pool. He waved at someone and a woman a few yards away responded.

It only took Mattie a few minutes to reach the terrace balustrade. She slung her camera over her shoulder and started climbing the wall.

Henry reached over to help her with the last few steps, and pulled her onto the terrace.

"How about using the door?" he said, as he held her in his arms.

"Too boring."

She slid her arms around him and squeezed tight. "So where is Harris sending you this time?"

"You know I can't say." He brushed his lips against her hair and kissed her forehead.

"But you're not leaving tomorrow?" There was a hint of anxiety in her voice.

"Nor the day after tomorrow."

"Something else on your mind, then?" Mattie asked.

Henry shook his head. "I still find it tough that you can read me so quickly."

Mattie ran her fingers over his face and through the hair that had grown back to its usual thickness. "I love you, that's all."

He held her tighter; that was the best response he could give to such a frank admission of feelings. Mattie didn't seem to mind. She had proven to be surprisingly patient.

"There was a murder..." he began, "it was a long time ago, during the Troubles in Northern Ireland."

"Did it involve the old IRA?" Mattie rested her head against his chest.

"That's right."

"And you want to find out more?"

He lifted her face, cupped it in his hand and looked deeply into her eyes. "I'll never be free until I find out who killed my father and why."

Dear Reader,

I hope you have enjoyed RED RENEGADE as much as I have enjoyed writing it!

So, perhaps you would like to know more about Henry Crowne. What are the ghosts that haunt him? What is it in his past that made him who he is?

Delve into HENRY CROWNE PAYING THE PRICE series with

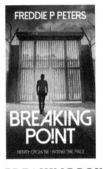

COLLAPSE:
mybook.to/COLLAPSE

BREAKING POINT:
mybook.to/BREAKINGPOINT

NO TURNING BACK:
mybook.to/NOTURNINGBACK

HENRY CROWNE PAYING THE PRICE, BOOKS 1-3:
mybook.to/HCPTPBKS1-3

 SPY SHADOWS:
mybook.to/SPYSHADOWS

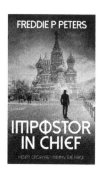 IMPOSTOR IN CHIEF:
mybook.to/IMPOSTORINCHIEF

Or check out my new series
A NANCY WU CRIME THRILLER:

BLOOD DRAGON:
mybook.to/BLOODDRAGON

ACKNOWLEDGEMENTS

It takes many people to write and publish a book… for their generosity and support I want to say thank you.

Kate Gallagher, my editor and story consultant, for her immense knowledge of good language and of what makes a book great. Ryan O'Hara for his expertise in design and for producing a super book cover – yet again. Danny Lyle for his patience and proficiency in typesetting the text! Charlotte Gledson for her precise and yet creative copy-editing and Abbie Headon, for her eagle-eyed proofreading.

To the friends who have patiently read, reread, and advised on all matters book: Kathy Vanderhook, my most excellent beta reader, Bennett Little for inspiring some fun repartees and dispensing his knowledge about Inner Mongolia so generously, Simon Heath for his immense knowledge of the Tech world, any mistakes made in portraying that world are clearly mine, and Caz Woolley and Simon Fairfax, authors in their own rights, for their support during the book production and, of course to my very cool ARC team.

It's also time for me to ask you for a small favour...

Please take a few minutes to leave a review either on Amazon, Goodreads, or Bookbub.

Reviews are incredibly important to authors like me. They increase the book's visibility and help with promotions. So, if you'd like to spread the word, get writing, or leave a star review.

Thank you so very much.

Finally, don't forget. You can gain FREE access to the backstories that underpin the HENRY CROWNE PAYING THE PRICE series and get to know the author's creative process and how the books are conceived.

Read FREE chapters and the EXCLUSIVE Prequel to the HENRY CROWNE PAYING THE PRICE series: INSURGENT

Go to https://freddieppeters.com and join Freddie's Book Club now...

Looking forward to connecting with you!

Freddie